Evolution's Race

BOOK I

The Runners

By

L. Pelletier

DEDICATION

This first book in the Evolution's Collection, which just happens to also be my very first book in general,

is dedicated to my husband Scott.

I won't lie to you and say that he was thrilled when I left my day job without a new one anywhere in sight. I won't pretend here that he was a giggly cheerleader when it came to me spending hour after hour on my laptop, drinking wine and happily escaping reality.

Let's face it, I'd have thrown me out.

So, for being a better person than me and *not* throwing me out before I could finish it, I will be forever grateful to you. Your patience was invaluable.

Love you.

ACKNOWLEDGMENTS

Writing this book was a real labor of love, from beginning to end. It'd been living in my head for far too long and I had to get it out of there. I needed the room. While I truly enjoyed every minute of it, I didn't have even the slightest clue of what I was supposed to do, or how I was supposed to do it. So I just started writing!

However, I believe it was also that freedom from the knowledge of "proper procedure" that was largely responsible for the fact that I managed to finish it. In the beginning I had to be okay with the possibility of some slight imperfections. It was more important to get it to you, the reader, as soon as possible, and I have no regrets.

Though if you're going to write a book without having a clue *and* self-publish it, then at the very least you'd better have a world class friend/sounding-board/proofreader by your side. Luckily, I was fortunate enough to have had the very best. So a *HUGE* thank you goes out to my SIL Lauren, for being the best support staff I could've ever asked for! I can't thank you enough for your endless willingness to read version after version, without complaint, even when your own life occasionally required your attention. I may *never* have done it if not for your help and encouragement!

I also want to acknowledge some of my favorite artists who inspired the ultra-important soundtrack to my tale. I absolutely could not have told the story without it! Thank you Adele, Alex Clare, C+C Music Factory, Chicago, Kelly Clarkson, Eric Clapton, Fleetwood Mac, Dave Mason, Jason Mraz, Joss Stone, Paolo Nutini, REO Speedwagon and Bob Seger. But *especially* Matchbox Twenty, specifically for *"Overjoyed"* from their album *"North."* I truly hope you guys will be happy that I included it in my book. It was as if it was *written* for this story!

Also, a general thank you goes out to everyone around town who in some way inspired a character or a scene in the book.

You'll know who you are. ☺

REFERENCES

I imagine lots of people start a book with tons of highly organized research. That however, is not how this book began.
I just started writing one day for fun and went along with the story as it played out in my head. I didn't try to steer it, I simply enjoyed the amazing ride.
I did decide after the fact, that it might be a good idea to go back and give it a few connections to reality. Maybe even include just a couple of accurate facts here and there. In that endeavor I have to acknowledge and thank the few resources that I gratefully took advantage of.

To The New Hampshire Department of Environmental Services for the "The New Hampshire Water Resources Primer" that I found on their website.
https://des.nh.gov/organization/divisions/water/dwgb/wrpp/primer.htm
It was extremely informative, especially Chapter 4.

I would also like to acknowledge the
United States Environmental Protection Agency
and the National Service Center for Environmental Publications
(NSCEP)
for the "Ground Water Issue" article on their website:
https://nepis.epa.gov

EPA/540/S-93/503
February 1993

The "Suggested Operating Procedures for Aquifer Pumping Tests" article was my main resource for what little information on pumps and water testing that I did actually read.

Again, it is important to clarify, that any and all inaccuracies or situations that are just plain fiction are my responsibility alone, not the sources and of course *are* in the end, after all, fiction. ☺

PROLOGUE

Evolution: The change in the inherited characteristics of biological populations over successive generations.

The following story is just one example of the completely subconscious place that every living human has in the perpetual race to be the best possible version of itself that it can be. Of the outside forces that continually shape and mold us all in the eternal weeding of the weaker traits of the species. And of the unconscious hope that we all have to somehow be among the lucky ones' remaining, who possess the winning genetic attributes required for survival into an unknown future.

A tale of how this all happens without a single conscious thought from us.

All we ever know is that the journey through life is never a straight line. It's convoluted and full of obstacles. It also has an uncanny way of working itself out, but it's almost never in the way that we had planned.

Chapter 1

"Another glass of Pinot please, Dani." I said without looking up as the familiar petite, dark haired waitress walked by. I could see her in my peripheral vision as she jotted it down and moved on, unfazed by my inattention. She was used to me already.

I was trying to finish up my latest sketch. I still had at least three more to produce before I met with my client in the morning, and it was already getting late. It was a huge project and as much as I hated to admit to such a cliché, it was pretty much gonna make or break me at that point.

I'd been doing freelance landscape art for years but I'd always had a *"real"* job as well. There was never any pressure on my artwork to keep me alive and in wine refills. It was always just something that I loved and when someone gave over a space to me, I could let my creative side flow and that turned the tide on the emotional input from all around me. It was a safe place that I had found I could *create* all on my own. I poured my heart and my personal style into it and got peace of mind, at least temporarily, back out. It was a fair enough exchange.

I was always looking for more space that I could use to Zen out in. It was very therapeutic for me. I would ask friends, relatives. Friends of relatives. Even relatives of friends. I wasn't picky. So when I started to actually get *paid* to do it, well that was pretty awesome, I'm not gonna lie! But that had been the rarity rather than the norm, more often than not. I had still only done what I wanted to do, when I wanted to do it. Up until that point, that is. After that I officially didn't have that luxury anymore.

I was officially on my own. I had quit my *"real"* job five months prior to *"focus on my art/therapy full-time."* So something *"real"* had to come of it, and fast. It wasn't like I could afford to screw that job up and wait for the next one. I had pretty much just enough funds left in my account for the two months-worth of bills that I expected it to take me to finish the job, and that was it. There was no encore. If my client didn't like it and decided not to pay, I'd be all done. Might as well stick a fork in me. After that, I'd be looking at going home to my parents in the city. At least temporarily. *Ugggghhhhh God!*

Just the thought gave me the heebie-jeebies. I loved them dearly, with all my heart. But one of my main goals growing up had been to get beyond those four walls and I could not face the idea of going backwards at that point in life. It was simply too defeating! With the big 3-0 looming just a couple of short years away, it made every decision tythat much more important. I was starting to get the distinct and unavoidable sense that I was running low on "do-over's."

I wasn't sure what I would do if it really came to that, but I knew it was a rock bottom option. And I knew I had to be pretty damn close to rock bottom!

Anyway, it wasn't like I hadn't had plenty of time to get that first step done. We had discussed the project originally over eight months ago. Before everything else around me went and fell apart. I kept putting it off because it was a serious job. A paying one. That was important by then. Plus I knew I had tons of time. That was the worst for me. Too much time was always the kiss of death.

Get me under the gun and I will blow your freakin' socks off! Give me three weeks to do a three-day project and I can pretty much guarantee you that you will not see me for two and a half weeks.

The sketches were just the first step in the process and I still hadn't even gotten them all down on paper. Most, but not all. That was alright though. I knew I could pull it off. As long as I could hang out in my cozy little spot there in the back corner, away from the crowd. It was minuscule most nights, but I personally considered anything above ten people a crowd.

The ideas were flowing. They always did when I was there. It was the music that did it for me, I knew. I had the Magician, my favorite musician to thank for it and I had a good three more hours before he called it quits for the night.

My work quieted the flow, but only while I was actually knee deep in the earth or flowers, *working*. Not so much during the planning stages. I needed some outside help to concentrate on that part.

He was definitely larger than average size, but somehow he still seemed a much less imposing figure than one would expect, especially for a performer. He didn't make a habit of working the room or being overly social or anything like that. Still, he maintained a quiet presence that spoke volumes, even though he never did. And a stare! *(Insert head to toe shudder here.)* When that stare was in use it could be just as jarring as he was quiet. I avoided that stare 99% of the time. I didn't need the noise. Not in there. I didn't know what it was he was looking for all the time and I didn't want to know.

Just keep working your magic for me Mr. Magician, and you can keep your reasons all to yourself, I thought happily. I won't say *"boo"* to you. *I promise!*

He wasn't really called the Magician, though. Only I called him that and only in my head since I had never actually talked to him in person. Nope. He was handsome enough and all, but that wasn't what I needed from him. I just needed him to keep playing so I could keep working and maybe have one thing left in my life that wasn't total shit. It was the best I could hope for at that point and I would take it if I could manage to pull it off.

The Magician's real name was something like Ian or Ethan, I thought. Plain and simple. Nothing nearly as exotic as I felt it should be. He had jet black hair and eyes that were so clear blue they were actually a light gray. Combined with his pale skin and the fact that he almost always wore dark clothing, you could watch him on stage and almost imagine that you were seeing him in black and white. From another time and place, like he was there, but separate from the rest of us. I could tell that he liked it that way. Most of the time anyway.

In between songs, I could sense his need to continually "size-up" the room. After which, he would relax and go back to focusing on playing again. I would even recognize the stare visually sometimes while the music was playing. It was strange, but I really *didn't* want to know. I just wanted to sit there and listen to him play his wonderful music and get my work done. That was a lot already and I wouldn't ask for anything more.

He could play and sing almost any genre and I'd heard enough of them to attest that he seemed equally as comfortable in any of them. I didn't understand it, really. I had always thought that performers tended to have a *"style."* A type of music that their voice and personality were best suited to. Even if you could switch back and forth between one or two, most would generally only do one or the other really well. That didn't seem to apply to him though, and that was rare.

Whatever. It didn't matter to me what he played. As long as he played. On rare occasions, other musicians would sit in with him. Sometimes there were even a few backup singers that joined in. Most times though, he played alone. Just him and his guitar. The latter was the most fitting to the establishment, seeing as we *were* in a back woods bar in the middle of *almost* nowhere. But he could easily transform the atmosphere in the room completely when he switched sounds. It really was amazing for such a little hidden jewel.

My luck in the area had been remarkable so far. It made me more than a little nervous, actually. I had been keeping my minds' eye on that. It was always hard for me to trust something that seemed "too good." Meanwhile, I prayed every day that more people wouldn't find out about the place and ruin my little safe haven by crowding it up past my comfort level.

My Magician was there three or four nights a week and I had no idea how they afforded to pay him for so many nights with so small a clientele. But however they did it, I was grateful because

I needed them all. I also had no idea if or where he played the other nights but if I was ever desperate enough, I thought I might try to find out.

That night he had started with a country set and was well into a jazz section by the time I got to my second glass of wine. His deep voice rolled over the lyrics like a slow rumbling car on a winding road. It was the perfect white noise for me. The fact that I happened to actually really like it was purely a bonus. In fact, he'd yet to play anything that I didn't like and I'd spent a fair amount of hours there already.

When he wasn't consciously scanning the room, he mostly looked down at his guitar while he played and sang. Like he was really playing for himself, rather than for us. Sometimes he just closed his eyes and even through the music I could feel a deep longing and I would catch myself wondering where it is he goes.

I didn't spend too much time on it though because as long as he was making music, my thoughts and feelings could be my own. *If I let them.* I was grateful for that, since that was not always the case. That was not even *usually* the case. I got most of my work done there lately for that reason. Sometimes I felt like I owed him a special thank you or something, but really he just did what he did. He didn't *know* that he did more for me than anyone else in the room. Whatever, I did the best I could do which was to make sure I always tipped really well.

I had been starting on the next sketch when Dani came back with my wine refill. I was sure it was a bad habit to get accustomed to it being so readily available every night, but I wasn't ready to worry about it yet. Two glasses usually got me through my *"night shift"* anyway, and I could walk home if I ever really had to.

I had found the place by accident when I first moved to the area about four months prior. The little Eastern Mass town of Pinegrove that it resided in was only thirty minutes north of the city and yet the difference was like night and day. Twenty minutes into the ride you feel like you're truly in the country. Fields and farms and forests, oh my. It was beautiful and easy to forget that two million people were only twenty five miles south of there. Some people found that refreshing, others found it downright horrifying. I was firmly entrenched on the "refreshing" end of that spectrum. *Waaaaay* down on that end. I could breathe out there. I could think, and most of all, I could feel my own feelings and *know* that they were mine. That was something that I had learned long ago, not to take for granted.

You see, for a long time I didn't *know* why that was so hard for me. I was well into my teens before I started to figure it all out. Finally make some sense out of it. Try to learn to accept it, to live with it.

I was exiting my teens by the time I found out that there was actually a name for it. For what I was.

First and foremost, and this is very important to me, I am just an ordinary, boring but basically decent, person. But *besides* that, I am also what people would call, an *empath*.

Most people aren't familiar with what that means so I try to explain it, if and when I talk about it. I liken it to being the customs department that the emotions of everyone around you must pass through. Baggage and all, and the counter never closes.

Then of course, there's also the occasional dream, where my subconscious does the work for me. But those are usually much easier to deal with, so I don't mind them too much. The empath stuff however, was harder to get used to, to say the least.

I did though, eventually. After reading and researching every angle of what was available on empaths, which unfortunately wasn't really very much, I started to understand what was happening enough to at least take control of it a little better. I decided pretty early on that if I had to live with it, then I was going to live with it my way. I wanted to understand it as much as I possibly could, so *I* could make the rules. *I* would decide how and when it got to intrude upon my life.

That had been the plan anyway, but I found that the more aware I became of it, and the better my control got, the *stronger it* got. I hadn't counted on that necessarily

When I was really young, it had just been about being able to feel whenever someone was sad or angry or hiding something. Or when someone was lying. But by the time I was in my early twenties, it had grown to the point where it had become a constant awareness of the specific emotional state of almost everyone around me!

Most days that was just *TMI* dammit!

My main goal had always been to maintain as normal a life as possible. Always refusing to let it define me. But the truth was that it was mentally *exhausting* most of the time! I would be haggard and snappy by the end of the day, but when asked why, I could never seem to explain. My list of seemingly mundane tasks didn't sound difficult, but then they were never really why I was tired.

I figured out early on that crowds were the hardest. Too much stuff coming at me all at once. It made it difficult to control my own emotions when they were so over loaded with too many others mixed in. I felt like I was a filter full of holes and every emotion around me would pass right through me as people walked by. They got to be oblivious to me but I never got to be that way with them. The more people there were, the more stuff that poured through me. Sometimes a stray feeling would stick. I learned to how to shake them eventually, but it took a while because I had to learn how to *identify* them first.

Things like movie theaters were the worst. Especially if God forbid, the film was a tear-jerker! The sadness of 200 people would filter through me and no matter how determined *I* would be to hold it all together in front of my date, I would end up spending the entire movie wiping a slew of tears from my disobedient eyes. It could be *very* frustrating.

There were a lot of times though, that it could also be beneficial. Like when three angry ex-security employees decided to shoot up the mall ten days before Christmas. I could *feel* their anxiety and their anger bombarding me as they entered the building and walked determinedly past us.

I didn't know what was going to happen, but I knew it was going to be bad and that was enough for me to convince my husband Ben, that we needed to leave right away. I picked up our daughter and he pulled us both behind him as we walked out backwards from the mall. I called 911 while we ran to the car.

I didn't know what to tell them, but I knew that I needed to make them come, so I said I thought there was going to be a robbery. As the blue lights started to appear from around the corner, we could hear the first gunshots echoing out from inside.

I always wanted to do more. It drove me crazy that even though I could feel things coming, I didn't always have the means to stop them. Then it was just maddening to know! During times like that, I always felt so ineffectual. FIve people were killed in the mall that day before the police had the situation under control.

It was really hard to take at first. But we found out soon after that if the cops hadn't arrived when they did, it would have been a *lot* worse! Apparently they had enough ammo on them to take out a small country and they had a list of mall employees that they intended to "take out." That list had been 49 people long. Not including those who just got in the way in the process.

That part helped me to sleep at night again, but going to the mall still got a lot harder after that. I just didn't always want to *know* what was going on with everyone around me. Sometimes it was easier to stay home and order it online. The world *is* at your fingertips these days after all.

There was no denying that it had influenced my decision to leave my job as well. I had already spent years facing my worst fears, trying to prove that I wasn't a freak. That I could do normal things and live a normal life. Outwardly, I was trying to prove it to my family and friends. Inwardly, and more honestly, I was trying to convince myself that it was really possible.

In the name of that quest, I had worked directly with the public in one capacity or another for over ten years. I had scooped ice cream for the masses at the softball park at sixteen, and held the requisite job in retail at the mall at eighteen, fulfilling all of my teenage requirements. I had held various jobs at the University wherever they needed someone, from the library to the cafeteria. I even spent a summer in the enrollment office, and there was never a quiet moment there! I really felt at that point in my life, that I had fully overcome those particular demons.

I wasn't afraid of the world at large anymore. I was just tired of it. I had made my point and done what I needed to do and I didn't want to do it anymore. I just wanted some peace and quiet for a little while.

It made me feel kind of old, or like I was quitting in some small way. But I knew in my heart that neither was really true, and that it wasn't wrong to want some tranquility in my life.

Chapter 2

My latest and most important job had been managing a busy art Gallery in the city. I'd started out a total newbie at the matting and framing side, as well as the art of displaying and selling. But it was a whole new aspect to art and I found it fascinating! I eventually got used to the strong emotions that people tended to feel around really good art. Some days just walking from one end of the gallery to the other was a monu-*mental* task for me! Sorry, pun intended. I found it interesting too though, how seldom people expressed truly what they were feeling. Let me tell you, the world is a different place when you can sense all the emotions that we as people in polite society try so hard to hide all the time.

Like the well-dressed business man with the overly thin, perfectly coiffed blonde. He would talk softly of the beauty of the strokes while he thought in his head that the painting was childish and vulgar. Then he would proceed to his own vulgar thoughts about the blonde. All the while she would smile at him wistfully, a twinkle in her eye at her impressive catch.

I knew the truth. But I could never bring it up, so it was a one way conversation in my head, all the time. I would learn to perfect my acting skills along the way. That came in handy. You just aren't allowed to voice every intimate thought in *someone else's* head. Or to constantly react to them when you shouldn't.

So I practiced, and I worked hard at managing both sides

of my job. It had been a struggle for such a long time, but I'd always had a fire inside of me when it came time to tackling the challenges in life. I'm not sure why. It was something mostly akin to defiance, but whatever. It worked. And overall, I think I've done alright. That energy had served me well. But for quite some time, all I had been feeling was the surety that I was done there and that it was time to move on. I had tried to ignore it, but my feelings can be pretty hard to ignore.

It was a difficult change to make, to say the least. I was walking away from a *very* good job, in a *very* bad economy. "Yes, I was leaving for good," and "No, I wasn't crazy." These, I answered the most.

I couldn't change the way I felt, and I couldn't ignore it anymore either. If I had learned anything through all of my hard work at self-realization, it was that it did *not* pay to deny my instincts. They were there for a reason, and unfortunately I couldn't just leave all the empath stuff behind me. It went wherever I did. I had come to terms with that. I was determined to at least take it someplace quieter. Someplace where I could try to relight that fire. Maybe spend some time enjoying some of the good stuff that my situation had to offer. There actually are a few pleasant side effects. Besides the occasional life-saving episodes where forewarning makes all the difference in the world, there was also live music.

Although my experience with instrument lessons was mediocre at best, it had led to the subsequent discovery of the effect that music had on me in general, which essentially changed my life. I spent years' worth of free time exploring that area with great relish.

You have no idea what it's like to stand high on a hill at an open-air venue concert, with the elevated *good* vibes of 20,000 people washing up over you along with the reverberating music! *It's an absolutely* incredible *feeling!* I have felt many times, the power that music has to affect all of us. It's not just emotional either, as most would assume. It can be *physical* too. When it's really good it can be all-encompassing.

It is definitely more pronounced in some, than in others. But still for me, someone who is *so* susceptible to the effects of the music myself, to then also pick that up from 20,000 other people at the same time, well that was an absolutely *joyous* experience for me! There were barely even words for it! But *I got to feel that!* That part's pretty cool. I have to admit.

It certainly helps to balance things out a little. Balance was all that really mattered in the end. I am a big believer of that. People I have found, can endure almost anything, as long as the desire to continue is great enough and the hard stuff is punctuated by intermittent periods of relief. Anything can be overcome. All it takes is a little bit of lightness to balance it out and the will to carry on. I was no different. That had been my point all along.

So if balance made the world go round, then I could not really complain. It definitely wasn't all bad. Though it wasn't easy either, and eventually life in general got a lot harder for Ben and me.

In the beginning, he was duly impressed by my skills. And for a while, he was quite happy to take advantage of them. But before long, the times when he was grateful were gradually becoming less frequent than the times where he found it to be a huge pain in the ass. I was truly surprised when his attitude started to change, but he wasn't even always wrong and that made it really hard to argue with him. Anyway, at some point he realized that he didn't really *have* to deal with it.

Only I did.

It was clear to me then that I was on my own. Even before I left. Actually, *long* before I left. Ever since the day I realized that he had completely disconnected from a big part of who I was. I wouldn't have believed that I would ever see the day, but it was true and over time it became unavoidable. *He still loved me.* I knew that. But it wasn't enough anymore. Not for him, or for me.

Leaving Liliana behind, well that had been another thing all together. No matter what kind of struggles I had endured growing up, *nothing* compared to that particular hardship! It was the most difficult thing I'd ever had to do. It still rocked me to my core every time I thought about it and in four months it hadn't gotten even one tiny bit easier. It was equivalent to leaving half of my heart on the floor and walking away. I could never, ever do it if I wasn't absolutely sure that it was so much better for her. Or if she wasn't so well adjusted. But it was, and she is. And so somehow, I managed. I was managing.

I swear sometimes she really is five going on twenty five. I know now where those ridiculous expressions come from. She's such an amazing little person, that it was too easy to forget that she was just a child still sometimes. I didn't ever want to take that away from her though. I wanted so badly for her to keep that as long as possible! That was part of what helped me to deal with letting go of her a little. Just for now. I wanted her to have a real childhood. A *good* childhood!

Sadly, even at five she already knew that she was better off with the stability that dad could provide. She understood how important it was that he could go to the soccer games and not have to suppress the desire to kill everyone around him the whole time. *Literally.* He could also take her to the park after school without feeling the need to alert the police to the presence of every pedophile who walked by. But, think about it, could you ignore that kind of thing if you knew about it?

And, he could still take her to the mall.

In other words, dad was more fun. But that was okay. It was true. At least for the moment, and at five, fun was important. When the time came that she needed *me* more, I would be there for her. No matter what. In the meantime, I couldn't justify stopping him from being there, when she needed *him.* I just had to get through it. I needed to remind myself constantly that it wasn't Ben's fault and not to hate him. It was hard in the beginning, I'm not gonna lie.

It was a horrible situation but for the time being, there just didn't seem to be a better way. We would have to figure it all out though because she was too important to wait around for us to get our shit together. She was growing up more every day, so we had to too.

Ben wasn't a bad guy though. I was still pretty lucky as far as ex's went. I knew that. We were always on the same page when it came to what was best for our daughter. That was number one, and with that going for us I knew eventually the rest would work itself out and we'd be okay.

I still saw her most days. I could never function otherwise.

Whenever I could, I liked to pick her up and bring her to school in the morning or home in the afternoon. It was perfect because it was guaranteed alone time. It was often the best part of my day. I also said good night to her every night. Whether in person or by phone. It didn't matter as long as we got to say "good night" and "I love you." It had been a ritual between us from the time she was born, and I would never let the current mess get in the way of that.

We tried to eat dinner together at least a few times a week, but *always* on Fridays. Then she would stay overnight with me and play on the farm on Saturdays, which she loved. It wasn't nearly enough, but for the moment, it would have to do. She was the most important thing in the world to me and I would do whatever I had to not to screw her up. As long as she was okay, I could deal with whatever I had to on my end.

I tried to push it out of my mind, not wanting to waste whatever working time I had left before the Magician took his magic home with him for the night.

Chapter 3

Music had always been a balm for me. I had that one figured out by the end of my first piano class. Not only did I enjoy it immensely, but it seemed to fill the holes so-to-speak, so that less of the other things got through. It was a welcome discovery to say the least. It made it possible for me to focus on my own thoughts for a while then. Or sometimes, just to let my mind wander to whatever thoughts or mood the music elicited.

Either way, I could actually *think*. It was like a mental time-out. I always felt like it was kind of magical, how it worked in its' unseen way. I had counted on it more and more over the years for my peace of mind. It had gotten to the point that I preferred to have music on almost all the time and it had become practically impossible to do any work without it. It was a good thing I didn't have to. My future was still very uncertain, but I knew for sure that there would never be a Monday through Friday desk job under fluorescent lights in it for me. Not that I'm knocking that for those whose life it fits, it just didn't fit mine and I would never pretend that it did again.

I had stumbled in *there* after my first week in town, when I heard the music through my open car window. I had been driving around aimlessly, enjoying my Adele CD and the pleasant spring night. I wanted to get to know a few of the long, wooded back roads that those "in between" towns were so full of.

It had surprised me when I heard the music drift out over the night air, since there didn't appear to be much of anything around. I'd had the radio cranked and would surely have missed it entirely, but *"I'll be waiting"* had just ended allowing the sound to reach me in the quiet pause between songs.

I looked around me on the quiet country road and all I saw was what looked like an old trading post. Even though I wasn't sure I knew what one would look like exactly, that was the impression that I got. I slowed down as I drove by and on closer inspection, I could see that whatever it was in the past, it had since been converted into newer businesses. It was a dark brown, one story building. There was a small combo convenience/liquor store, a chiropractors office, and on the far end of the L shape, "The Tavern," where I currently sat.

It was set about fifty yards back and there had barely been enough light to feel safe parking in the lot, never mind to see it clearly from the road. But I could hear the music and that, along with the promise of a mental break and the cold beer advertised in neon, drew me in.

He had been singing a Bob Segar song originally when I entered. It was an "oldie" but a "goodie" and I got pleasant vibes from him right off the bat. You have no idea how important that is to me. It was like a breath of fresh air. Unexpected, and *nice.*

The place wasn't anything fancy, but I was okay with that. It was light enough to see what you needed to, but not so bright that it hurt your eyes. The decor was a combination of a "rustic cabin" motif, cross-bred with a seafood shanty. Complete with hanging nets, buoys and various stuffed critters. It was almost comical but mostly it was kind of homey.

I helped myself to a seat in the furthest, tall booth along the wall. They were sturdy cubicles made up of dark stained solid wood and double padded, espresso brown, leather seats. It was surprisingly roomy and comfortable. I found myself thinking that somebody had known what they were doing when they chose comfort over maximum seating capacity with the bulky, but high quality benches.

A perky woman in jeans and an apron had come over and smiled genuinely at me. She looked to be maybe mid-thirties at most, had huge, warm brown eyes and shiny black, shoulder-length hair. It hung down in spiral curls so tight that they had to be natural. Only her exuberant, happy energy could outshine her adorable demeanor.

"Hi! What can I get you hun?" She asked cheerfully.

"I would love a Coors light. Bottle please." Seeing the stand-up menu on the table advertising the traditional bar fare, I asked, "Kitchen still open?"

"Sure is! Would you like to see a full menu?"

"No, no, thanks. If I could just get an order of buffalo fingers, please. That would be great." I said happily.

Huge smile again. "I'll get that right in for ya, and my name's Dani." She said pointing comically towards her plastic name badge with a gleaming smile. "Just holler if you need anything else."

"Thank you Dani." I said with a genuine smile of my own then, and she was off like a flash.

By the time I was audibly *"mmmming"* over the blue cheese dressing, I was completely at home.

It was about halfway through my second beer, that I realized *why* I was so happy. As I sat Indian style, my shoes long ago discarded under the table, I suddenly understood. There was no *emotional* noise there. None *what-so-ever!*

Huh. Usually the music would *slow-the-flow*, as I liked to say, but to have it quiet all together was pretty rare. I had let my guard down completely and it was like a lazy Sunday afternoon in my head. I had felt a little guilty at the indulgence of hanging around so long originally, but it was so nice to finally have some peace that I stayed anyway. Until the music stopped.

He left the stage when his set was over and quietly walked off into the darkness backstage. I assumed that he left through a back door, but I couldn't swear to it, since I never actually saw him leave. I paid my bill and left the first of many good tips for occupying the booth for so long, then headed home. I had known as I drove down the long, dark road on my way home, that I would make that particular trip many times in the future. I would definitely be back.

It's what people like me liked to call a *"safe"* place. It was like home base in a game of hide-and-seek. Outside influences had no power over you as long as you were on home base. You were safe.

I was safe there. His music soothed the beast and I would bow to his magical matador skills. I hadn't had a steady safe place in a while. Ben was not there for me in that sense anymore and I'd lost Nann long ago.

My Nann had been a rarity though. I knew that by then. She was a quiet place, all by herself. She didn't need to sing or play an instrument or even tell a story, (which sometimes worked when I was young, if the narrator was good enough) to slow-the-flow. She just had to be near me and it was blissfully *"quiet."*

It had always been that way and growing up she had been my favorite long before I knew why. I think she understood though. She had seen it before, I found out later. In my great grandmother and my Aunt Clarice, and then in me. And in herself of course. If anyone in our family truly understood, it was her. I think she was the opposite of me though.

If I was like an antenna, then Nann was like a radio station. You couldn't help but feel what she put out. If the mood in the room turned sour, she could turn it around almost instantly. When Nann was happy, everyone around her was too. Whether they liked it or not. But I liked it. A *lot!* Whenever Nann worked her magic, nothing else would get through and I was always grateful for the break. She was one of the biggest reasons that I got to spend some time just being a kid, and I will always love her for that.

Of course if Nann was upset, well then everyone was subject to that as well. But that was rare. Sometimes it was even fun! When the adults would all start yelling and throwing things around the house! The cousins and I would hide and laugh until it blew over. She usually calmed her temper pretty quickly, or she would leave if she knew it was going to take longer than a minute. I don't know where she went, but I always felt bad for whoever was there. Wherever it was! Our family wasn't that big, but it sure was fun sometimes!

It was all far easier when I was little, but I still didn't understand it. Not then. I just knew that it was always more fun to be at Nann's house, or out somewhere with her. I had no notion of *why* it was better, I just knew, even then that it was. It kind of reminded me of Liliana and Ben too, which I had to admit worried me a little.

I still wasn't sure if my daughter had inherited whatever gene I carried that made me just screwed up enough to feel other people's emotions. I watched her for signs of it all the time. But it was hard to tell what was really more than ordinary empathy and what I might be projecting due to an overactive imagination.

We had agreed to try to relax for a while. Not push it on her either way, and just see how things developed. So far, so good and I knew we were both grateful for that. But then my childhood had been pretty quiet too. At least early on.

Then there was Ben's ability to be a quiet place that had always made him attractive to me. I had to at least consider that he could be having a similar positive, and therefore masking effect on her as well.

That could be why we couldn't see her abilities as much but it could also be another part of why she preferred to spend time with him, just like I had with Nann and she didn't realize why yet either. That possibility was also another reason that I didn't fight the current custody situation harder. If that's what he was for her, and I couldn't be sure that he wasn't, I certainly wouldn't take that away from her and replace it with a parent that embodied chaos. It could be the difference between a happy childhood, and years of turmoil for her.

I couldn't go back and relive *my* childhood, but I would do whatever I could to make hers better. Easier. If Ben was her Nann, then she would have him. I'd had mine. For a while, anyway.

With everybody else, my mood was always anybody's guess. There were whole years after Nann was gone, where my parents had me in and out of counseling because my mood swings were so erratic. I was never a *bad* kid, at least not on purpose. I was just highly emotional and painfully unpredictable. Disruptive is probably a better word than "bad." I always had a knack for having the worst days on the most important ones for them. I hated not being in control of it back then and I took it out on everyone around me. Mercilessly sometimes, but mostly whether I really wanted to or not.

L. Pelletier

My parents never gave up on me but they did eventually give up on the counseling. After a while it started to become more and more apparent that my mood swings were not really about my own moods, but were actually directly related to the moods of those I came in contact with. Sometimes it was with people I knew, that I should naturally empathize with. But just as many times it was the same with complete strangers.

They didn't understand it necessarily, but they were smart enough to realize that it wasn't something that a psychologist was going to be able to fix. My mother in particular, had heard just enough talk about such things growing up in our family, to realize that wasn't the answer.

As we eventually became more aware of what was happening, I started to be able to recognize better when an unexpected feeling would flood through me. It would take me a minute sometimes, to realize that *I* hadn't really felt that way, but that *someone else* had! Someone near me. Once I knew what it was and how to differentiate it, it was easier to ignore and life finally began to calm down some. Peace finally returned to our lives to some extent.

I was finally able to take some time to focus on other things a little. Be a regular teenager. It didn't go away, not by any means, but I began to learn how to move it to the background where it belonged.

We didn't talk about it much for a long time after that. It was really nice once we were able to enjoy a relationship again without that one element taking over all the time and no one wanted to force it back into the conversation.

My mom was, and still is a nurse in the ER, and she had worked long hours for as long as I could remember. But even through all the crazy stuff over the years, she somehow always managed to be at every school play or playoff game when it mattered. She made sure of it. Especially when things got better. Even if that meant switching for an overnight shift to make it happen. She didn't care, she would do it.

People always say I look most like her. We share the same long golden brown hair and warm hazel eyes. Her easy smile is all her own though and it was always simple to pick from any crowd.

Even with her inability to understand or develop my particular talents, she had been a better mother than I could even hope to be. She still was. And although she often had no idea what to do with me growing up, she had loved me unconditionally 100% of the time. For that, I felt the same in return. Liliana was lucky now too I thought, to have her for a Grandmother.

Even though she learned to accept it back then, she didn't want other people to take advantage of me or punish me unfairly for being different, so she always insisted that I keep my "special talents" to myself as much as possible. By that time I had it fairly well controlled, so it wasn't really that much of a stretch to just shut up. Not my strong point mind you, but I could do it when I had to.

Dad was a little bit of a tougher customer than mom had been when it came to me getting the most out of life. He was a professor at the University and as *"type-A"* as they come. He had chocolate brown hair that had handled well the addition of a few scattered grays. They only added to his classic *"New England Preppy"* good looks. He was tall and broad shouldered, with a strong jaw, but it gave a deceiving first impression because he was almost always soft spoken. He was truly a *gentle* man.

Sure he loved me. He couldn't hope to hide that. He spoiled me rotten. But he always expected 110% from me and then some in return. I think he thought that for every nutty tendency I had, I needed to balance it out with *two* equally useful life skills. I was happy to humor him for the most part. Especially once it was mostly under control. I felt like I had a lot of lost time to make up for. It was usually fun anyway.

Thanks to my Dad, I could play a half decent piano or violin. I had a strong brown belt in karate that still inspire a lot of my stretches to this day. I played only a passable shortstop in softball, but back then I could do a mean sow cow on figure skates. Though that one, not so much anymore.

He never acted like he was unhappy with me, quite the opposite actually. He just always pushed me to learn something new. "Anything you *really* want to do, you can do!" He's always saying. Literally, always! But I love him for it. It's a great attitude to instill in your children, I think. Mostly I was grateful for the looseness with which he held the reigns while I explored my newfound freedom. I know now, being a parent myself, that it couldn't have always been easy for him.

I know part of it was just his way of dealing with my particular issues. His plan of action was to keep me too busy to focus on anything but what I was doing in that moment. It worked too, to some extent. I think that's a very important, learned skill as well, the ability to consciously block out something that is beyond your control and function in spite of it. I always appreciated him teaching me that, even if that hadn't been his intention exactly. It wasn't always possible either, but when it was, it served me well.

He supported me too, any way he could. Whether it was through rides, regular spectator status or strictly by paying fee after fee for anything I signed up for. Whatever I needed, as long as I was doing something constructive, he was happy to provide.

Some things were harder for me than others, with my preexisting skill set. I was always willing to explore new things though, in the hopes of finding a safe place or two within the bunch.

Karate was hard to take, with the large crowd and the level of aggression, but I hung in there because I found that I loved the physicality of it. It actually kind of *helped* to focus in on all of the tension around me then turn it outward in the form of a kick or a punch. It wasn't something that you really got to do that often if you thought about it. To vent, *physically,* in a safe environment. I found it very cathartic.

Piano was by far the easiest. It was quiet then, always. That had been my first experience with the quieting effects of music in general. But out of all of that, I had still found the walks that my dad and I took together to be my favorite pass-time of all.

We started walking the neighborhoods and hills around our home after dinner to enjoy the view of the sunset. Either up on Outlook Hill, or down in the park. I found that if I walked at a steady rate long enough, that it worked nicely as a type of block, like white noise, and it could slow-the-flow as well.

It was a nice break. It was scenic, *and* fairly peaceful. So I would want to just keep going. He would always shrug his shoulders and say, *"I'm game."* and we would just keep going. Sometimes we walked for hours. People came to know eventually, that if we left for a walk not to expect us back for a while.

I loved that time together with him. He spent a lot of hours at the University, which was totally normal and to be expected given his seniority there. But it was nice that we always had some way to hang out together. Whether it was a ride somewhere, another activity or just a hike through the hills, we had our time together. So I didn't begrudge him all the good work he did. I was really proud of the way he managed to nurture both his career and his family. Both of mparents had been great role models in that way.

I had my issues sure, but I was still a lucky girl and I knew it.

By the end of high school, I had started to make more of the decisions about which things I wanted to spend my time doing. My interests by then had turned decidedly towards boys and the arts. In that order.

The boy part would take me years to get right, even though I really gave it my best effort to care about a few of them. Teenage boys seriously spend about 85% of their waking hours thinking about sex, even if they know better than to mention it out loud every time it pops into their head. The problem was *I* still knew it every time. I found it really hard to constantly overlook. I just didn't have the patience to be with anyone long enough for it to matter. It made it hard to form any kind of real connection with anyone or to even take them seriously, which wasn't always fair but I couldn't always help it.

I felt like I hadn't really had a guy's full attention since puberty hit and my chest had filled out. I had wondered back then, at what age it would get better.

Hah! Little did I know!

I liked the way it felt to create something though, whether it was on paper or in clay or seemingly any other medium they threw at me. So while I mostly failed miserably at the boyfriend part, the art part stuck.

It wasn't even the result so much that I cared about, as the action itself that I found I really enjoyed. I noticed pretty quickly how peaceful it was once I was involved in a project. I would stop feeling overwhelmed by the anger from the girl behind me. Who I had talked to enough to guess that her moody artist boyfriend Rafael, had most likely cheated on her again. The incessantly chipper waves of energy from the instructor would fade off blissfully into the background, where they belonged. And I would stop feeling amorous at awkward times from the mood floating up to me on my left, where Rafael sat enjoying his sexual daydreams.

It was very confusing to get turned on because you were feeling someone else's feelings, when that person happened to be turned on by *you*. At least I assumed it was me, since he stared at me half the time and smiled to himself the other half. Plus, I was pretty sure I was the only female left in the class that he *hadn't* slept with, so I assumed it was the thrill of the chase that he enjoyed. It was never going to happen, but it didn't stop him from thinking about it. Or me from feeling it when he did.

With him, it felt weird and narcissistic somehow. When I was interested in someone though and they liked me back, then those feelings would go back and forth between us, and end up doubling up for me. Then it was great! *Believe me!* Another little bonus of this particular gift of mine that I didn't mind. I had been a little overwhelmed by that discovery at first, I will admit. But after some privately conducted research and plenty of practice under the bleachers at school, I learned to get that under control too. Or at least adjust to it. Again, it was all about the balance. But when those feelings came at me from a stranger or even worse, a friends' boyfriend, it was just annoying. So it was nice to have found a way to occasionally block it out.

Ironically though, even though I was there for the act itself, the results actually weren't half bad. By the time I was sixteen they were good enough to get me into a few highly sought after classes around town. Even a few of the mixed age courses at the University, which is where I was lucky enough to work next to Rafael. Although I was sure that being Professor Harrington's daughter hadn't hurt my chances in that particular case.

I was still young, but I had *never* had the luxury of being *naïve*. That was just a fantasy for me, something I watched play out in movies.

I took oil painting, photography and sculpture classes and hung out with older brooding artist types while I explored the different effects each medium had on my psyche. Their emotional status was tiring at times but at least for the most part, it was usually predictable.

The loopy free spirits, I could take. It was the one's full of self-hate that I stayed away from. It hit too close to that self-pitying part of me that I tried not to give in to. I had mostly come to terms with my *"gifts."* I had accepted that I would always be a little different. But I refused to let that make me a victim. I didn't hide it, but I didn't focus on it either. I just tried to live my life with the best balance that I could find. Life was too short to focus any more than necessary on the negative. *That* I already knew for sure.

With that goal in mind, I managed to keep a pretty decent attitude most of the time and keep the empath part of me, at least mostly under control.

It wasn't until it was time to go off to college, and out on my own, that the subject really came up again seriously. My parents were good solid, hard-working, loving people. They didn't understand how things like my gift worked, but they weren't so ignorant that they denied it existed all together. My mother in particular, having been brought up in a whole family of believers, was never one to say something didn't exist even if it had never touched her personally. But they still wanted me to.

"It will just be easier." My mother would argue. "Save that kind of personal information for those who become more permanent in your life. Casual acquaintances don't need to know every single thing about you." She would insist.

As much as I hated to waste energy on the pretense, I finally decided that she was probably right. As frustrating as it is, mothers usually are. So I managed to keep it pretty quiet throughout my first year while I got used to the place, and its usual noise. I didn't go too far away. Only a two hour drive. But it was far enough to feel the separation for the first time. Back then, at that age, that had been the most important thing. I wanted to really feel like I was on my own. Completely. Just for a little while though. It was like a trial run because I knew I could go home at any time. It was strange at first, but I settled in pretty quickly. For every loud cafeteria, there was a warehouse sized library to make up for it. For every mind numbing mid-term, there was a party in someone's dorm room afterwards. Balance.

By my sophomore year, I had made a few friends who were close enough to me by then to notice. One of which was Vivianne, who is still my best friend today.

Then, she was like a long lost sister. Right from the day we met. Maybe in another life we were sisters, who knows. I felt like I had already known her for years. She would be there by my nursing home bedside when I died or I would be there at hers. However it ended, one way or the other, we would be friends until the end. That is just the kind of friendship that we have.

It isn't perfect and neither is she. But of course neither am I. That's why it works. We both know and accept each other's imperfections unconditionally. Everyone needs one friend on this Earth that they can count on that with.

She had been in the break area of the study hall when we met. She had jet black hair with a shockingly bright blue streak and she was sitting with her feet up on the table looking like she owned the place. I had spent so much time over the years just trying to fit in. It was very freeing to me to see someone who not only refused to do it, but also thoroughly *enjoyed* not doing it!

She smiled broadly at me. Most would have taken that as a challenge or a slight, but I could sense right away that there was nothing but honest, unabashed joy behind that smile. I knew right then that we were going to be great friends. She always says I am the only one who ever *"gets"* her.

Eh. So I cheat, so what? Every relationship has a reason that it works.

I ended up having a great time at college, but I did not necessarily come out of it with a plan. Or even a direction. My parents were a little disappointed when I came home with my art degree and not a clue of what I wanted to do with it.

And so I found myself, after graduation, without a current goal and without a steady boyfriend still. My dad was dealing with some major upheaval at the University at the time, with the Dean being asked to resign under suspicion of embezzlement. It was taking up all his time helping to cover shifts and handle scheduling conflicts.

Mom was at the ER as usual most of the waking hours. They didn't mind me being home. That was easy of course, because neither one was ever present to mind. They were happy to have me there at the moment to feed and walk the lonely pets, and water the poor wilting plants.

And so, I was temporarily given a reprieve from starting whatever would come next. For the first time since I was a little kid, I found myself with free time. I was pretty excited about that. I decided that I would just go and sit in the park and enjoy the sun for a while. In New England it didn't always last that long and we know how to take advantage of it when it makes an appearance.

I gave up on the boyfriend and the purpose for the time being. I was going to just be single and carefree for a while. See how that went for a summer.

So of course, that was when I met Ben.

Chapter 4

The park was about three blocks from my parents' house and it was the largest open natural area in the city, so naturally I gravitated there, even when I wasn't walking with my dad.

There were always at least a handful of people there. Picnickers, sunbathers, or Frisbee players. Even occasionally hikers. Though not serious ones, since the whole park was only four and a half square miles. It was pretty though, with the flowering fruit trees in the spring, and the beautiful maples and oak's changing colors in the fall. The city paid a local landscaping company to maintain the park and all its' meandering flower gardens and trails year round.

It was quite a scenic spot actually. There were benches and gazebos that ball-gowned and tuxedo clad people often pooled out of limousines to take pictures on.

It was far from private, but still so much quieter than any other public place nearby that I could think of to go to. So I spent a lot of that summer lying on a blanket, reading books and walking along the trails. There was always something to do, or somewhere to go with friends from the neighborhood, or with Viv who luckily lived nearby in the same city, but there never seemed to be enough time to just *chill*. So I was pretty happy to do just *that* whenever I could get away with it. I knew it wouldn't last. Life was a constant cycle. And usually I could feel the gravity of the circle start to shift, long before the tilt ever became apparent.

That one, particularly hot August day however, I had not seen it coming at all.

I was sitting by the stone fountain enjoying the sun on my face when a feeling of intense anger rushed through me. I blinked. It was quickly followed by an incredible sense of fear. I lifted my head just in time to see a group of teenagers come racing at me on their bikes. *Whoa!*

The two in back started screaming obscenities at the one in front, who was obviously peddling for his life. I didn't catch enough, verbally or emotionally, to know what he had done. Nor could I tell if he deserved the anger that was aimed at him or not. But it was just enough warning for me to jump out of the way before the fleeing cyclist ran right into me! Just *barely* enough. I had twisted to my left to get out of the way. But the fountain was still too close and I bumped the cement edge, scraping my knee, and fell into the flower bed beside it. If I hadn't felt their upset first, I wouldn't have even made it that far.

I had been admiring the beautiful rose bushes there and considering drawing them before my tranquility was interrupted. The same bushes that I could feel underneath me. I knew from the cracks that I had heard as I fell, that at least one of them was not going to be in good shape. I didn't expect the back of my white tank top to be anymore either, between the thorns that had ripped through it and the blood I could feel seeping into it. Unfortunately, all the karate in the world could not help you against a rose's thorns. Life lesson learned.

At first, I was pissed. But I quickly realized that there was no one left to be pissed *at,* so using a technique that I had perfected over the years, I took a few slow, deep breaths as I worked hard to let it go. I had decided at one point, that it made no sense to hold onto emotions that weren't even mine, and sometimes, even the ones that were. I took another deep breath, feeling that much closer to calm.

I didn't move right away. For the first few seconds, I was still stunned by what had just happened. The next few, I spent laughing at myself. After that, I was trying to come up with a plan of action for the best way to get out without doing even more damage. To the bushes or myself, especially since I did still want to be *wearing* a shirt when I stood up and it felt pretty well stuck.

As I contemplated my options, my favorite at the moment

being to just stay there indefinitely, a hand reached out to me. I was shocked at first because I hadn't noticed anyone approaching. Normally I would get *something* off of anyone near me. It was very unusual for anyone to be able to sneak up on me like that! So of course, it surprised me.

I looked up, curious to see who was attached to that arm and I found a pair of green eyes staring back at me. Smiling, emerald green eyes. He seemed harmless enough, but I still couldn't get a handle on him at all and that was very unsettling to me.

The eyes were surrounded by sandy blonde hair and a tanned face where the rest of the smile was lingering. It was a very generous smile, full of shiny white teeth. "Need a hand?" he asked, obviously amused.

"*Hmpf...* Uh yeah, thanks." I replied ever so eloquently as I took the offered hand. Oh well, I couldn't get a read on him but I was thinking that even if he killed me, he would have to get me out of the bushes first to do it, right? I'd start with that and hope for the best at that point. But as soon as I reached for his hand I immediately thought to myself, no wait. I suppose if you're going to kill someone, then the bushes would be a fine and convenient place to leave them, now wouldn't it? Oh well, too late.

As he carefully pulled me up I could tell that he obviously worked there in the park, as evidenced by his requisite uniform. The well-worn Levi's, complete with a tool belt full of clippers and shovels of various sizes. Combined with his work boots and darkly tanned, bare upper body, it was a no-brainer. I was embarrassed to find that the rest of him was just as handsome as his face and there I was lying in a rosebush, shirt torn and bloody. Awesome!

Not!

Normally, I wouldn't even be talking to a hunk like him. Too much self-love for me to stomach. Sorry for the generalization, but I've found it to be true more often than not when they are *that* pretty, unfortunately. But by the time we had finished laughing together at my misfortune, I could tell that he was different somehow. I couldn't put my finger on it at first... *then I realized what it was!*

It was *precisely* that I couldn't put my finger on it! I

couldn't seem to feel his every intention like I usually could with most people. Either he was an incredibly even-keeled guy or he was one of those rare people whose emotions didn't broadcast out much, or *at all!* They weren't super rare, but neither were they terribly common for me to come across.

At first I wanted to spend more time with him just to be sure that's what he really was. To try and figure it out. I realized that was obviously why I hadn't felt him approach originally. When it had finally dawned on me around seventeen, that *people* could actually be a *"safe place."* I finally understood that that's exactly what Nann had been.

And that's apparently what *he* was too, in a way.

Wow. That changed things for me. Just realizing that there were more people out there like that than I thought, opened up new possibilities in life for me. Things I thought that I might never really get to enjoy properly.

I also just enjoyed being with him. He was very easy to spend time with. Even without being constantly, overly aware of his private feelings, I knew what kind of soul he was. Honest and kind. It was apparent in everything he said and did. Even the little things that were harder to fake. I could also read his emotions easily on his open face like everybody else, but they didn't barge through me uninvited. They stayed in his head where they belonged.

I'm sure he thought about sex just as much as the next guy, too. In fact knowing him as I do now, I would have to say, probably more. But it didn't matter to me because for once, I couldn't sense it. I wasn't forced to try to sit and ignore it all day long. Being with him was so much easier than it had ever been with anyone else. I could just be myself and not spend the whole time blocking. It was a welcome change.

I'm not gonna lie. I was pretty excited at the prospect of spending time flirting with a guy, without knowing every thought in his head in return. There would finally be some mystery. Some fear of the unknown. A little bit of a challenge for me romantically, at last! Of course we all know you should be careful what you wish for.

When we hung out at first, it was more about that peace

of mind. He was older than me. Not a lot, he was 24 to my 20, but it seems like a bigger deal when you're younger and we still didn't date right away. Not for some time actually.

In the beginning, I was too obsessed with the work that he did while I watched. I was mesmerized by how intent he was when trimming the bushes into just the right shape. Or slowly nursing a carelessly broken rose bush back to health. I would sit and watch and we would talk. When he was done, the garden would be transformed.

He saw it as one big living entity and he would tell me that, "Once you started to treat it that way, it could to do amazing things with a small amount of help from us." He didn't just make up pretty things to say either. He actually knew what he was talking about. So I ended up asking him to teach me. To let me help in the gardens for free and learn to create a scene the way he did. I had free time and an eagerness to learn. He had plenty of work and was intrigued by the challenge. A deal was struck.

I could tell that he was interested too, even without knowing all his inner feelings intimately, but he was obviously also intent on ignoring that part. At least for a while. We were both attracted to each other, but trying not to focus on it.

For a long time, I was determined not to mess that up. I hadn't met too many other *safe* people in my life at that point, but I was eager then to see how many others I could find. In the meantime we would become friends, Ben and I. Good friends. And, well, I continued to have fun with the outside search, though most of my attention was still spent on the projects he let me help with in the gardens. It was a great way for us to spend time together without it being weird or needing more definition.

It was also my first taste of art and nature combined and I found I *really* liked it! It brought my two most satisfying things together. It wasn't just about being with him then anymore. Working silently within the black soil that lied just past the beautiful edging along the paths, I found a peace and a beauty that I hadn't felt since I was a child. It not only helped me to Zen out, it *refueled* me! So there was *that* too!

So the gardens became a very important place for me. Of course the more it came to mean to me, the more afraid I became that I would screw it up with any attempt at romance. The one thing I had never been particularly good at. So the temptation towards that lessened and the distance grew. It helped that he was feeling the same way.

He was fully enjoying the challenge of teaching me his craft. But even more than that, was the fact that fairly early on in our honest relationship, I had shared with him the existence of *my* unique talents. That had left him just as fascinated to learn more from me. It became a delicate balance of getting what we each wanted out of our meetings without pushing it too far and scaring the other off. We became surprisingly good at it due to the fact that we were extremely cognizant of it.

Plus, a part of me needed to be sure that I knew what I was comparing it to, if I did ever get a chance to be with him. I had a feeling that what we could have might be real and possibly even permanent. I wasn't ready for that yet. I didn't think he was then either. But when I was, I wanted to have a point of reference to be able to judge just how amazing he really was. So we hung out. A lot. We stayed close. We dated other people during that time, but we also worked a lot of hours in the garden together.

It didn't take me too long to figure out what it was that made him such a safe place either. It was because he was what I would categorize as a *fixer*. Yes, I have categories. Just basic generalizations. In my book, a fixer was someone who took in the wounded all around them and healed them.

In order to do that, I felt like he had to have an ingoing signal. So he would be able to pick up outgoing mental SOS's, like the one he would have gotten from me on the day we had met in the park. Most people generally had an *outgoing* signal. That would be all the stuff that I picked up all the time, so in truth, he was actually more like me than he realized. I kind of liked that. But whether I did or not, it was his thing and once I identified it, he didn't bother to deny it. He just shrugged his shoulders and smiled, at peace with his place in the world.

He was still studying to become a vet back when we met, even though he was gardening at the time to help pay for school. It didn't seem to matter what type of living thing he tended to though. Plants, animals or people. He was just as skilled at caring for all of them.

Sometimes his fixing was done metaphorically. Sometimes physically. Sometimes the stray in need of help was an animal, or a dying plant. Then just as many times it was a friend or even a complete stranger. It didn't matter. He didn't turn away anyone or anything in need.

It always amazed me that people didn't seem to take advantage of him the way one would expect. Probably just because he was a big strong looking guy, I guess. Who knows? But he holds his own, kindness intact. I have always found that, in and of itself, to be one of his most impressive qualities. He was smart enough to know that he didn't need to be physical to be in control of a situation. His goal in life was to fix things, not to destroy them. He treated all living things with the same care and attention, myself included.

That was a big part of why it worked between us for so long, why we were drawn so strongly to each other in the beginning. But I can also tell you now, without a doubt, that it was also largely responsible for eventually driving us apart.

When it came right down to it, Ben could never *fix* me. Eventually he came to know my issues and even more importantly, to accept them. But that meant that he would never succeed in that one vital area. I think it started to make him feel like a failure somehow in his own eyes, and I hated that. I couldn't fight that.

It had never really been his job to fix me. I knew that, but I had been content to let him try, for a while.

We had taken our time, and carefully managed to keep things platonic between us for about nine months before we finally lost the ability to stay apart physically.

We had each spent the better part of the winter involved with other people, but we had been working together almost constantly throughout. By that spring, neither of us happened to be seeing anyone anymore when we were completing a tremendously challenging project at a private home.

It was still only early spring, but it was one of those really hot *summer preview* days that we would get out of nowhere before the temperature would drop predictably back into the sixties again for a week following. But for this one glorious weekend in April, it was in the 80's, and it was practically a heat wave. Luckily for us, the owner of the estate that we were working on was one of those *super-on-top-of-everything* kind of guys when it came to household maintenance. That was why his beautiful, heated in-ground pool was already open and ready to go, even though the family was not due back home for another week and it usually wasn't warm enough to swim for another month.

By the time we had finished planting the hundreds of plants that the massive project had required, we were dripping in sweat and decided that it would be a shame to let the sparkling, beckoning pool go unappreciated.

We hadn't thought to bring bathing suits, but as it turned out, it hadn't mattered. We started out laughing and joking and ended up pushing each other in with all our clothes on. We laughed and splashed each other and had a great time. Until we found ourselves tangled together. Once that happened, it was too late to turn back. Passion lit off like a tinder box. Things got serious and the clothes floated off.

What we started in the pool, we finished on the warm patio stones in the long stretching, afternoon shadows of the surrounding arborvitae. We didn't go into it with a conscious decision, either one of us, but afterwards we both admitted we had no regrets.

We realized at that point that it was time to either take a chance and give it a shot or walk away once and for all. We made it pretty clear that day which way we wanted to take it. And we did. We went willingly and quite happily, for a while. Looking back it was almost as if we knew deep down that despite the intensity of our relationship, that it had an "expiration after opening" date. Maybe that was why we put it off so long, I don't know.

Though when he proposed on that first years' anniversary of our *first time*, I had no doubt in that moment that we would be together forever. It was a small but beautiful wedding in the park. We got married in the gazebo by a JP, and had dinner under the giant wooden trellis on the side by the fountain, where we had first met. The grape vines wrapped around the entire structure and mixed perfectly with the miles and miles of tiny white lights we had put up for the occasion.

My parents had always loved Ben, and his mom, June, was as kind and caring as he was. It was easy to see where he got it from. His dad had passed away when he was only five years old but his step dad Brad, affectionately known as *"Brad-Dad,"* had been a great role model and mentor, without ever trying to *replace* his dad. He was also madly in love with his mom and always treated her like a queen. Those two things had been key to a young Ben, and they are still very close today. Not only did we both like each other's parents, but our parents liked each other as well. They often got together without us for card nights and dinners. Things were good.

That was the case a lot of the time in the beginning. The best time of all being when Liliana came into our lives. We had been shocked to learn that she was coming, not having planned on starting a family quite that soon. But shock very quickly turned to love. I liked to say that "She wasn't *our* plan. She was the plan of someone a lot smarter than us." By the time she was born we couldn't wait to meet her. She had us both wrapped from the moment we saw her and has every day ever since. Our life wasn't all joy and rapture though. There were bad times too.

It didn't happen overnight, but it did become apparent pretty early on, that maybe I *wasn't* the person who would be able to make him happy. I mean *really, truly* happy. With nothing missing, or getting in the way. Not just *"passing-ly"* happy. I started to feel like maybe that really *wasn't* good enough for the rest of his life. Perhaps, I began to also realize, it was true in the reverse as well. That was a real surprise, to both of us I think and a *really sad* one. Neither one of us had seen that impasse coming.

We *had* taken a real honest shot though, at making it work. We had given it all we had. I really felt like our story was most like that Dave Mason song. *"There ain't no good guy, there ain't no bad guy. There's only you and me and we just disagree."* I couldn't bring myself to regret the love we shared. For however long it lasted, it was right at the time. And I knew for sure that my Liliana was absolutely meant to be! I'll say it again. I really believe that every relationship has a reason that it works. I know now undoubtedly that she was ours. And for her alone, I would do it all again in a heartbeat.

We had tried to ignore the disappointment in the beginning. When it became apparent that we couldn't, we tried to work around it like a good married couple should. We kept up the effort for quite some time before it became too hard to pull off anymore. It's so easy to be ignorant. It truly is bliss. It's a lot harder to *unlearn* something once you knew it to be true.

We both loved Liliana so much and wanted everything for her from the moment that we knew she existed. We knew that splitting, no matter how amicably, would divide her to some extent and we truly avoided it for as long as we could.

Eventually though, a few strained years of honest effort later, that original doubt that had started as a tiny seed had grown to the point where it had become much more toxic than separation was. It became obvious that it was just time.

We had taken a chance on love, a first for both of us and I know we had both worked hard at making it work. But I couldn't help feeling that, no matter how much you loved someone, it just shouldn't be *that* hard.

It was one of the saddest days of my life when we finally had to admit it. First out loud, to each other. Then to Liliana.

Her feelings, I feel as strongly as my own. Thankfully, that had made it very easy to care for her as a baby, before she could tell me what she wanted. But it also meant that on that day, my sadness was immediately doubled.

She knew it was time too, though. Had known it was coming, I could tell. There was sadness sure, but there was no surprise anywhere in her mix of feelings, no shock. Way down underneath that, there was even a little bit of relief. I could relate, but I really wished that she couldn't. Always so much more grown up then she should be.

I couldn't help thinking then, that she may have more of me in her than I wanted to believe after all.

Chapter 5

As my thoughts wandered back to the present once again, I heard the Magician starting up an acoustic version of Eric Clapton's *"Layla"* and I marveled at how long I could get lost in my own thoughts and feelings there. Maybe that wasn't always such a good thing. I took a deep breath and finished the last of my wine.

I tried to get back to my sketches but even with the music, the memories were proving to be too much and I couldn't focus anymore. I sat with my eyes closed for a bit, breathing slowly, trying to clear myself of all the emotion. Relying once again on my meditation techniques. Thankfully, it usually worked pretty well.

After a while I realized that the music had stopped. My Magician was done for the night, and so was I. As I started to gather up my pencils and my mostly finished sketches, a strange feeling washed over me from somewhere across the room.

I always hated when that first wave would hit me after the music or whatever had been blocking for me had stopped. It was silly really, but even now it still manages to startle me. Almost every time. It's like having someone tap you on the shoulder, when you hadn't seen or heard them approach at all!

What hit me then was hard to identify at first. Kind of a mix of things. A longing, combined with excitement, mixed with anxiety. I looked up. I didn't see anyone new at first. I searched the room myself then for someone else who was doing the same thing and I saw him.

He was young, probably not even old enough to sit at the bar. He was the only one over there and I was sure now that it was him that the feelings were emanating from.

He was cute. Surfer blonde hair, bright blue eyes. Tall, but still too lithely muscular in a way that only a *just-recently-grown* man could be. You know, still brand new. Everything freshly stretched to its' adult length, but not filled out yet. It always reminds me of Bambi when I see young men at this stage. Thrown into full size, fully functioning bodies with no idea yet how to use them. So beautiful and so awkward. It made me smile to myself.

I wondered briefly what he was searching for and I noticed the direction of his attention was towards the stage.

Then I noticed that the Magician had also looked up before locking his guitar case, and stared back at the newcomer for a minute. One of his patented *"look right through you"* stares. Then he grabbed his case and walked off back stage and surfer boy turned away and went back to his soda. I was still getting anxiety but it was quieter then. Patient. A minute later Dani dropped his bill on the table and I got nothing else from him. It was weird. Like he'd just shut down.

Hmm? Wonder what that was all about. Once I thought about it, I realized that it wasn't the first time. Something similar had happened two nights ago with a young girl. She had come in with three friends for dinner, but ended up sitting at an empty table near the stage by herself for a while, watching The Magician play.

Normally I wouldn't notice but whenever the music stopped, her fear and anxiety would wash over me. I kept wondering what had her so worried, but she never showed any outward sign of what it was, and I had no reason to ask.

I had forgotten all about it but what just happened had triggered a memory that I had of The Magician giving *her* that stare at one point during the night too.

One bad thing about *feeling* every situation was that I got used to always having an understanding of the things going on around me. My mind had come to expect an explanation for all things that it didn't always get. So when something piques my interest and doesn't present a suitable explanation, I find it very unsettling. I don't know how to mentally file it away, so I end up holding it in a virtual *"to be figured out later"* pile. When that happens, no matter how small a thing, it will stay in that "actively awaiting explanation" section of my brain until it makes sense. However long that takes.

It was popping up like a red flag in my mind then. Now I had two of those memories filed away.

I grabbed my portfolio and my bag and I left two twenties on the table. I walked out into the warm spring night, balancing my stuff on my left hip while I dug my keys out.

Then I felt it. A sudden rush of panic and desperation! *Yikes!* Someone was close by and determined to do... *something!* In a parking lot at night, that was usually not good. Even in a backwoods parking lot. Dammit, *especially* in a backwoods parking lot! *Ooooooh, not good...*

My gaze scanned the lot for the responsible party and it didn't take long to land on surfer boy coming around from behind the back of the building. I automatically dropped my stuff to the ground at my feet. My hands went up and my feet went into a semi-defensive stance at the surprise, my old karate lessons kicking in. I probably forgot more than I remembered, but I hoped that I at least still *looked* like I knew what I was doing.

"You have to make him take me!" He insisted emphatically as he thankfully came to a stop across the space from me. *"Please!"* He stood there with his arms outstretched at me, looking at wits end and I was not at all comforted by that.

"Look, I don't know who or what you're talking about, but maybe someone inside can help you." I offered easily, trying hard to be a calming force. I was still just picking up major desperation off of him and it wasn't reassuring me in the least.

"That's what *I* thought!" He shouted back. "But he said it was too soon. That I should come back... *but I can't... I can't come back...*" He finished weakly, rubbing his hands across his eyes. I took the moment to assess my opponent.

He may be new to his physique, and it may not have filled out yet, but he was broad shouldered, obviously very strong and *really* tall. That was still more than enough to be sufficiently imposing. Even at a good ten feet away, I felt like he was fairly towering over me. With that and an overexcited mental state, I had no doubt he could throw me across the parking lot if he tried. So far he hadn't thank God, but I had no idea what he was waiting for.

I was torn between running back inside or trying to make it into the car when he suddenly fell back against the building in a heap. He slid slowly down the side until he was sitting on the ground, his hands mercilessly gripping handfuls of his blond mop.

Now he was just pushing waves of defeat. *Ahhhhh?* What to do, what to do? My instinct, of course was to help him, but I had no idea *how* or if it was even a good idea. It still felt like a trap. *Hmmm.*

I didn't get to ponder it for more than a second before the decision was taken away from me. A small, fast looking, shiny black car flew up behind me and caught me by surprise. When I turned, I was even more surprised to see my Magician's face revealed in the small space that appeared in the window where it *whooshed* down a few inches.

Huh? I was no expert, but that did not look like the kind of car that belonged to a local singer in a small town bar. I was immediately distracted wondering what he did when he *wasn't* singing. Robbing banks? Dealing drugs? Something *worse?* Or was it as simple as family money perhaps? I hated things without obvious answers. He wasn't giving any off inadvertently either. Only thing I was picking up from that direction was strained patience. Nothing else what-so-ever.

He gave a short whistle to Surfer Boy and a quick waving motion for him to get in when he looked up. Surfer Boy did not hesitate. He jumped up, ran over to the passenger side as the door raised up like something out of a car commercial and he hopped in. The door went smoothly back down as the pretty little black car pulled away, and all was quiet again.

I was suddenly *very* alone in the empty lot. I exhaled in disbelief.

Did that really just happen?

Chapter 6

Ooooooookay?! I took a few deep breaths and waited for my heart rate to return to normal. *What the Hell was that all about?!*

Yup, that one was *definitely* gonna stick. Things were getting a little too weird around there. Even for me, and that was saying a lot. As I bent to pick up my sketch books and pencils that were scattered around my feet, I thought about the most unsettling part, which was that too many weird things lately had at least one common denominator, my mysterious *Magician.* That was number three, and the hardest so far to let go of.

I was so tired after all of that though, that I practically fell into my car. I had to keep the window open all the way home. I was glad that it was a beautiful night and that it wasn't far. Because as much as I didn't want to fall asleep at the wheel, I really *hated* being cold!

In no time at all, I found myself pulling down the long curving drive that separated the property where I rented my own personal little piece of paradise, hidden safely from the rest of the world. Once you turned off the street, and started on the first turn through the enveloping greenery, you could forget that the main road and the rest of the world even existed. I couldn't pull down there without feeling an instant sense of peace. It was inherent to the location and I loved it.

I didn't know where it generated from. If it was the many beautiful things growing there, like the mature fruit trees with all their springtime flowers blooming that made the area around the farm so peaceful. Or if there was something in the area that generated its' own good energy and in turn, gave life to all the beautiful things around it. It was like the chicken and the egg all over again. One could spend hours upon hours pondering it and still not know the answer.

Either way, I didn't have to understand it to know how lucky I was to find a spot like that in the first place. Never mind one that had a gorgeous little studio apartment that I could actually *afford* to rent! It had been fate for sure.

It all started one morning when I stopped at the little diner downtown for breakfast. Just as I was sitting down, I noticed a hundred dollar bill on the floor. I looked up to see an older man vacating the next table. He was the only other patron at the moment so it wasn't hard to guess who it must've belonged to.

He was probably early fifties, but obviously in very good shape for his age. He stood straight and tall to his full height of roughly six feet, his shoulders square and strong. His white hair was straight and shiny and was pulled back into a single, long ponytail under his baseball hat. Between his physique and the *leatherized* look of his neck and face that only a lifetime of working outdoors could give you, I could tell already that he was an honest hard-working man who surely couldn't afford to lose a hundred dollars. Not that too many people could. I would have done the same for just about anyone but I could personally relate to the hardship that it would cause this type of person even more, so it felt even better to be able to save him from that fate.

I searched the atmosphere around me for some kind of hint of mischief, in case someone was just messing around. I was new to the area after all. You never know. People can be weird. Hell, *I* was proof enough of that.

I didn't sense any anxiety or malice. Although, *Hmmmm....*

I decided to risk it. "Excuse me, mister?" I said as I left the chair I had barely rested in and reached for the bill on the floor. Picking it up and offering it back to him, I said, "Here, Sir? Looks like you dropped this."

He turned to look at me warily, but his attitude changed fast enough when he saw what I was holding. "Oh wow! Thanks!

I can't tell you how much I appreciate that, miss. I was headed to the feed store after this. I hate carrying around so much money, but they only take cash over there at Este's and I do like their stuff so much better than McGowen's, even if they do take credit cards. *Hah!* Imagine my face when I got there and had no cash to pay with!" He said as he shook his head and laughed at his own imagined misfortune.

I laughed with him for a polite amount of time. He seemed genuine enough for the most part. His emotions were somewhat guarded which was a little strange. I could tell that he was trying hard to remain neutral, but I had no idea why. Maybe he was just shy. I chalked it up to wariness over the stranger in town and smiled back at him.

"Well, thanks again miss." He said as he turned back and waved on his way out.

"No problem." I replied easily. I sat back down and went right back to my menu. I hadn't had a chance to eat breakfast yet, even though it was almost lunch time, and I was *starving!*

I had a quick but tasty and most importantly, affordable breakfast and then left on foot to go by the bank that I had seen on my way in. From there, I knew I could hit the post office across the street. It was a perfect plan. As I waited on the corner for the few cars present to pass by, I thought about how convenient it was to be able do all this on the way back to my car.

I was still amused that that *was* "down town." From where I could see to on my left, where the road bent out of sight and crossed the bridge over the Merrimack River, to where I could see to on my right, before the road curved back towards the neighboring town. That *was* down town in its entirety. Blink and you missed it. But stop and walk it on foot and you would quickly realize that contrary to appearances, everything you really needed was represented in some form or fashion within a couple of square miles. You didn't need to drive three blocks to get from the Police station to Town Hall. They were across the street from each other. The area served its' purpose perfectly without trying to be bigger than it needed to be. That was definitely part of the charm there. It was not only honest, but more efficient.

I had come through the little town quite a few times

recently in my search for a new place, and had admired the unmolested beauty each time. That's why I tended to stop there. For gas, or for food. I loved its' innocence. The diner and the quaint little duck pond in the center island. All the open areas that had still never been developed. That was becoming so rare and it was so refreshing to someone like me.

It was standing there on the corner that day that I had decided that it was where I wanted to stay. *If* I could manage to find a place there.

I didn't expect that to be easy. I was from the city. Like the majority of the population around there. But by then all I wanted was to get away from it all and live somewhere quiet. That's where the crowd divides in half. The ones' who dreamed of getting away like me, and the ones' who loved the city life too much to ever want to leave it. The problem was, even with just *half* of the city dwellers wanting to get away that was more than enough to drive the prices way up in towns like Pinegrove.

With forests and parks for hunting and camping, mountains for hiking and skiing, and so many beautiful beaches in between, it was easy to see why people thought that area of New England was a good place to take a break and enjoy life. Especially in the towns closest to the south where they could work in the city all week and still drive up in a few short hours or less on Fridays.

Then they could enjoy the weekends in their boats and RV's and cabins and at the spa but still be back at work in the city on Monday morning, making enough money to pay for it all. Places that fell into this golden range were the first to go and generally the most expensive.

One had to go *waaaaay* up usually to get past the overpriced *country-lifestyle/city-paycheck* bracket and really get anything decent for their money. But as much as I enjoyed solitude sometimes, I did not enjoy long car rides. The stress of worrying that I will have to stop and pee, always makes me have to stop and pee. Another vicious cycle.

More importantly though, I could only be so far away from Liliana. If she needed me, I could never be a four or five hours drive away. That was just too far. Ut uh. Ben had his practice and she had her school so it was up to me to find a place as close to them as possible. So as much as it made financial sense, going that far up was not an option for me.

Then you had what I liked to call the *"in-between"* towns. These are the band of towns past the first round of suburbs, that aren't far south enough to be part of, or considered *"close to,"* the city. They also aren't far north enough to really be considered *"vacation"* property. That was actually the most desirable area for me, partly *because* it was the least desirable to the general masses. But it was also because they were beautiful, stubborn little towns that had great pride in their community, and an even greater desire to keep the outside world from affecting their peaceful little oasis.

Most of the historic towns in the area *were* historic mainly because they had somehow managed, over the passing years, to maintain their usefulness without sacrificing their original integrity. At the same time, you could pick out so many areas that had at one point seen such grand successes, only to subsequently grow wildly out of control and eventually self-destruct. The beauty gone, crowds of unhappy people and steel jungles in their place.

Cities had personalities too and being the way that I was, I valued open spaces and less people per square inch much more than a coffee shop on every corner. Therefore this particular type of community that so staunchly resisted over development and uber-commercialism, was not for everyone, but appealed to me very much.

It was notoriously hard to get a place in one of these towns if you didn't already live here though. They were famous for not advertising listings at all, other than by word-of-mouth to each other. It was one of those towns that, even though it wasn't up in the mountains or down on the beach, property remains in high-demand. Even better, around there you were usually talking in acres, not square feet. That never came cheap in New England, and the residents lucky enough to own property around there, knew their own worth. If there was any marketable quality at all to a property, then there was no doubt that any agent with a license could get every penny they asked for.

It was depressing that the little town of Pinegrove was set firmly inside that bracket, because it made it impossible for real, regular people like me to ever hope to get a piece of it. It was something to work towards though. Someday, somehow, I had thought to myself at the time. I would keep it in mind for the future.

My *real* dream was to eventually build my perfect home someday, in the perfect place, on the perfect private plot of land and stay there forever. One that had enough space to not only breathe easy, but to also easily include family members. And then *their* extended families as well someday. Somewhere they would each have plenty of breathing room of their own, as we grew over the years.

Yup, that was the dream. Of course there was just me, and no *"we"* at the moment, but it was only temporary and I knew that. I tried not to let the thought destroy me in the abstract, just because it *existed*. I reminded myself again that things were the way they needed to be for now, but they *would* get better. I was sure of that. They had to.

I was leaving the post office and heading to the small lot adjacent to Main Street where I had parked when I saw what I could only describe as a crystal ball sitting against the curb. It looked as if it had simply rolled down the sidewalk and come to rest against the granite slab. It was mostly opaque ivory with an iridescent sheen that made the colors seem to move as the sun glinted off of it. It was so beautiful and so fragile that I couldn't walk by and leave it to eventually be destroyed in the traffic. I reached down, picked it up and turned it over a few times in my hands in wonder.

It was perfectly round, without any visible imperfections, even from its journey across the sidewalk, if that was indeed where it had come from. Even though it was much smaller than your traditional bowling ball sized crystal ball, only measuring equal to a small plum instead, it was much heavier than any plum of its' size could ever hope to be.

I looked up and turned to the doorway from which I thought it must have come. It was some sort of antique shop. There seemed to be one on every other corner two cities south of there, but they were rarer in that quiet town. I couldn't find a sign anywhere but it appeared to be open. I knocked on the door that stood ajar and called into the cluttered shop.

"Hello?" I didn't get any response right away so I walked in a little further. It was warm inside and full of racks and racks of vintage clothing and jewelry of all sorts. I was thinking then that I had been wrong with my original guess. It looked to be more of a consignment shop than an antique store. As I came around the corner, I could see a counter to my left with all sorts of stones and crystals displayed. It must be where the beautiful round crystal had come from, but it didn't really make sense for it to have escaped the glass counter and rolled around the corner to end up on the sidewalk. My face screwed up as I looked from the counter to the sidewalk and back trying to think of a logical chain of events. Before I got too far though, a female voice finally answered my original call.

"Hello dear! How can I help you?" A woman asked me in an overly cheerful voice as she came out through a set of hanging curtains. She was short and slightly round with a shiny brown bob and big pink glasses. What she lacked in height, she more than made up for in exuberance. She was feeling me out too. Wondering at my intentions in her shop. And something else...

"Are you looking for something particular dear?" she asked, distracting me momentarily from my analysis of her.

"No, actually I found this outside on the street and I thought it may have come from here." I held the polished stone out on my palm to show her and she smiled a genuine smile, obviously recognizing it.

"Why, thank you dear. I don't know how it could have gotten out there! I had it out on the counter to show someone and when they left, I had to run out back to answer the phone. It must have fallen somehow. It was awful kind of you to bring it back." She beamed.

I smiled back at her, even though I could tell that she wasn't exactly being entirely truthful. About which part, I had no idea. "Well, it looked like the kind of thing that someone would miss, so... Here." I said rolling it gently from my palm to hers. "It's really pretty." I couldn't help adding.

"Isn't it? It's a moonstone. It's always been one of my favorites. Well, thank you again, my dear." She said, still with that warm smile. That, oddly enough, seemed to be genuine. "It sure was sweet of you to go out of your way to see it returned to its' rightful owner." She added and it felt more like a proclamation than a thank you but I just smiled, not sure what that was about either.

"You're welcome. If it was mine, I know I'd want it back. Okay, well, I've got to run." I gave up on trying to figure it all out. "Have a good one." I said over my shoulder on my way out.

"You too dear." Still smiling. Much happier than she should be for reasons still unbeknownst to me. And it was going to have to stay that way because I really did have to get going. Liliana was due to get out of school in an hour and I was still 40 minutes away. That gave me just enough time to get back into town and stop off at the bakery that she loved before I picked her up.

Next time I stopped though, I thought to myself, I may come back and look at what else she has in that counter. I had seen quite a few large crystals and I had a great respect for how much the seemingly innocuous stones could actually help someone like me.

I walked the short distance back to my car, and was about to press the clicker to unlock the door when I felt the attention of someone behind me.

"Umm, miss?" Called a female voice from that direction. *Really?!* What a weird day! What now, I wondered impatiently as I turned around.

"Yes?" I answered warily at first, still trying to feel out the situation but I wasn't getting much besides a shy curiosity. What was this about? "Do I know you?" I asked trying to prompt an explanation of some sort while I searched her features for recognition. She was about 17, average height but curvy for her age. Not heavy, just what Hollywood would annoyingly describe as a *"bombshell"* rather than a *"beauty."* She was beautiful though with her long red hair and big green eyes that were still just staring back at me.

"I'm sorry, but can you tell me which way to go to get back to 97?" She asked.

"Sure." I said warily. "It's... right there." I added as I pointed to the main road in front of us, beyond the lot. It seemed kind of silly but maybe she didn't know that. I guessed that she would feel silly if that were the case, once I told her she was practically there. But I wasn't picking up any embarrassment or surprise, which I thought was kind of weird too. It was still just the curiosity, like that wasn't really the question that she had wanted to ask.

She smiled then. Not really *at* me, but almost in spite of my presence and then said quickly. "Okay, thanks." Then she turned and left.

I'll say it again. *Weird!* "*Doo-doo-doo-doo.*" I thought as the old Twilight Zone tune played in my head!

I felt better once I was back safely in my car. *All-righty then!* I started the car and put it in reverse while I experienced a strange deja'vu type of feeling. Did she even have a car? I didn't see her get in one and I had no idea where she had gone. Oh well. I'd had enough fun for one day. I looked behind me and backed out. I was out of there.

As I turned back and put the car in drive again I noticed something stuck in the windshield. I contemplated driving home with it in my wiper blade, but figured if I did it would probably blow out as I drove by a cop or something. I sighed, and threw it in park. I looked around, jumped out on one foot and grabbed it off the windshield. I hopped back in and then went so far as to lock the door. I really didn't know why but it made me feel better. I definitely didn't feel like I was "alone."

I pulled out of the lot and I didn't look at the card until I got back on the highway. It was a business card with the name of a local realtor. *Huh?* Why would he randomly give me a card? And how did he even know I was looking? Had there been cards on all the cars that were parked there? Damn, I couldn't remember noticing. The card portrayed the realtor as the top selling agent in the area. I put it in my purse and forgot about it for a while. It was a pipe dream at best.

Chapter 7

It was about two weeks later, after a long and unsuccessful day of apartment hunting, that I remembered the mysterious card again. At the time, I didn't think I would ever really find anything I could afford in that cute little town and didn't want to waste time. Theirs *or* my own. But I had been looking for two months, and I had just about worn out my welcome at Vivianne's by then.

She was still my best friend, but that was why it was time to leave. I wanted to keep it that way. We were driving each other crazy but it was her place, so her crazy won. I needed to return her space and her privacy along with her peace of mind. Viv was one of those people who wasn't good with anyone being in her personal space. It had ruined many a relationship for her over the years so I knew how much she cared about me when she offered to let me stay with her while I looked for a place of my own.

I tried to be as invisible and as unobtrusive as possible, but it was hard to not be somewhere when you *lived* there. I made it my goal to stay out of her way. But much longer, and she was going to snap and I really didn't want to be responsible for that. It was a crappy way to repay her generosity and I would never want to risk losing her friendship. Time was running out and I was getting so desperate that I felt like I had nothing to lose. So I dug out the card and I called.

A very high energy man had answered the phone, catching me off guard. He immediately insisted that he was the man who would find me a place in Pinegrove. After about two minutes worth of questions, he was equally as certain that he had *just* the place for me.

I hesitantly agreed to meet him the next afternoon and I hung up. I sat there for a minute, amazed at how fast that had all just happened. I was going to look at a studio apartment in Pinegrove tomorrow at 1:00. *Wow!*

When I drove out there the next day and saw the property that he was referring to, my hopes were crushed and I immediately thought that *good ol' Percy* was entirely crazy! From the road the place looked like a freakin' country club, with a farm and a big barn and stables off in the distance just for authenticity's sake. For some reason I pulled down the long drive anyway, thinking I would tell him personally that he was crazy and yell at him at least for wasting my time. Maybe even get him to reimburse me for some gas money for Christ's sakes.

As I pulled up closer to the main house I could see someone on my right, down a separate drive that split off of the main one, waving frantically at me. So I pulled down that side lane instead and instantly I could feel his excitement washing over me.

I took a moment to look around before I got out. There was a six car garage over there away from the big white farmhouse, with an obviously finished area above the entire space. There was another building that I assumed was probably a shed of some sort even though it was two stories tall, off to the left of the driveway. The buildings were also both white with shiny black shutters. There was an ornate oversized black door in the center of the smaller building and one on either end of the garage.

Percy had apparently waited as long as he was capable and was now on his way over to my car door. I took a moment to absorb his *vibes* before I got out and quickly realized that I was right. He *was* crazy!

He was way more excited than one would expect him to be. He was on the shorter side, though I would guess probably still a few inches taller than me and a little wide around the middle. He had a close cut, perfectly styled head of black hair. That was as far as the "normal" went though.

In that perfect hair, on one side starting at his temple and going back over his ear, was a lightning bolt shaped streak of hair that had been dyed bright orange. He was wearing a pair of pale yellow shorts with a coral colored polo shirt that had a very expensive label on it. This was complimented by various gold bracelets and rings, yellow argyle socks and white shoes that again had a better name than any dress currently hanging in my closet.

He looked like a cross between a high end show during fashion week and your worst childhood Easter outfit, with a little bit of super-hero thrown in for good measure. I took a deep breath and climbed out of the car.

His excitement washed over me again. For some reason, he was very happy! I wondered if that was normal for him. I imagined one would have to be pretty high energy normally, to do that type of work and actually excel at it. "You must be Simone!" He said with undue familiarity as he reached for my hand with both of his. "I'm Percy. We spoke on the phone."

Looking at the place close up I was guessing that it was his commission on a place like this that had to be making him so damn happy. "Uh, hi!" I said shaking his hand and then prying mine back as gently as possible. "So what's the deal with this place Percy? I think *someone* may have made a *huge* mistake." I said with a nervous laugh. "I'm pretty sure we're both wasting our time here 'cause this place is wa-*haaay* out of my price range!" I said honestly, cutting right to the chase. I appreciated that when people did it for me and I decided that I would extend that courtesy to him, even if he *was* completely insane.

He just smiled that broad smile at me again. Yup. *Rocks-in-a-big-ol'-crockpot*-crazy. I thought to myself, suppressing another laugh.

"I think you may be pleasantly surprised, if you would be so kind as to humor me." He said with a quiet confidence while holding his arm out in a grand gesture towards the tall, black, ornate door on the far right end.

"Oh what the hell, I drove all the way out here." I said showing my annoyance while I glared at him. "I guess I might as well see it. I'll bet it's just gorgeous!" I said with a cheerfulness I didn't really feel.

"Oh, you've hit the nail right on the head there darling. It's like you already know the place. I'll tell you what it is, its fate. That's what it is. *Ummm hmmm!*" He rambled on.

I just turned and gave him a one eyebrow stare to see if he was messing with me. Nope. I didn't think so anyway. All I was getting was patience warring with excitement. But it seemed to be based in sincerity. No *"gotcha"* vibes what-so-ever. I know it seems like I always assume the worst until proven otherwise, and that's just because... well, I always assume the worst until proven otherwise. Can't help it. It comes with the territory of always knowing way too much. People just don't do things without a reason.

I came up the stairs and looked around. It was larger than I would have thought possible, and for a pseudo-claustrophobic like me, that was a big deal. It was more than just spacious though, it was beautiful! The interior was one large open space right to the high, cathedral ceilings. It was painted entirely in soft tones of white and cream, with beautiful blonde hardwood floors that went on so long, I thought I could surly sell tickets to roller skate on them!

There was a living room area complete with a fireplace and a big overstuffed sofa on the right end, where we entered. I saw a compact but open and modern kitchen in the middle of the area, and a large, high, four-post bed behind a shoji screen on the far left end.

All three areas faced the most impressive feature of them all, which was the rear wall that was made up almost entirely of glass. There was one oversized set of sliding doors in each area, with double width, floor to ceiling windows in between. All that glass wasn't wasted either. It opened up the whole place to the beauty of the rolling hills, orchards and forests that sprawled out behind it. It would be a great place to heal and recharge. Ten seconds and I was already in love.

Ten seconds after that, I was really pissed at Percy for showing me something that I could never have and making me fall in love with it! It came out in my tone.

"Well thanks for the tour Percy, but even if I were still *married* I wouldn't be able to afford this place. It's been fun and all but I think I'll head on back home now." I said with a wave as I turned to leave, not wanting to look at the place any more.

"Aren't you even going to ask how much?" He coaxed,

playfully.

"I stopped and looked back with a *"get off it already"* kind of expression. "No." I said plainly, not willing to play his game anymore and turned again.

"You might want to rethiiiinnnk that." He continued in an annoyingly childish sing-song voice.

I sighed deeply, but I couldn't make myself walk away. It was just too awesome not to even ask. "Alright Percy, I'll bite. How much?"

"One thousand even." He spit out without hesitation. "Everything included. *Everything.* Not just heat, hot water and utilities, but cable and phone too! Everything. For a thousand bucks." His smile grew even larger. He was very pleased with himself. I could tell that he was relieved to finally let the cat out of the bag so-to-speak.

"A week?" I asked skeptically.

"A month." He answered quickly with that ever present smile.

I couldn't even respond at first, I was so surprised. But it turned to disbelief rather quickly. *"What?!* That's crazy." I said, waiting for the punch line but he just kept staring at me with that *too pleased* smile.

I scrunched up my eyebrows and cocked my head to the side like a dog trying to figure out human language. "Really? Why? You could get triple that for this place, easy! What's the catch?" I asked, suspicious as usual.

"Nothing at all. *Really!"* He insisted, seeing my expression. "Except that the owner is *very* particular. You see, he doesn't really need the money but he likes to see the place get used. His kids each took a turn living here but they've all moved out now."

It doesn't open up often. He prefers long term tenants. Once he finds someone that he trusts, that he *wants* on his property, he's happier to have them stay there as long as possible." He smiled that *"I've-got-a-secret"* smile one more time then said slowly, "And right now, he wants you." He crossed his arms then like he had said all he intended to.

"Alright, now you're just creeping me out there, Percy." I said with the suspicious feeling returning full force. What the Hell was *that* supposed to mean? Who was this guy?

"Don't go getting your panties all in a bunch now, darling, it's nothing like that." He assured me, and even though I just raised my eyebrows at his choice of words, he laughed and went right on, undeterred. "His name is Jack Kent and he owns everything you can see from here, including the stables and the farm off to the left and the apple orchards on the right. It's been in his family for many generations and I'm sure, once one of those kids of his settles down, it will stay that way. In the meantime, it's just him and his wife, Shirley. They're happy people who are quite happy to share what they have as long as they feel they can trust the people they share it with."

"They're well known around town for being extremely generous. But no one really knows the true extent of their philanthropy, since they are believed to be responsible for a lot of '*anonymous*' donations as well." He said making air quotes with his hands.

"Well, that's all well and good Perce," I said in a falsely familiar way. "But why would he want me? How does he even know me? Or that I was looking for a place? Can you explain that please?" But as I finished my question, I could feel a distinct sense of amusement rising up behind me. I turned in surprise and immediately recognized the pony-tailed man from the diner as he came up the stairs.

"I think I can explain." He said, still smiling as he reached the landing. He was wearing the same type of work clothes as he had been that day in the diner, but they were freshly washed and his pony tail wasn't covered by the baseball hat at the moment. He held out his hand to me.

"Jack Kent. It's very nice to officially meet you." He offered.

"I don't understand what's going on here. Does someone want to catch me up?" I asked, feeling more uneasy by the minute since I was obviously the only person not up to speed in the scenario.

Jack laughed again. "Sure thing. You remember me?" He asked.

"Sure. You're the man from the diner that dropped the C-note." I answered hesitantly.

"Right. Well, you'll have to forgive me my little quirks, but that was a test. Which I'm happy to say, you passed." He gave a small chuckle at that before he went back to trying to explain. "I had seen you there a few times before, always reading the apartment listings. I needed a tenant. You needed a place. But I need to know what kind of person I'm renting to, before any papers get signed. I have found that there are faster, easier ways of figuring that out. People don't generally think fast enough to *not* be their true selves when their guard is down. I could tell you were trustworthy and kind with that one easy stunt. My apologies for the deception, but I find that it's worth it more often than not." He smiled while I digested this.

I was stunned. I wasn't sure if I had been complimented or violated. But I was sure that the place was amazing. *And for a thousand dollars a month?!* Hell, maybe I was okay with it after all. I just looked at them both warily.

Mr. Kent extended his hand again. "Look, I'm sorry if I offended you in any way. But the bottom line is, if you can forgive me, the place is yours." He was serious.

I looked back and forth to each of them again. Percy was still oozing excitement, but Jack was just waiting patiently.

I looked out the back at the view again, and thought about Vivianne one more time as well. Then I put my hand in his and shook it.

"When can I move in?"

Chapter 8

A lot of my biggest decisions were often made that way. On the spot. I could be good at avoiding them sometimes too. But when I was sure, I was sure. As I drove the familiar route down the long drive though, I noticed immediately that the serenity I so greatly treasured was tainted. There was someone nearby.

By the time I reached the long section of the driveway that split off to the right where my apartment was tucked away, I knew who. There in my usual spot by my door, sat the shiny black car. Waiting.

What the ...? Would this night never end?

I had never even so much as talked to him. Even earlier that night! He hadn't even looked at me when he addressed surfer boy. So why would he just show up at my house? How did he even know where my house was?! I wasn't sure if I wanted to get out of my car. I dug my phone out and sat there as I considered calling the police. What a night! *Jesus!*

Just then, my cell phone rang. I turned it over to look at it. *Unknown.* The curiosity got the better of me.

"Hello? I said, tentatively.

"Hello yourself." A deep but cheerful voice replied.

I didn't know what else to say yet but I made a question mark with my face while I waited, like the person on the other end of the line could see me or something.

Then he broke the silence. "It's Ethan Stone. From The Tavern?"

"Okay..." was still all I had to offer.

"I just wanted to apologize, for earlier. But I figured that you might not want to get out of your car with a stranger in your driveway, to find that out." He explained as he laughed softly.

It made me laugh too, in spite of my better judgment, that he had been so right. "Good call." I agreed. "Apologize for what, exactly?" I asked.

"For Carson, the young blonde mess from the parking lot? He was looking for me, but you confused him." He added.

"Excuse me? I confused him? I don't understand. How exactly did I do that?" I asked.

"I'd love to explain, but if you feel safe enough, it would be a lot easier in person." He said.

How *did* I feel about talking to the Magician? Face to face. Alone. At night. Out in the middle of nowhere. Um, yeah, I wasn't too sure about that. I wondered for a minute if Jack or Shirley would still be up. Would they hear me up at the main house if I screamed? I can't help that these are the things that run through my head. If you always think of the worst case scenario, you just spend less time surprised. I try not to let it stop me from living life though, I really do!

I thought then, that at that point it was probably already too late. Unless I wanted to floor it in reverse and race back out of there, then I really was kind of stuck. He was too far away in his car for me to get a good feel off of him, and unfortunately it didn't work very well over the phone. It was still there, but it was more muted.

Besides that, I still hadn't invited *any* man inside my new little sanctuary and I wasn't sure that I wanted to be pushed into doing it then. But what could I say really? He had me on the spot and he knew it.

I resented having my hand influenced, but not seeing a better option, I reluctantly agreed. "Sure. See you in half a second." I said and hung up. I closed the phone and took another deep breath as I gathered my purse and phone. I left all my art stuff for the moment. I took one more deep breath and then stepped out of the car onto the familiar, gravelly drive. As I walked slowly up to his car, I thought about how much I loved the sound the rocks made under my feet, trying to distract myself and remain calm.

I had my head down while I walked and I wondered again at the car as I approached it more closely. *Holy shit!* A Mercedes McLaren F1?! *Really?!! You've got to be freakin' kidding me!* Who *was* this guy?

The only reason I even knew what it was is that a local artist who had prints for sale at the gallery where I had worked was also a huge car collector. He liked to photograph his collection and just the framed photos alone went for tens of thousands of dollars. He had done one particular series that included the top ten most expensive cars and the McLaren F1 had happened to be one of them. One I never thought I would see in person!

I was lost in my thoughts for a moment but his wary anticipation washed over me as I got closer and it brought me back to the present. I would ask about the car later. First, I wanted to hear his explanation for this Carson business. Once I thought about it, I was kind of glad that he was there. It was probably high time that I got some answers about a few other things as well.

His door whooshed up and one long, black denim clad leg, anchored by a scuffed, black leather boot appeared, swiftly followed by its' pair. He turned to face me as he got out and when he straightened fully, I was surprised by just how tall he really was! Damn! In all of the past few months that I had been relying on his musical talents, I had never stood that close to him. I was slightly above average height myself but I was certainly spending an awful lot of time that day feeling *tiny!*

He offered his hand in greeting. "Ethan Stone."

"Simone Harrington." I said back while I shook his hand, still getting used to using my maiden name again. I backed up just a tiny step. The urge was involuntary and I had to fight it. He didn't appear frightening, just... *strong!* A little overwhelming somehow. He was keeping himself very neutral and I got the distinct impression that it was intentional, but how could it be? How would he even know to do that? I wondered. Of course, he couldn't. I chalked it up to nerves and my over-active imagination. "It's nice to finally meet you." I said.

"Like-wise." He answered with a knowing sort of smile. He was pretty emphatic about that for just a moment, but I had no idea why so I took back my hand and started up the path to the door. He kept talking as he followed. "So how are you liking living on Kent's farm?" He asked congenially.

"I love it. Much more than I thought I would, even." I confessed. I wasn't sure why I felt compelled to tell him that. I must be tired. I'm going to have to be more careful around this guy, I thought to myself then. I could tell that he was already reading into even just that little bit of information. He certainly could not be accused of sleeping at the wheel. That got me wondering about him again. "And how exactly is it that you happen to know where I live?" I asked without bothering to hide the suspicion in my voice. He smiled at that and I found it very annoying. I hoped my expression was clear enough to convey that.

"It's a small town Simone. May I call you Simone? We are neighbors after all." He said, smiling again.

Why did I always feel like the only one out of the loop around there? "Sure. *Neighbors?*" I asked. There were no visible neighbors of course, but obviously the Kent land stopped somewhere. I just had no idea where that was.

We topped the stairs, and I dropped my purse on the side table and my keys in the bowl there. He put his hand on my shoulder to turn me toward the back windows. The contact caught me off guard. I didn't jump, but only because I was frozen for an instant. A wave of heat shot through me when his hand touched me. It was brief, but it was real. I quickly focused my attention on where he was pointing, wanting desperately to pretend that I hadn't just felt that. It was the last thing that I needed!

He kept the other hand around my shoulder while he explained. "Beyond the apple orchard and through the woods, to the right. If you walked for twenty minutes or so, you would eventually bump into my humble abode." He released me then and stepped back a step. I was beyond grateful. "We even share the same road actually, although our driveways are over a mile apart." He smiled again.

It was a bright, straight and easy smile and I was surprised by his casual use of it. He certainly didn't spend a ton of time on stage smiling, so it was a new look for him. Unfortunately for me, it was not a bad one. I had not been prepared to be attracted to him. I wasn't too hard on myself though. I hadn't been that close to *any* man in months. I *was* still a living breathing woman. I wasn't worried. I could ignore it. I didn't want it to get in the way of getting the answers he was supposed to be there to give.

I tried to shake it off mentally, and to return my attention to the task at hand. But just before I broke the stare and turned towards the kitchen, I felt a powerful wave of *his* desire wash over me. *Crap!* It was a quick wave but it was just as hot as my own had been. *Dammit!*

"Can I get you something to drink?" I asked both trying to be polite and to distract him. He shook his head no.

I reached for a glass and poured myself some water from the pitcher in the fridge. As I stood by the sink, drinking and stalling a little, he caught me off guard again.

"I apologize for that. I didn't mean to make you uncomfortable. But you can't blame *me* for the fact that *you're* hot. I can control what I do and *say.* It's a lot harder to control what I *feel."*

He said it so casually, like he knew all about me and we had been friends for years. *I,* on the other hand, almost spit water all over the wall! After a few coughs to clear what I had accidentally inhaled, I turned my top half and looked at him with raised eyebrows and undisguised surprise.

He ignored my expression and kept talking. "It was unexpected and unintentional, and *not* why I asked to talk to you. I promise I will do my best to stay on topic." He smiled that damn smile at me again.

Okay, now I needed something stronger than water to drink. I went back to the fridge for the open bottle of wine I had just moved out of the way to get at the water and poured myself a glass. It was weak I knew, but at the moment I didn't care. I wasn't going to offer him a drink again either. He was far too comfortable already!

After a few sips and a few deep breaths, I turned back towards the living room only to find it empty. I searched further and noticed the sliders that led out to the deck were open. He was sitting in the black wrought iron chair at the matching small round table where I liked to have my morning coffee, watching me.

Waiting.

"Alright. Answers please." I said sitting opposite him. I rested my wineglass on the tabletop while I pulled my knees up and caught my heels on the edge of the chair.

"What do you want to know?" He asked cooperatively.

"Start with your new friend Carson." I said. "What was that all about?" I wasn't ready yet to confirm what he seemed to know about me, so I would have to wait to ask him *how* he knew.

"He was looking for me. He wanted me to help him with something." He provided cryptically. Apparently he was going to make me work for it.

"With what? And how did I confuse him?" I asked specifically.

He took a deep breath and leaned forward with his elbows on his knees. He was thoughtful for a moment before he spoke again.

"I've lived in this town all my life. I've made a lot of connections over the years. Some of those connections are highly sought, but rarely shared. It can be difficult when someone comes a long way, hoping to attain something that they are then denied." He answered cryptically.

Connections, right. "Um hmm, and what kind of *'connections'* exactly, will get you a McLaren F1, may I ask?"

He didn't seem offended by my insinuation. He laughed instead and looked up at me, clearly surprised. "I'm impressed. Most people usually just think it's a Corvette. Anyway, what does it take? An uncle with a Mercedes dealership, basically. But I still paid through the nose." He laughed again and looked me in the eye, almost like he was waiting for me to decide that I believed him. Maybe he was.

"So it's not a perk for some crazy illegal organization you're running?" I asked, only half joking. I wanted to feel his reaction to this question too. My skills did come in handy at times. But all I felt was amusement still when he answered.

"No. The car is mine. And I bought it because I have a soft spot for fast things, no kids, and I can afford it. Simple as that. It's one of the few luxuries I allow myself." He turned serious after that though. "As for the other part of that question; Organization, yes. Illegal, no. Well... for the most part, anyway." He grinned mischievously at that.

"What do you mean?" I asked, wanting to hear more but dreading it also.

He rubbed his face with his hands and sat back in the chair. "I don't usually explain these things to anyone who isn't actively seeking them. It's weird though, because I've been expecting you to come to me, ever since I first saw you at the Tavern. I'm still at a loss as to why you haven't or what your deal is and quite frankly, the curiosity has been killing me!" He admitted with a humorless laugh.

I had been so intent on my work and my own memories, that I hadn't even noticed his curiosity towards me. A searching sometimes, sure. Though that seemed to apply to everyone.

"I can assure you that I do not make a habit of getting involved in peoples' lives uninvited, but it seems that fate is determined to throw you into mine." He said, referring to the situation with Carson. I took a slow breath before I responded.

"I want to ask you why on Earth I would have '*come to you,*' but the truth is, I'm not sure I want to know the answer." I decided then that I was willing to risk it, my need-to-know getting the better of me as usual. "What exactly do you think you know about me, Mr. Stone?" I finally asked, with dread spreading like ice through my veins.

"Well, to explain that would be a much longer story and I truly didn't intend to hold you up all night." He said with a slight smirk, getting off track again for just a second or two with that crude innuendo. Despite my lack of interest in such a situation taking place, a quick, *burning* hot image of him *literally* holding me up flew uninvited through my head! It was lightning fast and I shook it off just as quickly. But it registered just the same.

No-no-no-no-no-no-no! Such juvenile remarks did not usually have that type of effect on me. Boy, I must be tired! I thought in my own defense.

"And please, call me Ethan." He continued, more seriously now, without knowing the reaction his words had caused. "I just wanted to make sure that you weren't too shaken up. That you were okay. And also, I admit, to do a little damage control. It's important to me not to let anything jeopardize my situation."

"So you wanted to make sure that I don't go and file a police report, essentially?" I said, getting right to the point.

"To put it bluntly, yes. Although you don't really have much to report. It's just easier I think, in this particular situation, to nip it in the bud. Avoid any trouble to begin with. Hopefully."

"Well, I'm not giving you all night, but I have the rest of this glass to finish, so why don't you talk until I'm done." I suggested. I thought for a moment about my meeting so early in the morning, but there was no way I would sleep without some answers. I knew myself too well to believe otherwise.

He looked at me thoughtfully some more and then made up his mind. "Fine. The abridged version then." He said as he started. "I struggled when I was a kid. I was different and life is hard for a kid who's different. I eventually overcame my obstacles, but not without help. Help I wished I'd had when I was younger. Help most would never have. So I decided to do whatever I could to connect those who need help with a certain set of obstacles, with the people that I know can help them. It's my way of giving back I guess you could say." He was still keeping his feelings very neutral.

"It started out innocently enough. Just a small circle of caring individuals that I knew I could count on. A handful of people who knew my situation well enough, to recommend me to the rare people they would come in contact with who had similar issues. It just kind of grew from there." He was being honest, though holding a lot back, I could tell.

"What kind of issues, exactly?" I asked feeling cold again. I couldn't put it off any longer then. I had to ask. "And what makes you think that I would fall into that category?" He sighed resignedly before he spoke.

"Because it's what I *do* Simone." He answered softly.

"What do you mean? *'What you do?'* What exactly do you *'do'* Mr. Stone? *Ethan.* " I added grudgingly at his look. 'Because I was under the impression that you were a performer."

"Hmpf. That I am, for sure. But it's only part of why I'm there. What I *'do,'* is use *my* skills, to identify people who might

need my help. People like me. And yes Simone, people like *you*." He said that last part with quiet confidence and a definite chill ran up my spine. There was a familiarity there that shouldn't be.

"And what would that particular *'skill'* be exactly?" I wanted to stop. I didn't want to know the answer but I couldn't keep myself from asking. It was almost automatic.

"Well, with me it manifested in my head, literally. As a result, I have sort of *'extra sensitive'* senses. Extremely good hearing, an overactive sense of taste and smell. And if I focus just right, an extra layer of vision that other people don't have." He looked at me to see how I was taking it so far. *Could he see with his extra vision that I was freaking out?!*

All I was thinking then was that surely this was some kind of a trick to get me to admit that I was a freak or something. To drive me out of town like the King pin of some lynch mob. He could not be for real. I had *lived* a *"this could not be real"* kind of life and *I* still didn't believe him. I was wondering then just how I was going to get him out of there. At least we were outside, that should make it easier, I thought. I tested his vibes while he sat there waiting. All he was giving off was an honest patience. I couldn't find the negative intention anywhere, but I felt sure it had to be there.

"How long have you been able to read people like that?" He asked, finally getting right to the point.

"Like what?" I asked playing coy, even though I was shocked that he would act as if he knew that I was. I liked to decide who I shared my personal information with, like my mother had taught me and he was bypassing that choice for me. It pissed me off.

He smiled again. "To some extent, you've probably always been that way, but at some point it became much more prominent. Right?"

I wasn't even answering then. It didn't stop him though.

"It would have been when you were still a kid, most likely. Sometimes people are too young to have a memory of a distinct 'before and after.' But you seem to have a real good handle on yours so I'm guessing you were young, but at least old enough to understand the difference when it happened. Maybe...

8 or 9?" He guessed.

Again, I wasn't willing to voice the other side of the conversation. I just stared at him and past him at the moon and the stars that were lighting up the orchards behind us with a light blue glow. He kept going.

"Anyway. For you, it surrounds your hands." He said matter-of-factly, and I almost fell off my chair. My feet did drop out from under me where I had been sitting on them and hit the deck with a double thud. *Huh?*

Another chill. I contemplated continued silence, but I had questions of my own again. "Why don't you tell me more about *your* skills that let you know all of this?" I said very quietly, still not necessarily agreeing to anything.

"You've heard of people having an aura, right?" I nodded and he continued. "It's kind of like that, although I can't actually see auras. What I can see is layers of swirling colors, surrounding certain areas on some peoples' bodies. It only shows up in people who have been *'heightened'* by the virus, like me, and it always surrounds whatever area of the body that their particular skills originate from."

"It makes them very easy for me to identify. A complete no-brainer actually. I'm sorry for intruding where I wasn't asked in your case, I really am. But there is no faking it and there is no hiding it. Not from me anyway. It's either there or it's not and honey, *you light up like a Christmas tree!*" He was smiling broadly by the end of his statement.

I on the other hand, was definitely not smiling. I was sitting with my chin on the table at the moment. "What are you talking about, this *'heightened'* state you're referring to? What does that mean?" I asked.

"It's the term we use to describe the difference between people like us and the rest of the population. Sometimes it's having an extra strong sense like my sight, but there are tons of other manifestations. It's very different for everyone. It reacts much more vigorously wherever you are the strongest. Whatever your body uses most and fights the hardest with. That targeted area lasts the longest before giving itself over to the infection, therefore it is bombarded and exposed the longest to the effects of the virus and in the end, becomes changed by it. *Heightened.*"

"Not everybody has some underlying unusual strength that they, and it, can tap into though. So by default they don't get as sick. The virus won't last as long with nothing to feed on. Most people will be like that and will never notice a difference between life before and after. In others it is a marked and often difficult transition." He said with understanding in his eyes.

"But almost everybody *does* go through it at some point, as far as we can tell, kind of like chicken pox. Except it doesn't have a name, at least not an official one. Because nobody *'officially'* knows about it. We refer to it as the HgT virus."

I was just sitting quietly again, listening to his amazing tale.

"The process is initiated originally by this virus and if you've ever had blood drawn, then *they* already know whether you've had it or not. Most people have come in contact with it before they reach adulthood. They will either have been immune to its' *heightening* effects and think it was nothing more than a bad cold, or they will have had a full blown case of it. Either way they will test positive for the antibodies. Those who test positive go into a database... *somewhere.* It moves constantly but we know it exists. We've caught pieces of it a few times. Snippets here and there being uploaded, copied by different sources before it quickly disappears again." He provided.

"We?" I asked. "You and your contacts, who know all about this *'virus'* and help people who have had it, cope with any special abilities they may end up with as a result of it? Is that right?" I asked sarcastically.

"*Hmpf!* Pretty much." He said tiredly. "We know they know. We just don't know what they do with the information." He saw the look in my eye just then and immediately answered my next question before I had the chance to voice it. "'*They,*' assumedly being some top-secret branch of the government. Whether they are tracking an experiment of their own, as some would have you believe, or if they are tracking an '*unknown,*' we're still not sure. But they *are* tracking it. And now, so are we." He was quiet again for a moment.

I know what my face must look like as he's telling me all of this. I'm thinking that he's nuts and that I should never have let him in there to begin with! I should have just said no. He caught my deer-in-the-headlights look though. He just stared at me with that super intense *look-right-through-you* stare, seeing whatever it was he sees, and then his face softened. He took a deep breath and started again very quietly.

"Have you ever been really sick? Like *really* sick! Super high fever, hallucinations, passing out, *weird* feelings kind of sick? Think back. Even once when you were young?"

The worst part was that I could think of three or four times, easily. Maybe more. I was kind of a sickly kid. But I had set a pattern right from the beginning of always coming through it stronger. I had never let anything keep me down for long.

"There are lots of viruses out there." I said, though I knew again, it was weak.

He just smiled. "You know which time it was if you were old enough when you had it. *And you definitely had it.*" He assured me and again, it felt like a bit of a violation. He had a way of making me feel naked, even with all of my clothes on. It made me more defensive than usual. I glared a little but he continued like I hadn't.

"It changes from person to person, but there is always one time that is clearly distinguishable from all the others due to some particular anomaly. Whatever it may have been for them. Or *you.* "

"Simone. Do you remember a time that you got sick and your *hands* didn't feel right?" He was patient then.

A chill ran down my back because he had hit the nail on the head again. *He shouldn't know these things!*

There had been one particular fever when I was seven that had me seeing things for days. My mother had tried to feed me some Tylenol to bring my fever down and I woke up on the floor after trying to tip my head back to take it. I have fuzzy memories of a subsequent middle-of-the-night emergency room visit. My mother talking worriedly to her fellow nurses. After a long night of tests, they still didn't know for sure what I had, just that it was viral and not bacterial and needed to run its course. They gave me more Tylenol and some fluids by IV and then sent me home.

I had laid around in bed for days, frightened into hiding

by my families distorted, laughing faces. But the most memorable part of the whole experience was still and always would be, the way my hands had felt. I could never explain it after the fact and I still can't to this day. Not with any words I know. But I could *feel* my hands in a completely different way from anything else that I had *ever* felt before. They felt really... *big*, kind of... and *rock solid* in a different way that I *still* couldn't properly describe. Every nerve ending firing so that I felt every part of my hands at once. It had been one of the strangest experiences of my childhood.

That and that fact that everything had felt too..., I don't know... *loud*, I guess is the best way I can explain it. Like every time someone spoke to me it was *startling* somehow. Almost a physical assault. That had also contributed to my desire to hide in my room. It had made no sense. Had no context. I could never put any of it into adequate words after the fever. But I had understood it completely at the time.

I had always written it off as the rambling mind of sick kid. But to this day, whenever I feel something *really* strongly, whether it's physical *or* emotional, I also feel it in the palms of my hands. *Deeply.* Like a heat wave crossed with a cyclonic muscle spasm. I don't know what it is or where it comes from, but it's an *incredible* sensation! I've often wondered why I've never heard anyone else mention that type of physical reaction before. But no one else ever has, so I've kept its' existence to myself. I definitely enjoyed it very much whenever something came along that was strong enough to make me feel it though.

The whole thing was a very strange memory. One I knew I would never forget, no matter how young I had been at the time or how long ago it was. But no one had ever brought it up like they might actually *understand* it before and I had certainly never expected anyone to.

I just stared defiantly back into those piercing grey eyes, trying to block the strength of the feelings coming off of him right then so I could think straight. He could tell he had hit a nerve. I could feel both his intensity and his excitement and I was working hard to ignore both, trying not to react. How could he know about that when I couldn't even explain it? I could feel his barely controlled eagerness for me to embrace what he was telling me, but I didn't want the things he said to make sense. I had spent my whole life trying to prove that I wasn't a freak. Now he wanted to turn me back into one.

No. I wasn't having it.

I decided a long time ago who I was, and who I *wasn't*. It was also not just me and my own life that I had to consider anymore either. Being a mother was more important than anything else. Liliana was the most important thing in my world and I wasn't going to take any chances on exposing her to any type of organized wack-a-doos. Whether his little story made sense or not.

I was on board with everyone having the freedom to live their own life and have their own beliefs. But people who belonged to secret organizations in general, were not my cup of tea. I wished then, that I hadn't asked. Quite frankly it scared me a little. I just pictured a bunch of guys in the woods, dressed in camouflage, stock piling weapons and preaching paranoid propaganda while their wives hoarded food and supplies, chanted weird mantras and pumped out children to join the cause.

Alright, that may be a little extreme. But my mind never did anything half way.

"You can say no." He said, breaking the long silence. "But it won't make it less true."

I took a deep fortifying breath and then looked back up into his steel eyes. I smiled and answered him very politely. "It doesn't matter. None of this matters really, whether it's true or complete fiction. I just want to live in peace and do my work. I don't think I want to know any more about what you see or what you think you know about me. If you can just keep your recruits from accosting me in the parking lot, then everything will be fine."

"It wasn't his fault entirely." He started to explain. "His particular skill involves a type of visual recognition, sort of like mine, but different."

He seemed reluctant to let it go just yet and I wondered why. I sighed deeply before giving in to my curiosity again, and asking, "Different how?"

"He see's connections. Between people. I hear it's like a

string of light that shows up between them when they are near each other. Different colors for different types of relationships." He explained.

"As fascinating as that sounds, I don't see how it would lead to my confusing him." I said impatiently.

He sighed himself then. "I turned him away. That's not something I take lightly either but I was finally sure that he didn't really *need* my help. Unfortunately, he just wanted to learn how to hone his skill better as a weapon and he just assumed I'd help him do it. People are people. *Heightened* or not. Some just want to live in peace and be normal. Others just want to develop their gift and use it to manipulate other people. I have to try to tell them apart. It's not a perfect science like telling *height's* from *norm's* is for me, but I do my best. Quite frankly, I could really use someone like *you* for that, but that's another issue." He said tauntingly.

"Anyway, I knew already his head was in the wrong place, too much anger. I was willing to allow that maybe some of that was just due to his immaturity. I told him to come back in six months, just to test his ability to take direction on faith. It didn't take him long to fail and try to take matters into his own hands."

He hesitated for just a second, feeling wary and also like he was about to reveal too much. *Good!* I thought. It was about time that *he* felt a little of that.

"He didn't like the idea of waiting. He decided he saw a weakness and he tried to use it to force my hand." He stopped again and stared angrily out at the stars in the black sky for a minute. He was feeling a lot of things then. Resentment. Confusion. Curiosity. Fear. *Anger.*

"And how did he do that?" I had to ask.

"He left a note on the bill for Dani after he saw you leave, that I should come and rescue you in the parking lot. I don't think he ever really intended to hurt you. He just wanted to get my attention and he thought that you were the best way to do that." He still wasn't making any sense.

"Why?!" I practically yelled, my impatience starting to get the best of me.

He turned back to look at me before he answered.

"Because he saw a connection between us. Thought we were a couple or something." He just stared at me after that declaration.

"Uh... wh... eh... *huh?*" I stammered, feeling like I'd had the wind knocked out of me. "I'm sorry but I don't get it. I still don't want to go on record as saying that I believe any of this. But even if I do, that doesn't make sense. We hadn't even met officially, before tonight. How could we be *connected?*"

I laughed incredulously, and tried to pretend I had no idea why someone sitting in the Tavern might think I was connected to him. Secretly I was panicking, wondering if either of them could have somehow been able to see me using him as a block. That was crazy though, right? Then I wondered if it mattered if they did? Why did I feel guilty? I really hadn't done anything wrong. I had just wanted to keep his blocking ability to myself, that's all. He really made it hard for me to keep *anything* to myself so far though. He answered me then, but it didn't help.

"I don't know." He said. "I kind of hoped that maybe you could tell me. I've actually been wondering about you for some time now. You see, I know his talent is genuine. *I can see it,* remember? But he proved that I was right about him being too manipulative, after all. So I had no regrets telling him 'no' flat out after that. I brought him back to his car after you left and told him not to bother coming back in six months."

"It did leave me wondering however, why the only *heightened* person to ever come into the Tavern and *not* seek my attention or my guidance in any way, would be the one he would see me having a connection with." He was being honest and he was hoping for answers of his own, I could tell. *Aha!* I get it now, I thought to myself. That's why he was still there. He wanted answers too! *Hmmm...*

"So now it's got me curious, really curious, about who you are and what you're really doing here." He leaned back in his chair when he finished and I could feel the atmosphere change. He was less persuasive and more suspicious himself then.

Good. That was easier to deal with. I was used to that.

"You have a definite skill, but you obviously didn't come here for help. You have great control already and you seem to be doing very well. So then it makes me wonder who helped you originally, and why?" Still searching.

Wow, this was just great! *Seriously?* I'm glad he was so sure that I was doing well, I thought to myself with a mental laugh. So apparently he didn't know everything after all.

"So what, now I'm the enemy?" I asked.

"I don't know *what* you are." He answered. "That's the problem. You have to understand, Simone. I have worked a long time to get where I am today. There are a lot of people counting on me and I have too much at risk at this point, to jeopardize it recklessly. There are those who would destroy what we have built. Out of ignorance, fear or a desire to control those involved." He looked at me and I could feel the challenge coming from him then.

"What am I supposed to think? You show up at the Tavern, with *obvious heightened* talents. You're there as much as I am for Christ's sake, yet you never so much as *attempt* to speak to me, the very person the *heights* come there to see. So now I have to wonder. Are you there to keep track of who else comes in there looking for help?" He was going back and forth and I could see that not knowing was definitely making him nervous.

"Never mind Carson, you confuse *me!*" He said emphatically. "Why did you move here in the first place? Why did Jack give you this place? Why do you spend all of your free time at The Tavern? I can't figure you out at all even though I've spent the last few months trying! Then Carson comes along and sees a *connection* between us? I'm telling you right now, I want to know what the hell it is!" He insisted heatedly.

He was almost yelling by the end. Almost, but not quite. I didn't feel threatened, but unfortunately I could tell that *he* did! So I knew I would have to explain myself then. I hated that something so personal and seemingly innocent had him worked up into such a state. It wasn't fair of me to leave him worrying about all the good he claimed he was trying to do, *if* it was true, just because I didn't want to confirm his theories about me and confess my weaknesses all at once. But it was starting to look like I didn't have a choice.

"Alright, fine." I said, resigned to the corner I had been backed into. I got up and walked barefoot back in through the open sliders. I retrieved the wine bottle from the fridge and another glass for him. I came back out and sat back down heavily in my chair and poured him some without asking.

I waited until we had both taken a sip before I tried to speak. He had made me feel more vulnerable in one night than anyone else I could remember. It really was annoying how he had that ability. I didn't want anyone to have that over me anymore, especially not another man, but apparently I had no control over that either and that pissed me off even more.

"Look, I don't know if I believe any of this, or if it even matters. Either way the reality of it is, it doesn't change what *I* am. So I might as well just tell you that I'm an empath. I do try to keep that private, mostly just to avoid the obvious issues. But since that's supposedly not possible with you, I guess I'll just admit it and get it over with." He listened, but he wasn't surprised at all. That was even more annoying.

"Now, whether that has anything to do with what you're talking about here or not is irrelevant to me really. Let me assure you of that by also telling you what I'm not. I am *not* a science experiment. I am *not* a freak to be poked and stared at and I am certainly not some lost little girl anymore. I figured it out on my own then and I'm fine with keeping it that way now. I didn't come to The Tavern looking for you or for guidance, or for any other ulterior motive. I came for the music. *Period!*"

I could feel his confusion then and I was happy to share that feeling a little, but I went on and kept explaining anyway. There didn't seem to be any reason not to at that point. I felt like I had already been laid bare.

"I'm assuming you are familiar with what it means to be an empath, being in your supposed line of work and all." I said with a skyward flick of my eyes.

He nodded. "The basic idea, anyway."

"Good." I continued. "Well, music is a *'block'* for me. When I need a break from all the input, I find some good music somewhere and it helps to *'slow-the-flow'* to a varying extent depending on what it is. I really don't want to get into all the details with you, but for some reason *your* music is a *total* block for me. I don't know how many empaths you have come across specifically in your experiences, but I can tell you that it's not common. And I'm not gonna lie, I took advantage of it." I took another fortifying sip of wine and continued.

"See, I have a big job that I'm working on and it's really important to my survival that it go well. Not all of us can afford to splurge hundreds of thousands of dollars on sports cars." I said teasingly. "I've been... well, using you really, to keep things quiet while I work so I could complete this job on time." I cringed appropriately as I confessed.

"I don't know why your music works so well. I can't help wondering now, *if* there is any truth to your strange tale, if maybe this '*infection*' extended into your throat and vocal chords too?" I said with raised eyebrows. It was his turn not to answer so I kept going. "Anyway, I don't know if that is why your little *would-be-apprentice* saw some sort of connection between us or not. But that's all I've got. Other than that, your guess is as good as mine. *Really.*" I insisted easily.

He was thoughtful for the next few minutes while we both sipped our wine under the bright night sky. He was contemplating a lot of new ides in his head, but I had no idea what they were. I knew it had to be really late but I felt as if I'd had three cups of coffee.

We sat quietly, each lost in our own thoughts for a few more minutes. I was trying to absorb everything that he had said. I was surprised to find out that he had been curious about me. It was weird not to have picked up on it sooner but I had to write that off as a side effect of his music's total blocking ability. I really did tend to ignore everything else when I was there working. Still neither of us had ever intended to approach the other until it became totally unavoidable. I wondered about that for a minute until he broke the silence.

"I should go." He finally said. "I'm really sorry. For *all* of this unpleasantness. You need time. To let all this sink in, think it through. I've caused you enough trouble for one night." He stood up and grabbed his keys off of the table. He took a deep, tired sounding breath and spoke without looking. "I'll see you at The Tavern."

I could feel his remorse but I wasn't sure whether it was due to his upsetting me or because he didn't find out more from me.

He turned and headed towards the stairs that led off the deck but as he reached the landing, he stopped for a minute and turned back to look at me. He spoke again in a soft and annoyingly understanding tone. "But you should know that you *are* extremely gifted and that makes you very special. *Not a freak. Hmpf.* Especially not around here." He said with a crooked half smile.

"At some point, when you're done being pissed off, it's going to make sense for you to contact me." He left a business card on the table by the railing. "I'll leave you alone until then." He turned again after that and left without another backward glance.

I was still sitting there looking incredulous as I listened to his engine fire up and then get quieter and quieter as it sped away.

Had that really just happened? *Hadn't I already said that once tonight?* Jesus! Things were getting out of hand around there. I looked around the spacious deck, into my softly lit living area and then out across the green pastures behind me, sighing deeply. So much for my peace and quiet. I had never felt such relief in another place before but even the beauty and serenity of it all could not quiet the thoughts that were swirling madly in my head then.

Dammit! Why did all this upheaval, stress and drama have to come with what was supposed to be my beautiful, peaceful slice of paradise? Ugggghhhh!

It didn't matter because I had a meeting that did matter in... *Shit!* Four hours! Had we really been talking that long?! Sleep was out of the question at that point. If I went to sleep after the day I'd had, I'd be out until at least noontime. I could make myself get up, but I knew from experience that I would look worse than if I hadn't slept at all. Better to use what time I had to shower and eat. Maybe I could at least *look* like I'd had a good nights' sleep and not like I had spent the entire night engaged in one "*heightened*" situation after another.

I went inside to put my plan into action, and the whole other situation out of my mind.

Chapter 9

I managed to get through the entire morning and half of the afternoon before I thought about it again. The meeting had gone surprisingly well. The shower had helped immensely. I felt recharged after the long soak under the steaming hot water. I even went all out and made a real breakfast with the extra time I had from not sleeping. French toast with fresh strawberries and strong coffee. Between the shower and the breakfast, I was feeling almost human again by the time I left.

I met Mr. Wu Xing at his office promptly at 7:00 AM. My current client was as old fashioned as his name made him sound and he was also big on punctuality.

He was the owner a five star hotel, but it wasn't just a hotel. It also had a five star restaurant and spa as well. It sat regally up in the rolling hills of the *real* resort country of New Hampshire. It was about thirty five minutes North of Pinegrove, and it was a truly beautiful retreat from the rest of the world. Wu Xing Gardens covered thirteen acres of the twenty one acre property and were some of the finest in the country with their highly exotic flora, intricately woven "*living walls*" and multiple award winning designs.

I, like most of the general population, had walked through them in awe a handful of times over the years. It was a great place to waste a sunny afternoon. What existed there was breathtaking already, but he wanted to add to it. Again. Just as each generation before him had done.

Each section of the Gardens had been done by a different

designer, in their individual style. Each hired by a different family member from a different generation. It reminded me of the traditions carried on by the ancient Pharaoh's with their pyramids. I personally thought it was an admirable tradition and the next decedent, the current Mr. Wu Xing, had chosen *me* to do the next new section. It was a huge honor, but also held a tremendous amount of pressure. The bar was already set ridiculously high.

The only consolation was that each section had been free to have its' own personality. There were a total of five separate gardens already, and you couldn't really compare any of them to another. They were each too different and too spectacular in their own way.

That was my one saving grace. My plan was to keep with that tradition and just go with my gut. Forget about the amazing gardens that already existed and just keep true to myself. He obviously liked my work. He had hired me, right? It was the only way I had any hope of holding my head up afterwards. Whether I succeeded or not, the plan was to do it my way and walk away with no regrets.

Mr. Wu Xing had liked my preliminary sketches though and that certainly went a long way as far as my state of mind was concerned. We would see. It was probably the scariest project I had taken on to date, and I had just about everything riding on it.

It not only needed to be, but it also deserved to be the recipient of my undivided attention. I knew that and yet I still couldn't stop the things that Ethan had said as they started running through my head. I had been working hard to keep them quarantined in the back of my mind all day long, where they couldn't poison the rest of my thoughts and I couldn't do it anymore. As much as I wanted to discredit him or chalk it up to over exaggeration, his words rang too damn true and I couldn't ignore that fact. Even though I *really* wanted to!

I wondered about the things that he claimed. About himself. About *me!* Was it really possible that he had at least some of the answers that I had all but given up on ever finding?

That alone was very tempting for me. Much more than anything else. But it felt like he knew, like really *knew* that I would come to realize he was right. That he ...knew *me* somehow!

Anditpissedmeoff! Dammit!

I had never given him permission to know things about me. I liked it better when I had control over how much of me someone was allowed to see. Not that I could give others that same choice or control, but I still wanted it for myself. Maybe I wanted it more because of that. I don't know.

He understood that about me too apparently and was seemingly willing to wait while I found a way to get over it. I still felt slow and juvenile and even more pissed off for being behind him in that thought process as well!

Was this the normal pattern one would follow, when they find all this stuff out? Or did he really have that firm a grasp on my psyche? How could he? Even if he *could* see some weird trace of some weird virus in me and everyone else who had it. That still wouldn't give him the same insight into my personality. So why was he so sure that I would contact him?

Well he was right about one thing. I *would* see him at The Tavern.

I couldn't decide at first if it was worth it or not. If it would even really be possible to go back to using him, admittedly, without talking to him. But at the end of the day I had just as much right to be there as anyone else. And not only was he aware of that, but he knew that I would be too. Of course. That was why he had said he would see me there, but also that he would leave me alone until I wanted to talk to him. I was already pretty sure that he was a man of his word. *From what I could tell about him so far anyway...*

I thought about it and realized that I could keep fighting it, which I know from experience can be exhausting, or I could accept it and find a way to "see the bright side" so-to-speak. Any time I am given a choice, I will choose the bright side. Brighter was always preferable in my book.

So I made up my mind. I had too much work left to do still and no time to try and find a better place to get it done. Of course I could always stay home and put the radio on. It was spotty though depending on what came on, how well it worked. Even though there was no crowds' worth of emotional noise in my apartment, I still needed to be able to focus and his music had been the best conduit for that lately. It was just easier at the Tavern. I needed easier at the moment.

Sure, I could always put on CD's too, but my favorites were so sorely worn out by then, that I dreaded it. I wished then that *he* had a CD that I could take home with me. *Hah!* That would solve everything! I laughed again to myself. I'd have to ask Dani if he'd ever made one. Later.

Until then, I had something more important to do. As I pulled my car up to the next available spot by the curb, that very important something ran eagerly up to my car and hopped in. She pulled the heavy door closed and waved to Mrs. Mason through the window before she turned her giant smile on me. Her energy hit me first. Her emotions were so pure and untarnished by time that it was always a welcome sensation. "Hi mama!" Liliana said with a smile as bright as sunshine.

"Hi yourself there kiddo! How was school? I asked as she hopped across the seat to hug me.

"Great! We got to hold turtles and spiders today!" She said excitedly.

"You did?!"

"Yes! And snakes and alligators too! They said they were curious creatures, but I don't know why because they mostly weren't as curious about us as we were about them." She said totally serious, and it made me laugh. She did that to me a lot. She was way too smart for her own good, but still too young to realize it. I knew there was a company that came out to the schools with plastic bins full of creepy crawlies to give the children a little hand's on time. I also knew the name of the company was *"Curious Creatures,"* so I got the joke, even if she didn't.

"I'll bet they were just a little shy." I said with a conciliatory smile. I watched as she climbed into the backseat and buckled herself into her booster seat. It was Friday and I had my baby girl all to myself until tomorrow at five. Nothing in the world made me happier.

"Did you miss me a lot, mama?" She asked me then, and I could feel her worry for me, her fear that I might say no, and her own sadness all at once. It broke my heart a little. I was quick to recover though. The last thing I wanted to do was to let her worry that I would ever stop missing her when she was away from me.

"*Soooooo* much!!" I said emphatically. "I miss you *every second* that we're apart. But I know it's going to be okay, because all I have to do is think about what you're doing right then. Like if you're in school or home with Daddy or even with your grandparents. I know where you are and that you're safe and happy and doing all the things that a five-year-old should be. It always makes me feel better until I get to see you again."

"See sweetie, we are not always going to be right next to each other, like this." I said pointing at us inside the car. "But we will always be close together in *here!*" I said pointing to my heart with one hand and hers with the other. "No matter what or how far apart we are. It doesn't matter. Because we are always connected here. You have to promise to always remember that. Okay?"

When I finished she smiled and I could feel her relief and her security grow.

"Okay, mama." It was very rewarding to actually *know* when you had gotten through to your child. I'm positive that if I could bottle and sell my gift, it would be parents wanting to understand and communicate better with their children that would be lining the streets to buy it. Men and woman for the most part could hear each other's thoughs all day and still never understand each other.

"Alright, it's just you and me girlie!" I said happily. "First stop, the market! Should we get stuff for a fish fry or pizza?"

"Fish Fry! Fish Fry!" She yelled, hearing her favorite choice.

"Fish fry it is." I answered with another wide smile, and we were off. We made our way back to Pinegrove first and as soon as we got off the highway that familiar peacefulness washed over me. I breathed a sigh of relief.

We continued through downtown and over the bridge where the market and the fish truck were. Some people were too afraid to buy fish off the back of a truck that sits parked at a gas station, but people around here know that it happens to be the nicest, freshest and most fairly priced seafood around. It came straight off the boats in the surrounding fishing towns every morning.

Doug, or *"The Fish Guy"* as we all affectionately called him, let Liliana pick her two favorite pieces of haddock from the big cooler, and we chatted while he weighed and wrapped them. We thanked Doug and then we headed off to get cracker meal and some relish to make tartar sauce from the market next door.

The supermarket was one of my least favorite places on Earth, except for the rare quiet moments at like 10:00 on a Tuesday morning. Unfortunately, it was also one of the most unavoidable. I've learned to get in, get what I need and get out as fast as humanly possible. That night was no different. Liliana knows me well enough to know this about me, and was as cooperative as usual. She was never one to waste time asking for every item on the shelves while we went up and down each and every isle. She was a dream child for someone like me. I wondered constantly how I ever got so lucky.

Back at my apartment with our feet bare and our sleeves rolled up, we breaded fish chunks side-by-side and laughed for the better part of an hour. It wasn't the fastest food prep in the world but I didn't care. I loved to cook and I loved to cook with Liliana even more.

Ben and I both tried to keep to her normal schedule whenever possible. It was another one of the things we had agreed upon very early on in hopes of keeping the turmoil from touching her any more than necessary. But things were a little more casual on the weekends. Then we would plan to eat a little later while we watched a movie. We called it "dinner theatre" and it was her favorite game to play.

We cranked my favorite Andrea Bocelli CD while we cooked, even though he was just as worn out as any of my other favorites. A little repetition was okay when I was cooking. Especially when I knew what worked for what task, and Bocelli always worked when I cooked. I absolutely loved his music and I didn't think I could really ever get tired of listening to him anyway.

I sliced the outer rings of the onion to fry. Then I chopped the onion heart and drained the liquid from the relish to mix into the mayo for our tartar sauce. In our area, the tartar sauce was just as important as the fish itself and I had a recipe that I had guarded carefully over the years.

Actually, it came from when I worked at the best seafood restaurant in town for a while during my twenties, while landscaping was still just a hobby. After months of hard work and loyal service, I was taught the recipe for what was in my opinion, the absolute *best* tartar sauce in existence.

That may not mean much to you, but around here it's a *BIG* deal. There are contests and competitions held regularly over things like that and loyalties are often defended to the grave. I am definitely not the only one who takes my food seriously. I would never give the recipe to anyone else, the secret was safe with me, but it was mine forever, fair and square.

She stirred and I fried and we danced around each other as I sang with the CD even though it was completely in Italian. I had listened to it so much that I could sing the whole thing in its entirety. It made us both laugh when she asked me what I was saying, because I had to admit then that I had absolutely no idea! We both laughed and continued singing gibberish together a little louder with our arms up in the air.

When the concert was over, we left the finished pieces on the plates covered in paper towels to drain and cool while I mixed some chocolate milk for Liliana. I set that down and grabbed a bottle of Coors light for myself. We sat our plates, piled high with the fried fish and homemade onion rings, on the coffee table. I went back for the all-important bowl of tartar sauce and the coleslaw from the fridge that I had mixed before we started cooking. We finished it off with copious amounts of napkins. Then we plopped down onto the pile of pillows stacked up around the table to eat.

"What should we watch?" I asked coyly, even though I knew the answer I would get. It had been the same for the past month, since she had first discovered it and fell in love. It would probably hold that coveted spot for another few weeks yet to come. That was generally about how long it took before she grew tired of her new 'favorite' and moved onto the next. Right now it was...

"Finding Nemo!" She practically screamed. I just laughed and hit play, already having the movie perfectly cued and ready

to go.

She never made the connection between our dinner choice and our entertainment, thankfully. We sat and ate and watched and laughed, sunshine pouring in through the windows. I thought to myself that those really were the absolute best things in life. Everything else was just what we had to do, in order to earn and enjoy the simple times like those. I was reminded again of my feelings regarding my family when I was growing up, and they were still the same today. We had our issues, sure. But we were all still *very* lucky. My father would always also jokingly say, "It's better to be lucky than good!" and he was probably right.

After watching Dory and the little clown fish find Nemo for the hundredth time and only crying *a little*, I got up with a slight groan and cleaned up. Once I had the dishes rinsed and loaded into the dishwasher, I went back to the living room and pulled the sofa bed out while Liliana changed into her jammies and brushed her teeth. She had wanted to sleep in the big bed with me when she first started to stay over, but we had decided that while it was fun once or twice, it was not the best habit to get into.

We'd always had a very strict rule, Ben and I, about not bringing the baby into the bed when she was young. We knew too many couples whose children still wouldn't spend an entire night in their own beds, even at seven and eight years old. That idea did not particularly appeal to either of us.

We felt like it was better to comfort and cuddle and then return her to her own bed so she could learn how to get back to sleep on her own, no matter how hard it was for *us*. And for the most part, it had worked really well. We had no problems later when it came to Liliana going to her own bed and going to sleep at night. It was a blessing and it had been worth a few nights spent tiredly pacing floors in the wee hours back in the beginning.

I grabbed her and swooped her up as she came out of my bathroom and carried her out to the couch where I pretended to throw her out the window. She squealed loudly and landed safely in the middle of the queen sized sleep-sofa. She laughed and bounced merrily for a few seconds then scrambled under the blankets and grabbed "Ellie" her favorite stuffed elephant and snuggled up to the pillow. I tucked her in and gave her a kiss. "Goodnight. I love you." I said, the same way I did every night, in person or otherwise.

"Goodnight. I love you, too." She said back, the same way she did every night and all was right with the world. Later I watched her for a few minutes, sound asleep with her white blond hair lying in a silky river on her pillow behind her and her mouth hanging open just a little. Her beauty was always a pleasant surprise to me. I had never thought myself ugly or even unattractive. I do fine. But neither had I ever considered myself to be *"beautiful."* But *she* was. Ben was admittedly more of a looker than me but still a fairly regular guy. I remained amazed that somehow the better parts of each of us had combined to make a new being far superior to the two original halves.

After checking on her one last time, I shut everything off except for one small lamp by the couch and one by my bed. I walked out onto the deck and sat down in the same chair that I had sat in just the night before. Talking to my Magician. *Huh...* I was thinking that maybe my fictitious title applied to him more than I had realized.

The moon was still almost full and the view was bathed in the same light blue glow as it had been the night before. I suddenly felt like I was right back there again and he was still sitting across from me waiting for my response. I looked at the empty chair while the memories ran through my head until I couldn't take it anymore and I had to turn back to stare out at the empty, un-accusing orchard instead.

He wasn't even there and he had managed to make me feel vulnerable again. I sighed deeply and sipped my beer trying not to think at all. It was hard though, especially in the quiet times. The only bad part about the peacefulness there was that there was no noise to stop my own powerful feelings from rising to the surface. I had thought that I wanted that originally but I wasn't so sure anymore. I sighed then and decided not to fight it.

I thought again about my childhood. There were others in my family who were like me, so there was a genetic thread for sure. No one would ever convince me otherwise. But I was willing to consider the possibility that maybe some of us were touched by this "virus" in addition, and that was what made it so much stronger in just a few of us. I didn't know what the odds were that some of us would be affected and some would be immune, but I supposed it would be the same as the odds for only some of us having a gift in the first place. It was worth at least considering, in the abstract anyway.

My mind loved to puzzle out any and every answer and I was still missing an awful lot of those where my abilities were concerned. There weren't too many experts out there reporting regularly on the subject. Just a small group of organizations trying to connect over the web that I mostly chose to keep away from. Basically just for the sake of my own privacy. But again, it's also to separate myself from the "freak-factor" as much as possible.

If I chose to believe what Ethan had claimed, then that meant he represented a whole other group of freaks that would try to lump me in their pile. Why did I have to pick a pile or a label at all? Why couldn't I just *be?* What was wrong with that?

The only thing I could think of was the other half of my heart that was sleeping so soundly a few yards away. Would *she* inherit the family trait someday? Would she also be infected by some virus that would eventually *intensify* it?

Would I need someone like Ethan to help me, help her get the most out of life? Was he really even capable of making a difference with something like that? Was *anyone?* What a fantasy that had been of mine when I was young. To have someone even *understand!* Never mind be able to really *help* in some tangible way.

Or was she better off with just Ben and I, and the advice and help that we could offer her in the privacy of our own home. Well, "*home's*" then, but still. It had been enough for me in the end. A set of loving and understanding parents and I had turned out just fine. For the most part.

Still, I couldn't help but think about all the ways that it could have been better. *Easier.*

All of that was irrelevant then though and I truly hoped that it would remain that way, but I couldn't deny that it was at least a possibility that she would follow in my footsteps. Would he really be able to help? Would it be too late to forge a connection with him later, should I change my mind, if I turned him away in the meantime?

So many things were swirling in my head that I finally decided I had better just go to bed and sleep on it. Give my conscious mind a break. Maybe my subconscious mind would work it out. That happened occasionally. I would go to bed thinking about a problem, and I would dream about a situation that would lead me to figuring out the solution.

I closed and locked all the doors like I always did, even though it probably wasn't necessary. I just couldn't invite opportunity like that. Not there or anywhere else. After brushing my own teeth and washing my face, I turned my light off. I left Liliana's on in case she woke up in the middle of the night, and I went to sleep.

Chapter 10

The next morning I woke to a pair of giant emerald green eyes staring gleefully at me. Liliana was standing on her tiptoes, trying to reach the top of the bed, and that was about all I could see of her.

"Well good morning, sunshine!" I said with a smile as I stretched and yawned. I turned to look at the clock. 7:04. Liliana knew that she shouldn't wake people up before 7:00 AM. We had taught her that that was the earliest *"polite"* hour to expect interaction from someone. Whether it was me, Ben or one of her grandparents. As usual she was very mature about it and would entertain herself in her room with a book or a toy until then if she woke up early. But once that magic hour had passed, as far as she was concerned anyone was fair game. Saturday morning or not.

I reached over and pulled her up on the bed with me and under the covers. I snuggled her neck and pretended to snore while she giggled.

"No, mama! You have to get up now. It's seven o'clock!" She insisted.

"Alright." I said playfully as I tickled her one more time. "Let me brush my teeth and get some coffee going and I'll make you some breakfast. K, kiddo?"

"Okay mama." She agreed easily. "While I'm waiting, can I put a movie on?" She asked.

"Sure. What did you want to watch?" I asked, innocently, as if I didn't already know.

"Finding Nemo!" She yelled, right on cue while I mouthed

it where she couldn't see me and laughed.

After her millionth viewing of "Finding Nemo" and breakfast, we both got dressed. I put on a pair of old jeans and a well-worn black t-shirt. Liliana chose a plaid button down shirt and her favorite dark purple denim capris, with matching converse sneakers. I pulled her hair back into two adorable blonde pigtails then twisted my own up into a quick and easy knot and clipped it on top of my head. I went into the kitchen to grab the last thing we needed from the fridge. I took the carrot and headed to the back door where she was already waiting.

I looked down at her. "Ready?" I asked.

"Ready!" She confirmed and we headed out the back sliders to begin our adventures for the day.

I walked and Liliana skipped across the deck toward the stairs that led to the driveway. Instead of crossing the gravel expanse at the bottom, we took the path that started at the grasses edge, in between the garage and the shed. We followed it across the wide green lawn that expanded in almost every direction. It went all the way up to the farm house on our left and over to the stables and horse paddock in front of us. It also went beyond the fields, past the orchard and all the way up to the forest's edge on our right. It continued past the structures in front of us until it eventually met the forest there as well. It was almost impossible to be down while surrounded by such natural beauty. That was one of the reasons that I loved the place so much.

As we approached the riding area, I could already see Jack waving to us with one hand. He was standing in the center next to a horse, holding its reins in his other hand. We both waved back and Liliana looked up at me eagerly, knowing I would feel what she was feeling without her having to say it out loud. Her eagerness ready to overflow.

I simply nodded and handed her the carrot. She ran off ahead of me joy spilling out everywhere. I just smiled to myself, as usual. She knew how to appreciate the bright side too, my smart girl. She didn't think twice about taking advantage of my skills. She had never known anything else, so it made sense that she would simply take it for granted. It was never an issue to her either way. It just was. Unconditional love. Luckily for me, it worked both ways.

The gentle mare, whose name I knew was "Cookie," came over to accept the treat that Liliana offered. She nibbled slowly, taking her time, much to Liliana's giggling delight. I climbed a rung or two myself a few sections away and leaned over the top rail to watch with a contented smile on my face.

"Farm living suits you, girl." Jack said softly as he watched both of us from ground level.

"It sure is peaceful here. Can't complain about that." I said by way of explanation. He just smiled at me and started over to Liliana.

"I think she might be ready." He said then, referring to the mare and not Liliana, I knew. She had been ready to jump on since day one. Jack had patiently explained to her though that the mare needed to get to know her and accept her first. As usual, she was very mature and understanding about it. She would wait and get to know her first. Because that was the right way to do it. As long as she was aware of what the right way was in a given situation, she would always try to do things that way.

She was only five and she made me so proud already. I wanted to take credit for it, for molding her into such an amazing person. But I knew for a fact that most of that was just her. That's just who she was. So we had a head start. So what. I knew we were still willing to work our asses off to make sure we didn't screw her up.

I looked at her expectant face and asked. "What do you think? Is she ready? Does she know you well enough to know that you care about her, and that you won't hurt her? Does she trust you yet?" These were the important points that we had already discussed.

She looked back at me with those giant green eyes shining brightly. "Let me see." She said, and climbed down off of the fence. She ducked under the second rail and stepped inside the riding area. I was leery but I spotted Jack right behind Cookie with the reigns tight in his other hand. He nodded at me and I relaxed a little. I looked back down at my brave little soldier and nodded at her once more.

She took one big step toward Cookie and held the

remaining half of carrot up for her. She click-clicked to her and the mare walked the rest of the way to finish eating the carrot. She looked back at me and smiled bigger than I had seen in a very long while. I was practically bursting with pride then.

"You did it!" I said, my joy at her accomplishment, clearly coming through.

Jack came up beside her then and handed her the reigns. "Here you go, missy. You're in control from here on out. You got her?" He asked one last time, before letting go.

She nodded, serious then and I smiled again. I couldn't help it. She walked over to the stirrup and reached her left foot as high as she could trying to set her purple sneaker in it. Jack lifted her up under her arms and swung her the rest of the way up and over. She grabbed the horn of the saddle and sat up straight and tall. She looked absolutely *tiny* up there!

I was nervous, but excited for her too. I could feel her excitement as well. I remembered how much fun I'd had trying new things when I was growing up. I also thought again how much I admired my parents' ability to *allow* me all that exploration. It was harder than it looked, that's for sure.

Jack started to slowly lead them around the large square with one hand resting gently on the bridle. I knew he thought it was important for Liliana to hold the reigns herself in order to have the proper amount of understanding of her responsibility. To herself and to the animal that was entrusted to her.

He explained all of this to her again while they moved slowly in a circle. I just watched in awe while I leaned on the top rail and chewed happily on a long blade of grass. It was pretty cool. I could feel Jack's beaming pride at her accomplishment. It mixed in with my own happiness, while the sun burned down on my cheeks and arms. The birds were chirping all around us madly and the smell of the coming summer was carried in on the soft, warm breeze. Which currently, happened to be keeping those same cheeks cool.

Life was starting to feel good again. I was relieved to know that I had been right to have faith. Things *were* getting better. I found myself hoping the trend would last for a while.

After a few dozen laps around the paddock, it was time

to call it a day. At least for riding, anyway. Jack showed her the proper way to brush Cookie after her ride. Then she helped him get her fresh hay. He was not only teaching her the importance of trust between her and the animal, but also the necessary care that went along with the fun. She was a little small for cleaning out stalls yet, but I had no doubt that as soon as she was big enough, he wouldn't hesitate to hand her a shovel. I liked that about him.

It reminded me of my dad. I thought then, that I would have to introduce them soon. They would definitely get along. Once she was happy that she had fulfilled all of her new "equestrian duties," she hugged and thanked Jack.

"She did really well today." He said to me in a quiet voice, as we hugged goodbye. "Picks things up real quick. Reminds me of someone else." He said cheekily with a backwards stare at me. It hadn't taken Jack very long to figure out how *"sensitive"* I was. Oddly, and well thankfully, it hadn't seemed to matter to him one bit. Then louder again he said, "You should bring her back for Movie Night on Friday."

"Movie Night?" I asked. Unfamiliar with the term.

"Yup. It's nothing fancy. Just some small town neighborhood fun. The wife and I get the projector out and shine it up on the side of the barn for the masses once or twice a month during the nice weather. Everybody brings a beach chair or a blanket and parks it on the lawn. We generally try to keep it family friendly. And you're in luck, this week we're showing *'Shrek.'* He said with a comical grin and a sly look over his shoulder.

"Shrek?!" Liliana asked excitedly from the edge of the stall where she was still petting cookie. She had seen it before. In fact it had even held the coveted spot of *"favorite"* for a few weeks last year when she first discovered it. I could tell she thought it was a great idea, but I was still confused.

"Um, neighborhood?" I asked again, wondering what neighbors he might be referring to since none were readily visible.

"Yeah, you know, friends around town. Business associates. Neighbors. Around here we personally consider anyone less than ten miles away a *'neighbor.'* He explained and instantly it brought me back to the night that Ethan was in my apartment. When he had pointed out that we were in fact *"neighbors."* I had thought that he was joking at the time. *Hah!* Guess not. I remembered the heat too. I didn't want to, but unfortunately the memories were connected. Jack thankfully snapped me back to the present again.

"You two should come. It's fun."

Just then Liliana ran up and asked, "Oh, can we Mama?"

There were lots of times that I had known that a certain social encounter would be too much for me but being there, at least so far, had not been. Maybe "Movie Night" wouldn't be either. I wanted to try. I wanted to be able to get excited about those kinds of things. They were the things that I wanted so badly to be able to enjoy with her. I sighed and agreed before I could change my mind. "Sure!" I was dreading the crowd, but I knew that I was outnumbered at the moment anyway. Oh well, at least if it was truly terrible, I wouldn't be too far from home. We told Jack that we would see him next Friday and then we headed back along the path across the lawn towards my apartment.

We had a quick lunch of PB&J and then went to walk around the orchard where she liked to climb the trees. After that we picked some wild flowers for Shirley and walked them up to the farmhouse to give them to her.

She had been hanging sheets on the line out back of the farmhouse when we approached. I knew she dried all her clothes indoors in an electric dryer like the rest of us, but she had explained that she preferred the smell of fresh air on her sheets. It helped her to sleep at night. Oddly enough, I could totally understand.

Her straight, silver hair blowing in the springtime breeze, made her look like a stately grandmother. But it didn't hold weight up close. Her soft smooth face was that of someone much younger, who just didn't care for hair dye. She never seemed to have even a worry line at the corner of her eyes. I didn't know how she did it, but someday when we were close enough, I planned to ask.

She was extremely gracious and thankful for Liliana's sake, to receive flowers that were essentially already hers. As usual, I was grateful. It was clear that she was a mother first, and obviously a darn good one. She made us stay for cookies and lemonade.

By the time we got back, it was time to gather up her

things for the trip back home. Well, *her* home. It was a beautiful day for a drive and the radio was cooperative enough with the good songs. Still I was slightly tense and a little sad. It was always the same on the return trip.

I couldn't help it. That was always the hardest part. Bringing her back. Letting her go again. My heart gave a painful squeeze just thinking about it. I swallowed it down and tried to enjoy the Fleetwood Mac song and the breeze through the open moon-roof. *I would get through it.* It *was* getting better.

I pulled up out front of my former home and retrieved her things from the trunk. She gave me a big hug and a kiss and then I watched her run up and jump into Ben's waiting arms. It was obvious that he loved her as much as I did. It was painful, but it was also comforting. It was hard but it helped.

He looked over her shoulder and winked at me. I waved and turned to get back in my car before the tears in my eyes betrayed me by jumping ship. I cranked up Adele and headed back to the highway.

I debated going back home and just going to bed, but I was too wound up by the time I got back to Pinegrove. Right then, I really *didn't* want to be alone. I needed to try and readjust the balance a little. So I headed to The Tavern instead.

I knew that Ethan would be there, but I didn't care. I had to get that first sighting over with sometime. And since I had decided that I *would* go back rather than sacrifice my favorite work spot, the mood I was in presently was perfect. It couldn't get any worse. Might as well kill two uncomfortable birds with one stone.

I pulled up and parked in the same spot that I had been in on my last night there. The night that Carson had approached me. The night that Ethan had come to my house and told me I was different. Again. Not even just an empath anymore. Like that wasn't enough.

I sighed, turned the ignition off, pulled the keys out and headed inside. He was playing REO Speedwagon's *"Take It On The Run"* when I walked in. It was perfect. I just shook my head and gave an ironic half smile. I should have been angry. I should have been feeling resentment and indignation. Instead, I instantly felt better. I knew I should be pissed, but I couldn't work it up.

I sat heavily in my usual booth and waved at Dani, who understood what I wanted without a word.

I sighed and dropped my head in my hands while I waited. I really needed to get some work started on the technical plans for the Gardens at Wu Xing's, but I was too distracted and emotionally fried to do anything remotely responsible at the moment. I just wanted everything to stop for a while. The anxiety. The sadness. The jealousy that I felt towards Ben when she went home. The guilt for feeling that. The pain. The sense of failure. All of it. I just wanted it all to stop. Just for a *little* while. *Pretty please?*

He only looked up at me once. I felt his tentative searching. I couldn't be sure, but I thought he may have actually flinched at what he found. Whether I imagined it or not, he kept his word. He left me alone after that. I was glad. I relaxed a little more.

It was comforting that I could still count on my Magician for emotional relief. But as good as it was, I couldn't deny that it was different. There was an awareness there that hadn't been present before and try as I might, I couldn't ignore it completely. Thankfully though, I was just too tired to do anything about it, including worry.

I sat and sipped, staring emptily at nothing and reveled in escapism until the music stopped. When that happened, I put a ten dollar bill on the table and walked silently out the front door.

I called Liliana from the car to say goodnight, and then I drove home on auto-pilot to the soothing sounds of Paolo Nutini. I walked up the stairs and went into my bathroom to undress and shower. I brushed my hair out and brushed my teeth. I threw on a tank top and some shorts and turned out all the lights. I walked the short distance to my bed and fell deeply asleep as soon as my head hit the pillow.

Some days just needed to be over.

Chapter 11

The following week went by faster than usual. I brightened at the sight of Liliana the few times that I saw her, but was brought low again each time I had to say good bye. I tried to remind myself that I would have had to let her go off to school every day anyway, even if she were still with me full time. Not that it guaranteed I would have handled it any better.

I laughed when I remembered how I used to get choked up at putting her on the bus for preschool in the beginning. I would have to remind myself that she would be back in a mere few hours so I could laugh at myself.

It was harder at that point though, since it wasn't just for a few hours when I dropped her off anymore. Harder to laugh at my own absurdity. It was just hard.

I realized then, with some resolve, that I had to stop acting as if every goodbye was forever. It was affecting her as well. I could feel it. That was unacceptable. I would have had to let her live her life at some point anyway. I was just learning to do that a little earlier than I would have liked, I told myself.

Alright, a *lot* earlier than I would have liked. But she would be better for it in the long run, I added resolutely. Just like her learning to sleep through the night on her own.

Coping. I was supposed to be coping. I could do this. *For her.*

Deep breaths.

I started to get a better handle on it all by mid-week. Work was going well at least. I had been at The Tavern the normal two nights so far and I had been pretty successful at ignoring Ethan and focusing on my project. I was starting to get excited about the design by then. It was my favorite part of the project. I was past the "discovery" stage, where I needed to decide what type of plant life was right for the area and then design it into something desirable.

I was at the point then that I had to take it from the concept stage, to the actual 3-dimensional design. That part was easier though. There were measurements and specific requirements involved. It wasn't up to me so much to *decide*, as it was to just *determine* where things belonged and I had someone who knew more about it than me to help with a lot of that, Micky. I would dream it up, and she would help me make sure it would actually survive. She was due to do just that for this job, as soon as I finished the next round of drawings.

It was mostly based on mathematical equations and predictable levels of light and water. There were absolutes and rules to follow. I knew the basics by then but I always deferred to an expert when necessary. It also took some of the pressure off of me for a little while. There at The Tavern I got lost in the peace of mind that Ethan's music afforded me and within two nights, my part was done.

Very soon it would be time to start the actual work in the dirt. I was beyond excited. But I was just a little bit apprehensive, too.

I would be spending a *lot* of time at the sight for the next two months and a lot *less* time at the Tavern, once that that part of the job was finished. That *should* be a good thing. It had been a stroke of luck finding the place and it had worked out beautifully. It had served its purpose, but I couldn't deny that I was going to miss being there.

Truth was it was really good to have a public place that I felt comfortable hanging out in. Even though some days I definitely needed a break from it all, I don't actually *want* to be by myself all the time. I do crave human interaction or even just the presence of other humans sometimes, just like everyone else. I just don't always have as many good options to make that happen as everybody else does. So by default, I get a lot less of it.

But I was supposed to be trying to find ways to enjoy my life more, to relax a little, and The Tavern fit the bill. Of course there was no reason I couldn't still go by for a drink and a song whenever I wanted to. I would just have to find the time.

I decided then, that I *would* find a way to keep that. To fit it in somewhere. I needed to make those things a priority for a change. The things that I *wanted* in my life. I don't know why I am always so happy to take the things that I really want and put them off a little while longer. Why does every other thing always have to come first? Let me just get here, finish this, do that for them, *then* I will be ready to really enjoy my life.

Screw it! I was ready dammit! Unless someone had found a way to make aging go backwards for a little while whenever we wanted, I was wasting time. Not anymore. Only get one life and all that. The only thing I wasn't willing to consider enjoying was Ethan. That part of me was on vacation. And I wasn't expecting her back anytime soon. As long as I could keep that from being a problem, I thought to myself, the Tavern was a good thing. I really needed to start keeping the good things.

It was on Thursday afternoon that I decided I'd spent enough time thinking about it all. I was worn out but I was also finished working for the time being, so I decided that I'd had an adequately productive week and deserved to take the night off. From everything.

I immediately called up Vivianne and invited her up. Of course, she immediately accepted. I stopped off at the dreaded market for nacho fixin's. Then the liquor store for margarita mix, which was also just over the bridge in the same plaza. I really did love that about that town. I would hate to have to give it up. I was feeling like a kid again by the time I headed home. It was exactly what I needed. A *"Viv-*id experience," as we liked to call it. It had been a while and I was overdue.

Vivianne was the one person who could always make me laugh. In spite of whatever other crap was going on around me at the time. She can be so overwhelming in her exuberance, and her commitment to her comedy, that she was like a one woman show. I *loved* that about her.

I heard the high pitched chirp of the horn in her Corolla

bleat a few times in rapid succession and I bolted down the stairs like a little girl.

I burst out the door at the bottom screaming and running with my arms out in front of me. I spotted her, with her long black hair, still with the multi-colored streaks, up in a high pony tail. As if that wasn't enough, it was tied with a scarf that was colorful enough to rival her hair. She jumped out of the car with her own arms outstretched in my direction. We ran screaming toward each other and hugged and spun around until we couldn't help but laugh hysterically at our own absurdity.

I stood back and took her in for a minute feeling like I hadn't seen her in months, when in reality it had only been weeks. She had on a denim micro-mini skirt with black knee length leggings underneath that kept it from being indecent. On top she wore a graphic purple tank top that Liliana would love, and sneakers that she could probably borrow.

Vivianne was the only grown woman I knew that could still shop in the juniors department and come out looking amazing. Between the hair, the tattoos and the piercings,' she wasn't in any danger of looking even remotely juvenile. But even without all of that, no one would *ever* mistake Viv for a little girl. Her body was that of a woman for sure. I had always been a little jealous of the way she could eat anything she wanted and never gain an ounce. *Anywhere.* She was a perfectly petite size 3 with a 36 C chest. Some things in life really just weren't fair, but I loved her in spite of it, because her painfully honest personality balanced it out.

"You are just too damn cute! Look at you! If Liliana was here she would be so jealous!" I said honestly while I grabbed her overnight bag and threw it over my right shoulder.

"I think that's a compliment?" She replied with a confused smile.

"Of course it is!" I said adamantly. "Liliana is one of the most stylish people I know!" I added emphatically.

"Yeah, you're right. Okay." She agreed and then we both laughed because it was true.

We topped the steps and Vivianne took in an overly dramatic deep breath. *"Ahhhhh!* I can't believe you get to live here! Every time I leave, I forget how beautiful it is! It's selective amnesia, of course." She admitted backhandedly.

It made me happy that she truly appreciated my little piece of paradise. "Me either, believe me! You should come up more." I urged honestly, even though I knew she was too damn busy and it would do me no good.

She had taken *her* art degree and used it to open her own tattoo parlor in town. Of course her straight-laced parents thought she was insane, and still do to some extent. But she had shown all the doubters that she *could* in fact do whatever she wanted, and still be successful. And she was. Very.

She had two other artists working for her by then and she still had enough appointments to keep her there six days a week. She could fill up seven easily, if she hadn't chosen to draw the line there.

That was a big part of why she valued her alone time and her personal space so much, when she finally got a chance to be in it. She wasn't an empath like me or anything, but she liked to have time away from people in general, to decompress. Except of course for those times when another person's presence was *required* for the *"decompression process."* Those days I had *really* made sure to get out of the way! And to not come back till the next day, at the earliest.

I understood. She had been very generous to me and anything I could do in return, I tried to do. But that night wasn't about any of that. It was just for fun and Vivianne was the right person for the job.

I set her things on the chair in the corner of the living room, and then went straight to the stereo to turn on some upbeat music. I got some Joss Stone cranking and then danced my way over to the margarita mix to *"Jet Lag."* Viv helped out by slicing limes while I mixed and we both sang along unabashedly while we filled our glasses with ice. Sometimes it wasn't about blocking anything. Sometimes it was just about enjoying the music.

I skipped *"You Had Me" and "Spoiled"* on the way by, because I wasn't in the mood to think about Ben and they always reminded me of him. We poured the lime green liquid over the ice and took a test sip while we rocked out to "Don'tcha Wanna Ride?"

"Mmmmmmm!" We both said in unison.

We danced together until we reached the railing at the far edge of the deck. There we clinked our glasses and drank whatever was miraculously still left in them.

"This place is good for you." She said, being serious for a second.

"Mmmm. Mostly. *I think...* I don't know. I'm not sure anymore." I confessed, feeling the need to clarify. I would have agreed with her in a heartbeat a week ago. But did I still? There were obviously more sides to Pinegrove then I ever knew and I didn't know how deep below-board they ran. Would I ever know? Would I still think it was good for me if I did? There were just too many variables for my comfort level. Though I hated the thought of having to give up my little piece of heaven, just to escape the other people who ruined it by being there.

But I *would.* Leave... *if I had to.*

"What'cha thinkin' Lincoln?" She asked in true Viv fashion, while she nudged me with her elbow.

"Ooof" I said dramatically, stalling at first. I sighed heavily then began the rest my confession. I always felt that way with Viv because for some reason she never had any trouble getting anything out of me. "I met *'The Magician'* the other night."

" *The* Magician? The one from the infamous *Tavern?*"

"Yup."

"And...?" She prompted.

I just sighed again.

"That bad, huh?" She guessed correctly, sensing my hesitance.

"It could be. I'm still not sure yet. I can't decide if I even want to find out or not." I explained.

"What's the problem? He's cute right?' She asked with a smile and another nudge.

"Oh yeah. That's not the problem. Or maybe it is. Part of it, anyway." I rambled incoherently. I sighed deeply and started again. "I'm not ready to get involved with anyone yet. No matter how cute they are." I said honestly. "The divorce isn't even final yet." I said, picking up our glasses and going in to make the next round.

She followed me in and kept up the inquisition. "Alright, so don't get involved then. Just use him for *'decompressing.'* Then send him home." She said with her eyebrows raised. She loved to use our secret term for sex, whether we were in public or not. "It's been *too long* girl! You're still human! Everybody needs a little *'stress-relief'* now and then." She said and winked. Even as she said it though, I could sense when her eagerness changed to feelings of regret.

I looked at her with a raised eyebrow of my own then. "Is someone else having trouble in the *'stress-relief'* department?" I asked, glad for the chance to change the subject.

"Are you kidding me? I get all the *'stress-relief'* I need. Trust me. Especially now that there isn't anyone in my apartment, cramping my style." She said teasingly, trying to play it off. But she knew me as well as I knew her and she gave up once she saw the look on my face. "Who cares if he gets just as much from other sources..." She admitted and I felt her disappointment wash over me.

"Jeff?" I asked making sure I had the correct sometimes-boyfriend in mind.

"Um hmm." She confirmed with a nod. "The one and only. Apparently, he is too much man for just one, occasional girlfriend, so he felt the need to spread himself around. All around the tattoo parlor to be specific. I lost two customers and I had to fire Andrea."

"No! You fired Andrea! She's been with you the longest!" I said in real surprise.

"Well, I never expected loyalty from Jeff, just boundaries. But I certainly expect loyalty from my employees." She said and laughed before she took another long sip of her drink. "But we were talking about you, and your magic problem. Nice try, though." She winked and went to the kitchen and started opening cabinets. "Shouldn't there be some nacho fixin's around here somewhere?"

"Over the stove." I answered directing her to where I had put the chips while I came in behind her. "Well that sucks. I'm sorry, Viv. About Andrea anyway. Jeff? He's on his own." I joked as I grabbed a platter from under the sink and veggies from the fridge. I started slicing up peppers and onions to sauté.

"He sure is!" She said and we both laughed. "Thanks though. It was time for a little new blood around the shop anyway. I start interviewing next week." She told me while I drizzled some olive oil into the frying pan. "I think I may go for a guy this time around." She said with a wink. My eyes went wide at that statement.

"Really? What happened to wanting to destroy the stereotypes and help other women in the business and all of that?" I asked, reminding her of the business principles that had meant the most to her five years ago.

"Screw them bitches!" She joked and we burst out laughing again even though we both knew she didn't mean it.

"Yeah right. You're just hoping to find a new *"stress-release"* partner." I accused. I noticed that the oil began to ripple and I started throwing vegetables in. The sizzle and the smell made me hungry even though I hadn't been before. We continued to talk while I stirred and chopped tomatoes and shredded a block of cheddar cheese.

"Hmmm. Maybe." She got lost in thought for a moment and I could tell it was good even before she smiled to herself. She snapped out of it then and began again. "So when are you going to tell me what it is you're *not* telling me about your little meeting with the *Magician*? I know you, if it was just the sexual tension thing you wouldn't be worried about it. You're used to that." She stated matter-of-factly, getting straight to the point.

"Damn you for knowing me so well." I said only half joking. "It's *Ethan*, by the way. His real name." I explained when she looked momentarily confused. "I don't know. It's a long story and I don't really understand enough of it to explain it to you. Even if I did, I don't think it's mine to tell. I'm pretty confused right now. It shows, huh?"

"Uh, yeah. To me, anyway. So what's his deal?"

"Well, without saying too much I hope, apparently in addition to performing at The Tavern, he also has this whole sideline of trying to connect and help people like *me*. People with *"extra"* abilities." She was looking at me like I was playing with her.

"No sir! He knows about you! *Already!* It took me almost a year to get into your personal stuff." She said indignantly.

"I know, I know. It all sounds crazy. Believe me, I'm with ya. It took me off guard too because I certainly didn't tell him! That part really pissed me off, I have to say. He made me wary, suspicious and defensive. More than anyone else has in a very long time." I confessed with some of that fear in my voice. But I knew it was more than that and so did she. She waited for the rest more patiently than I would have.

"Well, a lot of what he said made sense. And I know he's telling the truth. At least as far as he knows it to be. That's the part that bothers me the *most*. I don't want to go into too much detail. The truth is I don't even *have* a lot of details. That's where I'm stuck. I can't even decide if I want to find out more or not." I stirred the almost done vegetables while I talked.

"You know most people would just sprinkle some shredded cheese on a plate of chips and nuke it for thirty seconds." She laughed at her own joke. "Lord knows you are not most people though, are you now? Nope. Not our Simone. *Mmm-mmm*, but damn if that don't smell good! Hurry up, would ya!" She begged.

I laid the big restaurant style white corn tortilla chips out over the platter and started layering the veggies over them, and then the cheese. I popped it under the broiler for two minutes to melt the cheese while Viv made more "*mmmming*" sounds instead of me for a change.

When I took it out, I sprinkled on the tomatoes and the scallions. On top of that I dropped a few generous dollops of sour cream and then said theatrically, "*Wah-lah!* With a flourish of my arm directed at the finished platter. Viv was a very appreciative audience and clapped heartily while jumping up and down.

"C'mon. We'll take our '*dinner*' out on the deck." I said haughtily while she grabbed our refilled drinks. We sat at my favorite little table and proceeded to inhale the entire platter of nachos like two truck drivers who hadn't eaten in three days. We laughed and fought over all the best chips.

It wasn't until the platter was empty and we were moaning in pain, that the conversation picked back up again. "So is he for real? You would know. Is he truly the *"helping"* kind? Or do we just not care?" She asked, knowing that I would have gone all over this in my head already.

"I still don't know really, but I can't sense any deceit or any *"Muah-ah-ah-ah"* in his attitude at all." I said with a laugh that Viv shared with me. "And believe me, I searched. *Hard.*" I sighed and sipped my margarita. "He saw me searching, by the way." I said with a look that was part skeptical, part amused. She shared the look with me immediately but added 'surprised' to the mix. I really did love her.

"At least that's what he claims, anyway. That's *his* thing. Being able to actually *see* something that gives someone like me away. I'm sorry that I'm telling you all this because it also means I have to ask you not to repeat a word of it to anyone. Like I said, I'm still not even sure I want to know myself, but I really did need someone to talk to. I don't know. I still can't seem to trust any of it. But I think it may only be because I don't really *want* to." My face fell even further after that and it didn't go unnoticed. "

"What does he do for these people? Why all the secrecy? And why are you so afraid to at least find out?" She asked, knowing that I was holding back still. I finally let the worst part out.

"I thought I was coming here to get away from all of that stuff overwhelming me and controlling my life. I thought I was going to blend quietly into the beautiful background. Enjoy some peace and tranquility. Get some distance from everything for a while!" I sighed heavily but kept going.

"If what he says is true, than all I really did was jump out of the pot and into the frying pan, dammit! *No, the pressure cooker!* Jesus! Why am I always so good at finding the worst possible place to be or the last person I want to meet, without even trying?!" I shouted without really expecting an answer. She offered one anyway. Real friends were like that.

"Or the *best?*" She suggested bravely.

I looked at her with one eyebrow raised in warning but she was undaunted by my threat. "Hey. You don't know. You can tell a lot of things honey, but the future still ain't one of 'em." She smiled beautifully at the end in her confidence. Then I saw her falter for a second, obviously remembering my *semi-prophetic* dreams. "Well at least not everything, or all the time anyway." She backtracked a little. "Have you dreamt about him yet?" She asked curiously, knowing that if he was important, he would inevitably come up in my dreams. Every important person in my life factored into my dreams at some point. Sometime.

"Not yet." I said, and she continued.

"Maybe you should at least find out what he's really about, before you consider relocating again." She suggested diplomatically. After that, she just sipped her margarita while I contemplated the scenario from her point of view a bit. In the meantime I could tell that she was feeling very content.

There are so many reasons that I am friends with this woman. But her unique and intimate knowledge of me was one of the most invaluable when I needed an honest and unbiased opinion. I didn't always *like* it, but I definitely *needed* it sometimes. And I could always count on Vivianne to give it to me.

We sat together, un-bothered by the quiet while we enjoyed the rest of our cocktails and watched the sun setting over the trees. When the mosquito's started to come out, we finally got up. It was such a beautiful night and we hated to go inside but we both hated being the next meal even more. So we changed spots to the coffee table in the living room on the other side of the screen doors.

"Alright, you've avoided it long enough. Get the board." Vivianne said when we plopped down on the same pillows I'd had dinner with Liliana on last week. It tended to be the favorite spot of anyone I had over.

"You want a piece of me?" I asked tauntingly.

"You bet your ass I do. Let's go, I'm down one and you know that doesn't sit well with me." She said, referring to the running tally that we had kept over the years.

"Alright. You asked for it." I said, getting up to get the "*Sorry*" game from the closet. "I don't want to hear any crying when you have to go to bed a loser again." I teased. Of course it worked beautifully. I could see the fire rising in her eyes. The fact that we both had such a competitive nature made game playing between us an Olympic event at times, and "*Sorry*" was one of our favorites. There was only one thing more satisfying than wiping your opponent off the board just as they were about to enter their home, and that was getting to say *"Sorry!"* sarcastically while you did it!

"Just let me call Liliana and say good night while you set it up." I requested. Five minutes later, the slaughter began. We were truly the biggest cutthroat *"Sorry"* players you could ever meet. We would repeatedly pass up an opportunity to go into our own home or to get a man out, in order to kill the other player instead. It was ridiculous and it was *tons* of fun! We played three games in rapid succession.

We killed mercilessly and we laughed uncontrollably. It went on until the glasses emptied for the last time and we wore ourselves out completely from laughing. We laid down on the floor in the end and stared up at the ceiling while we caught our breath.

"Alright!" She said tiredly. "I give up! But only until next time!" She threatened menacingly as she jumped up and into a defensive stance. She ruined it by wobbling though. We both laughed again as we got up to get ready for bed.

I changed into a long t-shirt and boy-shorts and Viv came out of the bathroom wearing black silk shorts and a hot pink tank top under her short silk kimono robe. It was black with the most beautiful fuchsia colored flowers. "Geeze Viv, even going to bed you look freakin' adorable!" I wondered silently at how she managed to remain single. "Jeff's an idiot!" I said shaking my head back and forth on my way by her into the bathroom.

"Well I'm glad someone is around to appreciate what he did not. Though no offense honey, but after tonight I think I might get a new handsome virile male to fill that role." She said without any real apology as she followed me in and we laughed some more. The CD player randomly cycled to Chicago's *"Stay The Night"* and we sang mockingly to each other as if we were each that prospect for the other while we brushed our teeth.

"Just To have you near me. Here by my side." The toothbrushes and hair brushes became microphones. *"Just to have you near me... Stay the night! There's room enough here for two. Stay the night. I'd like to spend it with you!"* We sang like we were

teenagers again until the song ended and when we finally stopped laughing, we both spit and rinsed.

Just that simple act in the quiet moment, suddenly reminded me of being there doing that with Liliana and I wasn't quick enough to stop the sadness that came over me for just a second.

It was still long enough for Vivianne to notice. "I know I'm not *your* favorite sleep-over pal either. Don't worry. I don't let it hurt my feelings." She teased as she elbowed me again. I laughed as I pushed her forward and she pretended to go flying from the bathroom.

"I'm so lucky to have you." I said to her back.

"I know you are." She replied confidently over her shoulder and we both smirked at her lack of modesty.

I pulled out the sofa bed and threw on new sheets. She fluffed her pillow, tossed it over and throwing her feet up in the air in front of her, jumped in after it. It was only slightly more mature than one of Liliana's typical entrances. I said good night and locked up. I closed the blinds too, so she wouldn't be up with the first light of dawn. Liliana typically didn't mind. She was usually up anyway.

I shut off all the lights except for the bathroom, and I cracked the door in case she needed to find it in the dark.

I made my way back to my bed and flipped the switch to the ceiling fan that I was quickly becoming addicted to sleeping with, since it was warming up. I laid back and slid my bare legs and feet back and forth a few times across the cool, crisp sheets.

I stretched out and took a long deep breath then let it out in a huff as I threw my arms up over my head and fell fast asleep.

Chapter 12

It was dark. I was uneasy. I could feel the warm night air, but for some reason I couldn't see. I had thought I was alone. But then, *I could feel him.* Close to me. I could feel the heat coming off of him. He leaned in closer.

"What are you afraid of?" He asked me quietly in his deep voice.

I was startled at first by the richness of it. Then by the closeness. I didn't want to answer. But reluctantly, I did. "I don't know... You... *All of it.* It's too much." I replied defensively.

"Too much *what?*" He pressed, leaning closer.

"I don't know. *I can't think straight!*" I proclaimed vehemently.

"Why not?" He asked. Softly. Seriously. His face dipped lower. Closer.

"Because...*uh huh!*" I started, but couldn't finish. I tried again. My breath was coming faster. I turned around to face him and the bright grey center of his eyes was all I could see in the absolute darkness. "*You...* you... distracted me..." I managed shakily.

"*How exactly did I do that?*" He asked tauntingly, mimicking a question I had asked him originally. His breath fell on my neck while he spoke. He was *that* close.

"*Really?! Hmpf!!*" I huffed and tried to back away, but found I couldn't. There was nowhere to go. "*Stop!*" I said then, closing my eyes. "Why are you doing this to me?" I asked in a high pitched voice.

"What am I doing?" He asked softly, calmly. But the words fell like *fire* on my skin.

"Oh God! *Seriously? C'mon!*" I yelled. It was crazy! I couldn't do it! *I needed to get away.* But how? I was thinking frantically, but for some reason my brain wouldn't come up with one thought on how to actually do that.

"Where do you want to go?" He asked me sweetly. *Infuriatingly.* Even though I had not voiced my need out loud.

"Stop doing that!" I demanded.

"Doing what? *Reading you?* Like you read me?" He challenged as his hand came up beside me to rest against the wall behind my head. He didn't even touch me and the heat was palpable on my left side. "It's only fair." A soft, warm breeze blew over his hand and across my face from somewhere nearby and a few loose strands of my hair fluttered around my face. I could see a full silver moon on the edge of the darkness along with his bright grey eyes. They didn't even blink.

"Ugghhh!" I finally tore away and escaped out into the night.

The next instant I woke with a start and a huge intake of breath in my own bed. I jumped in reflex and found myself drenched in sweat. I sat up in the bed and looked around the screen to see if I had woken Vivianne up. I didn't see any stirring or hear any noise other than my own pounding heart. I relaxed again. I reached over to turn the fan up to high and then flopped back down and tried to get back to sleep.

I laid back, breathing deeply and tried to relax. *Geeze!* Nice job conjuring him up in my dreams with our conscious suggestions! It had to be all the talk about him and my dreams earlier that had triggered *that* dream. At least that's what I tried to convince myself of as I lay there waiting for my heart to return to normal so I could fall asleep again.

When I woke in the morning, it was as if a mere few moments had gone by and the dream still haunted me. It was lurking right behind my every thought. I looked at the clock and was surprised to find that it was 9:30. Vivianne loved to get a few extra hours of sleep when she came up but she would never sleep past 10:00. That was where she drew the line between enjoying a weekend day, and missing it.

I got up to check on Viv and put some coffee on. She was draped over the bed under a blanket, with a book next to her but I couldn't tell when she had been up reading or if she was asleep still or not. I decided to leave her be for the time being and jumped in the shower hoping to drown out the memories of the dream.

I knew it wouldn't work though. It was one of *those* dreams. Try as I might to deny it or explain it away, I knew I couldn't. These kinds of dreams didn't *go* away. At least not until after they came to fruition. Then they would move over into the memory category in my brain.

The dreams weren't always as clear or as reliable as my empath abilities and I tended to focus less on them. But they existed anyway, periodically at important times in my life, and they would stick with me until I figured out what they meant. A dream that I can't shake or figure out, can distract me for weeks if I'm not careful.

About half the time, they were more metaphorical. Real people and places, but full of symbolism that I would have to decipher. They were a little harder to connect to the eventual reality without giving it some real thought. When the light would finally dawn, and the pieces would start to fall into place, it always made perfect sense. It was an, *"Ohhhhhh!!! I get it now!!"* kind of thing.

But until then, it was usually just a confusing collection of scenes and impressions. That is why I tried to just ignore them sometimes. Too vague. Too much work. *Too frustrating!*

Other dreams were more literal though. Specific. *Real.* With locations. *Feelings.* The things people will say, or do. I'll see them playing out. Those were the ones that I paid the most attention to. Of course they were less common, but they were also easier to recognize when they came up in real life and they tended to come up an awful lot faster. This felt like one of *those* dreams and I wasn't anywhere near ready for it to come up.

I had absolutely no idea what I would do about it, either.

I let everything run through my head over and over, during my shower. The possibilities. The options. The consequences. It went on until I realized that I was in danger of leaving Viv with no hot water for her shower and I still had no answers. I decided to try to be a good hostess. I gave up and turned the water off, grabbed a towel off the rack and pressed it to my face.

When I came out of the bathroom in my Bermuda shorts and tank top, I noticed that Vivian was already dressed and sitting on a stool at the bar. She saluted me with a tip of her cup. So she had been up already.

"Did we have sweet dreams?" She teased right off the bat and I knew then that I *had* woken her up last night after all. *Great.* She must have already showered way before me, I was guessing by her combed out, almost dry hair. The way she had been laying on the bed before, I couldn't tell. *See!* I was distracted already!

"Sorry. Was I loud?" I asked, with one eye closed in embarrassment.

"No, but if that was *Mr. Magician* that you were finally dreaming about, than I officially enter a vote for hearing him out." She said with a wink and a knowing smile.

"That's not funny." I groaned and went to the coffee maker for a cup of my own.

"Who's kidding?" She asked with raised eyebrows. "It was a pretty specific one, I'm assuming." she guessed correctly, familiar with my different dream categories.

"*Mmm.* Think so." I confirmed while I sipped.

"So it won't be long then. Do you know what you're going to do?"

"*Hah!* I wish. I'm not even sure there *is* a good option at this point." I sighed. In a few seconds I was lost again in thoughts of his breath falling on my neck and of how soon that was apparently going to happen.

Dammit! Now what? Should I stop him? Did I really want to let him get that close to me? A part of me, traitorously, screamed yes! Should I just be happy that it was even possible to feel that way again so soon after getting my heart stomped on so completely? Or should I just run away *from all of it,* and never look back? Before it could get out of control. What I really wanted in my life just then was control. Maybe just for a little while?

That is not what involvement with *him* promised to get

me though. The exact opposite would be much more accurate, I was willing to bet.

"Don't worry. You'll figure it out." Vivianne said, interrupting my fruitless thoughts. "You have Lil tonight?" She asked and I brightened immediately.

"Yes. We have *Movie Night!*" I answered with a smile and a wiggle of my eyebrows, trying to act excited about it.

"Oh right, *Movie Night!* Well, have some popcorn for me and try to have a little fun while you're at it. You never know!" She laughed. "Alright. I'm gonna get going." She said after that. She got up, put her mug in the sink and hugged me. Then she pulled back and looked me in the eye. "You let me know when you decide what you want to do because I cannot *wait* to hear how all of this stuff plays out." She said with a genuine smile. "Thanks for the hospitality. It was fun and I needed it. You officially owe me one less. Now I will go and try to forget about this place again until the next time I get a chance to come back up." She joked.

"Thank you for the company. It's been extremely *Viv-id* as usual." I joked back.

"I am a true original!" She said touting her own praises with her hands in the air, her backside swaying wildly at me.

"Thank God!" I said and we both laughed. "Do you want help to your car? I offered.

"No, I'm good." She insisted. She grabbed her things that were already all packed up and sitting by the door and then kissed my cheek. "Don't worry so much. Be smart and stay safe and all that, but don't forget to live a little too!" She insisted happily.

"K." I agreed.

And she was gone. Just like that it was so quiet I almost couldn't stand it. I still had hours before I could go and pick up Liliana. I looked out through the glass at the beautiful day visible behind me and I decided to go for a hike and kill some time.

I changed into a pair of old jeans to cover my legs and threw on some socks and my hiking boots. I grabbed my cell phone, a granola bar and a water bottle. I was always annoyingly aware of the constantly repeated warnings about not heading off into the wilderness alone, but I loved the outdoors and being on my own schedule too much to listen. There wasn't always someone else around that wanted to go when you did. What are you gonna do? Not go? *Pfft!* Not on a day like that!

Though I didn't invite disaster either. I always made sure I had a mace canister for bears which I also grabbed and my fully charged cell phone. And I *always* called someone and told them I was going. Usually that was my dad. Then I would call that person again when I got home. It was a deal I had struck with my parents long ago when they realized that being alone wouldn't stop me from going if I really wanted to go. I called my dad and wished him good luck on a grant he was trying to get and he wished me a good hike. I promised to call him later and hung up.

I started on the stone path that cuts through the great expanse of lawn, but I veered off at the orchard and headed into the woods. I purposefully headed west, away from where Ethan's place supposedly was. I definitely did *not* want to "bump into it" or *him* at the moment.

The Earth was still soft under my feet from the snow that had melted away and the early spring rains that had fallen since. It was starting to bloom and to spread over with color, but it was still in the honeymoon phase. When everything was new and bright green. Soft and fragile. Full of promise, but not fully established yet. Only half of the things thriving then would survive the next few weeks when it inevitably turned cold again, and the weather presented us with a few more storms to drown out and wash away vulnerable new sprouts. The hot summer sun would then burn out the weakest of those left after that. I enjoyed it while it lasted.

I took a deep cool breath into my lungs and the crispness of it was very refreshing. There was the definite smell of summer in the air though, promising that the chill would soon be long gone. For a while anyway.

I made my way along the wide trails. It always amazed me how few people I would come across on those paths, since they were obviously years and years old and well-traveled. I saw people on horseback more often than on foot back there, but that was okay too, as long as I watched where I walked.

The birds were singing in the trees all around me and I

could hear the sound of a small stream gurgling as it ran alongside the trail for a distance. The combination was very tranquil. I walked for quite a while. It didn't matter. I just followed the trails mindlessly, killing time. Watching the small animals scurry by and the birds fly overhead. I stood next to trees that were taller than five story buildings and I felt so tiny. It always put things back into perspective for me.

My problems were microscopic in the face of the big scheme of things, and life was way too short to spend so much time fretting. I decided to just let it all go for the time being. Maybe the right thing to do would suddenly present itself. *Hmpf!* Sure. Anything could happen, right?

I reached the area where the forest opened up and I walked over to climb up onto a big rock that sat half in and half out of a large pond. The sun beat down on my face and shoulders. I closed my eyes and breathed it in. I sat back like a happy lizard as the heat from the sun and the rock warmed me to my core. I felt more relaxed than I did after a full nights' sleep.

I stayed there for some time. Until my arms got too tired to hold me up anymore. I thought about laying back on the warm rock but I knew if I did, I'd surly fall asleep and just then I got the feeling that I was not completely alone. Not close, but there was someone out there somewhere. Nope, I definitely wasn't crazy enough to fall asleep out there.

I sighed deeply, opened my eyes and leaned forward to give my elbows a rest. I thought about seeing Liliana soon and that reminded me again of movie night. I smiled thinking about it. I still wasn't sure what to make of it, but I guessed that I was going to have to go and check it out to find out what it was all about.

I pulled my phone from my back pocket and checked the time. It was close to 1:00. Almost time to get Lil. I decided to head home. I hefted myself up off the rock and jumped down to start the hike back.

Chapter 13

If I'd had hopes at all that she might have forgotten about Movie Night, they were immediately dashed. As soon as she jumped in the car, actually.

"What time does Movie Night start?" She asked eagerly.

"Huh, I don't really know." I had to admit, "But surely not 'til after dark. That gives us until at least 8:30. In the meantime, what should we eat?" I asked.

"Ohhh! Can we make mac & cheese?!" She asked with as much excitement as most people reserved for things like lobster and filet mignon. I smiled broadly.

"Do you have any idea at all how precious you are? *Huh?*" I asked her teasingly, as I squeezed her cheeks. She just giggled. "Yes we can have mac & cheese, and *hot dogs too*, if you want."

"*Really!* Yay!" she shouted happily. And I couldn't help wishing then, that it had been that easy to make *other people* that happy, as memories of the good *and* the bad times with Ben ran through my head. I had been all through that though and I had already decided that there was no point in wallowing in the *"what if's"* anymore. There was no future for me and Ben. It sucked. And it was sad. But it *was* the truth. You can't fight the truth, only postpone it. That was then, this was now. I was finally getting used to that.

"Alright, ready? You buckled?" I asked in typical New England shorthand. She climbed into her booster seat and buckled herself in. Then she smiled up at me, happy as a clam and my heart melted. Again, my problems felt so insignificant next to the joy I had in her.

"Buckled!" She confirmed with a smile. I returned it wholeheartedly.

It's funny. I think everyone always assumes that the weekend parent is the one who cares just a little bit less about *being* a parent. Sure no one would ever dare say it, but they think it. *I* was guilty of that assumption myself. *Before.* Now I *was* that parent and I realized firsthand that sometimes the one who loves them and cares the *most* about their wellbeing, is the one who has to find the strength to let go. A little.

I definitely saw things differently by then. I wasn't nearly as quick to judge as I used to be.

The ride back was quick and blissfully, traffic free. The weather had warmed up nicely, as I had predicted and once we got off of the highway we had the moon roof open the rest of the way home.

Back at Kent's Farm we got the water boiling for the pasta while *Finding Nemo* started its' hundredth play on the DVD player. After boiling and slicing the hotdogs into small discs, I mixed them into the mac & cheese. Then we filled our bowls and ate in our usual pillowed spot on the living room floor.

After Nemo's friend's made their big escape into the ocean, we went to the kitchen to clean our bowls and pop some popcorn to bring with us. We both used the bathroom one last time and then I got the bug spray from the cabinet. It was almost dark by then. I grabbed a quilt from the hall closet and draped it over my arm. "Ready?" I asked, already knowing the answer. I could feel her excitement which could not possibly be contained inside her small body.

"Ready!" She confirmed loudly as she jumped up in the air to give it even more emphasis.

"Well then, let's go." I said, and we went out through the same back sliders as last time. Only this time we also needed a flashlight or two. I grabbed one off of the table by the back door and turned it on to make sure it worked. Its light shone brightly into the night so I handed it to Liliana. I took the next one and repeated the process, keeping that one for myself. We shone them all around and up at the sky like lasers before we set them down to put some bug spray on. It was not always fun to be covered in bug spray, but it was never fun to get eaten alive and the early spring mosquitoes were notoriously ravenous! After that we grabbed our flashlights again and headed down the stairs and across the lawn.

As we approached the big grey barn, we could already see other beams of light flailing around in the night sky and a few glowing neon necklaces, bracelets and earrings as well. I had been right. It had warmed up to a downright balmy 78 degrees during the day and it didn't feel like it had changed very much with the setting of the sun. It was probably still 70 out, which for that time of year was fantastic. It was obvious that everyone wanted to take advantage of it and be outside. I started to feel the waves of emotion hitting me from all of the various people that I still couldn't see, but for once I didn't mind.

In fact, I had to admit to myself that so far I was enjoying being there, feeling that particular crowd. It was actually nice. I was getting... *relaxation... joy... playfulness...* There were lots of feelings that were of a romantic nature floating around everywhere too. Yup, spring was in the air alright! People in general were just having a good time. I let out a breath and with it, the last of my anxiety. I smiled down at Liliana then and walked with a little less hesitation.

When we got closer I could start to make out figures on blankets. Some arm in arm, others wrestling around on the ground. I could smell the horses, but I could smell all the popcorn too. It was a unique mix to say the least, but not entirely unpleasant.

It reminded me of summer and even though we had a ways to go yet, I loved that feeling. I spotted Shirley waving to us beside the barn where she stood with a group of people. We went over to say hello.

"What a gorgeous night!" I said honestly while she hugged me, happy I didn't have to fake it for once.

"It sure is! It's gonna be a great movie night! And crowded too! You two better go and get yourself a spot before they're all taken up and you end up watching it up in the hayloft." She said, and then she winked at me. *Okay...* Whatever that meant.

She was being playful yet serious and I didn't understand. But there were many others vying for her attention so I acted appropriately worried and hurried off saying we'd talk to them after we set up our spot. We headed back toward the large group of people camped out on the lawn. I was surprised to recognize more than a few smiling faces in the crowd as we walked past them. There was the waitress that I knew from the diner, laying on a blanket and laughing with what I assumed was her boyfriend.

The nice man from the post office was sitting in a lawn chair surrounded by blankets and bags of popcorn. He looked like he was there with a handful of grandkids. There was the bag-boy from the supermarket, who was sitting on the fence next to one of the checkout girls. And I was pretty sure the woman sitting in the low slung beach chair was the same one I had met in the consignment shop. Her, and the woman from the pharmacy were sitting together in matching chairs. From that distance I couldn't tell if they were lovers, friends or sisters, but it was obvious that they were very close. I saw them notice me and then speak briefly to each other. They waved and smiled at us before they went back to talking. *Huh.* It really *was* a small town. I even spied Percy sitting in a bright orange soccer chair with another gentleman that I didn't know beside him. I waved to him as we walked past and he blew me a kiss.

There were so many others but they all seemed to know each other somehow. They all seemed like family, with the little ones running around the blankets and the adults chatting and joking with each other. Teenagers hanging all over the paddock fence, flirting with each other. I paid attention to the interactions in the crowd, recognizing certain connections that I knew and mentally noting new ones.

When we reached an open spot, along the edge of the mass of people, I set our stuff down and started to spread our blanket. In the next second, Jack came up from behind us and scooped Liliana off her feet. He lifted her squealing, high up into the air and then set her back down again. When he dropped her, laughing to the ground, he looked back at me and asked, "Can I steal her? It's so crowded tonight, I'm gonna put all the little ones up on the hay bales in the back of the tractor trailer so they can see over the crowd. S'at alright with you?" He asked expectantly.

I didn't have the heart to say no, even though the thought of sitting there all by myself, was not at all appealing. I wouldn't keep her from having a good time though just because of that. I couldn't be that selfish.

"Sure." I said. "Go ahead. I'll just be right here if you need me." I said to Liliana who was *extremely* happy then. As always, it had been worth it.

"Why don't you find a spot up in the hayloft?" He suggested seriously, which confused me.

My expression said as much. "I thought that was what I *didn't* want to happen." I said with a furrowed brow and a perplexed smile.

Jack just laughed. "That's just what we want people to think sugar, because they're the best spots and we don't want everyone fightin' over them. It's actually kind of a running joke. Most people know that we really save those spots for family when they come, close friends, or our favorite neighbors. You know, people who won't sue if they fall out." He finished with a sly smile. "Just follow the stairs on the far side of the building. You have a flashlight, right?" He asked.

"Yup." I held it up.

"Perfect. You'll need it to get up and down. There's no electricity over there. Now go, relax." He ordered then he scooped Liliana back up and over his shoulder as she let out a peel of laughter, and he was gone back into the crowd.

I could see the tractor trailer full of hay bales over to the left of all the people. It sat up against the wall of the stables and there was a spotlight shining directly down on it. I realized that it was no mistake that, *that* was where all the little ones were seated. It was easy to keep an eye on them from almost any spot, and they were up and out of the way of the screen at the same time. It was perfect and the kids just thought it was *way* too much fun! Jack sure was smarter than one might give him credit for at first glance, I thought, and not for the first time. I had already learned not to underestimate him. That was part of his charm, I was learning.

I spotted the stairs over at the end of the building, just within the door. I picked up my blanket and popcorn and headed in that direction. On my way over, I watched Liliana jumping and playing with the other kids like they had known each other forever. She seemed really happy like she was just enjoying being a child. I couldn't ask for more than that I thought, feeling more and more satisfied with my choices of late.

I entered the building and could see the first few stairs but not much else. I turned on my flashlight and looked around a little. The flashlight did very little to illuminate the large space. I couldn't see much of interest, besides some worktables and the open beams that held the loft up. I gave up on the site-seeing and I started up the stairs. I was about halfway up the unstained wooden planks, when everything suddenly went black. I mean *really* black! I stopped short for a second and shook the flashlight. It came back on, but one step later it died again and I gave up. *Crap!* Oh well, I thought I was almost there and it would be easier to keep going rather than to try and turn around on the uneven stairs. I figured later I could find someone who had a working flashlight to walk back down with.

I put my right hand on the wall and one step at a time, I kept going. Once I reached the top of the stairs. I would have been lost in the darkness, if not for the sound of voices traveling along the loft. I turned with my hand on the railing. I headed into the darkness in the general direction of the voices and the barn, where I knew the movie would be playing. Once I got past the stairwell, I put my hand up and found the roughhewn wall to my left. I slid it carefully, mindful of splinters, along the wall to find my way to the front of the building. There it finally opened up out into the night.

I could see the light from outside reflecting off of the hay in the front area and I was relieved that I was almost there. As I came around the wall that separated the main area from the open area, I could see the four high access doors that were all open to the night air and offered a perfect view of the barn. It wasn't *bright* or anything, but by the open bay doors it was at least light enough to see more easily.

I greeted the other people who were lucky enough to be invited up there, in the *"good"* seats. There weren't too many, for which I was thankful. Just five or six. They were happily tucked into nests of hay covered in blankets, snuggled up together awaiting the start of the movie. They said hello and waved, their happiness and excitement pouring off of them.

I only recognized one person from one nest. The half-full one closest to me. She was a bubbly blonde who was always full of energy and was as sweet as could be. A little flaky at times, but her heart was always in the right place. I knew her name was Gabby, having met her two months ago at the supermarket. We tended to shop on the same day and it didn't take her long to come up to me and strike up a conversation. I was put off at first, naturally, but I could tell right away that she was genuine and just naturally curious about "the new girl." Lots of people around there were, but most wouldn't dream of coming right up and talking to me. *Thank God!* But Gabby did, she was just like that. I waved to her separately and she smiled a huge lipstick covered smile and waved back.

I picked the empty pile of hay closest to me, spread out my quilt and flopped down. I looked out through the opening and noticed right away that I could see both the tractor where Liliana was and the "screen" easily from there. I relaxed a little bit more, grateful for Jack's judgment in both our cases and watched as the movie started. I was pleasantly surprised to find that it was actually pretty comfortable. I had given one bag of popcorn to Liliana and kept one for myself and I opened it up and started to munch on it while I watched as Shrek began his helpless fall for Fiona.

I was amazed at how good the movie looked up on the side of the barn that Jack and Shirley had covered in white sheets that were sewn-together. It reminded me of being at the drive-in back in my younger days. The quality was great! I would have to ask them what kind of projector they had exactly. It was certainly better than the kind *I* grew up with! I settled a little deeper into my nest and switched to crowd watching for a while. Everyone was clearly enjoying the beautiful night. That and the simple joy of getting together with friends for some pure, guilt-free fun. Not to mention that it was just plain *'free.'* It was at times, much more interesting to watch them than the movie.

The warm breeze was blowing just enough to make it comfortable and the mood up there as well as down on the ground was pretty relaxed. Of course, that helped me to relax. It sucked always being at the mercy of the moods around you but when it worked in my favor, I didn't complain. I put my feet up on a smaller pile of hay to my left and threw some popcorn in the air and caught it in my mouth.

I heard Gabby clap and I looked up to find her coming over. "How are you?" She asked exuberantly.

"I'm good. Actually kind of enjoying myself." I replied with a chuckle. "This is nice, huh?" I asked.

"Sure is! I never miss a movie night if I can help it, especially one on a night like this! So I have a thermos full of wine and I see you have a whole bag of popcorn and I'm wondering if you want to form an alliance?" She joked with an eyebrow waggle and a nudge, making a reference to the reality TV shows.

"Sure." I said laughing and putting the bag down in between us while she poured some wine into small plastic cups.

"Cheers!" We both said, and clinked plastic before sipping. We sat back and enjoyed the movie. We talked a little and laughed a lot. It was pretty impressive we decided, that Eddie Murphy's comedic chops carried over so well, even as an animated donkey!

I could see Liliana the whole time. She had spent a fair amount of time in the beginning, jumping around with all the other kids but she was sitting quietly then. Watching intently from beside the seven year old boy Jonah, who was obviously her new best friend. We had talked to him a few times before, when he came for riding lessons on Saturday's. He had seemed like a good kid. He wasn't automatically bossy or dismissive of Liliana, just because he was a couple years older. That right there said a lot about him to me. His feelings towards her were always kind and polite. At least in the time that I'd known him which wasn't very long, but I considered myself a pretty good judge of character.

Anyway, she seemed very happy sharing her popcorn with him. I was really glad again then, that I had moved there. Alright, so it wasn't perfect. It still had a lot to offer! A lot more than one would ever guess just by driving through. Maybe it wouldn't be quite so easy to give up after all.

Gabby said she was sorry, but she couldn't stay for the

end. She was meeting somebody for official drinks somewhere else at 10:00. She hugged me and thanked me for the popcorn and then snuck out quietly.

I spent the rest of the movie in blissful peace and quiet. I only watched Shrek occasionally, having seen it so many times already with Liliana. Instead, I spent a lot of time just staring out at the night sky. I was vaguely aware of some of the other people leaving the loft, and a few new ones who came up. I was so relaxed that I ignored most of the activity. There were a few playful pranks now and then and I picked up some amorous angling between a few of the teens coming and going, but for the most part the mood was just happy. So in general, I didn't pay too much attention to the details for once.

I was watching the movie the least though and that was why I didn't notice right away when it ended. The sudden clapping gave it away. I looked down and noticed that the side of the barn was solid white again and a few more of the outdoor spotlights had been turned on. People didn't seem in any hurry to disperse though. I could see why. I felt the same way. I looked toward the trailer and saw Liliana and the other kids tumbling around happily again in the hay. I stretched lazily for a minute before I finally pulled myself up out of my comfy spot.

I picked up my blanket and shook it out as others around me were doing the same. I folded it up and bent to grab my popcorn bag when I heard the teenage girl squeal loudly and run towards the stairs. The boy grabbed his blanket and went running after her. I just shook my head and laughed. Ah, to be so young and carefree again, I had thought wistfully.

I was looking behind me into the dark towards the stairway, when I suddenly realized that I had forgotten about my flashlight predicament.

"*Oh shit*" I said out loud but to no one, since by that point I was the only one left. I should have walked Gabby out and asked to borrow hers, I thought. Then I thought about how nice it would have been to have thought of that *sooner!* I sighed heavily at my own stupidity. That's what I get for letting my guard down. Apparently, my brain went with it.

"Oh well, here goes nothing." I was openly talking to

myself then in a lame attempt to make me feel less alone. I started walking slowly into the absolute darkness, keeping my right hand on the wall that time as I went. But before I reached the stair railing, I could feel that I was not really alone.

Ut oh.

Chapter 14

I could feel someone, off to my left in the darkest corner of the huge loft. They were agitated and I didn't even want to know why. What I did want to know was why *they* didn't have a light! I couldn't think of one *good* reason for anyone to be hiding in the pitch black loft without a flashlight.

I wondered then if it was simply the teenagers again, waiting to scare each other. That actually made *sense* and I started to feel better for about a second and a half while I tried to feel out the energy and see. Then the person in question spoke and I had my answer. That was no teenager.

"What on Earth are you doing skirting around up here in the dark?" A deep male voice asked from what sounded like a good twenty yards away. I had nearly jumped right out of my skin! But then I recognized the voice *almost* immediately.

It was Ethan and at that realization my heart began to race for reasons *other* than being startled. It bothered me that my body reacted to him at all. I felt like yelling at my traitorous body. "*You don't even know him, so just knock it off!*"

"I could ask you the same thing." I answered without really answering.

"Me? I came for Movie Night, like everybody else." He said and chuckled. "Originally, anyway. I was bringing Shirley some more citronella tiki torches, when I thought I saw something colorful and familiar around someone who was headed this way. I know the kid, and his parents. So I wanted to check it out. *Quietly.*"

"How can you tell, in the dark?" I asked, partly curious and partly wanting to trip him up.

"It's actually easier with less light. It shows up better than in broad daylight. I have to work harder to see it then." He said openly and I thought about the dim lighting that was preferred at The Tavern. I guess it made sense.

"Which one?" I asked, just to make sure he wasn't making it all up as he went along. That would really surprise me at that point though. Even though I was *terrified* of how he made me feel, it'd never been because I'd gotten *"creepy"* vibes off of him. I'd hate to think that I had missed something like that. But he answered quickly, easily. As usual.

"That kid that was up there on the end. The pale kid with the dark crew cut?" He coaxed patiently.

"The nervous one who was more interested in the blonde than the movie?" I supplied, questioningly. I hadn't noticed everything that went on up there, but I had noticed that!

"That would be the one." He said and I could feel him smiling even if I couldn't make it out.

"And?" I asked, wondering what he had found in spite of myself.

He didn't answer right away. "Have you decided that you want to know about these things then?" He challenged in return.

"No. Never mind." I said quickly, since I really hadn't decided anything at all.

"Well then it's your turn, because I really have no guesses as to why you would risk your neck walking around up here without a flashlight." He said, seeming more upset about that than I would have guessed.

"Easy. It died on me." I said lifting it up and shaking the useless thing back and forth. I could hear him laugh then at my misfortune. It was a quiet laugh full of obvious relief. He was closer by then.

"We missed you last night." He said referring to my night off, but I could tell that he meant himself and he immediately regretted saying it out loud. I thought about how there would be a lot more of those nights soon and found myself wondering if he would miss me more or just forget about me. Then I decided that

I shouldn't care. That I *didn't* care. Alright, maybe I cared, but I wasn't going to let *him* know that, because it didn't matter.

"I'm ahead of schedule. Decided that I needed a night off." I explained.

"From me? I thought I *was* "time off" for you." He teased again.

I could hear that he was a little closer again. Maybe ten or fifteen yards away then. My rebellious heart beat a little faster again. I could feel the desire coming off of him by then too, that he was trying hard to contain. *Oooooh,* that was not good!

It was weird to be reading someone when they were trying hard to hide their feelings, even though they knew full well that you could feel them anyway. Should you pretend that you didn't in an attempt to make them more comfortable, even though you both knew the truth? It was awkward at best.

We were still conversing in complete darkness.

"You know, it's a little disconcerting trying to have a conversation in the dark. Don't *you* have a flashlight that you could turn on?" I asked, trying to change the subject.

"Nah." He answered and I was surprised to see that he wasn't lying. "I grew up around here, remember. I know this place like the back of my hand. After all, I *was* that teenage boy once. I spent many a night hanging out up here in the dark back then." He said, nodding towards where the teenagers had been snuggling. "Not to mention, I can see in the dark a *lot* better than most people."

My hopes were dashed once he admitted that he didn't have a light either. I noticed though that strangely, talking about his teenage escapades made him momentarily less amorous and more reminiscent. For that, I was grateful. "Okay, well I'm going to just keep feeling my way out of here and go get my daughter, Liliana before she starts looking for me." I said, hoping that it would be enough to get me out of there fast, but he wasn't playing along.

"Is that your daughter? That cute little toe-head with Jonah?" He asked.

"Mmm hmm, light of my life." I said with a smile even though I didn't think he could see me. I was surprised to get a little

wave of joy a second later.

"I saw her down there. She's adorable. And she's also *fine* and you know it. I don't know her personally, but if she's like any other kid I've ever met, then you're going to have to drag her out of here kicking and screaming." He declared confidently. We both knew it was an exaggeration, but not by much. His feelings changed quickly to frustration then.

"When are you going to stop running away from me?" He demanded, impatiently.

I couldn't see his face but I could feel his anxiety over revealing his interest. He had put himself out there, when he obviously didn't want to. *Huh.* I guess I wasn't alone in my hesitation.

I still didn't have a good answer though. "I'm not." I lied. Because *I* could get away with that. At least I thought I could.

"That's bullshit, and I don't need to be an empath to know that." He announced mercilessly.

Dammit! One thing he made me very aware of was the way people who know me must feel all the time. Because I really hated the way he always knew what I was feeling, or what I would say or do, without my telling him. It was actually quite annoying. I kept silent in the dark.

"What are you afraid of?" He asked softly and suddenly the whole dream flashed through my head along with the heat that was coming off of both of us by then. *Oh no! Not now!* Dammit! Dammit! *Dammit!*

I tried to take a deep breath, but I was panicking a little, trying to remember which way was out before things could get out of hand. He was coming closer still and even though I couldn't see him, I started to back up a little instinctively.

"I don't know." I said, trying to answer him. Thinking then maybe he would stop coming. "You. *All of it.* It's too much..." I faded off in the end as another wave of his desire washed over me. It was hotter than before and I felt a quiver go through my whole body and finish in a tight swirl in the palms of my hands. It happened in spite of the fact that I knew full well the feeling wasn't mine. I *felt* it, just the same, and it was *that* strong! *Damn!* He was still trying to contain it, but he wasn't trying as hard anymore. It really wasn't fair. He *knew* that!

Uggghhh!! My eyes of less impressive ability had finally adjusted enough to make out vague shapes within the black and I could see him standing about ten feet away. "Too much what?" He asked sounding genuinely interested in the answer.

"I don't know." I answered lamely, struggling to keep my thoughts separate in my head with the feelings battling for dominance. It's not like I was new at it, but his feelings were *much* stronger than I was used to and mine were not helping matters! "I can't think straight..." I finally admitted.

"Why not?" He asked. But he was walking closer as he said it and he knew why. He was letting it go a little more then. He was getting closer and it was getting hotter. He was enjoying the effect he was having on me.

His question annoyed me but I tried to answer it so maybe he *wouldn't* know just how much he was affecting me. "Because...*uh ahhhh!*" I started, but couldn't finish. I tried again. My breath was coming faster then. I tried to look away to clear my head but it was useless. He was too close. Not only could I feel him, but I could smell his clean male scent. It was faint but familiar already in a very pleasant way. I turned back to face him again and the bright grey center of his eyes was all I could see reflecting in the darkness. "*You...* you distracted me..." I managed shakily.

"*How exactly did I do that?*" He asked with a smile that I could see reflected in those grey eyes. He was teasing me again, referring to a question that I had asked him during our first conversation. I remembered most of it from the dream but it made more sense then, as usual.

I still didn't know how to stop it. Aside from running out, which I couldn't do. He was standing right in front of me. So close that I could feel his next deep breath fall across my chest. I tried to remember what had come after that but I couldn't find it in my memory.

"*Really?!* Hmpf!!" I huffed and attempted to put more space between us, but I found the wall right behind me and the stairway railing to my right, which was the direction that I *really* wanted to go in. I was trapped. "*Stop!*" I yelled, panicking a little and closing my eyes. He did stop. Right next to me. Touching his hip to mine, pressing me up against the wall, just slightly. Just enough to make me want a little more. *Ahhh!!!*

"Why are you doing this to me?" I asked in a high pitched voice. My eyes were still closed. I was afraid to look up and see his face so close to mine, even if it was just the shadow of it.

He spoke very close to my ear and his breath washed over my skin as his words shot through me. I remembered that part then. "What am I doing?" He asked in a calm voice that made it sound like he had no clue. Though he clearly knew exactly what he was doing.

"Oh God! Seriously? C'mon!" I yelled. It was crazy! I couldn't do this with him! I thought frantically. *I needed to get away!* But which way was away? I was trying to remember. In spite of my lack of interest mentally, my body was apparently still too weakened by such long a span without sex to function properly. I couldn't seem to think straight long enough to figure it out. My head said get out of there, but my body said, *"Yeah sure, just one minute..."*

"Where do you want to go?" He had asked and it surprised me. How did he know? How did he always know? Was there more to his *"talents"* than he let on? What the hell?!

"Stop doing that!" I demanded, hating how vulnerable it made me feel when he knew things that he shouldn't. I had worked too hard to gain control over my life. Too long, not to feel like a victim of circumstance. Why did being around him always seem to bring those feelings back again?

"Doing what? *Reading you?* Like you read me?" He challenged, as his hand came up beside me to rest against the wall behind my head. He wasn't touching me but I could feel the heat on my skin as if he was. *"Hmpf! I wish!"* He said emphatically. "It would certainly even things up a bit wouldn't it? It would only be fair if I had free and total access to all of *your* feelings, the way you do to mine."

Just the thought was like a waking nightmare for me!

"Don't worry. Unfortunately, it's just *you.* I've spent too much time thinking about you lately, wondering why you do the things you do. I think I'm starting to get you a little bit and that scares the hell out of you, doesn't it?" He asked, still much too close. I could feel the warm breeze blowing through the loft and across my skin and I was extremely grateful for it. I looked up at him and I could see the silhouette of his shape. That was all that I could see in the dark besides the moon through the front of the loft. I looked back and focused on his shape in the darkness.

"Look, I'm not scared of you. Or this." I said defiantly. "I'm just not looking for any of this right now."

In the darkness, I could see his eyes reflect what little light there was. They didn't so much as blink while they stared down at me.

"I know you want me just as much as I want you." He said flat out, once and for all. No hesitation in his voice.

"I don't want to push you, Simone. I admit, I don't know what's going on in your life or in *your* head right now. But I can feel what's going on in the *rest* of you, when we're close. *And I like it.* I like it a lot! *I want more.*" He said without a hint of humor in his voice. "But I can wait." He said confidently. He didn't stop there.

"I'll take it as slow as you want me to. *But I'm not going anywhere.*" As he said it though, he contradicted himself by backing up and giving me my space. I felt his intention, even without the gesture, but I took advantage of the situation anyway and made my escape.

"*Ugghhh! We*ll thanks because right now, *I am.*" I said, as I felt along the railing and slid past him. I could feel his disappointment running through me, but he didn't try to stop me. When I reached the top of the stairs, I looked down and I could see a faint light at the end of the tunnel. In that case, it was the doorway at the bottom of the stairs. I felt a little cowardly, leaving it like that. He was quiet then. Mentally and physically. *Passive.*

As usual, a lot of what he said was true but I just couldn't *do* that then. Even if I wanted to, which I really wasn't sure I did. Still, I felt like I should at least *try* to explain that to him. I wasn't sure how to do that without it sounding too much like the *"It's not you, it's me"* speech, but I gave it a shot.

"So you don't know what I'm feeling, *thankfully.*" I laughed, trying to lighten the mood a little. Judging by the feelings I was getting though, it hadn't worked. "So I will just *tell* you straight out, okay. That's fair enough, isn't it?" I offered. He didn't say anything then either so I kept going.

"I'm not sure what I think about you or your ...*situation*, but it doesn't matter right now. And as for what you felt between us... well, I'm not ready. I don't know when I will be or if I even *want* to be." I looked back at the blackness where he was still standing. Where I had been standing with him just a moment ago, and continued quickly before my courage gave out.

"I'm not *denying* anything. I just can't right now." I finished weakly but honestly and then I headed down the stairs. I felt just a small taste of his satisfaction before I went. Oh well, at least he felt better. What the Hell, let him have that I thought. It was the truth, after all.

On my way down I heard him say. "Take your time, Simone." Then just as I was stepping out the door. "Just hurry the hell up already, *will ya?*" He added and then he laughed. A deep but happy laugh. I laughed too and shook my head as I made my way out into the warm night air.

There were too many good points to him for us to keep having encounters like that. I knew I wouldn't have the strength to keep getting myself out of them for long. Not in my current, weakened state anyway.

Frustratingly enough, I soon found that Ethan had been right again. It had taken me almost twenty minutes to get Liliana down off the trailer and ready to say good night. Nobody appeared to be in a hurry to get home and small groups were lingering around here and there. No one seemed to have missed me at all either and I was thankful not to have to explain where I'd been.

I hugged first Jack and then Shirley, who handed me a bag full of baked goods. I took the bag, knowing it was pointless to resist. Her mothering instinct appeared to be at peace as long as she knew I was being fed. I thanked them again, telling them honestly how surprised I was at how much fun I'd actually had. I knew they weren't offended. They understood. And they knew I meant it and that I would *know*, when I told them what a great thing they had there. But of course, they knew that already.

Liliana said one final good night to Jonah and we were

off down the path, hand in hand. "Did you have a good time?" I asked. Not because I didn't know, but because I knew I should. That she would want to tell me.

"Yes! That was the best time ever, Mama! Can we do it again? Next time they have one? Can we, please? Jonah says he's coming next time too! Oh please say yes!" She managed all in one breath.

I just laughed. "Just how many cups of coffee did you drink on that hay wagon?" I joked. She just laughed harder and danced around in circles ahead of me down the path towards the back deck. It was nice to be able to do something with her that made her that happy. It had been a while, but things seemed to be coming back around again for us. It helped me to breathe a little bit deeper again. Little, tiny, micro-bits at a time, it was becoming just the slightest bit easier. I hoped it would continue.

We went up the stairs using her flashlight, which thankfully still worked. As I climbed, I tried not to think about what I had encountered at the top of the *last* flight of stairs. I let out a big sigh. I took the batteries out of the bottom of my useless flashlight, and threw it into the recycling bin under the table by the door as we passed by. It landed with a very satisfying *crash*!

Liliana looked back, startled by the noise.

"*Whoopsie!*" I said playfully and purposefully changed the subject. "Did someone let a horse in here?" I sniffed around like I was pretending to try to find the source. I got close to her and sniffed her neck until she laughed hysterically. "It's you!! *Hah!* No wait, it's me!" I said acting surprised. Liliana laughed some more.

"It's both of us, Mama!" She yelled and we pretended to be horses while I went and grabbed what we needed for a quick shower. Liliana galloped her way in and got started. I helped her wash her hair and then left her to finish the rest on her own. She was a *"big girl"* after all she had said. And yes, she was she confirmed, a 'girl' again, once the "horse" was all washed off. I just grinned and left her to it.

After her teeth were brushed and I had her all tucked into bed, I went back to take my own shower. Then I fell exhausted into my own bed. I reached up to switch the light off and the fan on. I laid back heavily, expecting to drop off quickly but before too long it became apparent that, that was not going to be the case.

Partly because the things he had said were still running through my head, but also partly because I was afraid to go to sleep and dream about him again. I felt like I couldn't get away, either way. *Again.*

I tossed and turned all night. At one point I did hope spitefully, that I wasn't the only one not sleeping! It was petty, I knew. Truth is, I'm not nice when I don't sleep. I tried until the sun came up. Once I heard Liliana pouring a bowl of cereal, I gave it up and got out of bed. It was going to be a very long day.

After all of the excitement of the night before, Saturday was comparatively quiet. We both ate cereal for breakfast and then went to the riding area again so Liliana could spend some time with Cookie. It had cooled off considerably from the day before but it was still sunny and generally nice out.

After her riding lessons and her grooming were done, we went home and had a quick lunch of tuna sandwiches, chips and pickles. We capped it off with an ice cold can of caffeine free coke, which she still didn't get to drink very often. It had been one of my favorite lunches as a kid, though I got the fully caffeinated version, and it was now one of Liliana's too.

We took a short walk through the woods for a while, pointing out the different birds that we saw. We even had time to draw a few, back at my apartment before it was time for me to bring her back. It had been a good day, so I tried not to ruin it by being sad. We put on the Kelly Clarkson CD and sang *"Stronger"* together on the way. It kept me up beat all the way there.

I gave her a big hug and a kiss and handed her backpack off to Ben. I got back in and waved before I pulled out, proud of myself for finally getting a little better at that.

Chapter 15

Once I got through the rest of the boring weekend, the next week actually flew by. Even faster than the last one had. After I got the approved plans back from Micky on Monday, I spent the first two days ordering plants and materials from various suppliers. I was covering over two acres of land in foliage and that translated mostly to a lot of paperwork at first. Or virtual, digitized paperwork anyway, since I did it all online. Then there was all the hardware, lumber and other various supplies that would be needed to make my vision a reality, too. But with the ordering done, there was nothing left but a few days of waiting for things to show up at the site. I had some time left to kill in the meantime, so on Wednesday I decided to take a ride into town and get caught up with everyone while I had the chance.

I went by my parent's place and they were thrilled to see me as usual. Of course they were also getting ready to go out to some fundraising brunch, *as usual.* We chatted briefly about my new project, but there wasn't time to get into anything else. That was probably just as well, since I had no idea what I would even tell them at that point. I hugged and kissed them and said I wouldn't keep them anymore.

After that, I went by Viv's shop and surprised her with croissant and egg sandwiches and iced coffees for lunch. She was happy for the excuse to take a break. She told her other artist Carol that she was taking lunch and we went to sit in her little curtained off lounge area in the back of the shop.

We plopped down on a sofa that was barely visible under

all of the colorful scarves and throws that covered it from end to end. I put the warm bag and the cardboard tray with our iced coffees on the appropriately named coffee table in front of us. I took the sandwiches out of the wax paper bag and placed one in front of each of us.

"So, how's the search going?" I asked, referring to her hiring a replacement for Andrea, while I put straws in the cups.

"Very well!" She said enthusiastically. "I think I may have found my man!" She said with a grin.

"So you're really going through with it. You're going to hire a *man* to work *under* you?" I asked teasingly.

"Hopefully!" She said and laughed a little too loudly. She covered her mouth then, remembering the few customers who were still out there. "We'll see." She said more quietly, but still smiling. "He has some hurtles left to make it over. And what about you and the *Mysterious Magician?*" She asked, wasting no time. "Have you talked to him again?"

"Sort of." I sighed before answering fully, as I remembered our encounter and thought about what to say. "We had a little *run in*. In the pitch dark hay loft on *movie night.*" I said, rolling my eyes but otherwise letting the circumstances speak for themselves.

"The dream?" She asked excitedly.

"Oh yeah! And then some!" I confirmed. "I managed to escape unscathed for the most part, but I'm not sure what will happen next time." I admitted, keeping up my tradition of confessing.

"Will there be a next time?" She asked with her eyebrows raised in amusement.

"Not if I can help it. But he does seem to turn up at the darndest times!" I laughed and shook my head. "I don't know, but I guess at some point I *will* have to stop and figure it out. *Ecchhkkk!*"

I screwed up my face at the thought, then I sighed. "I just don't know if it's really even worth it. You know what I mean?" She nodded. "I know everyone feels like that sometimes, but the fact of the matter is it's a lot more complicated for me and I'm just not sure anymore if it's *really* worth the trouble. I really think I could be happy being by myself." I said honestly. "As long as I have Liliana in my life and my work. I could be content with that." I insisted. "That's still a lot! What's wrong with that?" I asked rhetorically, but I knew that Vivianne being Vivianne, she would answer me anyway and she didn't disappoint.

"Nothing. If you've passed menopause and have a nice condo in Boca Raton! But you my friend are not done living yet and I will not let you eliminate the one part of life actually *worth* living *for!*" She said and then laughed at her own joke. And even though I hated to encourage her, I couldn't help laughing with her, customers be damned.

I left there as clueless about what I would do as I had been before I came, but I felt better anyway.

That brought me to Thursday. I had been trying not to think about it. I didn't want to dwell on it. It was part of why I had kept so busy.

D-day. Ben and I had a meeting at 2:00 to officially render our marital contract null and void.

It was time. It was the right thing to do, and it needed to be done. But I still didn't want to do it. I wished I could just wake up when it was over. That wasn't going to happen though. Time to suck it up and get it over with.

I showered and made some coffee. I tried not to think about anything at all while I dressed in a pair of black dress pants, a lightweight, grey, cashmere V-neck sweater and my grey suede ankle boots. I figured if I couldn't feel good, I could at least try to *look* good. It helped some.

I left early when I ran out of things to do and drove much more slowly than usual. I still made it to the lawyers' office twenty minutes too soon. I wasn't alone. Ben was also early and was parked three spaces away. We both waved and smiled weakly at our situation. That made it a little easier too.

We got out and he came over to me and hugged me hello. "I bet this isn't the funnest thing you've ever done, huh?" He said sarcastically as he stepped back. He looked good, but a little tired too. Just like me, I supposed.

"Not the funnest, no." I agreed. "Do you think it will get easier, *after?*" I asked him in return, more seriously.

He took both of my hands in his. "Yeah." He said quietly looking down at our hands. Then looked back up at me. "I do." He answered nodding, serious too at first. But then we both looked at each other and started to laugh at the absurdity of his choice of words. He shook his head. "Come on, let's get this over with." He said and we walked in together, still holding hands.

It was a strange way to end a relationship, but I was glad. We needed desperately to be good to one another or we would just end up hurting Liliana and I know neither of us wanted to do that. We had never wanted to hurt each other, either. That was why we had put it off for so long in the first place. We had finally faced the facts though and once we ripped that Band-Aid off we could both try to get past it and get on with living the rest of our own lives.

It was surprisingly quick. A few handshakes, a few signatures, a few stamps, a few more handshakes and it was done. The life that we had vowed to share together forever was thereby canceled. It was all business as usual for the lawyers and I even felt the need to thank them afterwards, which was just plain weird. Ben and I walked back out together and hugged one last time before getting into our own cars.

Once inside, I threw the papers on the seat and took a deep breath before I started the car.

I put on my *"Alex Clare"* album and cranked up *"Too Close"* until I couldn't hear anything else, even my own thoughts.

You know I'm not one, to break promises
I don't want to hurt you, but I need to breathe
At the end of it all, you're still my best friend
But there's something inside, that I need to release

Which way is right, which way is wrong
How do I say that I need to move on
You know we're heading separate ways

And it feels like I am just too close to love you
There's nothing I can really sa-aaay
I can't lie no more, I can't hide no rmore

Got to be true to myself
And it feels like I am just too close to love you
So I'll be on my way...

The intensity and the beat carried me all the way home on repeat. I cried for a while, but not the whole way. It helped. By the time I got off the highway and back in Pinegrove, I felt better. A little bit relieved even. *It sucked.* But at least it was done. It was freeing too, in its' own, desolate way.

Once I was home, I changed into my favorite super-soft gauchos and a comfy V-neck t-shirt. I slipped my flip-flops on and picked up the drawings that I had been tweaking. I grabbed my keys and headed back out the door. I drove straight to The Tavern and sat heavily in my usual booth when it finally opened up. I asked Dani for a beer when she came by and as I waited I felt Ethan's attention for just a quick second during a pause in the music.

I ignored it and sat back staring blankly into space. I just wanted to get back to my drawing. I refused to consider what came next. Not yet anyway. I was taking the rest of that day off. Completely, physically and mentally.

I promised myself that I would finally take a moment and attempt to figure all of that stuff with Ethan out, but it wouldn't be that day. I slipped my flip-flops off under the table and pulled my feet up underneath me. I was still had one time out left, I thought stubbornly, and the buzzer had yet to sound. I closed my eyes. I just needed to sit and enjoy the music for a while longer.

Tomorrow. Everything could wait until tomorrow. I just hoped silently that Ethan would be as willing to put it off as I was, because I really needed the mental break that his music always managed to afford me.

He appeared at first to be in a cooperative mood. He looked over when his song ended and acknowledged my presence with a slight smile, but he didn't make a move to come and talk to me. I wanted to just be grateful and finally relax, once and for all, but he stared at me for a few more quiet heartbeats before he started to play again. That made me a tad bit curious in spite of my lack of current interest.

He maintained eye contact as he began to play and I was slightly uncomfortable and a little perplexed at first. Then I recognized the song.

It was a softer tune called *"Overjoyed"* and I was a little surprised and further impressed that he even knew it. It was a Matchbox 20 song and they were one of my favorite bands, so of course I already had the CD and knew the whole song word-for-word. But I suddenly felt every one of those words take on a whole new meaning as he sang them slowly, seemingly directly to me.

"Feeling my hands start shaking.
Hearing your voice I'm
overjoyed.
I'm sorry
but I have no choice
You're only
getting better."

"Baby you have
your reasons.
Maybe you're scared you'll
be let down.
Are you crying when there's no one around?"

"Well then maybe, baby if you hold me,
baby.
Let me come over.
I will tell you
secrets
nobody knows.
I cannot
over
state it
I will be overjoyed"

He strummed his guitar in between verses while I sat practically frozen in my spot by words that he could have written just for me. I knew for a fact that he hadn't. I happened to know that Rob Thomas had written them along with his band mates Paul Doucette and Kyle Cook. So why did they appear to speak directly to me and *specifically* of our situation so perfectly? How did he *do* that? I just smiled at his uncanny choice and even that seemed to play right into his hands as he started the next verse.

"That smile on your face
like summer.
The way that your hand keeps
touching mine.
Let me be the one to make it right
And maybe, baby let me hold you,
baby.
Let me come over.
I will tell you
secrets
nobody knows.
I cannot over
state it
I will be overjoyed."

"And if you want
we'll share
this life.
Anytime you need a friend
I'm gonna be
by your side.
When nobody un--der--stands
you,
Well,
I
do"

I just sat quietly, staring at him as he went into the last

round of the chorus, asking me again to *"let him hold me."* I couldn't deny that the urge to do just that was quite strong. It was just too complicated. I tried to deal privately with the things he made me feel, even as it seemed as if everyone in the place must know that the whole thing had been aimed at me. I felt so raw and overexposed that I thought I might-as-well of been standing up on the stage next to him. But when I looked nervously around the room as he finished, I was surprised to find that no one else was paying attention. No one else had even noticed. How did he *do* that?!

I just shook my head in relief. I was grateful for his *"offer"* but as easy as his song had made it sound, I knew that wasn't really the case. I didn't know when I would be ready to handle the things he was offering me. All I knew was that it was not an option at the moment. No matter how much better it might make me feel, I thought with some real regret.

I paid my tab, gathered my things and I stood to leave. I could feel his slight disappointment mixed with his amused, desire infused patience as it hit me from behind when he stopped singing. I looked back over my shoulder and just smiled weakly at him in apology for what we both knew was really just my cowardice.

Before I had a chance to reconsider, I turned and walked out.

Chapter 16

When I woke on Friday, I felt more like myself again. Whoever that was.

I was happy though, that it was time to get to work. The first shipment of materials would be arriving on site. I could finally go and get my hands dirty. I *loved* that part the most!

I pulled out a pair of my work jeans and threw on a fresh t-shirt. I washed my face and threw my hair up in a ponytail. Then I rubbed some sun-screen on my face and arms and went to the closet to grab my tool belt and my boots, smiling in anticipation.

It felt good to lace them up again. It had been too long a stretch and the closer I came to working in the dirt again, the more I realized how much I had missed it. Work during the daytime and my Liliana at night. All in all I thought, a good day.

I drove up to the site in record time and was there long before the first truck rolled up. It was one of those cooler spring days I had predicted would come that reminded you, you were still in New England but that was actually good. Once we started working we would warm up fast.

I parked next to the construction trailer that would act not only as my office and home base during that job, but it also happened to be where my bathroom was. There were the always the usual Jiffy Johns on site of course, and the guys had no problem using them. The ladies and I however, needed something a little sturdier and slightly more private. Since it would hardly be appropriate for us to traipse in and out of the hotel covered in dirt numerous times a day, I was as grateful as ever to have our own permanent "ladies room" arrive on site.

I got out walked up to the edge of the clearing where I greeted first Mr. Wu Xing and then the crew that I had hired before we got to work.

It would be a long day of directing truck after truck to where everything should be unloaded for the time being. The crew just had to get everything stacked and covered with tarps as things were delivered. It was a fairly small crew for a project of that size, but it was more than enough for what I had planned. I mostly just needed help with the lighting and the construction phase and after that, only with the most basic and time-consuming of landscaping procedures. The adding of fill or laying and moving of rocks and gravel over large areas, that sort of thing. Most of the plant work, I would do myself. That was the most gratifying part for me and I didn't like to share. But there was going to be a lot more construction than usual so I knew there'd be plenty of work to go around.

All of the people on the crew were people that I had worked with before. I knew their work and more importantly, their work ethic. They also knew me and how I worked and I trusted them.

All together there were seven of what I liked to call my *"regulars"* working with me on that project. I could have used ten or fifteen, just based on the square footage of it but I wanted even more control over it than usual, so I would make due. For that reason, I was careful to pick the best of the best.

There was Tom. He was a soft spoken but knowledgeable "uncle" sort of guy, somewhere in his early fifties. I had met him originally when he was still working with Ben in the park. He was quiet but he really knew his stuff so when he did speak, people listened. He had an easygoing manner and we had hit it off right away. Much to my delight, we have had many opportunities to work together over the years.

He had been with that same company for ten years before he started his own business. He specialized mostly in trees and shrubs and at that point I couldn't think of anyone else I would rather have working on trees for me there. They were going to be a *very* important part of the project.

Then there was Sharon and Dale. They were a package deal. Ben and I had gone to a landscaping expo three years ago and we had both been blown away by their display. They were the local landscape lighting experts. They had created a dark tunnel out of plastic light blocking material that people could walk through to see their samples. Sharon knew exactly where to put a light to get the full effect and Dale could make them practically invisible. He could design a landscape light to look like almost anything. I knew basically what I wanted the lights to look like and roughly where I wanted them to be. Making all of that a functional reality would be their job.

Mack, Doug and Anthony were all extremely valuable to me for their versatility. They were my top, go-to guys. They could do it all. I knew from past experiences how crucial it could be to have a few players with the flexibility to shift where ever I needed them the most. That was especially important when you were working under a deadline like I was there. Of the three, not one was a "specialist" of anything *per se,* but I still wouldn't trade any one of them for even three other men apiece. They worked with me on most of my jobs and I wouldn't dream of taking on something like Wu Xing Gardens without them.

Other than that, there was just Micky, my aforementioned botanist. *"The brains of the operation"* to be more specific. I knew what I liked and what I wanted to it do. She was always there to help me figure out what would actually survive where. That part is pretty important. It's one thing to do over someone's outdoor space and have a positive, dramatic effect at the unveiling. It was another thing all together to have it live for more than a few weeks after you've left. That was important.

I had started my plant passion late in life and I didn't have the patience to go back to school to learn everything there was to know firsthand. Especially when it had been just a hobby for so long. Luckily, I found that I could hire someone else *who had*, to advise me and learn as I go. It had worked out beautifully over the years. It was a pretty cushy job for Micky, since she was only needed sporadically. But her expertise was invaluable to me, so I didn't begrudge her a single penny that I paid her.

Everyone was present and accounted for and as excited as

I was to get started. There had been a lot of hugging and joking at first, like there always was when we hadn't seen each other for a while. We had sat and talked and got caught up a little while waited for the trucks to arrive. Once we got started though, we went straight out until lunch.

We stopped and ate sandwiches that the restaurant up at the hotel had graciously prepared and brought out for us. Along with potato salad, macaroni salad, Greek salad and every other kind of salad that you could want. All set out buffet style, under a shade tent, precisely at noon. All courtesy of Mr. Wu Xing. I asked the waitress to please express my sincerest gratitude to him after lunch and then I got back to work.

As it turned out, that would become a daily occurrence and as much as I insisted repeatedly that I would like to pay for my crew's lunch, he would never take a dime for it. It was a real gift to work for someone with such impeccable integrity. Inside and out.

I met with Mr. Wu Xing every few days, just to keep him informed on how things were progressing and what he could expect, noise or traffic wise. I didn't mind. Meeting with him was never something that I had to dread. He was a peaceful man and he had a quiet and kind temperament. Whenever he was giving off strong emotions, they were generally things like concern or expressions of hospitality. It made it very easy to go to work there every day.

The work itself was moving along nicely, but after the first full week, it still didn't look like much of anything to the naked eye. I liked that though. I liked the way you could tear up all the ground around you and move huge boulders and implant trees and flats upon flats of plants, and it would just look like a giant mess through most of it. Right up until the end. Then all of the separate random things would finally all come together and suddenly make perfect sense. It reminded me of my dreams that way.

In the end you would have something beautiful and people were always pleasantly surprised. I liked to see their faces when they had been watching the project unfold the whole time and yet they are still in awe at the finished product. That was another part that I enjoyed. Being able to make *other* people feel good things was a great way for me to improve my own atmosphere, so it was mutually beneficial. Definitely win-win.

We weren't even close to that moment there. No, not yet. We still had a long way to go for that. Thinking about it didn't bother me one bit, until I thought about how much I was actually missing The Tavern and Ethan's music. And if I was honest with myself at all, Ethan. I really didn't want to admit that, that was part of it, but I wondered who I was supposed to be kidding when I pretended to myself that it wasn't.

I hadn't been in once during the week and I was starting to worry about how it looked. Like I was avoiding him, even though I was way too old for that kind of shit. The truth was, I was just too damn tired at the end of the day.

I didn't want him to be thinking that I was afraid to face him, or worse, that I was upset with him for being straightforward with me. But I also really didn't want to drag myself down there after a ten hour day at the gardens, just so I could fall asleep on the table and embarrass myself. I still didn't know what to say to him anyway. In spite of my promise to myself to sit down and think it all through, I had been so busy that I had done everything but. I liked to pretend that was a coincidence.

Since no good solution magically presented itself, I had just continued to put it off. It was Thursday again that I sat thinking about it but that could actually be a pretty busy night there sometimes, so I figured he wouldn't miss me. Without having any work that I was desperate to finish, I didn't have the same motivation or excuse to show up so often.

I had let my mind wander casually over these things until I was done at the gardens for the day. I was beat as usual, but in the best kind of way. I just wanted to go home. Shower, eat and sleep, in that order hopefully. But that reminded me that the eating part would be tough since I hadn't had time to do any shopping all week. I would need things before Liliana came the next day anyway. It wouldn't be good to have her pour a bowl of cereal at 6:00 AM, only to find that we had no milk. She would certainly feel justified in breaking the 7:00AM rule then. I smiled to myself and gave in to the idea of one last task.

I stopped off at the dreaded market that I could no longer avoid on my way home. After pushing my cart with the shaky wheel up and down isle after isle of bored kids, frustrated moms and unappreciated workers, I couldn't get out of there fast enough. I put the bags in the trunk, annoyed that there were so many because I had gotten the *put-two-things-in-each-bag* kid. I gave the carriage one big push into the corral and let it make its' own space. I dropped into my car and finally headed home. That was enough for one day.

Once I was back in the safety of my sanctuary, I turned on the radio, put away the groceries, showered and fixed some dinner for myself.

I took my plate and sat Indian style in the center of the overstuffed sofa that I tended to ignore, with my plate of angel hair pasta and vegetables on my lap. I twirled pasta and flipped through the channels until I found a true crime documentary that I hadn't seen. Yes, it was worth it to take in all of the shiver inducing, stomach turning images and devastated feelings that came through so easily, to learn how each one had been successful in accomplishing their crime. It was like homework to me. I always felt like I wanted to expose myself to as much of it as was available, in order to learn how each one thought and acted. So I would recognize it when it came around. I had always found it extremely upsetting and absolutely riveting at the same time.

I was halfway through the show and all the way through my pasta when my phone rang. I picked it up and looked at the display. *Unknown.* But it wasn't unknown to me anymore. I had seen it once before. *Ethan.*

A million thoughts went through my head. So many reasons to answer. So many reasons to ignore it. *Hmmmm.... Ahhhhh....* and then finally, "Hello?"

"Simone. It's Ethan. I'm sorry. I wouldn't have called you again... I meant what I said. But *I need your help.*"

Chapter 17

My guard was immediately up. "Help? With what?" I asked, more than a little afraid of the answer.

He sighed heavily. "You remember the kid from the loft? The one I suspected of being a *height?*" He asked.

"Yes. I remember." I said warily. I also remembered saying that I didn't want to know about him. I wondered why he was telling me anyway.

"Well, I was right. Long story short, I've spent some time with him since then, trying to help him figure out his skill. I already knew it was in the visual recognition category. Seems to be popular lately." He said referring to himself and Carson. I think we've confirmed pretty conclusively now exactly what variety of recognition and it's a doozy. He's going to need what I have to offer more than most, but he got spooked and took off before I got a chance to really talk to him. Explain that I could help him. I had wanted to talk to his parents first." He sighed and sounded disappointed with himself.

"I've known his father for years. But I wasn't aware that things have been coming to a head for a while now over there, and it all blew up before I had a plan in place to help him." I was just listening quietly on the other end. "Here's the thing, I don't know if his parents are telling me the truth now or not." He admitted worriedly.

"Their old friends, and I love them dearly, but they're stubborn and proud people. That is not always a good combination. There's a part of me that's worried that they think they're protecting him by lying to me. If they think they're doing the right thing for him, they'll defend it to the death. If I'm right and that's the case, he'll *never* get the help he needs." He was angry at himself again. Even over the phone I could feel that.

"Simone, they have family in Germany. Family who live in a very remote area with very limited resources. I'm afraid that if they get the chance, they'll send him there. They really do think they're helping him, I know, but they have no idea what they're condemning that boy to if they do that. I need to somehow make his dad understand, before it's too late!"

"I've seen this skill once before. It's not common. And it's not going to be easy to acclimate to. Some kids do just fine without outside help, as you know. Not him. I promise you that he won't make it without my help! I *have* to help him. You have to *help me*, help him. *Please, Simone!*" I could feel him desperately longing for my compliance as well.

"What can *I* do?" I asked warily.

"You can come with me and meet them. Tell me if they're being honest with me, or if they're hiding him. That's all I need to know, but I need to know *now!* Normally I would never ask you, but in this case tomorrow could be too late. I didn't know what else to do. They could have him on a flight in as little as a few hours if that's what they decide is necessary." I could hear the panic in his voice too, even more than I could feel it over the line.

"I have contacts all across the country, but not very many overseas. I'm not really equipped to go chasing teenagers internationally. Especially ones who don't think they need or want my help. You can't exactly *force* them to come back to America, you know? The international police frown upon that type of behavior at the border." He said, obviously stressed by the whole situation.

"Why are you so sure that he won't be able to handle his '*skill?*'" I asked. "Don't forget, I grew up without any specific guidance and I survived. Some do, as you said." Even as I said it though, I thought about my years of somewhat helpful counseling. Not to mention the two loving, attentive parents I'd had. "What exactly *is* his skill, anyway? I already know more than I wanted to, so you might as well just tell me." I said, giving in a little.

He sighed deeply before answering. "He see's illness." He said sadly. "He can look at any person and see any ailment they may have. Whether they were previously aware of it or not." He was quiet after that for a time, obviously lost in his thoughts. It wasn't awkward though. I was thinking about it too.

I came to the conclusion that it *was* sad. I didn't even want to know about people's *feelings*, and here *he* was forced to see their most intimate physical vulnerabilities. Things they maybe didn't even know themselves yet! With that ability, he would also always be the first to notice any problem that appeared in a loved one. Not exactly a desirable designation to always be the bearer of bad news. *How would someone adjust to living like that*, I wondered?

It was funny, how it was always so hard to understand how other people managed to overcome their individual struggles. The things they face always seem so incredible and insurmountable to those around them. Meanwhile, from the other side of that same coin, we tackle our own obstacles without ever even considering the *possibility*, that they could be insurmountable.

They say God only gives you what you can handle, and if you believe in God, that's a pretty handy explanation for the phenomenon. I do believe in God, in my own personal way, but I still didn't buy it necessarily. I still think it's up to us what we do, and how we live with whatever we get. That's really the only part we have any control over. Not what life hands us. Just how we react to it. To believe otherwise is foolish.

Whether it's God, fate, or just Karma and some cosmic universal energy, there *are* forces out there greater than us at work. I believe that wholeheartedly but I have no illusion of ever knowing all of those answers in this life. So I try to focus instead on what I *can* control. It's a pretty good game plan and it serves me well for the most part.

I couldn't control what the boy's skill was. No one could. I knew that better than anyone. Ethan really believed that he could help him deal with it better though, and that would go a long way towards making him feel that there was something that *he* could control. That should help. *If* he would let Ethan help him. Right now the ability to help was being taken out of Ethan's control. I could tell that it was hurting him to be at such a frustrating dead end.

Apparently *I* could help with that. *That* was within *my* control. As resistant as I had been all along to even *know* about such things, never mind let it touch me personally, I found that I couldn't turn my back on him. I was sure that it wasn't about me, or about *"us."* It was nice not having those suspicions get in the way and muddy up my decision. I would know if he was just using the situation as an excuse to see me. He knew that too. So I could agree to help him without having to worry that it was all just a ploy. Removing all of that made it easier. And faster.

"You still there?" He asked quietly.

"Yes. Alright. I'll help you." I said quickly, before I could change my mind. "When?" I asked.

"Be there in five." He said, then, "...and Simone... *Thank you!*" He breathed heavily, and hung up.

I ran to my closet and traded my jammie shorts for a pair of jeans and threw a sweatshirt on over my tank top, once I had put a bra on underneath. I threw my hair up into a pony tail and put on my socks and shoes. I grabbed my cell phone and my keys, and went downstairs to wait for him. True to his word, he pulled up almost exactly five minutes later.

The compact shiny car drove up beside me and the door whooshed up.

"Really?" I asked, a little embarrassed by the pageantry of it.

He just smiled. "Hop in." He said, looking up at me.

I just rolled my eyes and got in. It was dangerously low to the ground and I felt like I was getting in a bobsled more than a car at first. But once I settled into the body hugging leather bucket seat, I found it was actually very comfortable. Maybe too comfortable for someone who was considering going to bed a half hour ago.

"This seems like an odd choice for someone involved in clandestine operations." I said, buckling my seatbelt as he pulled back out onto the main road. "It's not like it *'blends in'* or anything." I said with a chuckle.

"I've found the easiest place to hide is often in plain sight. And the best way not to attract attention is to invite it." He looked at me and smiled more broadly. "When you're flashy, people look right away, but get bored surprisingly fast. Especially when they see only exactly what they expected to see. Then they stop paying attention." He drove fast, but not recklessly. He never left the yellow lines on a single corner and never once did I feel the need to reach up for the "oh shit" bar to hold on. Still, we somehow made it to the farthest edge of town in just over seven minutes. It would have taken me at least fifteen I was sure, and I don't exactly drive slowly.

He kept me distracted most of the way by explaining the situation the best that he could in that much time. He told me that the kids name was Hoffmann, Jeremy Hoffmann. Ethan had known him since he was born.

"Jeremy has always been the kid who had a tendency to find the bird with a broken wing, or the stray cat that just happened to be pregnant. He always had one thing or another recuperating in his garage in a cardboard box with holes poked in the top. Everyone just assumed that he'd be a doctor someday." He smiled a little at the memories.

"He's a smart kid. He does well in school. He loves baseball, and he has always been surrounded by tons of friends. And plenty of *girls!*" He added with some amount of pride for his friends' son.

"Then he got sick. *Really* sick! And no one seemed to know what it was. That was a few months ago." The light went out of his voice then.

"He'd had the high fever, the hallucinations, the whole nine yards." As he said it he looked at me meaningfully, knowing that I knew exactly what he meant. I tried to ignore that it was even more reinforcement that the unimaginable things that he had told me were actually true. "He was even admitted into the hospital, but it was mostly just for observation. They just kept telling everyone that there was nothing else that they could do. That he would either pull out of it, or he wouldn't but that it was up to him at that point." He was remembering being that sick himself.

So was I.

"Apparently he had been there for a week, fighting the fever. He was so sick that they had him in an induced coma during a large part of that time, to keep him from suffering and to let his body rest and heal. Thankfully it seemed to help and he finally pulled out of it a few days later. Though instead of driving the doctors crazy with questions, like he would normally do, he acted withdrawn. *Scared* even. All he wanted to know was when he could leave.

I remembered what it had been like in the beginning for me, when I was young and didn't understand the strength of the things that I was experiencing. Having all those feelings coming at me at once and having no idea why or how to control it. It was enough to drive you crazy if you let it, I knew. Still I couldn't imagine what it would be like to not only suddenly see graphically, the illness in anyone you looked at, but to wake up to such astrange new reality in a *hospital!* Of all places! Where half of those around you would register one kind of illness or another. The fear and confusion must have been completely *overwhelming!*

"I was out of town when he got sick. But I talked to some of the doctors there when I got home." He confided. At that I raised my eyebrows, wondering what happened to patient confidentiality. He just winked and continued. "They said the illness was definitely viral, but that his psychological behavior afterward was an anomaly." He frowned as he took the next corner.

"I had been keeping an eye on him at first, but it takes time for it to show up in the beginning. It comes on in stages, and continually grows stronger over the first year." He explained. I thought back and didn't disagree, I just digested it for later analysis.

"Anyway, I hadn't seen him in a couple of weeks when I went to movie night to check up on him. I knew if anything would get him out of his room, it would be the promise of spending time with a special female in the dark." He turned to wiggle his eyebrows at me and I just rolled my eyes at the overly vivid memory. He wouldn't use that situation to further his cause in that area, but he had no problem bringing it up. He didn't let himself get distracted though. He kept to his train of thought.

"Though we're still waiting for the official confirmation from our sources that it was in fact the HgT virus, I think we can safely reason now that it was." He turned down another long wooded street that looked identical to the last two we had been on.

"His family said that when he first came home, he was different. Not his usual resilient self. Didn't want to go out. So eventually, family members had started to come over to see him. Hoping it would help. He had an issue first with one cousin that visited, then with an uncle." He added another right turn to the green maze, then continued.

"No one could say specifically what it was about, but I got the distinct impression that they thought he was *afraid* of them. He yelled at them to get away from him. I checked and found out that they had both been sick with a cold that was going around at the time. Most people just wrote it of as a fear of getting sick again so soon after his illness, but I know now that it was more than that. Soon people got word, and family stopped coming to see him. Everybody just left him alone for a while, myself included." I could feel some guilt at the fact that he had agreed to wait, for whatever reason.

"Then I saw him walk past me at movie night. He only had eyes for the blonde that he was following, but all I noticed was the blue and purple glowing mist swirling around his eyes. That's when I knew for sure, once and for all." His jaw tightened at that.

"No wonder he was so scared when I first tried to talk to him. I wonder what *I* looked like to him." He mused out loud. Then he looked at me and I knew we were both wondering the same thing.

"And you're not at all worried that the sight of the two of us *together* might send him right out a second story window?" I asked, only half joking.

"It's possible, I can't deny it. But if I wait too long it won't matter. I just know that if he runs away now he's never really going to come to terms with it. There's a window of opportunity, before the damage that can be done is so deep that it becomes permanent, irreversible. But it's small." He was worried for him again.

"He needs to know that this doesn't have to ruin his life." He said, staring at me for as long as was safe while driving. "Not everyone gets there on their own, Simone. Lots of *heights* don't ever get there at all! Another reason I'm so impressed by you." He admitted. We locked eyes again for just a second. After that, he pulled down a long dirt drive and then stopped. We were there.

"You just nod yes if he's telling the truth and no if he's lying. Okay? I will try not to ask more of you than that." He said feeling a little sorry about using me. Hell, I guess I owed him a bunch of turns there though, if I really thought about it.

"Alright." I agreed and took a deep breath before getting out. The house was a naturally stained two story split and I rolled my eyes at my own prophetic choice of words. That wasn't one of my special skills though. Just a weird coincidence.

They had chickens and goats in a small pen off to the left, near a small barn. There were more car skeletons scattered around than there were working vehicles, but the property was otherwise well kept.

As we got out three large dogs came barking wildly down the front steps towards us. I stopped short in my tracks, never a big fan of strange dogs. Especially not when I happened to be on their turf. Before I had a chance to really panic, Ethan let out a high pitched whistle and they all changed course and ran straight for him. He bent to pet them while they happily licked his chin. I let out the breath that I hadn't realized I'd been holding.

The owner was at the door then, and seeing that his attempt at deterring us had failed, he called the traitors back into the house. Gee thanks dude, I thought with a bit of an attitude.

"Stone? I thought I told you we were all set. What are you doing here?" He asked in a less than friendly manner and I could tell right away that he was hiding something. I looked to Ethan and caught his eye. I shook my head from left to right, just slightly and he sighed. I could tell that it was out of disappointment and not relief. You always want to believe the best of people. Especially those you love. But I knew only too well that it almost always turns out to be exactly what you feared the most. After all, there are always real reasons that you have those fears in the first place.

"I just want to help, Pete." He responded calmly. "Can we come in?"

"Who's 'we?'" Pete asked skeptically. *Shoot!* I hadn't thought to ask about what we would tell them about me.

"This is my friend Simone. She lives out on Kent's farm." He answered, keeping it simple.

"So? Why did you bring her here?" He asked stubbornly.

"This would be easier to explain if we weren't yelling across the front lawn, Pete." Ethan said and Pete finally gave in and held the door open for us. I couldn't help but notice what a knack Ethan had for being persuasive. I could see now how often that must come in handy.

Once inside, we waited in the living room while he went and put the dogs in a back bedroom and closed the door. He came back and gestured to the well-worn sofa. "So you want to tell me what you and your friend are doing here?" He was still holding out, defensive.

"Sure, but first can you tell me where Jeremy is? He asked purposefully.

"He's not here." He answered and I knew right away it was a lie. Well that made it easier anyway, if he was still there after all. I looked at Ethan and shook my head again ever so slightly and he released his breath in quiet relief.

"I need you to listen to me Pete. You know I wouldn't steer you wrong. We've been friends too long." He sighed and I could feel his exhaustion. "Look, you've asked to be kept out of my business over the years and I have always been perfectly happy to comply. You *know* that. My discretion is absolute." I could feel Pete becoming more relaxed, but he was still fighting it.

Ethan gathered some steam from somewhere deep within and kept going. "That was then Pete, and this is now. Now it has become clear that you are in need of my particular services. *Let me help*, Pete." He implored passionately. "Just let me *do*, what I *do*. I *can* help." He was being completely honest, but Pete couldn't know that.

I wondered then, how many times that same scene had played out for Ethan. Over and over again. It must be so tiring constantly fighting against those you were trying to help. I wondered if anyone ever accepted it easily. Pete wasn't. I certainly hadn't.

"What do you know about what Jeremy needs? You've only seen him a few times a year since he was little." Pete accused. "You're not exactly a leading expert. I'm pretty sure your girlfriend here knows even less about him than you do." He said, gesturing towards me as if I was less than useless. For the most part, he was right. I didn't bother to correct his other assumption. It wasn't important at the moment. He was still very resentful. Of Ethan's presence. Of my presence. But mostly of the whole situation that was tearing his family apart.

Pete seemed to be a straightforward, meat and potatoes kind of guy. It was easy to understand his feelings about all of the sudden moodiness and unexplained erratic behavior in his eldest son. It had really caught him off guard. He was at a loss and he hated to admit even that. Though there was more.

There was fear for his son coming from a few *different* directions. I didn't know why yet. Maybe he considered Ethan to be a threat also. I didn't know, but I wanted to then.

So I decided to take a chance. "I'm sorry for barging in here on you in the middle of an already tough time. *Really.*" I said sincerely, hoping he would listen. He didn't say anything, so I kept going. "But you need to know, it's not his fault." He looked up defensively but I continued undaunted. "It's not yours either." That was probably the most important thing, as I could feel his unnecessary but overwhelming guilt. I reassured him as much as I could. "It just *is.* You can hate it. You can even try to ignore it. But it won't go away. Jeremy will just be left trying to deal with it all alone. And he won't last very long on his own." I said sadly.

"Who *are* you?" He asked again. He looked to Ethan for explanation but he just smiled, obviously content to let me take that one once he could see that I had allowed myself to care.

I laughed and shook my head. "No one important, I promise you. I'm just a 'nobody' who happens to know exactly what you all are going through. *I know* it's not easy. Been there, done that." I said simply by way of explanation, with my hands up in the air. "Let me just tell you though, that I would have given anything for what Ethan is offering, if I'd had the opportunity when *I* was young and confused and scared." I said honestly, looking up at him. I felt confident saying that even though I still wasn't sure exactly what that was, specifically. I knew that between his heart which was pure and his genuine desire to help, combined with the determination that was always pouring off of him, that he had to have it right. He really would help, if he could. However it was that he did that. I did decide though, that after that night, I was going to find out once and for all just what that entailed.

Once I felt the comradery from Pete and I knew that he considered me an ally, I let my gaze drop from him and sweep to Ethan. He had definitely paid attention to that whole exchange and I could feel his happiness at my statement. I knew that it was true though. I hadn't lied and I wouldn't take it back. I didn't mind helping him in that instance, because I really did wish that I'd had someone like him who could have helped me. Someone who could have made it all easier somehow.

Pete seemed to be stubbornly ignoring me, but I could tell he was actually considering my words. That was one hurtle down, but there was more in there still. I didn't know what it was though, so I couldn't comment on it. It wasn't long before Pete finally offered it up.

"It's not just the changes in him that I'm worried about. There are other things to consider here. Like the Fed's who've been nosing around. Supposedly they're with the CDC. They keep asking to see him. Wanting to examine him. They want to take blood samples and such. Run tests." He was upset by that, I could tell.

"All he wanted Eat, was to get out of that hospital and come home. There's no way I'm going to let them put him through that again. I told them that, too! So of course they're trying to say it's a *'public safety issue'* and that they have the authority to take custody of him if they need to." He made eyes at Ethan and got very serious then. "I don't like to be threatened Eat. Doesn't sit well with me, if you know what I mean." He admitted in a low voice. Ethan clearly understood.

Ethan nodded once, but was thoughtful for a moment. I

could feel him considering that it was worse than he had thought. He didn't seem scared by that revelation, just more determined. I needed to remember to ask him later, why. He spoke up then.

"Just give me a week Pete, before you give up and send him away. I can protect him. I promise." Pete looked up, shocked that Ethan had figured out his plan so easily. Ethan continued, fortified by his small victory. "If you think he's not doing *measurably* better by then, I'll back off. Give you whatever help you need to do it your way." He finished with his hands up in the air.

I could feel that he wanted to agree, but something was still holding him back. "I have always been able to handle my own son, 'Eat.' Teach him right from wrong. Take care of him. We've done a good job, his mother and me! He's a *good* kid! I just don't know what the *hell* has gotten into him lately! But I know I don't need *'big brother'* to come along and figure it out for me." Pete said, feeling angry but defeated.

"You're right. You don't. Together, we can handle this. And Jeremy. You can't blame him *or* yourself for any of this." Ethan insisted. "Simone's right about that. You should listen to her." He could tell that Pete felt that he was being placated. He didn't even need me for that. But he didn't give up.

"You don't have any experience with any of this Pete. How are you supposed to know what to do? It's not something that comes with a manual unfortunately. Most professionals don't even know what their dealing with or how to proceed. At least not the one's without their own agenda, anyway. I found that one out the hard way myself. These kids need a safe place to turn. That is *why* I do what I do, Pete." He was softening, recognizing the ring of truth in Ethan's words.

"I *was* Jeremy once, and I was alone. It was *hard!* A lot harder than it had to be. I know that now. And I 'm not going to lie to you, what Jeremy is facing is going to be even *harder.* But if what I went through helps me make it easier for him, or someone else like him, then at least it wasn't for nothing right?"

He let out a sigh and gave one last request, mostly to help Pete save face, I could tell. "Let me have my purpose in life, will ya?" He chuckled in the end and Pete eventually laughed with him, loosening up at last.

Ethan sighed wearily and continued. "Look Pete. I can't make this go away, but I *can* make it a lot easier to live with. I promise you. *Let me help!*" He practically begged. There was no pride at all coming off of him then, only good will towards Pete and without knowing why, I was suddenly very proud of him. It was painfully obvious to me how hard he works to try and help others. *Especially* when they kicked and screamed and insisted that they didn't need it. Then he worked even harder.

I was pretty familiar with that particular response, and that recognition had me feeling more than a little ashamed for putting him through a very similar scenario. I *still* hadn't accepted it fully. Not *officially*.

I also didn't like the answer I got when I asked myself the question, '*What had I ever done to help other young, struggling empaths?*' Hmpf. I wouldn't even commit to joining the damn website! It was tough to swallow, but it wasn't the time or place so thankfully I was able to stuff it back down to deal with later.

"Please Pete. Where is he?" Ethan asked calmly.

"Alright, 'Eaten,' Pete said, using another variation of his odd nickname. "One week." They shook hands and shared a look between them. I could feel the threat along with the wary trust going from Pete to Ethan just then.

"He's upstairs. You might as well go up. It would take too long to get him to come down. By then your week could already be up." He said with a smirk and a healthy dose of dry humor.

"Good luck." He said lastly. He wasn't being sarcastic anymore though. He meant it.

Chapter 18

We walked up the stairs and down the hall, past the sound of other smaller children playing in their rooms, to the last closed door. Ethan knocked softly, then called out to Jeremy so he wouldn't be startled by us entering unannounced. "Hey Jer! It's me, Uncle 'Eaten.' Can I come in?" I looked at him and raised my eyebrows at the unusual nickname and he mouthed, "I'll explain later." to me. He was waiting for a response before turning the knob. Finally we got one.

"No. What? *Why?*" We heard him say from behind the closed door, sounding as if he was sleeping. I knew otherwise though. There was no sleepiness emanating from that room. Just fear, anxiety and sadness. I looked at Ethan like my heart was about to break and he understood. He opened the door and entered as he spoke.

"Alright bud. All I heard was *"come in,"* so look alive!" It was a typical teenage boys' room. Deep denim blue walls. Solid wood furniture. Posters of muscle cars with half naked girls on them. Baseball trophies on every available surface and clothes stacked in every corner. He had a full size bed with New England Patriots sheets on it that was pushed up against the far wall. His back was to us as we entered, but he was fully dressed and obviously not asleep. Well, obvious to me anyway. I looked to Ethan to tell him but it was obvious then that it was clear to Ethan as well. He didn't need my help for that either. He walked right over and plopped down on the end of the bed.

"Hey dude. You've got company. Aren't you going to say

hello?" He shook his leg as he talked and Jeremy reluctantly started to turn.

"What's up Unc?" He tossed out weakly, trying to act fine and failing. Badly. His eyes were red and swollen like he either hadn't been sleeping or he'd been crying. Probably both. He sat up a little by leaning his left shoulder against the wall that he was facing. But that was as far as he was willing to go and he still wouldn't face us completely.

"Well first off, I need to tell you that I'm sorry I didn't get a chance to explain about all this better before. I wanted to, but you're parents are my friends. *Good* friends and I thought I should work things out with them first." He started explaining.

"I was wrong. I should've worried about you first and them after. That was my mistake and it won't happen again." He sighed and I could feel his guilt over the turn the situation had taken.

"It's just that this was the first time it's ever come up involving people I was so close to. My loyalties were momentarily divided. Now this is not meant to serve as an excuse, just an explanation and an apology." He kept on before Jeremy could argue. "But have no doubt about it from here on out Jer, I'm here to help *you*. If you can forgive me, I *will* help you." Jeremy looked doubtful, defeated. "I know you are completely overwhelmed right now, but I promise you that it won't always be like this."

He was just staring at us. When he spoke, it was through dry, cracked lips. "You can't help me. Thanks anyway." He said his good upbringing evident even then in his attempt at manners. Pete was right. They had done a good job.

He wasn't being rebellious. He was being honest. "No one can help me. I'm... *sick.* I'm not ...*right* anymore." He said sadly, staring at the wall and I could tell that he believed it wholeheartedly.

I couldn't take it anymore. I knew exactly the things he was feeling. I also knew for sure, that Ethan was right about something else too. I *was* very lucky to be where I was now, since I had also been in that same state of utter despair at one point in my life. I recognized it immediately when I felt it. Then I thought of my Liliana someday facing a situation like that and the pain was so great that I couldn't stand by quietly any longer.

"You're not sick Jeremy. There's nothing wrong with you. But you're right. You're not the same as you were before." I could tell it startled him a little when I spoke, but I didn't let it stop me. I was far from being an expert on the subject, but I felt secure supporting Ethan. I felt like I had to do *something* for this tortured soul!

"Life will be different now, but it *will* go on. And that doesn't have to be a *bad* thing." That part at least, I was sure of. I knew I needed to make him believe me too, since I could sense his desire to maybe *not* do it anymore. I could tell that he was finally curious about who I was though once I had him pegged so perfectly, so quickly.

"I know you don't know me from Adam, and I know you have no reason to believe me, but I've been right where you are and I managed to get past it. It wasn't easy or always fun, but I got through it. You can too. I don't know if I can do anything to help you in any way. I just want you to know that you're not alone." It seemed like the most important thing to tell him at the time.

"It doesn't matter. I *am* sick. You can't lie to me. I can *see* it!" He was insistent, agitated, and the anger was actually a good strong emotion. Sometimes it helped you to feel stronger. I know it often worked for me. But he petered out again just as quickly. When he continued he was just sad again. "Just like I see it in everyone else now too. So you can't try to tell me that I'm not sick! *Hah!*" He didn't really laugh though. He was hurting terribly.

"I don't want to see it anymore, I really don't. But it won't go away. *Because I'm sick.* Something in me is *broken!*" He closed his eyes and laid his head against the wall again.

Ethan spoke then. "What do you see Jeremy? When someone is sick?" He asked gently.

"It's weird. You wouldn't understand. I can't explain it." Jeremy said quietly without looking up.

"Try me." Ethan encouraged patiently. "Do you see colors around them?" He offered and Jeremy did look up then. I felt his surprise register. He was curious enough then to answer.

"Yeah, kind of. It's like a layer of their skin almost. It stays tight to their shape, like spandex pants, but the colors move all around. Like, like oil over water. Except when something's wrong." He said more solemnly. "Then the colors don't run over that area. Then it's just black there. It's like its' cut off from the rest of the bodies energy or something. I don't know. I told you it was weird." He said and I could feel him immediately wishing that he hadn't told us. I wanted to reassure him but Ethan was obviously going somewhere with his questioning and I didn't want to interrupt.

"Okay. That's a lot like what I see." He revealed and Jeremy's forehead scrunched up like he thought he was being punked again.

That made him more defensive. He fought back the only way he knew how. "That because there's something wrong with you too, Uncle 'Eaten,' *and* her." He said pointing at me. "I don't know what it is though. It doesn't look the same as the other sick people." Again, he had started out strong but he just sounded beaten and confused by the end.

"You just look *...weird.* Like *I* do. I told you, I'm sick too... So you see why none of this matters. Just leave me alone. I just want to be alone." He finished and he was feeling like he just wanted to go to sleep and never wake up and that *really* scared me!

I looked at Ethan with a desperate fear in my eyes and he was adequately spurred on. "Jeremy, what happened to you is permanent. But you can learn to live with it. You can learn to control it better. Maybe even use it to *help* others. It has a good side too, I promise. You just have to decide to find it. *Like I did.*" Jeremy opened his eyes again at that. Good, at least we had his attention.

"Do you remember what I was telling you before? About the virus that you had?" Jeremy nodded. "Well, I had it too. And so has Simone here." He said gesturing towards me. "You say that I look sick, but it's not the same, right?" He nodded again. "*Learn to trust what you see.* It doesn't just *look* different, it *is* different. What you can do now, what you see, it's not a sickness. It's a skill. A very special one. You just need to start looking at it that way. Tell me, what you see when you look at me." He pressed.

"There are no broken spots in the colors, they're just... *different*." He said, sounding unsure.

"Different how? Specifically?" Ethan pushed.

"Most people's colors are completely random, always mixing. Never stopping in one place. Yours are concentrated in certain areas. They don't mix as much, I guess you could say. Maybe it's the beginning of something, and it's just starting to die out there? I don't know." He was feeling a little more confident talking about it by then though. "But specifically," He continued, "You have almost all blue around your head, and *only* blue around your eyes, which is weird since they are grey." He said with a weak smile.

Was he actually making a joke? That was a good sign. "It doesn't really ever go away though. It just stays blue all the time. It just kind of gets darker and lighter." He seemed remorseful, like he was confessing to a crime and I guessed that he had seen it a while ago but had never planned to admit it.

"That's because that's where my skills are centered. My sense of taste, smell and hearing are all *heightened*, but my vision is the strongest." He said with a smile. "Okay. Now, what do you see when you look at her?" He asked, pointing to me. I suddenly felt over-exposed again, but I would suck it up that one time if it helped. Plus I had to admit, I was curious. Would he see what Ethan had claimed to see?

He looked over at me where I was still standing by the doorway, leaning on his bureau. "Well, she has prettier colors than you. That's for sure." He said, smiling a little, but it didn't last. "But her hands are mostly just red and gold. None of the other colors go there. I don't know why, but it's not right. Sorry lady." He said, obviously feeling bad for having seen it. He didn't know what it meant but he was sure about what he saw and so far everything he saw had all been illness based therefore bad. The biggest difference was that their color variations were temporary.

I myself wasn't so sure before, if I believed all of that or not.

I knew I did *then*.

Feeling him as he confessed made it all too clear. He wasn't in ca-hoots with Ethan. His pain was genuine. He was being honest when he said what he saw. I had to face that whether I wanted to or not. Anyway who was I, *an empath*, to *not* believe anything? I wasn't sure what it would mean for me or my life yet. But I did know that from that moment on I couldn't ever go back to not knowing. Even though I think that's what I had been hoping for, for some time.

"Alright." Ethan said with a slight smile of his own. Now tell me what you see when you look at yourself."

He didn't look down at himself when he answered. It was apparent that he didn't have to. "I look just like everybody else." He answered confidently, at first. "Until I look in the mirror and see my eyes." He said softly, like saying it out loud somehow made it more real. "They kinda' look like yours Unc." He said with a hint of a question in his voice. "Except that mine are always bright blue and yellow. *It's... just not right.*" He looked thoughtful for a minute. "It's permanent?" He asked then. Ethan just nodded.

"So the colors still run everywhere? On each of us? There are no black spots. No "dead" spots. The colors just don't mix, right? Okay, so if you think about it that way, then it makes sense for you to realize that we're not actually sick doesn't it? You see "energy" there, if you want to think of it that way, it's just a different *kind* of "energy" in those areas, *right?*" Ethan took his time, not wanting to push Jeremy too hard but I could see things starting to make sense for him at last.

He nodded. "I guess.

"So *I'm* not sick. I promise you, I'm the healthiest I've ever been." He said confidently and I couldn't help but agree silently. I didn't know him before, but I could find no fault with his physique as it was currently. Once I realized where my mind had gone, I proceeded to derail that particular chain of thought. I didn't want to go there. Thankfully, he was unaware of my wayward musings and he went on.

"Simone is not sick either Jeremy. I see the same thing around her hands that you do and I can tell you that it's been that way since the first day that I saw her. That was months ago, and she's still perfectly fine. It hasn't changed one bit and it's not going to." He gave that a moment to register and he stole a look at me while it did.

"So, if I'm not sick, and she's not sick, and you look just like we do... What do you think that means for you?" He asked and there was no way that Jeremy could *not* see it then. He was suddenly very relieved. I looked at Ethan and nodded just slightly, indicating that he had gotten the point. He continued.

"What you are seeing, what you are able to see now, are the *heightened* areas in us. Just like *I do,* but that's all I see and I know that you see so much more. Eventually you will learn to tell the difference between all the things that you can now see. You just have to be patient. That kind of refinement takes time." Jeremy was working on rearranging his point of view to fit what Ethan was telling him. Ethan gave him a moment to digest it all before he moved on to the next issue.

"Now that you know that you are going to live, you have to decide how you want to do it. Are you going to hide in your room for the rest of your life? Cause' from what I've heard, the ladies will be sorely disappointed to hear that." He said with a jovial elbow to Jeremy's ribs. His taunt had the desired effect though.

"No, I guess that wouldn't be fair to them, would it." He said with a half-smile. It faded just as fast though. "I don't know what else to do though. How am I supposed to go around acting normal when I can see things that I shouldn't be able to see? Things people don't want you to see! How do I do that?" He asked, starting to panic again.

"You'll be fine. Trust me." Ethan said in a very calm voice. "It just takes a little work and a little bit of help. That's where I come in." He said smiling again. I will get you the help that you need, from people who know what you're going through. We will help you in every way we can to get through this in one piece. It won't get better overnight Jeremy. I won't lie to you. But if you're willing to listen and accept the help that's available to you, it will get better. I promise." He was nothing but calm and encouraging as he spoke.

"How do you know?" He challenged, still unsure.

"I know." He said with no hesitation. "You're a smart kid Jer. Caring, too. The truth is that your skill is not an easy one to live with. But if anyone has what it takes to handle it, it's you. It's already part of what makes you, *you,* to begin with. It's always been there, to some extent. It's just a little stronger now." He finished with a chuckle.

"Hah! Try a LOT stronger!" Jeremy said, but he laughed too. I could finally feel a glimmer of hope coming off of him. *Ahhh.* If you can count on the young to be anything, it was resilient. "But I guess you could be right. I could *try* to get a handle on it, somehow. Maybe... With your help... I don't really have a choice, do I?" He was at least coming to terms with that.

"Nope, but that doesn't mean it wins. How you live with it is up to you from here on out. I'm going to put you together with the right people to teach you. They will help you develop other skills too, that will help you get back to as normal a life as possible, as quickly as possible and it *is* possible."

"Once you've accomplished that though, you still have to decide how you want to handle it. What you want to do with it. The good news is that at least that part is up to you. I have faith in you 'Jer Bear.' You're one of the good guys." He said while reaching over to rustle his hair like he was still a little boy.

Jeremy pushed him away but he laughed too. His mood had done a one-eighty since we'd first arrived. For the first time I felt like we could walk out of there and not worry that, one way or another, he wouldn't be there tomorrow. I really felt like he was on the road to being okay just by having someone who understood. Everyone wants to feel like they belong and that separation had been doing a lot of damage. I knew what Ethan meant then about "the window of time" before they were too far gone. I could tell that just having a sense that he wasn't alone anymore had gone a long way in bringing him back around. Again, I was so proud of Ethan for taking the time to do that for him.

It wasn't just Jeremy, either, I reminded myself.

He thanked me shyly as we left, and I smiled. "You're very welcome. Just hang in there, okay?" I requested and he agreed readily with a quick nod.

Ethan told Jeremy that he would be back in the morning to pick him up and get started, then we headed back downstairs. We talked briefly with Pete and his wife Helena. There were handshakes between Ethan and Pete, and hugs between him and

Helena. When he introduced us, she hugged me too. "Thank you! We're so grateful for your help. We just didn't know what to do anymore!" She was trying to be polite but she was mostly just worried. I could relate.

"Don't worry." I assured her. "Ethan will make sure he gets through this. Jeremy's very lucky to have such a great Uncle." I said smiling at him. Again, I really didn't have a lot of experience to back up those statements but I really felt confident that they were true. She had known him a lot longer and apparently had no problem agreeing with me.

"Yes. I think we're all lucky." She said without hesitation and I could tell that she was very fond of Ethan. I got the sense that she had not been on board with the plan to keep him away from him. She was very glad that it had all worked out and relieved that Jeremy wouldn't be going quite so far away after all. I could easily tell that, that had been the worst part for her. I certainly understood.

They talked a little more about Ethan coming in the morning around ten to pick up Jeremy and then we said goodnight.

It was fast approaching midnight when we got back in the car but as usual, I felt energized rather than tired. Still, I was quiet most of the way home. There were a lot of things for me to think about. Things that I couldn't put off anymore.

He finally broke the silence. "Sometimes the quiet *after* the storm can be just as scary." He said, referring to my silence. "Are you okay?" He asked. I could feel his genuine concern as he tried to comfort me.

"I know you weren't sure about all of this, but I want to thank you. I couldn't have pulled this one off without you. Jeremy is very lucky that you were willing to be pulled into this and help me despite your reservations. *I* was lucky. I mean that." He said quietly and he looked me in the eye for a moment to make sure I believed him. I did.

"You're welcome. I didn't really do much, though." I said, feeling silly taking credit for his hard work.

"That's not true. Sometimes the smallest things can make the biggest difference and your presence tonight helped in more ways than I had anticipated. I know you would prefer to stay in the background of life in general, but the truth is you could do a lot of good in my organization. If you ever changed your mind about all of this, that is." He was serious, but not hopeful when he threw it out there.

He had no way to know how much had already changed for me. He was about to find out though. My decision was made at last. On *that* issue anyway.

"Show me." I said simply, and looked him in the eye.

"Show you what?" He asked, confused.

"Everything. Now that I've gone and vouched for you, I want to know exactly what it is you do and how you do it." I just stared at him as he came to an abrupt stop in the middle of the road with his mouth hanging open.

Good thing there was no traffic at that time of night! *Geeze!* Alright, there was no traffic there during the day either, but there *were* occasionally other cars and stopping dead in the middle of the road was never really a good idea!

I just laughed. He was actually speechless for a second and a half, but that was all. It was fun to turn the tables a little for a change. I enjoyed it while it lasted.

Chapter 19

"Really!?" He kept staring, his disbelief evident.

"Really." I was the calm one then. "I'm still not sure how I feel about all of this. But I can't pretend that what you say doesn't make sense anymore, as much as I'd really like to." I said, ending in a mumble.

"Besides, after seeing what you go through just trying to help people like '*us.*'" I said purposely. "I'm hesitant to be yet another member of that '*resistance*' that you constantly have to go up against. Besides, I find that I'm suddenly very interested in exactly what it is you *do* to help these kids." I admitted. "I guess I just feel like it might be time to stop standing with my fingers in my ears yelling *"lalalalalala"* over and over, if you know what I mean." I took a deep breath. "But for now, could you please just take me home?" I asked with a grin. He grinned back.

"Absolutely! It's the least I can do." He said happily, but he was clearly still surprised by my revelation. "Wow!" He drove the rest of the way home without another word.

He was feeling surprise and excitement, but also confusion and he was trying to keep it under control as much as possible. I left him to it. There was still too much swirling around in my own head for me to discuss it intelligently with him yet.

When we pulled into my driveway I really wanted to invite him in, just for the company, but I wasn't sure it was a good idea. I knew I wouldn't sleep for some time and I could tell that he was just as keyed up as I was but I didn't know how he would take it. I didn't want to mislead him, since I still *hadn't* made up my mind about *that* yet. I decided it was too risky and was about to just give it up and get out when he did it for me.

"I don't know about you, but I could really use a nightcap. Problem is the packie's are closed, and my place is dry at the moment. I'd really hate to let myself into The Tavern after closing, just to drink alone. Normally I would just suck it up and go home, knowing a woman would never buy such a convenient explanation. Since we both know that I can't pull one over on you, I don't have to worry about that do I?" He asked with genuine amusement in his voice. It reminded me of my own thoughts earlier in agreeing to come out. "*Huh.* I really do like hanging out with you." He said honestly but with some surprise. "So what do you say? You up for a drink?"

He was right that I could tell he was being honest and it made me laugh. Especially since apparently he would *"see"* me *"checking."* What a pair we were, I thought with a shake of my head.

"Sure, come and keep me company for a bit. Truth is I was sort of thinking the same thing. It will take me a while to wind down now. Provided no one *else* calls me with an emergency tonight." I said sarcastically as I got out.

We climbed up the stairs and I kicked off my shoes at the top. He followed suit behind me. After that, he walked over and dropped heavily onto the sofa where I had originally been when the whole crazy night had started. "I'm having whatever you're having." He said as he laid his head back and closed his eyes. I could tell that he was checking out mentally, just for a moment. I knew the feeling.

I took out my ponytail and I walked to the kitchen. I sighed as I shook my hair out. I fixed us both my special concoction that I saved for days when I didn't want to mess around with sipping wine. I called it a "BomBright." It was basically my version of a gin and tonic, made with a higher end brand of gin that I liked, called *"Bombay."* Of which I used only the *"Sapphire"* variety. That part was extremely important since it was of a high enough quality that it wouldn't leave a hangover behind in its' wake. Also in my version, I liked to mix it with Sprite instead of tonic water. Just because I liked it better and I could. Finish with a wedge of lemon *and* lime. Wa-la! BomBright! Sounds complicated, huh? But that's what I liked about it. It was simple, but *good!*

I just had to be careful *never* to drink more than two. It was one of those drinks that went down so easily that you would have no problem downing three or four before you knew what hit you. And it *would* hit you, I had learned, *hard!* I would never make *that* mistake again.

I was busily making the drinks but I was really doing a good job of distracting myself from thinking too hard about *him*. Being there. Sitting on my couch. I wondered then, if maybe it wasn't such a good idea after all, but only for a second. I was tired, but wired and his company made me feel better. I decided I was beyond feeling guilty about it.

I brought the glasses over and set them down on the coffee table, then plopped down on the sofa. I pulled my socks off then tucked my feet up underneath me as I leaned forward to take a sip of my drink. I set it back on the table but kept poking at the fruit with my tiny straw. He opened one eye first, then the other, joining me mentally once again. He leaned forward to pick up his glass.

"Gin?" He guessed correctly with a sniff and took a sip. *"Mmmm,* that's pretty good. What's in it?"

"I call it a BomBright. It's my own special concoction." I said. "I could tell you, but then I'd have to kill you." I added completely deadpan. Until *he* laughed, then I broke character and laughed with him. I leaned forward and sipped my drink again. Then I put it down and leaned back next to him. "Nothing fancy I promise. So where exactly will you take him tomorrow? I asked, changing the subject.

He started with a deep sigh. "Well the first stop's sort of an intake evaluation, just to get the basics down. A complete physical exam of our own, along with a discussion about who our contacts are where he's involved. That sort of thing. From there it's a no-brainer. The next step is always the psychiatrist that I work with on these cases. He's a *height* himself and he's *very* good at getting through to frightened and confused kids. In the beginning they usually just need someone that they can talk to about it, more than anything else. Someone who will actually listen. No shock.

No judgment.

Acceptance is the first step on the list of things they have to accomplish. It's important and it's not always easy." He looked at me when he said that and we both smiled. "Once they get past that, it depends on the individual and their particular skill. What their needs are. Since Jeremy's skill is visual, I know one of the next steps will be a visit to a certain Ophthalmologist that I know for a much more detailed exam. Once we get those results and see how he's doing psychologically, we'll go from there." He was quiet for a minute after that while he was considering something he thought was risky. When he spoke again I was a little bit surprised by what it was.

"You can come with me if you want." He offered. "I think Jeremy trusts you already anyway. He might actually feel better with you there." He reasoned. "Even if it's just as a reminder of what he would be missing. It's definitely good motivation for him." He said and laughed.

Either way, I didn't need to think about it for very long. I was already emotionally invested in the outcome of that particular case. "I think I'd like that actually." I admitted. "If you're sure that I wouldn't be in the way." I added, lifting and turning my head to look at him.

He shook his head no. "I'm really glad that *you* finally decided to accept all of this too." He said, suddenly serious. "When did you do that, by the way?" He asked, both surprised and amused.

"I'm not sure exactly. Somewhere in between *you* telling me about the crazy things you saw in me and Jeremy *also* telling me that he saw the same thing. There's just too much about all of this that makes sense, that now I feel very childish trying to deny its' existence."

I looked him in the eye, serious myself then. "My parents had never experienced things like this before me. Not firsthand anyway. But they're strong people. They never tried to deny its' existence, just to make life easier for themselves. *Hmpf.* I hope to be half as good a person as either one of them someday. You'll have to forgive me for being a little slow though. I'm still working on it." I admitted honestly.

He looked at me for a long moment and I could feel that he was feeling extremely proud of me but I wasn't sure why it was so strong. I was busy puzzling that out in my head when he reached out to swipe a lock of hair off of my face and the innocent contact was like a match striking on my skin. I inhaled quite audibly before I could stop myself and that reaction set off a fire storm in him. He reached up further with the same hand and slid it behind my neck to pull me towards him. I could have stopped him. It was like it was happening in slow motion. But I found that I wanted to see what would happen next too much to do it.

He leaned in slowly, until he was only a hairsbreadth away, savoring the intensity. Then he finally closed the small gap, his lips landing squarely on mine. It was unexpected but so pleasant, that I still didn't stop him. He closed his lips over mine repeatedly in small, soft nibbles. It was slow and it was nice and it made me instantly want more. Just as I was about to fall closer to him in surrender, he pulled back abruptly.

He looked up into my eyes and I could feel both his surprise and his passion register. He sat back and sighed deeply, a little angry with himself. "Sorry." He said in a deep, quiet voice. "I didn't mean to do that." I could tell it was the truth but that didn't make it any easier to forget. I tried to catch my breath.

"That's okay." I said quickly. "I didn't mean to let you, so we're even." I grabbed our glasses and jumped up, heading back towards the kitchen. He didn't let me off that easily though. He jumped up too and followed me.

"Wait!" He said coming up behind me. He grabbed me by the shoulders and turned me around. When he did I backed another step away from him again. "No!" He said and pulled me back closer. "No more running, Simone. *Look at me!*" He insisted.

I set the glasses down but I was afraid to look up. I wouldn't even deny it then. He could tell. As usual. He placed his hand under my chin and gently lifted it until I was reluctantly looking him in the eye.

"So we already know that we're both interested *involuntarily.* But that's not what I want. I want you to *tell me* that you want this as much as I do. Completely *voluntarily.* All of this back and forth is too confusing. I'm too old to play these kind of games, Simone." He said honestly and I couldn't fault him for it. Hadn't I thought nearly the same thing about myself just recently? I did always appreciate straightforwardness, I thought bitterly. He didn't stop there.

"You need to be honest with me, once and for all. With *yourself.*" He moved in closer to me before he continued. Then when he was standing right up against me, he asked. "Do you want this, or not? Am I alone here? If I am, just tell me and I'll go. You *know* I will." His voice was quiet and very serious.

I could barely breathe with him standing so close and I still had no idea yet what I wanted to do about my feelings for him, if anything. But I did know one thing for certain by then. If I was really going to be honest with myself, I had to admit that I didn't want him to leave. *Damn it!* It had just been way too long since I had wanted to be that close to *anyone.* I didn't know how to fix that though, other than the obvious. It wasn't fair. I sighed in surrender.

"You're not alone." I reluctantly admitted, but I stopped there, still unsure. The heat that was sinking into my skin through our clothes was nothing compared to the waves of desire that I was experiencing. And they weren't just his.

Who exactly was I supposed to be kidding, anyway? It was ridiculous to try to deny the attraction between us. We were adults, after all and it was obvious that we both felt it.

I was tired of fighting it. I wanted more too. But the problem was I still wasn't sure *how much* more I wanted. I was more afraid then, of what would come *after.*

I had just very recently become single again. I would never have the same type of casual attitude towards sex that Vivianne enjoyed, but I wasn't ready to go straight back into a full-blown commitment either. Was there some kind of *"in between?"* Should I try to find out? I wrestled with those things mentally while he waited patiently.

If my body had a separate vote, than there was one for yes already. If you counted Viv's, I guess that made two. *Oh what the Hell...*I thought finally! *Life was short!* I wondered what I was waiting for anyway, a guarantee that I wouldn't get hurt again? Yeah, I was at least smart enough at that point to know that, that was not likely to materialize.

At that thought, I made my decision. I lifted my hand and slid it over his shoulder and up to the nape of his neck. From there, I spread my fingers up into his hair. The dark curls were soft and thick and I grabbed a silky handful to hold onto. He was so big and so full of masculine energy, that the ridiculous softness surprised me a little and made me smile. His eyes closed halfway but he was still looking at me. Still waiting for an answer.

"I don't know how much I want to get involved. I'm sorry. That's the truth." I paused to make sure that he understood. He didn't leave right then though so I took a breath and continued. "But I do know that I want you *to stay.*" I finished quietly but intently. "Is that alright?" I asked, wondering how he would respond. Thankfully, what I felt from him never wavered.

"That's more than alright." He said, sliding his hands up onto my hips to pull me even closer. His lips were very close to mine again then. I was suddenly remembering how good they had felt and I could no longer resist them.

"Good. We finally agree on something." I said as I pulled him closer with my hand behind his head and I leaned up on my toes at the same time. I brushed my lips lightly across his and he groaned a little, deep in his throat. His lips were also surprisingly soft and he moved them slowly over mine again, savoring our first *intentional* kiss.

It was funny to me when I thought about going from our first kisses, straight to our *first time.* But I think we both knew all along that one would lead to the other. Things between us had been on a slow burn for far too long. I was smart enough to know by then how that would end. I had some experience in that area after all. One spark and it was gonna burn hotter than last years' Christmas tree on the campfire!

Right at that moment, I was on board with that! As long as I was truly going to let go of the last of my reservations and indulge, it might as well be worth it. I had tried for so long not to think about that happening, or about how it would feel. But once it was happening, I suddenly couldn't think about anything else! I found I was okay with that too.

His hands left my hips but only to reach up and hold

gently on either side of my head while he kissed me back. He then began to trail kisses down the side of my neck. My head fell back even more and my eyes drifted shut. His left hand slid lightly down the side of my neck and then across my shoulder. When he reached my tank top and bra strap, he slid his nimble fingers underneath and pushed them both down my arm. His lips followed then, very lightly, over the newly exposed skin.

I was shocked by how sensitive that generally ignored area was. The sensation was remarkable and I felt it reverberate all the way down to my core and back out again where it settled intensely in the palms of my hands. That familiar tight ripple ran through them, making me gasp just a little at the pleasure of it. I closed my fists tightly with the desire to hold onto it, even though I knew it was futile. My breath came faster already and my knees actually felt a little shaky.

"Unless you plan to hold me up, we'd better move this to a more suitable location." I said in between breaths. He just laughed.

"*Mmmm.* I can do that." He said, and I could tell by the determination mixed in with his passion, that he was only half kidding. I didn't even try to process that.

"But hold on just a sec. *Hmmm. That* was certainly interesting." He said slowly, surprise evident in his voice.

"What?" I asked, curious what he was so amused by.

"*Your hands!*" He said taking one into his and flipping it over, palm up. "I saw it in the hayloft too, but I didn't realize it was *connected!* He held my hand there while he came forward and grazed his lips against mine. I was trying to figure out what he was talking about but he was making it very hard to concentrate.

"What?" I mumbled against his mouth. He just ignored my question and kept on sliding his lips back and forth slowly over mine. I wasn't even kissing him back then. I was just holding my lips still, slightly parted, while he rained wonderful sensations over them. It was incredibly soft and amazingly slow and when he finally connected fully again that last time it felt so good that it swept right through me and ended squarely in my aching palms again.

"*That!*" He said looking down at my hand that he still

held. "I've certainly never seen *that* before!" He said with an amused grin. "That's *amazing!*" He said and looked back up at me.

"You can *see* that?!" I asked, totally incredulous. No one had ever even understood its' *existence* before, and he could *see* it?! "How? It's not me using my empath abilities. It's just a physical reaction. How can you see *that?*" I wondered out loud.

"*Hmmm.* That's some reaction!" He said with his eyebrows raised and a sly smile. "But I can see it because it's connected for you. A lucky coincidence for me, I'll admit." He was obviously very pleased with the circumstances.

"It's unusual, I'll give you that. But it makes sense if you think about it. Your skill is rooted in your ability to *feel* things." He held my hand up again and drew small circles in the center of my palm with the pad of his thumb as he spoke. "The fingertips and the palm of the hand are the top tools that we have to *feel* what exists around us. We test first with our fingertips. It is not until we trust and embrace something fully that we allow ourselves to feel it with our more vulnerable entire palm. Hence the whole, '*More than a palm-full is a waste,*' cliché." He smiled. "Not that I believe that for a second." He said with a wink at my "*more than a palm-full*" physique. "But it makes one understand where the notion comes from." He just grinned as he went right past it.

"Anyway, because you have *height* energy in your hands already, the energy there is visible to me, even when that energy changes gears. By default, I can see the new energy too, because it exists in the same area. Right in front of your 'open window.' *It's fascinating* really!" He said with his grin reaching epic proportions.

"See, the *height* colors that I see always react and change just slightly with people's state of mind. It's the only way I can hope to do even a tiny bit of what you do and tell what people are about. It really only works if I know what their "*normal*" is to begin with though and that takes time. So it's not a totally reliable system for me, but I pay attention to it and I'm always trying to improve on it. I have to say though, of all the different color combinations that my gift has allowed me to see over the years, *this* particular blend is *by far* my favorite!" He insisted, looking very pleased.

"*I could watch your hands light up all night!*" He added

with a very satisfied smile, kissing first one and then the other. "All I have to do is keep *making* them light up." He said into my neck and I did almost collapse then. He just held me tighter. *Man* that felt good!

I lifted both arms up over his shoulders. Then I bent my elbows and clasped my hands behind his head. With them out of sight momentarily, I had his undivided attention again. My lips found his and our kisses suddenly weren't so soft anymore. The height difference was a little tough on my neck until he lifted me up and wrapped my legs around his hips like a reverse piggy-back. A *piggy-front* I guess you would call it. I really wanted to laugh at that thought but his kisses were drowning out the areas of my brain that controlled simple things like laughing and talking. Again, I was okay with it.

I was also surprised by the ease with which he held me. I was never the girl on the top of the pyramid. I was always the sturdy one on the bottom. Being held so effortlessly was new for me, but I couldn't really focus on that for long either. He walked us towards my bed while he kissed me and then he gently set me down beside it.

As my bare feet came to rest on the floorboards, I looked up at him questioningly. "We're stopping here?" I asked, clearly surprised.

"*Mmm hmm.* For a bit." He answered vaguely. He slid his hands around my waist and then ran them slowly up under my shirt and over my ribs. He hooked his thumbs on the outside of the bottom hem of my tank top and lifted it as he went. He paused and looked up at my face when he reached my bra. I smiled slightly, lifted my arms and he continued slipping it up and over my head.

Okay, I get it, I thought nervously. I wasn't usually big on things like letting someone else undress me, but I was too mesmerized by his attention to want to stop him, *again.* He sure was fun to watch.

His hand slid down over my collarbone. He continued with just his index finger, slowly, down along the center of my breast bone. He reached the clasp that happened to be in the front on that bra, the first one I could reach to throw on earlier, and he easily unsnapped it with one hand.

"Showoff." I accused lightly.

"You ain't seen nothing yet, sweetheart!" He said with a wicked grin in a deep, raspy voice. He ended that with a wiggle of his eyebrows. Again, I wanted to laugh but it wouldn't come. I could feel how serious he was and a shiver of anticipation went through me instead. *Damn!* I tried to close my hands again, to draw his attention away from my overly obvious pleasure but he wouldn't let me. He slid his hands through mine and opened my fingers back up. Then he left them open at my sides while he went back to his task.

I felt a little nervous, a little over exposed then, which I was getting used to with him. It wasn't in a bad way and certainly not because of my impending nudity. I was actually much more content in my own skin then than I had ever been in my youth. I still had things I was working on, but I didn't beat myself up over them too much anymore. I was okay with "me" by that point. No it was an *emotional* vulnerability that he had made me feel and *that* was scary dammit! Still not scary *enough* for me to stop him though.

He looked down at the unsnapped bra and slowly slid his right hand up under the black lace fabric and over my bare skin underneath. His palm warmed my skin where he touched me and my eyes closed of their own accord. His thumb was the last part to pass as his hand finished its' trip across my breast and it was just the right height to brush the tip of it on the way by. My breath rushed instantly, like I'd been passed through by a ghost. He slid my bra down my shoulder and off of that arm. I opened my eyes again and I took a shaky breath, wondering how much more of that I could take.

I hadn't always been able to enjoy being so bold, so open and uninhibited. I'd had to work up to it over the years with Ben by building comfort and trust. I had no idea why I felt it so easily with Ethan, right off the bat. I wasn't sure if it was just part of my getting older, or if it was simply him that brought it out in me. Either way, I found that I *was* enjoying it. A *lot!*

His left hand came up on the other side then and slid under the remaining material to sweep it away. I was eagerly anticipating the contact that time when his thumb made its' way by, but he carefully avoided the contact at the last second. I was so physically aware of what I was anticipating that I felt the *absence* of his touch just as surely as I had his *actual* touch. It was *staggering!* I just stared at him wide-eyed while I tried again to catch my breath.

He smiled at me and brought my hands up to his lips and kissed each palm appreciatively. I could feel how much he was enjoying teasing me. He released my hands again and reached up to slide the second strap off my other shoulder. My bra fell to the floor, immediately forgotten. Then he pulled me closer and bent his head to my chest. When the heat of his mouth covered the formerly neglected spot, I gasped again and instantly forgave him. I would have fallen back on the bed right then. If he had let me.

"Not yet." He whispered deeply, holding me tightly to him. "I've waited too long for this. I'm taking my time, remember?" He said slyly, and I wasn't sure if I was glad or annoyed.

I just groaned. "What are you trying to do to me?" I asked impatiently.

"Oh, I think you know exactly what I'm trying to do." He responded with a wicked smile. "And if you let go, and *let* me, I promise I will do my very best to succeed." He said in a soft but serious voice and I had no doubt at all that he meant what he said!

"Far be it for me to stop a man on a mission." I said with my hands up, acquiescing to do things his way. I realized then though that, that was a whole other tantalizing position for him. It made me instantly hotter, watching him, watching me. I was sure my hands lit up quite nicely again just then, but it was too late to try and hide it.

He smiled broadly. "That wasn't so hard now was it?" He said jokingly and I did manage a chuckle that time before his hands found my waist again and the laughter died in my throat. He undid the button and then the zipper on my jeans but he didn't try to remove them. Instead he slid his hands inside, around my hips and down onto my lower back. He bent his head to kiss my neck again and then his hands went lower still, until they were tucked snugly inside my jeans, happily cupping my backside between the denim and the thin cotton of my underwear. He let out a soft groan into my neck before he gave up on that distraction. He used the leverage he had to pull me closer once again and held me tightly to him while his mouth came back up and devoured mine some more.

"Does this work both ways?" I asked breathlessly, when we came up for air. I slid my hands up along his sides and inside his t-shirt. I had yet to see his body bare but I had already known that he was a fairly healthy guy. Even three layers of winter clothing he wore when I first saw him couldn't hope to hide that. Still, I was a little surprised by the completely flat, rock hard stomach that I found, quivering lightly at my soft touch. It was really quite impressive for someone who *wasn't* a *"just-grown, young man"* anymore. I was curious about the severity of that, but I was momentarily more amused by the effect that my super-light touch was having on him. "Someone ticklish?" I asked with a devious smile.

"Nope." He answered quickly, with a telling grin. Even without the smile, I would have known he was lying.

"Hmmm... Really?" I said disbelievingly. I ran my fingertips even more lightly up his sides and his abdomen shivered even stronger than it had the last time. "Not ticklish at all, huh?" I teased until he finally confessed.

"Alright, alright! Maybe just a little." He chuckled. "I'll do whatever you say! Just stop. *Please!"* He joked. I just raised my eyebrows at his surrender agreement. He was surprised himself.

"Hmpf. Sleeping with someone you can't ever lie to could be tricky, huh?" He realized out loud.

"Hah! You have no idea! *Really."* I said, a lot more solemnly in the end. It didn't seem to reach him though. His mood didn't change at all. But he could tell that mine had.

"Simone, it's not an issue for me." He said calmly, with no trace of regret or deceit that I could feel. "Do you want to know why? Because I can see that you're reluctant to believe me, but it's simple really." We were still standing together by the bed and he took a step back and held my hands in his. He looked back up at me then and said with confidence. "I'm not afraid of the truth." He leaned in and kissed my lips lightly. "What am I feeling now?"

He asked with no hint of embarrassment at his finally-freed passion. "The bottom line is, I have nothing to hide. *Not from you,* anyway." He said with an easy shrug of his shoulders.

"However much of me you decide you can take..." He winked then went on. "...you are more than welcome to." He finished with a smirk.

"Really?!" I said sarcastically, in a very obvious *"seriously?"* kind of tone at his dramatic boast. It was actually more of an *"Awe c'mon!"* kind of thing, but he replied *very* seriously.

"Really." He said softly, which was much more effective than if he had shouted and I knew that he was referring to his remark about his openness and not his genitalia. It was a funny thing to joke about though, I thought to myself. Especially when he knew that I would find out, one way or the other, momentarily. I just shook my head.

"Why?" I couldn't help asking, even though I knew his response had the potential to ruin everything.

"I don't really have a good answer for that. It's just the way I feel. There's no point in trying to put on airs around you, so I don't have to bother with any of that. It's actually a relief to have one person that I can completely relax around. Be myself. *All* of myself, with no secret parts to keep hidden. It's very refreshing for me." He admitted, clearly surprised. *"Is that alright?"* He asked in the end, mimicking me again.

I didn't want to fall into the trap of constantly comparing him or anyone else that I might date, to Ben. But it was obvious to me then how completely different the dynamics would be with Ethan where my skills were concerned. It was like night and day. That was also very interesting.

I wasn't sure if it was really possible for him to look that good *and* say all the right things, but since he was currently pulling it off I decided to just go with it. I pushed the rational worries and fears into the back of my mind and hoped they wouldn't find their way back out before daylight.

"It's more than alright." I replied quietly, mimicking him back while I pulled myself up to him again.

He brought his hands up to pull my face closer to his and

kissed me. I grabbed his shirt and pulled it up and over his head. Then I slowly slid my aching palms across his stomach, careful not to tickle him. Well, at least not *much*. Just enough for it to be fun for me. I didn't torture him though. That was not the feeling I was going for. I slid my hands up his chest and over his bare shoulders. *Geez! He was in good shape all right!* Even in my head, I couldn't help another mental *"Damn!"* from slipping out.

I leaned closer and let my lips wander across as much of his chest as I could easily reach. Then I leaned up on my tiptoes, so I could reach more. I slid my hands down his smooth back and pulled him even closer to me. His skin was as hot as a rock in the sun and like a happy lizard, I instinctually wanted to be closer to it.

His breathing was coming faster by then too and I felt his passion reaching higher and higher levels. It swept into me and lifted me up a little more each time it passed through. As it flowed in and out, it continued to mix with my own growing desire until soon I couldn't tell them apart anymore.

I pulled back and I tilted my head up. I grinned at the fun I was having. Still wanting to be touching more of his skin with my own, I arched my lower back and pulled his hips closer, until our bare skin was touching at our navels. I leaned in closer, slowly. Rolling up a little at a time, until our bare chests finally came together as well.

He started out watching, with a smile on his face. But once I rested completely against his chest his eyes closed and his hands tightened, pulling my hips even closer to him. It felt so good that I reached my own hands down inside his jeans and pulled him closer too, while I rose up on my toes in a valiant effort to reach his mouth. He met me half way and groaned as we kissed and things began to pick up pace.

His hands weren't satisfied with caressing me through cotton anymore after that. He pulled back and stood straight, holding me at arms' length. I didn't like the distance already.

He reached the tips of his fingers under the elastic at the top edge of my underwear and then slid them apart, across my navel. *His* super-light touch sent a shiver through my entire abdomen and he enjoyed the *Hell* out of that! I just smiled. He didn't pursue it, but I could tell that he filed the information away for future use.

His fingertips followed the inside edge of the waistband all the way around to the back. There he flattened his hands against my hips, looked me in the eye, and then slid everything down at once. He bent at his knees and squatted down in front of me. I stood still while his strong hands slid down my legs. When he reached my ankles, he carefully lifted one foot, then the other and slid everything off in one pass.

I wasn't sure how I remained standing while he made his way back up. He didn't hit any vital areas specifically, but everywhere he touched me felt so good that he may as well have. His kisses made a trail all the way up my inner thigh and the heat of his breath set it on fire! My legs were actually shaking a little by the time he stood in front of me again and I suddenly felt overwhelmingly vulnerable once more.

Again, it wasn't about being shy. I actually caught myself wishing it was that simple. No, it was the unexpected intimacy of it all that startled me the most. The way he made me *feel*. It was powerful, and new and beyond my control. That was a tough one for me.

That was part of what made it both perfect for me and a perfect *disaster* at the same time. It was so rare for me to give up my hard won control. The fear that I had tried to shove down, had made its' way back up and it must have shown on my face for a moment, because he stopped suddenly. He stood tall in front of me and tilted my chin up again. It was fast becoming a habit I noticed.

"Hey. You still with me?" He asked gently.

I nodded. I was petrified of what it might come to mean and apparently not very good at hiding it, but I didn't want to stop any more than he did. He was right about that too. I did want it just as much. And it was time to accept that and deal with it somehow. I also needed to reassure him of that, once and for all. My own fears and weaknesses were just that.

I grabbed his belt loops and pulled him a step closer to me. "I think I'll feel better once we even things up a bit." I said calmly while I tried to undo his jeans.

He ignored my hands and focused on my face though, annoyingly. He also kept my chin tilted up and focused on him, so that I would have to look him in the eye again eventually. I could feel him waiting and as much as I wanted to ignore it, I knew it was impossible. I gave up on the button for the moment and hung my hands from his belt loops again. I finally gave in and looked back up with a sigh of impatience.

"Simone. Are you alright?" He asked seriously. He refused to just breeze over it and let it go. At first I was pissed that he was being so stubborn, but then I felt the deep sincerity in his concern. That unfortunately made a lump form in my throat and that made it so much worse.

I nodded but closed my eyes and breathed for a second while the flood of emotion passed.

"Are you sure?" He asked worriedly. "We don't have to do this. Just say the word. I promise I'll survive, *somehow.*" He said with his own hands up then as he laughed a little. "You know how I feel about this." He added more seriously then. "I meant what I said, Simone."

"I know." I opened my eyes and smiled at him. "I'm okay, Ethan." I said, calmer then. *"Really.* I wouldn't be here if I wasn't. You should know that much about me already." I said with a confident grin. Then I sighed deeply. *"But thanks."* I added sincerely, pulling him closer. "It's just... part of the joys of being me. Sometimes it's all just a little too much, you know? I just needed a little breather." I said, trying my best to explain.

"Besides all that, it's been a while. It takes a moment, to... *readjust."* That was honestly the best I could do with it just then and I really hoped it would be enough.

I took a deep breath and continued, a little more convincingly that time. "It's nice to know though, that my new lover is so thoughtful." I said with a smirk, hopefully making it clear once and for all that I was *not* changing my mind. I reached up behind his neck and wrapped my arms around him. The skin on skin contact finally did the rest for me. He was on board again.

I slid my hands down his back and inside the waistband of his jeans, which represented the last of the clothing at that point. I slid them around in between us, careful that time not to tickle him. He seemed grateful. I slid my thumb along the edge of the button and pushed it through the hole. He didn't try to stop me but he was still holding back quite a bit. I wasn't sure why, but I was not. Not anymore. I was done waiting and he would just have to catch up. I was also done with the pretense, I just slipped my hands right under his tight boxer briefs.

That is when I knew for sure that he hadn't really talked out of turn with his boasting. He wasn't Ron Jeremy proportioned, or anything nearly as ridiculous but he was definitely a healthy man with no reason for hang ups. Well, at least not anatomy-wise. I leaned up to kiss him and he finally responded wholeheartedly once again. His hips rocked closer and closer with every sweep of his lips. I reached around and I slowly pushed the denim and cotton fabric down over those hips a little bit more each time they came closer to me. It didn't take me long to push it all off completely.

Again I thought, my mind wandering slightly as usual, it's all about the balance. Right? Some aspects of his life had been a curse. Pure hell. But in other areas, clearly one could say that he had been blessed. *Balance.*

While I was prepared to be an appropriately appreciative fan of his newly revealed anatomy, I wasn't ready for the up-close and personal introduction just yet. Fortunately for me, I was dexterous enough to finish the job with my feet. I pushed his clothing the rest of the way down and kicked it away when I was done. He just stepped out and laughed at my reluctance to bend down in front of him. I didn't know about him but *I* needed a little time to warm up to such things. One hurtle at a time.

I found I wasn't the only one who was appreciative of the view.

"God, you're beautiful!" He said breathlessly while stepping back and staring openly. I was relieved that he thought so. Even though I wasn't the same tight little hard-body that I had been before Liliana came along necessarily, I had spent a few years doing some real, hard work to get back to where I was then. Content and comfortable in my own skin again.

As reassuring as it was to know that he actually agreed, it was still a little embarrassing to stand around discussing it. I tried to distract him at first, but when I looked back at him *looking at me*, I forgot the rest of my inhibitions completely.

Not only were his words having an unraveling effect on me but I could also *feel* his genuine appreciation and his rising desire *physically*. He didn't even need the words, the overall effect was quite the seduction. I was staring openly at him and I couldn't help returning the compliment.

"You're pretty easy on the eyes yourself there mister." I said, putting it *ridiculously* mildly. Nature had obviously been good to him but he had clearly not taken it for granted either, I thought as I took in the sight of *all* of him. He was in *really* good shape. Did I say that already? *Geeze!*

"It's just my way of trying to outrun father time." He answered modestly.

"Well, it seems to be working, so I won't tell him where you're hiding." I said playfully. I was surprised at how easily we were holding a conversation, of sorts anyway, while standing in nothing but what God gave us. But as soon as I thought the thought, he reached the end of his patience. *Finally!*

He came forward and held my face with one hand while he kissed me again. Harder that time. I let out a sigh and when I did his tongue swept inside and across mine and I felt him finally let go. *Really* let go! When he did, it hit me like a *MACK FUCKING TRUCK!*

I'd thought that he'd been letting it go *before* but *boy* was I wrong! I understood then, why he had still been holding so tightly to his control earlier. Because when he let it go fully, my knees suddenly felt as useful as cooked pasta! I was actually afraid that I might not be strong enough to stay standing any longer and I reached my arms around his shoulders to hold on.

The intensity coming off of him eased back a little and I opened my eyes. He stared back at me and held me tighter. Instantly the intensity flared again. I let out an involuntary gasp and held tighter around his neck. My palms were throbbing and I was struggling to hold on. I took a few deep breaths until I could feel it ease off again.

When I opened my eyes a second time he was a little calmer. He was trying to reign it in a bit. *Phew!* I took the opportunity to get a nice deep breath in. Then he reached down with both arms around my waist and lifted me up again. There was nothing to come between us and our *"piggy front"* that time but the heat. Suddenly that name didn't do it justice anymore but I was too preoccupied to try and think up a better one.

I was immediately thankful that he really *was* strong enough to hold me up! He obviously hadn't been kidding about that. Once I knew for sure I could relax, I let go completely. My head fell back and I let my breath out with my chin hanging slack like I had lost all muscle control. He had one arm underneath me, holding me up. The other one came up my back and held my head for me while he kissed my neck some more.

Just then a memory flashed through my mind of a very similar scene I had unexpectedly imagined once, on his first night there. *Huh,* was all I had time to think, before he lifted my head back up and our lips met again, beyond hungry for each other then. *Starving!*

He turned toward the bed at last and rested one knee on the mattress, then he laid me down in front of it. I was *extremely* grateful at that moment for the soft bed beneath me and I was sure that, that sensation was also no mistake. He was *very good* at what he was doing and for a moment I wasn't sure whether I should be repulsed by his extensive experience, or if grateful was the correct emotion.

Grateful won out pretty quickly. I had a past too, after all. If all of that was the means to bring us to that place, where we could make each other feel like *this? Well* then it was all both necessary and worth it as far as I was concerned. *Well worth it!*

I was grateful for his experience and wisdom once again, when he reached down to where his pants were and retrieved a very important accessory from his wallet. It was so nice not to have to ask.

When he finally came down over me at last, just the weight of him pressing me down into the soft mattress felt like heaven. I reached my arms up around his shoulders and let out a satisfied, closed-mouth sigh into the crook of his neck.

I was pretty flexible, both figuratively *and* literally, and generally game over the years to try new positions. I haven't had a *ton* of action or anything but I like to think I get my fair share. Life is short and all of that.

But no matter what I have tried in the name of fun over the years, I have always remained a big fan of the classic missionary, man-on-top position. I know, not very exciting right? Wrong.

There's just something about the warm, enveloping weight that is *deeply* satisfying in some very primitive way. I imagine it's a lot like how most people would absolutely hate to be completely bound up tightly, head to toe in a blanket. But to a newborn, nothing feels more secure.

Likewise for me, a great weight pinning me in place would normally send me into a massive panic, never mind my finding it pleasing. But for some reason when it was the full weight of the right man, at the right time, nothing was more satisfying. I knew it wasn't the sexiest position or the most adventurous, *but if it ain't broke...*

I could feel him, resting against me then and it was obvious that he was more than ready but he didn't attempt to go any further. He looked down at me, breathing heavily. His feelings practically boiling over. He was reluctant to let go and dissolve down into them just yet though. He was having too much fun still. I smiled up at him.

He reached his right hand over my head and up under my hair on my right side. He raked his hand through my hair, pulling it up and off my neck. He swept it across the pillow. Then he brought his hand back so he had one on each side for leverage again.

I could feel the breeze from the ceiling fan hitting the newly exposed area and it felt wonderful. Then he bent down and started to slowly kiss and nibble that side of my neck and that felt *even better!*

He pulled back up onto his arms after that and looked at me hungrily. "I'm not going to lie. I've thought about this once or twice." He grinned. I grinned back. He was lying.

"Alright. Maybe I've thought about it a *lot!*" He admitted reluctantly. "Sometimes it was so hot, even just in my head, that I would wonder why I was torturing myself." He looked down at me and I could feel his appreciation for the situation fill me. "But being right here, right now, all I can think is... *Hmpf! I wasn't even close!*" His breath came faster at saying it out loud. So did mine. The intensity from each of us ran through me and I breathed it in.

He leaned back down then and spoke softly next to my ear. "And that it was well *worth* the wait!" He said emphatically and I couldn't agree more! I could *feel* exactly what he was describing, from *both* of us, so it was quite easy for him to make his point.

"I was too afraid to go there." I admitted with a laugh. "I actually tried really hard *not* to think about it." Then I looked up at him again. "*Much.*" I admitted in the end, and we both smiled.

"I'm afraid I won't be able to *stop* thinking about it now though." I said more warily, softly, next to his ear. That admission was a little harder to make. I instantly went from being afraid to commit, to being afraid he would think I was too clingy. Thankfully, he reassured me quickly enough that it wasn't necessary.

"*Good!*" His support was deep and vehement. He pulled back and looked me in the eye. "Because I don't see myself feeling like I've had enough of you any time soon!" He kissed me again and the intensity took us over completely then. There was no more witty banter after that. The only sounds then, were the involuntary ones that escaped on their own.

A while later I was happily lying on my stomach, practically in a coma, with my head on a pillow near his thigh. He was half sitting against the headboard, running his fingertips lightly up and down my back. We rested there, perfectly blissful for a while before he broke the silence.

"I'm gonna go." He said softly. "Let you get some sleep."

I thought about it for a minute. I could tell he wasn't trying to run out once he'd had his fun. I already knew him too well to believe that anyway. He was worried about me for some reason. I was dead tired, but I didn't want to throw him out once I was done either.

"You don't have to leave." I said, thinking maybe he just didn't want to crowd me.

He looked back at me for a minute, clearly surprised.

"Thanks." He said seriously. "But I *do* have to go. Because I want you to get a few hours' sleep while you still can." He said, and then his mouth was by my ear again as he leaned in closer. "And as long as I'm here, *you're not going to.*"

I felt a familiar tightening deep down, at just the memory of what he was suggesting. *"Mmmmm...* Yes, I definitely think you should stay." I said with a smile, even though I was too tired to keep my eyes open for very long. He just laughed.

"I'll be back around seven to get you, okay? He slid out of the bed and got dressed as he said it.

"Mmmm." Was all I could manage at that point. "Seven..." I lifted my head, reached to turn on my alarm and dropped back down again. "See you then." I may have been asleep before I finished my short sentence. I couldn't be sure.

Chapter 20

I slept like the dead and when I woke, I felt brand new even though it had only been a little over four hours.

I put on a pot of coffee and quickly jumped in the shower. When I got out, I called up Mack and asked him to oversee things for the day and possibly the next couple. I just told him some personal stuff had come up but I'd be back before they missed me. Of course he knew that there was nothing happening yet at the site except for deliveries and clearing anyway. Truth was, he could handle the next few weeks without me but I wouldn't be busy that long. I thanked him, hung up and got dressed.

I had a moment of indecision then, since I had no way of knowing what type of attire would be appropriate. I finally just settled on jeans, but I paired them with a fitted black, V-neck sweater and my tiny flat black sneakers that could almost pass as shoes. I figured it was close enough to either end of the spectrum of dressy and casual, to pass.

I was ready by 6:55 and I was pretty pleased with myself. I threw my phone and a house key in my small black pocketbook and downed the last of my coffee. I was downstairs waiting when Ethan pulled up.

"Good morning, beautiful!" He said with a broad smile and I was suddenly a little embarrassed, remembering everything that had happened between us the night before, there in the light of day. I know I blushed but I refused to act like I was unhappy about it. *Any* of it.

I noticed then that he was wearing his normal attire. He

had on dark grey jeans, a deep blue t-shirt and his black boots. It seemed I had done fairly well on that choice anyway. So far so good.

"Good morning." I replied. "Did you sleep well?" I asked teasingly while buckling my seatbelt.

"Not long, but *well!* Yes, v*ery* well." He smiled deviously at me and I could tell that he had been surprised by that for some reason. I didn't get it, and I said so. He answered me easily as usual. At first anyway.

"Eh, sometimes I have a little trouble sleeping. No big deal." He started to laugh it off, but he stopped himself. I could tell that it had been a knee-jerk reaction, something that he had gotten used to saying. He looked at me and smiled a little. He decided to start again.

"Actually, I guess I qualify as somewhat of an insomniac." I could feel that there was still more to that but he changed mental gears too quick for me to really get it. As soon as he looked at me again with a hungry look in his eyes, I completely forgot about my curiosity. "But I seem to have found a prescription that works wonders for me." He raised his eyebrows and the devious smile was back.

"How about you? How are you feeling today?" He asked. "Let's start with emotionally. *Any regrets?*" I could tell that he was really worried about that and I was relieved to be able to answer honestly.

"Nope." He was very pleased by that, I noticed.

"Okay. Then next up, how are you feeling today, *physically?*" He asked that part with one eye closed as if he was afraid of the answer. "Um... *Too rough?*" There was actually some pink in *his* cheeks that time. I smiled and looked up at him through lowered lids. I didn't trust my voice just then but I happily shook my head no again.

"*Phew!*" He said playfully. "Because quite honestly, that could get worse before it gets better." It was a genuine warning. He was serious. *Holy...*

"Okay, *focus!*" I said, bringing us both back to the task at hand. "I thought you told Jeremy ten. Why did you tell me seven?" I asked, purposefully changing the subject. Thankfully, it worked.

"One, I have to get things ready. And two, we need breakfast." He just grinned and looked back at the road. It was apparent that he wasn't going to be forthcoming with more information than that.

Whatever, I was content not to ask for once. For the moment anyway. As I sat quietly, lulled into relaxation by the steady hum of the engine, I did wonder warily what on Gods' green Earth the day would hold.

Was I ready? Oh well, it was too late then. "In for a penny, in for a pound." I thought to myself. Then I laughed at the ridiculousness of that and Ethan just eyed me curiously. I wondered why in times of stress, those silly cliché's would always pop into my head.

Anyway, I was committed to helping Jeremy at the very least. I would just have to see what that meant and take it from there. I started to enjoy the drive. We wound smoothly down the wooded roads for a while, sun shining in the windows. I found myself thinking again, how all those roads look the same in the warmer months, once the greenery fills in and covers everything from street to sky. I was happily watching a hawk that was flying slowly overhead when I finally noticed that he had slowed down. I wondered if an animal had run in the road or something, because I didn't know why he was slowing. Then, unexpectedly he turned down a road that I hadn't even noticed was there!

"*Whoa!*" I said, clearly surprised, flipping my head back and forth to take it in. "Where did *that* come from. I've driven down this road a hundred times and I've never even seen this road before!"

He grinned again. "Been right here the whole time." He looked at me and then explained. "People tend to see only what they are looking for. No one's looking for a road here, so they don't see one. Unless, of course, *I tell them* to." He said meaningfully. I turned my attention back in front of us, watching as he appeared to be driving into nothing but wilderness.

We continued slowly down the little one lane dirt road that had nothing but forest on either side, as far as I could tell. Even in the winter months, you wouldn't see anything there but

L. Pelletier

the trees. After about a mile and a half of winding back and forth, we finally came up to the first man made thing I had seen, a metal crossbar blocking the little road. He pulled out his phone and touched the screen a few times and it swung open. We drove through and he touched the screen again and I watched it close behind us. I still didn't see anything yet to keep people out of.

He touched his screen a few more times as we went, but I saw no obvious reactions anywhere that appeared to be connected to his actions. Apparently though I was realizing, there was a lot more going on there than met the eye. I sat in anticipation, feeling the excitement build as we rolled slowly on. He just watched my face and the small road intermittently and smiled quietly, giving nothing else away.

After about another mile, it opened up. I could see three buildings then, set back on the left. All under the darkness of the towering evergreens. They were log cabin type houses, but more grand, like a golf course clubhouse or a ski lodge. They were log cabins on steroids. In front of us there was what looked to be a fenced off riding area. That was the only thing that was out in the open, and except for some weathered piles of lumber, it was currently empty and looked abandoned.

On the right side there was a row of what looked like extra-large storage units, also tucked completely under the canopy of trees. All had oversized garage style doors, and were painted completely in a camouflage pattern that made them blend in nicely with the forest behind them. I just looked at Ethan with a surprised look on my face. I felt like a little kid seeing the North Pole. I was slightly giddy even, but I was willing to admit that it could possibly just be an after effect from the night before. A chill ran through me again at the sudden memory. I shook it off physically and he noticed. I just grinned and looked away. *Focus,* I reminded myself.

He touched his phone again and the first garage door opened up. Just that one unit was about the size of my apartment. The walls were covered with various power tools and shelves full of plastic bins. The floor was also half full with various toys. Snowmobiles, motorcycles, and four-wheelers covered every inch of the left side. But a big part of the right side was perfectly clear and his car fit comfortably.

He pulled in and parked and we stepped out. He walked around to my side and held out his hand to me but didn't say anything else. I took his hand and let him lead me out of the garage. He left it open and we crossed back over the dirt road to the buildings on the other side. He pulled up a few more screens on his phone on the way over and I wondered what he was controlling then, but I didn't bother to ask. There was so much else I wanted to ask first.

"Where *are* we?" Was the first question, the *need-to-know* side of me finally winning out.

He chuckled. "Welcome to our "Camp of Great *Heights.*" He said with a flourish of his arms, the child in him that gave the place that name shining right through. I suddenly thought about what an irresistibly, adorable little kid he must have been. I could almost see it. I just shook my head at the typical wayward thought. Something about him literally made me act like a crazy person sometimes.

There were three cabins side by side. They weren't painted in camouflage like the storage buildings were, but they were the next best thing. They were made up of deeply stained, dark wood and artfully done stone work that appeared as a natural extension of the forest. "It's beautiful. You really seem to be serious about your shade though." I said, referring to all the buildings being tucked so tightly under the trees.

"Keeps us invisible to satellite." He explained. "'Google Earth' is very popular these days." He said with a smile. "From the sky, all you can see here is woods. If anyone did notice anything, or find the road, they wouldn't get past our 'security.' If they decide to check online to see where they can't drive, all they will find at the end is an old, unused riding paddock. Those are a dime a dozen around here." He explained.

Looking at the cabin, I could tell that the windows were tinted and I noticed that they also appeared to be non-reflective. The closer one looked, the more obvious it became that nothing there was accidental.

"All this is for helping *heights?*" I asked, finally giving in to using his terms.

"For the most part." He answered. "Essentially it is here to accommodate *heights* in need, and it does. When I take in someone new, they will often stay here in the beginning, while they get a handle on things. It's easier to absorb all of that internal upheaval, if you take away all of the external turmoil for a while. Let them focus on one thing at a time. Then there are the rare times that we need to keep them safely hidden for one reason or another. Here they can generally stay invisible for as long as we need them to." He seemed uneasy about that, but didn't go into any more detail on the subject, so I didn't ask.

"The main goal though is always to get them back to living their normal lives as soon as possible. So their stay here is only as long as necessary. It's empty a lot of the time in between." I was spinning slowly in circles, taking it all in while he talked.

"I tend to come here even more then. To be alone." He said with a shrug of his shoulders. It's very peaceful. So technically, it serves dual purposes." He reached out for my hand again and when I took it, he pulled me toward the cabins. "Come on. I'll show you." He said with obvious excitement.

I smiled back a little more nervously as I followed him up the stairs of the center cabin.

When I stepped through the door that he held open for me, I was surprised by the modern interior. It had an open floor plan with a living area straight ahead and a kitchen off to the left. There were two more rooms on the right behind closed doors. The high, vaulted, beamed ceilings were covered in a high gloss varnished wood that looked to be cedar. The walls were done in a soft gold throughout. There was a stone wall that rose from the center of the building that was really a large stone chimney for the built-in fire place. It was designed with glass doors on both sides so it could be enjoyed from either side. The large space was full of beautiful furniture pieces that looked handpicked. Most surprising of all was how well-lit it was by just the skylights that dotted the ceiling, despite its' placement deep under the thick canopy of trees. It was still bright and uplifting but also very comfortable and cozy. It had a *homey* vibe.

"How is it so bright in here? I don't get it." I said looking confused as usual.

"I used a special type of skylights." He explained looking up. "They're designed to make the most of even the lowest amount of light. It's done partly by catching light from greater distances with mirror's and reflections and partly by amplifying the little bit of light they do pick up." He explained.

I walked straight through to the back wall that reminded me of my apartment a little, being that it was all glass. Only that one was a tall, "A" shape of tinted glass instead of a wide, clear, rectangle. Looking out through the glass, I could see a long back lawn that reached down to what had to be the Merrimack River! I was shocked to see that there. "We're on the river?" I asked, clearly feeling disconnected. He just smiled, since the answer was staring me in the face. There was a good size dry dock housing also, hanging high under the trees where It wouldn't be visible there from the river or the air. It looked large enough to house more than one water-craft.

"You sure do seem to have quite the selection of transportation options." I said with a smirk.

"It's good to have options." He answered with a grin of his own. "You never know when you might need a backdoor, or a plan "B." He was walking with me but not crowding me, just letting me explore.

"I like being here. I like the solitude of it. Our neighborhood is *great*, don't get me wrong. I'll never sell my property over there. But sometimes I just want to go where I don't have *any* neighbors. Just for a little while. *No offense.*" He said apologetically as he came over to where I was standing then.

"None taken." I said truthfully. "I certainly know the feeling. Look where I live. I don't even know who my neighbors are unless they come and tell me." I reminded him with raised eyebrows. "And, for the most part, I *love* that."

He just laughed.

He came up behind me then, and wrapped his arms around my waist. "Why don't you take a walk and have a look around. I'm going to call in the troops." He paused to nibble on my neck. "Then, I'm going to make you breakfast while we wait." He moved my hair back and ran his tongue lightly up the back of my ear and a chill went through me.

"Mmmm. Or I could just have *you* for breakfast. You taste pretty damn good." He teased, whispering in my ear. It felt *really* good to have him holding me, but it was still a little unnerving as well.

"No way!" I said twisting out and turning to face him. "I was promised food and since I don't see a Dunk's out here anywhere, I sure hope that cooking proves to be yet another of your many amazing skills." I challenged. As usual, he was undaunted.

"Of course! You don't think I keep this physique living off of drive-thru food, do you?" He joked. It made sense though. As far as I knew, he lived alone. He would pretty much have to cook or eat out twenty times a week. I loved to cook but I still chose the *let-someone-else-make-it-for-me* takeout route at least a few times a week just to break it up, but my waistline often paid the price.

"I will happily be the judge of that!" I said with a smile. "So go. Call. Cook." I said turning. Any deadly security traps that I should know about before I go wandering around aimlessly and set one off?"

"Not at the moment." He said with a wink, but I could tell that he was totally serious. I was sure then, that was what he must have been doing on his phone. I just rolled my eyes and headed towards the door in the center of the glass that led outback.

As I walked out onto the wooden deck, the birds in the nearest tree flew up and away, one after the other, giving the illusion that they were connected on a long, invisible string. It was another nice spring morning. There was a slight chill, but again it was one that would burn off during the day, you could tell. I strolled across the deck, taking my time.

There was a built in grill and a fire pit on the right side of the deck. There were also four low, love-seat type benches surrounding the fire pit with fat square cushions in a simple beige fabric. There were more benches built into the front and side railings bordering the low deck as well, as if it could seat a great crowd if necessary.

I walked down three steps to the brick patio at ground

level and I could see a full size built in pool further down in front of me. It had a solar cover over it. I didn't know how much sunlight it would catch down there but it certainly seemed to work well as a leaf catcher anyway. I looked up into the tall trees surrounding me then and I noticed that everything I was seeing was under the cover of various shaped camo-print tarp's that were hung high up in the branches.

They were arranged at different levels, like real trees would be, and seemed totally random. But I could tell, looking up, that when put together from above they would fit together like puzzle pieces and cover everything underneath them. I could also see from where I stood that they had fake leaves woven into them to make them even more invisible. I marveled at the set-up as I passed. It actually reminded me a little of what I was working on at the Gardens and that made me smile. I was thinking suddenly, that if he knew what I had planned, he would definitely approve.

Once I stepped off of the patio, I could see the back of the other two houses, and except for the pool, they looked much the same. So did the trees above them. Okay, so they did gather in the woods, but at least they did it in style and with true stealth. I could appreciate that.

All of it reminded me that I still needed to ask Ethan exactly where all the money came from. I wouldn't say that it was thrown around there lavishly or unnecessarily, but it was quite obvious that nothing was half-assed or cheap. That spoke volumes.

I continued on down by the rivers' edge. There was a rock wall where the grass stopped and it dropped about four feet down to the sand. I stood at the top, looking towards the shore. I knew the river was much better suited for boating than for swimming, at least around that area. Not that I could recognize specifically where on the river it was! I didn't even realize the road we were on ever came that close to it.

I had been up and down the river a handful of times on friends' boats over the years, but I didn't recognize that section at all. There were no other structures visible anywhere near there that I could see. I tried to do the mental geography and place it in relation to the landmarks that I knew, but I was too disconnected way out there to do it successfully. It really was a beautiful spot though, wherever it was, I decided and gave up.

After what couldn't have been more than about twenty minutes of sight-seeing, I heard a loud, high-pitched whistle and I turned back toward the main house smiling. When I got back inside, I could smell coffee and bacon and I was immediately ravenous. There was also something else, something wonderful. As I came around the wall to see the table that he had set, I found the source of the fabulous smell.

"Pancakes! Oh yay!" I said appreciatively. "Are you serious? How long was I gone?" I asked, clearly surprised by the spread.

He laughed. "Well I cheated on the bacon. I had some I had already cooked and I just threw it under the broiler for a few minutes. But the pancakes are from scratch and I'm not responsible for any addiction that may occur as a result." He joked.

We both sat down and it didn't take me long to see what he meant. "Oh my God! That's crazy! *What's in these?*" I asked through a mouth full of the lightest, yet sweetest pancake I'd ever tasted.

"I could tell you, but I'd have to kill you." He joked back to me and we both laughed.

"Is everything I say to you going to come back and bite me in the ass?" I asked with a chuckle and a shake of my head. He just grinned and chewed and wiggled his eyebrows.

We carried on a conversation, but it was slow, and sporadic. Stunted in between bites. It didn't matter. It was still informative. "*This whole place is crazy!*" I said after I swallowed. I still can't figure out exactly where we are, but I know that we can't be more than like, fifteen minutes from town?! *How!?...* ...can all of this be *here,* on the river without anyone noticing?" I asked incredulously.

"It's a lot easier than you would think. People just aren't as curious as you assume they are. For the most part, they're just too busy. They drive right by without ever noticing. Some on a daily basis. They are on their way to work or home or to their kids' soccer game. They're not sightseeing off in the woods. They're basically just wishing that the guy in front of them would go faster or just turn somewhere already." He provided honestly.

"Hah! You have no idea how right you are!" I said thinking of some of the very strong emotions that I tend to pick up while driving in traffic. I laughed and then shoveled more food into my mouth. *Mmmmm!*

He took a bite of bacon before he continued. "They cruise right by the high dock ninety percent of the time. If they do happen to catch a glimpse, they have no way of knowing who owns it. And even if they *do* wonder, there's no way to trace it. The land is all in the name of trusts and corporations, and the road is not on any map. It's invisible, and unreachable without an *expressed* invitation. It doesn't exist." He forked some pancakes into his mouth and chewed happily.

I just shook my head back and forth again while I ate. "Wow, this really is good. Alright, so you can add cooking to your resume as well. Is there anything that you *aren't* good at?" I asked through lowered lids with loads of innuendo in my voice. He grinned mischievously.

"Not that I'm aware of." He boasted playfully and we both laughed. He grew more serious after that though. "But I'd better tell you that you *need* to stop looking at me like that right now. Unless of course, you don't mind not having a *shred* of clothing left on your beautiful body when the team shows up here in..." He looked down at his watch, took a deep breath. "...less than ten minutes." He looked back up at me and grinned like the Devil himself. He said it as if he were joking, but we both knew that he was not.

I allowed myself to wonder for a second just what the *"team"* would have to say about that. I would have laughed but then I made the mistake of picturing it myself. Just for a second! That was enough. I was suddenly very conscious of my hands and the feelings throbbing through them. It didn't seem like a good idea to advertise that though, since I had every intention of being fully clothed when I met these people for the first time. I placed my fork and napkin down on the table and then slid my hands underneath it and onto my lap. I took a deep cleansing breath and pressed them, palms down, onto my thighs.

He let out a low groan and said, "That's probably smart."

He shook himself physically and then got up and took our plates to the sink. "Come on." he said, turning back around. "Come help me get set up.

I took another nice deep breath and then stood and walked over to lead him out the front door that he held open for me. We walked down one front porch, across the dirt and up the next. I could see though, that it was just the outside that was the same once we entered. Unlike the last cabin, the far right cabin was not designed to look like a home on the inside. It was all business. There was a medical suite on the left where the kitchen would be, and another that looked less clinical and more therapy related on the right. The back area again was a large, open space. It was mostly filled by a four piece curved leather sofa set, that put together, made a circle. It looked like an obvious choice for a *"group therapy"* area. That, or a place for all of the different doctors to sit together and have a pow-wow.

He walked in ahead of me and held the door again. I followed him in and waited while he went into the room on the left and switched on the lights. "It's not quite as bright in here unfortunately. Over here we needed privacy and separate room's more than natural lighting." He explained.

He kept moving as he spoke, turning on lights in the side rooms and made his way over to the circle. Apparently it would be the conference option that we would be utilizing. We sat down and he touched the screen of the remote sitting on the table and it came to life. There was a slight chill left to the early spring morning and I heard the heat kick on. He touched another button and a fire sprang up in the fireplace that unlike his, was built into the far wall of that cabin. I thought of something then. "What about the chimney and the smoke?" I asked wondering how he could hide that.

"It's a real burning fire, so it gives off real heat but it's a gas fire. Clean burning. No smoke." He explained. Unless someone is using a scanner that looks for a heat signature, which no one should have reason to do around here, it's still invisible."

He kept going, turning on the rest of the lights as well as the ceiling fan to spread the heat around faster. I looked up as it turned on. The memory brought me right back to the night before under my own ceiling fan. Visions of his long chiseled frame intertwined with mine flew through my head and I struggled for a second to find the strength within me to wipe them away.

I could easily see him traveling along the same train of thought. Just as I considered sitting on my hands the front door opened and I was glad for the distraction.

Phew! It was a *crazy* situation! I had no idea how to handle having someone who could *see* my strongest feelings all the time! Once again he had much more access to me than I had ever intended to give him. He sure had managed to turn the tables on me. But when I thought about it, I had to admit that it wasn't really his fault. He was as much a slave to his ability as I was to mine. I also knew that there was absolutely nothing that I could do about it. Aside from not being around him and that wasn't so appealing an option anymore. Though I wasn't sure how I felt about that realization *either.* Dammit.

"You in there, 'E'?" A male voice called from the entrance.

"Yup, come on back, Dr. J." He called out.

"Does anyone besides me actually call you Ethan?" I asked with a perplexed smile. I was even more curious when I remembered that I hadn't always called him Ethan either. I didn't say so out loud however.

"Sure. *I think.*" He answered, looking like he didn't bother to notice. He shrugged his shoulders. "Morning Dr. J. How goes it?" He greeted his new arrival warmly.

"It goes, 'E,' *thankfully*, it still goes." He said and laughed at his own joke.

"Dr. J, I'd like you to meet Simone. Simone, this is John Jeffries, or Dr. J, as we all like to call him. He's our irreplaceable *resident* psychiatrist. He leaned over the table and reached his hand out to mine and I shook it. It was a big hand, as he was a tall man. He was on the thinner side though. He had slightly graying, short curly hair and an Abraham Lincoln looking beard. I guessed he was somewhere in his late fifties. He even had the round, rimless glasses that one would expect. His handshake was firm but his hands were soft. His nails long, but neatly manicured, like someone who played a guitar. He was dressed in a short sleeve button down shirt and pleated trousers. The shiny leather loafers finished the look. It was slightly reminiscent of Mr. Rogers' style but somehow on him it worked.

"*The* Simone? From The Tavern?" He asked looking slightly surprised. I was pretty sure I looked the same at the moment. *Ethan had talked about me?!*

"Um ...yeah?" I said looking to Ethan with a furrowed brow.

"Well, then. I'm not surprised." He said, like that explained everything.

Huh? I looked over to Ethan again and he was just smiling at me like I had finally realized there was no Santa Claus.

"I may have mentioned you once or twice in conversation." He said with a shrug of one shoulder, but it was obvious that the nonchalance was just for show. He laughed, but then he came clean. "Sorry, but I spent a lot of time trying to figure you out. I had to talk to someone! Dr. J here is a very good listener."

"Oooookay." I said but that was all I had at the moment. He sat and Ethan handed him a folder and I was temporarily forgotten.

"Honey, I'm home!" Came a female voice next from the doorway. I looked up and saw a beautiful, thirty something looking redhead come sauntering in. I felt her surprise when she saw me.

"Oh, are we already at work?" She asked. From her slight embarrassment, I could tell that she was wondering if I was the new *height*. She was wearing dark blue jeans and a mint green thermal Henley shirt under a plaid blue button down. She had the sleeves on both pushed up and the top three buttons undone. It was easy to see that she would also completely blow the *"more-than-a-palmful"* theory. I instantly wished that I hadn't noticed but it was hard to miss.

She was wearing a pair of Timberland hiking boots but still managed to look womanly in them. She sat with one thigh resting on the back of the circular sofa, waiting to be filled in and looking completely at home. For some reason I was extremely aware of that. Good or bad, I wasn't sure. *Her* feelings were carefully neutral at that point.

"No. Roxy, this is Simone. Simone, Roxy, our all-around "Medical Specialist." *Hmmm.* No *"Dr."* Roxy? I wondered silently.

"Ohhhhh! Simone, Simone? She said with a sly smile at me.

We stood and shook hands. We were both sizing the other up. I barely needed my skills to tell that.

"She's helping out on this one." Ethan said and I noticed he couldn't help but smile to himself at that. I was glad for that small bit of encouragement because I was wondering again just then, if it was all really worth getting involved with. *Was I crazy?*

"We discussed some of the different types of skills that are known to be connected with the hands." He said to me by way of explanation, while pointing his chin at Roxy. *"Hmpf!* Who knew I'd find a whole *new* element to add to the list..." He said smiling. He said it quietly and mostly to me, but no one had missed it. *I* knew what he meant, but I could only guess what they would *think* he meant and I just rolled my eyes again.

I cleared my throat and tried to be personable despite my embarrassment. "It's nice to meet you. Both of you." They smiled back at me expectantly, like parents watching a child on prom night. I wondered again what the big deal was. I took another deep breath and looked at Ethan again with wide, questioning eyes. He just laughed. But then he threw the remaining folders down on the table and diverted everyone's attention. *Thank God!* He could be generous when he wanted to be.

"Alright folks! Incoming. Jeremy Hoffmann: Age, 15. We do have parental consent but also a deadline to show results. One week. No prior therapy. ETA: 10:00. Skill is visual. Category: *now-defined.* He has the ability to visually detect any and all physical abnormalities. That includes illness*es* as well as *height* recognition." They all locked eyes when he said that. It seemed he wasn't the only one who was surprised and/or upset by Jeremy's fate. He continued, all business. "New onset: Approximately four months. DOI: early this past February. I've downloaded what we have for medical files to date onto the system. Roxy you're up first, but keep it as quick and painless as possible. He's still pretty fragile right now, especially where doctors are concerned.

"Got it." She answered all business then too.

"The most important initial psychological work up will be up to you, Dr. J. He's going to be spending most of his time with you at first, in fact. He's new and he's still working on step one." And to both, he said. "He's a friend. The son of a *good* friend." I could tell by the looks and the feelings around the table that, that was also unusual. And apparently a *really* big deal.

"This one's going to be a little tougher than normal folks. "A" games all around, okay?" At the end of his little speech, everyone got up and they each went off in their own directions with a nod.

He took my hand again and stood up. "Come on. Let's go get our newest camper."

Chapter 21

We went outside and headed back toward the garage. "What's 'DOI'?" I asked, my curiosity winning out as usual.

"Date of infection. It's not an exact science, but there is a rough time line for the way these things tend to develop so it can be important to us when treating someone. At least in the beginning.

I just walked quietly next to him, rolling it all around in my mind. I automatically headed for the open garage, but as I got closer it closed. I looked back, surprised and saw him on his phone again. I could feel his excitement and I was suddenly dreading whatever was behind door number two. I was too quick to judge though, I realized. I was pleasantly surprised by the sleek, black, SUV that was revealed as the metal door rose silently.

"We're gonna need room for luggage." He said. With one more screen, the vehicle bleeped and unlocked. *Handy.*

Climbing up into the spacious cabin was the opposite of getting down into the F1. I slid across the leather seat and felt like a small child in an adult sized chair when I buckled my seatbelt. I looked over at him and noticed that he fit quite nicely. It was funny to me then as I thought about it, how comfortably he fit in the F1 at his size. I wondered waywardly for a minute if he'd had to make modifications for that to be the case. A customized F1. Yeah, I'm sure that was *wicked* cheap! Was that even possible? I wouldn't be surprised at that point I realized. He took the keys from the center console and started it up. It didn't take us very long to get back to Jeremy's house, but we did have time to talk on the way so I finally had a chance to bring it up.

"Wow. Nice." I said rubbing the heated leather seats appreciatively. "That reminds me of something I keep meaning to ask you." I said with my eyebrows raised at the luxurious interior. "Where exactly does all of this stuff come from? These things that you have scattered about here don't come cheap." I stated with amusement.

He looked at me and was thoughtful for a minute. "I built the Camp originally on my own. It was a combination of money I had saved from working, some of my inheritance and some money that I had from a court settlement." He looked at me again. "But I think I'll save that story for another day, okay?" He asked honestly and I could feel his deep sadness for just a minute, and then something else.

Whoa! What the hell was *that?* I wondered as it flashed through me. He was quick to squash it but I felt it for just a split second and it wasn't good. Then I wasn't sure I even wanted to know. I nodded.

"Okay." I said. He continued like it hadn't happened. Or like he was used to ignoring it. *Hmmmm.*

"I don't charge the *heights* that I help. I do it because I want to. But it wasn't long before people who became involved one way or another wanted to donate to the cause. It means different things for different people. Some give of their time, expertise and knowhow. Like the good doctors you just met. They also occasionally donate some of the equipment that they need to use, like x-ray machines and defibrillators." He made a left turn then continued.

"Others donate services, like installing state-of-the-art outdoor security systems." He confided with a smirk, confirming my earlier assumptions. "Then there are those who have nothing to barter but they have more than enough money to share." He was feeling protective of them when he said that. I wondered why, but not for long.

"Believe me. When someone has everything they could ever ask for materially but still can't help their own child, it starts to mean nothing to them. Their money and their status can't get them the specialist's they need. But *we* can. They would give it *all* away by then, if it would make a difference." I understood then, that he accepted the donations to help the parents feel like they were doing *something!* As weird as that sounded, it made sense.

"At least here, they don't feel so powerless anymore. They know we can help their children when no one else could. So they do whatever they can to help us. Who am I to turn away the help that others want to offer to the cause? I always put any resources donated to the Camp, *into* the Camp. One way or another. *Always.* With that, I've been able to make improvements here and there and it has accumulated over the years." He was very matter-of-fact about it.

"I'll say!" I agreed. He was very comfortable with all of the tools he had at his disposal, but I could tell that he thought of it all as just that. Tools. Things he might need to do his job.

"How long ago did you start the Camp?" I asked next.

"It will be ten years this fall." He provided.

"Is everyone associated with your organization a *height?*"

"Most. There are *norms* too though. Parents, as well as the occasional sibling, related professionals interested in contributing, that kind of thing. Oh, that reminds me of another important point I need to mention. If you should run into an associate from Camp somewhere else, you don't know them. Unless of course, you happen to have another reason to know them. Understand?" He asked. I nodded.

"That's just standard policy. Complete discretion is imperative. Our attitude is, 'You don't have to worry about saying too much if you just don't say *anything.'*" He turned another corner then looked at me intently and I could feel how important it was to him.

He looked back at the road again. "I trust you Simone. I know you would never do anything to jeopardize Camp on purpose. I just need to make sure that you understand. I've worked very hard over the years to keep this a safe place for *heights.* It's important that every single person involved with it feels exactly the same way. One mistake, one person tells the wrong person just once and we could lose everything." He looked back at me again for just another second.

"Wow. No pressure or anything." I said, trying to break

the tension a little but he wasn't amused. "I understand Ethan." I
assured him seriously then, holding up my hand to stop his
complaint before he could voice it. "I know all too well the value
of saying nothing. Believe me. I have been very good at it, for a
very long time. Well, with everyone but you, anyway." I tried to
sound like I was joking but I think he knew I wasn't. He also knew
me well enough now to know that it was true, and that I would
not have told him about myself if he hadn't told me first. Even
then, I hadn't wanted to confirm it. Yes, I could tell he felt secure
that the strength of my stubborn need for privacy would carry
over to his cause as well.

"Alright, let's go see how the Hoffmann's are faring this
morning." He said with a smile. I felt him relax again. He could
tell that he had gotten his point across and he was moving on. I
was happy to follow his lead.

He put it in park and we got out. As I climbed down from
the high seat, I felt a little like Jack descending the beanstalk. The
dogs greeted us again as we hopped down onto the driveway but
much more happily than last time.

We pet them as we walked up to the door. It opened as
soon as we reached the top step. It was Jeremy that time and he
was ready. His bags were all packed, sitting by the door. He
looked excited and like he had actually slept, at least a little. I felt
his mood lighten when he saw me. I was glad for that. That I did
help in some small way. There was a new hope coming off of him
as he stood there holding the door and it was very reassuring to
me.

It was obvious that his parents had noticed the change
already as well, and they were feeling at least reservedly hopeful
too. They weren't *confident* or anything, but they did have hope.
It was more than they'd had yesterday.

We didn't waste as much time on pleasantries that visit. A
few quick kisses between him and his parents, hugs all around and
we were off. We helped Jeremy with his things and were loaded
up and back in the spacious SUV in under five minutes.

No one seemed to question the fact that I was there, so I
didn't bring it up. I was relieved. I still didn't know what I would
tell them if they asked me more specifically what my place there

was. The truth was, I didn't have one. Yet I still felt the need to be there. To make sure that he was really okay. I had been where he was and I knew what was on the other side of okay. I couldn't help the need to keep him away from there.

We drove back into Camp and I watched as the whole amazing introduction played out again, but for Jeremy that time. I enjoyed watching his face light up as much as I had felt Ethan enjoy watching mine. It was hard to believe that it had been just a few short hours ago. It was very interesting to me how quickly I had flipped from one side of the coin to the other. I found myself thinking that it had been *far* too easy. Was that good, or bad?

I watched as he spun in circles in the middle of the clearing in an all too familiar way, taking it all in. It was almost as if I could feel the ripple in the fabric of time by switching perspectives that fast. It was a strange thought and I was glad to let go of it when Jeremy finally spoke.

"Wow Unc, I can't believe you never brought me here before! This place is awesome!" He said and Ethan chuckled.

"Someone seems to be feeling a lot better today." He said to Jeremy.

"Yeah, I guess. It's like you said. It is what it is. I just gotta learn how to deal with it, right?" He was still a little despondent but nothing like the day before. His spirits picked back up again while he looked around. "But I guess if I get to do that here, that's pretty cool at least!" His smile was back. He was actually a handsome kid when he wasn't so depressed. I could see then for the first time, why he did so well with the teenage girls.

We went inside the public cabin with the offices and the introductions were made once more.

"Dr. J is going to be your best friend here for a while." Ethan explained. He's not only a top notch adolescent psychiatrist but he's also something else. Can you tell me what?" He asked lightly, testing him.

I could see Jeremy looking up at the doctor and squinting just a little bit. He was nervous, but not about his answer. "Um, a *height ...person ...thingy?*" He answered feeling a little more sure of himself.

"Yes, I'm also a *height.*" Dr. J answered for himself with a warm smile. "That's very good, Jeremy. You're a quick study." He said with a warm smile. I could feel his self-confidence lift up a notch at the compliment.

"I'll see you in a bit once Roxy has had a chance to get your initial exam done. Don't worry, it's nothing too intense." He assured him with a warm smile. "Our initial talks won't be either. We just want to make sure we're getting the basic facts, so we know that we're going about helping you in the right way. That sound okay to you?" He asked gently.

"Yeah, alright." He answered, a little less wary than before.

"Excellent. Then I'll see you in a bit." He said, and then he went back to his office/exam room.

Ethan continued with the introductions.

"Jeremy this is Roxy." He said, holding back his grin.

He was looking at Roxy already and I could feel his arousal register pretty quickly. I just smiled and turned my head and looked away as if to give him the privacy that I could not. Of course, Ethan noticed. He smirked and shook his head silently in amusement.

"Hey Jeremy, are you ready?" Roxy asked him sweetly.

He just nodded. He looked at Ethan again and then he walked after her as she headed back towards the front of the cabin. I watched as he followed her into the other exam room and she closed the door.

"She going to be okay in there?" I asked with a laugh and a look back at the closed door.

"Oh yeah. Don't you worry about Roxy! She's been dealing with that sort of thing for a very long time. Since middle school actually." He said reminiscently and I was instantly a little jealous. I didn't miss the fact that he remembered *exactly* when the attention had started. But I reminded myself that I had no reason to care about that or to protest in any fashion, so I let it go.

"She'll let him moon just long enough to get what she needs out of him. Then she'll set him straight." He laughed. "I actually feel kind of bad for him." He admitted, as if he remembered from experience. I hoped then that he did. "It's just another rite of passage he will have to get through here and the sooner the better."

We hung out while Jeremy finished his exam and his initial session with Dr. J. As we sat together on one section of the semi-circle sofa, I remembered another question that I still didn't have an answer for. "So tell me about the nickname." I said with a smirk.

He looked back at me and then at his watch like he was wishing he didn't have time to explain but we both knew that he did. I just shook my head. "Ut uh mister. Answer the question." I challenged.

He laughed and laid his head back to stare at the ceiling. "Alright. It's really dumb though. You're gonna be sorry that you asked." He warned but I wasn't deterred. I just stared and waited. He laughed again but eventually began the tale.

"Well, I met Pete when I was turning eighteen. It was a pivotal time for me and Pete was the first real friend I'd had in a long while outside of the Kent's. With all the issues that I had, I was a bit of a late bloomer when it came to girls." I looked at him and my expression clearly stated how hard I found that to believe. It was his turn to be undeterred.

"We clicked right away as friends, but Pete was almost two years older and always wanted to go out looking for girls. I was working pretty hard at the time. As soon as I would finish for the day, he would show up and want to go out. I on the other hand, always wanted to go and get something to *eat*. I was still a growing boy then." He said un-apologetically. "And so after a while as a play on my name, he just started calling me *that*. C'mon *'Eat.'* Let's go *'Eat.'"* He would say, mimicking me. "Get it?" He shook his head. "I told you it was stupid." He laughed.

"Anyway soon after, he met Helena and a few years later, Jeremy came along. When he was first learning to talk, he would hear some people call me 'Eat' and he would hear others call me 'Ethan.' He was not even two at the time when his little brain combined them. Then he started calling me 'Uncle Eaten.' I don't think *he* even knows why!" He laughed harder. "But my friends enjoyed the joke so much that it stuck. Aren't you sorry you asked now?" He wanted to know.

But I wasn't and I shook my head no. That was probably the most that I had managed to really learn about *him* so far. I was grateful for the insight. I just grinned.

"So Roxy and the good doctor both seem to know about me and my *skills*. Does that mean that it's okay to ask you about theirs?" I wondered out loud.

"Well, it depends. Sometimes that can be tricky. Asking them about you was more of an... ...*emergency* situation." He said with a half-smile. "The emergency being that I wasn't able to figure you out on my own." He laughed then. "Normally though it's more of an individual thing. Like with Roxy. Bottom line with her is, if she wants you to know she'll tell you." He laughed a little at that but rolled his eyes like he wouldn't mess with it. "I'm sure you have no problem understanding and respecting that though, right?" He asked me with a knowing grin. Of course he was right. Fine, I thought pouting just a little.

"Dr. J on the other hand doesn't mind at all. He's never been one to keep it from other *heights*. His openness is a big part of why people trust him so easily, especially since you would be hard pressed to decipher his skill otherwise. It's an intellectual skill. Meaning it originates from a certain area of his brain, one of the many that we as modern day humans don't usually utilize." I digested that.

"In his case, he has the ability to grasp any given social situation completely. Not only from the many different angles of each participant, but also in its' entirety as it stretches out through wave after wave of resulting reactions. Most people would lose sight of the cause and effect of a situation after it's once or twice removed from the central figures. But Dr. J can perceive the effects of an action through *generations.*" I could tell he was impressed by that but then so was I. I had never even conceived of such a thing.

"It goes a long way in determining what makes someone tick and how to best reach them when they have been seemingly, irreparably damaged." He said, clearly feeling admiration for him while he said it. I also felt that deep dark... *something...* again. Just for a second, but it was there. He didn't stop to wallow in it though, and just as fast it was gone again. He kept going.

"He really is invaluable when it comes to helping *heights* assimilate back into the real world, after things become decidedly *unreal.*" He was quiet then and I could feel how grateful he was to have the doctor on his team. But it seemed to be more than that. He was feeling affectionate towards him as well. More like he was a family member. *Hmmm.* That was also very interesting. I was mulling that new information over when the back room's door opened.

"How we doing so far?" Ethan asked as Jeremy came back out and we both stood. He walked over and laid an arm around his shoulder.

"Pretty good. Doc's alright." He said, sounding a little surprised.

"Yeah? Good. Then what do you say we get some food into you now?"

"Oh yes! I'm starving! He answered enthusiastically, in true teenage fashion. Ethan laughed at his predictability. Just then we could hear more people talking outside, greeting each other loudly.

"Come on. I hear Cook now. We'll say hello on our way over to get you settled in. Meanwhile, someone can get the grill going." He tightened his arm around Jeremy's shoulders and started to walk out the front door of the cabin. Then he looked back over his shoulder and reached his other hand out to me. I felt a little useless and like he was having to cater to me too much, when he should just be worrying about Jeremy. A small part of me was still very grateful for the consideration. I walked over and hooked just one finger onto his and followed them out.

Dr. J and Roxy were already standing on the dirt road out front greeting the two new *"troop"* members. One was a sporty looking guy who appeared to be mid-thirties. He had sandy colored hair with blonde highlights that reminded me momentarily of surfer boy. He was taller than Roxy, I noticed when they hugged, so I guessed around six feet. He was wearing brown cargo pants and a black long sleeve thermal under a short sleeve grey t-shirt. He also had on hiking boots.

I thought how funny it was that everyone looked like they

were *actually* camping around there. But then when I thought about it for another minute, I realized that it actually made perfect sense, since they were walking in the woods and what not. Possibly four-wheeling in and out too for all I knew, since I still didn't see any other vehicles anywhere. Either that or I assumed they all had their own spot in a garage.

The other person hugging and shaking hands, was another story all together. He was a full head taller than the others and that head was even more easily visible since it was completely bald. All the hair on his head was on his face in the form of bushy eyebrows and a salt and pepper Fu Manchu beard that was about five inches long. He wore dark grey cargo shorts that came down to the middle of his meaty shins, heavy black army boots and a thick button down flannel. Now *he* looked like my minds idea, of a stereotypical backwoods militant. *Yikes!* I was definitely a little more nervous then. For the first time that day, I worriedly wondered what I had gotten myself into.

As we came closer they both stopped to get a look at me. Suddenly I felt like the pariah again. I was starting to get the idea that Ethan hadn't brought very many women there, if their reactions of thinly veiled shock and amazement were any indication.

I still wanted instinctually to be just a little bit afraid of *Big Guy* over there, but as we came closer all I felt from him was concern and protectiveness for Ethan. *Fierce* protectiveness, underlined with a deep caring. My worry started to melt away again. Huh. If anyone should have known by then *not* to judge a book by its cover, it was me. I was instantly disappointed in myself for that but I was still human after all. I make mistakes. Ethan spoke up then and introduced me to the ones that I had mentally named "*Tony Hawke*" and "*Big Guy*."

"Simone, this is Mr. Kyle Cook." He said, referring to "*Tony*." "Around here we all just call him "Cook" since coincidently, that's also what he does best." He added with a sly grin. I thought he must be kidding but he wasn't. *Hah!* Okay.

I leaned forward and shook his hand. He was curious, but otherwise fairly neutral. That was actually reassuring. I would gladly take neutral at that point.

"Nice to meet you." I said and he agreed politely with a nod.

"This behemoth is the top dog of my security team, Mr. Hank Perry. He also shook my hand with a slight nod but no words, still suspicious. I actually liked that he was so protective of what they were doing there. I also liked his level of loyalty to Ethan. I decided right then that I liked him too, even though it was clear that he wasn't so sure about me yet. That was alright, he'd get there eventually. I smiled genuinely.

"Nice to meet you Hank." I could feel that he was at least a tiny bit impressed that I hadn't shied away from him and his cool appraisal. *Eh.* Better than nothing.

We both stepped back and Dr. J got the crowds' attention from the first cabins front door by announcing that the grill was lit. They cheered and we all headed over there.

Once inside the first cabin I could see that it was also different in design from the others. That one was obviously meant to act as the *"barracks."*

There was a kitchen on the left again but it was designed to be more utilitarian and less *"homey."* There were built-in double ovens and two different stove tops set into the long countertops. There was also an oversized Sub-Zero side-by-side fridge and along the opposite wall sat three sets of booths, instead of one main table.

To the right side, there were two separate rooms again. I could see through the open doors that they had three sets of bunk beds in each. I guessed from the decor, that it was most likely a "boys' room" and a "girls' room." There were two separate bathrooms side by side in between, with one door facing each way. Like the other cabins, it also had a main open lounge area in the back. In that particular cabin it included a pool table, a full-sized shuffleboard table, a foosball table and four big screen TV's hanging on the walls.

I hung back a bit as the rest of the people walked right through and headed out onto the back deck. All except for Cook, who went whistling away straight to the kitchen to put lunch together. I held tight to Ethan's hand as we reached the back of the lounge area and he held back with me.

"Maybe I should go?" I offered once we were alone, voicing my earlier thoughts. "I really don't want to be in the way. I think I might be more work than help for you now and Jeremy seems to be adjusting really well today."

He just shook his head. "You're right, he is. But don't think your presence has nothing to do with that. You're his reminder that he's not alone, or *a freak!*" He joked dramatically knowing how I felt too. You're another *height*, living a normal life. That's like a lifeline to him right now." He insisted. But I could tell that wasn't all.

"Besides, I like having you here." He confessed with a smile. "It's a little strange for me, I'll admit. I've always kept it separate before now. I'm sure you've noticed the reactions from my moronic friends." He said with a chuckle. "They're not used to me bringing anyone here that doesn't *belong* here. That's the crazy thing though." He said looking seriously into my eyes again. "You *do* belong here. Even if that's not *why* you're here. You still fit. Do you know what I mean?" He asked softly.

"It's weird, but I think I do." I admitted.

"Good. Because I *do* like it." He came closer and held my other hand. "Having you here with me. I really like being able to share all of myself with someone for a change instead of just a few select parts." He grinned and I rolled my eyes. I knew that he was trying to laugh it off, but that it was quite a serious thing for him.

"I understand." I said thinking about how I hadn't wanted to give up The Tavern, which was the one place that I had felt comfortable. It wasn't exactly the same but I understood the need to have that kind of place somewhere, to be able to let your guard down once in a while. I didn't want to make the mistake of reading more into it than that.

"Come on, Cook's making "*Laurel Burgers*" and if you don't get one when they come off the grill, you don't get one." He insisted heatedly. I laughed, sure he was kidding that time but he looked back at me completely serious.

"No, really! You don't understand! His wife Laurel makes these hamburger patties from scratch with really fresh, really lean yet somehow still juicy beef, and her own special blend of, *whatever* it is that she puts in them. I'll tell ya, people around here can't get enough of them. You watch, any respectable town cookout will be serving them. Hell, part of the reason I *hired* Cook was because he's married to *Laurel!*" He finished with his devious smile. "Right Cook?" He said louder.

"Yup. But that's okay, 'cause I'm only here for the pool." He called back in return without looking up or missing a beat. He just kept on whistling and slicing tomatoes.

Ethan laughed and pulled me out the door.

I couldn't argue with the way they smelled as we relaxed on the deck while they cooked. I was shocked to be so hungry after the breakfast that we'd had, but then I realized with surprise that it was somehow already after 12:00 and it made more sense. People sat and chatted. Some catching up, others just getting acquainted. Cook cooked, but he talked too while he flipped. Ethan stayed near me while we waited and I liked the comfortable feeling I was getting off of him while sitting next to him.

People *definitely* noticed. He noticed them noticing too but he just shook it off with a laugh. Of course he knew I noticed them noticing but he never let it make him feel uncomfortable, so I decided not to either.

He purposely gave Jeremy some space so he could begin getting used to the place and the people on his own.

Before long it was time to eat. After two bites I had to agree that he had been right again. The burgers *were* unbelievable! They were cooked perfectly to begin with, that much I had to rightfully credit to Kyle. They had a nice char on the outside, but were still light pink and super juicy inside. Not hockey puck fat. Not dry, tasteless cardboard, thin. Truly just right! *Mmmmm!* I felt a little like Goldilocks but in a really good way!

I had been leery at first. I consider myself to be a *giant* foodie. I can be sort of snobbish sometimes with food though. Even a bit of a purist, especially when it comes to preparing great, fresh ingredients. I don't like to mess with the good stuff too much. I like to be able to actually taste whatever it is I'm eating. But to *"Laurel's"* credit, whoever she was, she had done it right.

They weren't weird, or fancy, or flavored with anything overpowering. They were just perfectly seasoned and perfectly tasty without being too much of *anything*. The roll was amazing too which helped immensely. I love a good burger as much as the next person, but I am a *huge* fan of good bread. Sometimes what's holding the sandwich can be just as important as whats in it for me. These were soft, seeded rolls that were buttered then toasted on the grill. With a slice of cheddar melted on top of the burger, a little lettuce, tomato. mayo, and ketchup and I was one happy girl. There was potato salad and grilled corn on the cob too that just topped it off perfectly and I was sure that I *"mmmmm'd"* out loud more than a few times while I ate.

In the time that it took me to finish one, Jeremy announced that he was on his *third!* I almost didn't blame him. I saw what Ethan meant about not getting one, when I noticed he wasn't far behind. I could swear that there was a dozen on the platter originally, if not more, and there wasn't a single one left. Just puddles of enticing juices on the plate where they used to be.

I sat back with a dramatic sigh. "Wow! If I had stayed here as a teen, my next stop would have been *fat* camp!" Everyone gave a hearty laugh at that and I was a little startled. I had been so intent on my burger and blocking out the rest that I had kind of forgotten about the crowd. I hadn't meant to say it so loudly, but at least they had enjoyed the joke I thought gratefully. It could have just as easily gone horribly wrong. I have a habit of speaking long before I think things through. Much more often than I would care to admit.

For some reason, I felt comfortable there too. I wondered for a moment if it was just a matter of being wherever Ethan was.

Wow! I thought to myself then. *That was fast!* Jesus, I needed to get a grip! I decided that it was just the peacefulness and the red meat talking.

After lunch, we walked around the grounds with Jeremy, and Ethan explained the areas that were and weren't *"safe"* to go beyond once the alarms were set. I tried to pay close attention to that information for future reference. It would be just like me to accidentally set something off. Something loud. Or something silent that got a lot of people out of bed.

After that, we went back and he picked the center bottom bunk in the boys' room and unpacked some of his stuff. It was nearing time for me to get home and get my car. I had told Ethan when he picked me up, that I needed to be back at my place by 2:30 to pick up Liliana. He had promised that I would be and I trusted him to keep his word.

Jeremy was quiet for a minute sitting on the edge of his new bed. He was feeling a lot of things then, but mostly gratitude. *Genuine* gratitude. The kind you always hope your own children will feel for you someday when they're old enough to understand. He was grateful for the peace that the place afforded him at last and more importantly, for the fact that he didn't have to hide anything there. He felt like he could actually relax for a while.

"Thanks Uncle 'Eaten.' I really don't know what I would have done without you." He was embarrassed but he was trying to suck it up and be honest. I felt just a hint of the despair from the previous day in his voice as he thought about it, but he was stronger than that already.

"Hey, anything you need. You're in the club now, dude." He said knocking knuckles with Jeremy. "And it's a lifetime membership." He smiled and Jeremy smiled back. I felt his confidence pick up just a tiny bit more at that. Ethan really was just good with people in general.

We left Cook, Dr. J and Hank behind to take care of '*The Camp of Great Heights'* newest resident and headed back to my place, comfortably nestled in the F1 again.

Getting out of the car was the first time it was truly awkward. He wasn't my boyfriend after all and I was not his girlfriend. I didn't really know *what* we were. It was going to be tough to complain about that though, since *I* was the one who wasn't ready to put a label on it. I had to admit that it was a little confusing.

Thankfully, he didn't leave me to my thoughts long enough for me to self-destruct. He spoke up, but as usual it wasn't what I expected.

"I'd love to meet her sometime. Whenever you think it would be okay. I mean, I don't want to intrude or confuse her or anything like that. But she seems really bright, sweet. Like her mom, and I'd love to get to know her. You know..." He said looking up at me meaningfully, bravely. "...*just in case.*"

'It can run in families and it's easier sometimes, if they

trust me already." He explained, and it was enough for me to know what he meant. He was considering her future and what it may hold. I was resentful and touched at the same time. I didn't want his consideration to be necessary but that didn't mean that it wouldn't be.

"Sure. I guess that's probably not a bad idea. I'll figure it out. I'll let you know." I could tell that he was feeling placated. "No, *really!*" I said. "I mean it." I smiled. "I just want to do it right." At that, I turned and got out. I looked back at him but I was quiet. Still not sure what to say.

"Call me whenever you need me." He said with a wink and I smiled. I backed up and he pulled away.

I shook my head as I headed up the stairs but it didn't help. There was too much spinning around in it again. That seemed to be my new normal. At the top, I stopped to pee then grabbed my car keys and headed back down, hoping the drive would help clear my head.

Chapter 22

The drive was easy and surprisingly, traffic free. I was distracted though. It was hard to go from the altered reality of Camp *Height,* back to the world of everyday things like traffic and *Liliana!* I felt slightly disconnected. The things he introduced me to had a way of not seeming real when he wasn't there. *But they were real!* And even though I knew that for sure, I *still* had trouble digesting it.

It was easier when I got to the school and Liliana came running up to the car. I was instantly brought back to my own reality again. She opened the door and jumped in and everything seemed just as it should be. She smiled that beautiful smile at me and all was right with the world.

"Hi mama!" She said with unbridled excitement.

"Hello baby!" I said just as happily back at her. She had gotten too big to want to be called *'baby'* anymore about a year ago. But at the moment I couldn't help it. She seemed to be in a mood to let me slide.

"How was school?" I asked innocently.

"Oh it was great, mama! I got to be the weather person at the morning news time but Jennifer had to sit in time out for being mean to Marcus!" She exclaimed vehemently.

I remembered when such trivial things were the center of the universe for me too. I longed secretly, just for a minute, for the simplicity of those days. They were long gone for me but I could see it all so clearly through her eyes that I could almost pretend it was still really all that mattered. For a little while.

L. Pelletier

"Good for you, honey! And it serves Jennifer right for being mean to Marcus in the first place, doesn't it?" I asked.

She agreed easily enough. "Yup. Mrs. Woods told her if she took his paper again she would have to go in time out and she just did it again anyways! Right away, too! She's always doing stuff like that to Marcus, pretending not to like him. But you know what, Mama? I think she *does* like him. A lot! Because she sure doesn't ever leave him alone!" She said innocently and looked out her window. Again, I noticed that she was much smarter than she realized.

I wondered for the millionth time how much of that was her natural perception and intelligence and how much might be from being able to *feel* what was really going on. Like I did. I knew she had a basic understanding of what mommy could do, but she had still never mentioned anything similar having happened to her yet. At least not that she had *noticed.* Sometimes though, in situations like that, *I notice!* And I wonder, and I wait, helplessly, for whatever will be to present itself.

"Are we going, Mama?" Liliana asked and I snapped out of it. "Yup!" *Deep breaths.* The only way to see the future clearly was to live it, I reminded myself and I pulled away from the curb. "I was thinking we could make our own pizzas tonight. What do you think?" I asked her then.

"Pizza! Yaaayyy!!! Oh can we get pepperoni and mushrooms?" She asked excitedly. "Oh, and those hearts of choke things too!!" She yelled and it made me laugh so hard that I forgot about my worries again. For the moment anyway.

"You mean *ar-ti-choke hearts* honey." I corrected her gently and I smiled at her in the rearview mirror.

"Oh right! *Ar*-ti-choke hearts." She said slowly. She smiled back at me then, pleased with herself for getting it right. She kept me similarly entertained for the rest of the ride and throughout the market as well.

Back at my apartment we rolled dough and laughed as we tried to toss it in the air. It was a good thing I had washed my floors recently.

Once we had it stretched out, we laid the dough flat on the pizza stones I had put out and we each made our own. We spread the sauce and then the slices of fresh mozzarella. Then we topped that with our pepperoni slices, fresh mushrooms and the all-important artichoke hearts. We sprinkled a little bit of shredded mozzarella on top with a drizzle of olive oil and a sprinkle of oregano, then we put them in the oven. We cleaned up while we waited for them to cook.

We sat and ate our pizza on the deck and watched the sun set instead of the TV for a change, since the weather was starting to be a little more dependable. We had a contest to see who could stretch their cheese the farthest and I let her win. Watching her laughing and chewing so happily, I knew I had already won everything that mattered. I knew if anyone could read my mind, they would call me super cheesy, just like my dinner. But in the privacy of my own head, I didn't shy away from the overly sappy feelings. They were the best ones of them all and for the most part, what I lived for.

We stayed out long enough, even watching the bats eat mosquitos for a while, that it was bedtime for Liliana by the time we went back inside. She brushed her teeth while I made up her bed. When she came out, she ran over and jumped in with a diving roll. I gave her a 7.8 for her high degree of difficulty and we laughed together for a minute before I tucked her in with one light sheet.

"Good night, I love you." I said.

"Good night Mama. I love you, too." She replied.

I shut off the other lights, grabbed my sweatshirt and went back out to sit on the deck for a while longer. I sat on the bench with my feet up and my hands in my pockets, happily watching the clouds move in front of the moon. I couldn't help thinking about Ethan again once I had a quiet moment to myself. I was still trying to digest all of the amazing things that I had seen. I also couldn't help remembering the night before and the amazing things that he had made me *feel.*

As if I had conjured him with my mind, my phone vibrated in my pocket. I took it out and looked at it. It was a text message, from *"Unknown."* I really needed to fix that. I slid the envelope shaped like a puzzle piece across the screen and dropped it into the puzzle piece shaped hole to open the text. A yellow talk bubble popped up on the black screen.

"U still up?"

I texted back and a blue bubble popped up underneath it.

"Yup. Sitting on the deck. What's up?"

"Liliana?"

"Sleeping."

"K. C u in a min."

He wrote back. I was wondering what it was about and still waiting to hear his car pull up, when I saw him come running across the orchard five minutes later instead.

Of course. He would have no problem jogging through the woods in the dark. At least not in seeing where he was going anyway. I wonder how he would fare when he saw a bear or a coyote coming at him though. I'd have to remember to ask. He slowed to a walk about fifty yards away to cool down a little before he stopped.

I waited until he reached the bottom of the deck, then I went down to meet him.

"Hi." I said, walking onto the patio under the deck, not bothering to hide my surprise at seeing him.

"Hi." He said back, through a few more deep breaths. *"Whoooh!"* He was wearing a black tank top, black running shorts and black sneakers. If it weren't for his pale skin practically glowing in the moon light, he would have been invisible running over there.

"Sorry." He said, still a little breathless. "It's hard to text and run."

I laughed. "Night time really doesn't mean much to you, does it?" I asked with a smirk. He was sweating but not profusely, just enough to look like an ad for the sneakers he was wearing. He really should consider some modeling on the side I thought, my mind wandering to unexpected places as usual.

"It means lots of things to me." He said shaking his legs out a little. "Sometimes it means it's time to go to work. Sometimes it means I'll get to sleep a little. *Other times...*" His sentence trailed off as he remembered what we had spent the *previous* night doing. He walked up closer to me then and grinned deviously. "Other times, I find much better things to do!" He said deeply as he came close enough to kiss my neck lightly. Then I was remembering it again too as familiar feelings ran through my body. I did stop it before it could reach my hands that time though and he laughed when I closed them up tight.

"Sooo, out for a little midnight run?" I asked looking around him at the nightscape questioningly.

He put his hands on the wall on either side of my head and my heart started to pound in anticipation. I held my breath for a second when he started to lean forward. But then he dropped one leg back and I could tell that he was just stretching his calves, using the wall behind me for leverage.

Okay! Breathing again. *Geesh!* I could feel his arousal when he came closer, as well as his amusement at not doing what I had expected him to.

Apparently that was going to be quite typical of him also.

"Mmm hmm." He answered, reminding me that I had asked him a question. He switched legs, but his face stayed very close to mine. "Had too much pent up energy left over to sleep and since you weren't *available...*" He trailed off while he came back up on both legs but he kept his face next to mine. He did lean in and kiss me then. Once, lightly on the lips.

I closed my eyes and shook my head a little afterwards. Deeper breaths then. I looked at him again. "How's Jeremy doing?" I asked changing the subject, since what was on both our minds then was not an option for that evening. He took the hint.

"He's doing well." He provided, as he dropped his arms and stepped back a little. "I went back to check on him before he went to bed. He was pretty tired. Cook, Hank and Dr. J had him all worn out from playing volleyball in the pool. He was a lot more like his old self again. *He's good.*" He smiled a little in the end and I could feel how happy that made him.

"I'm glad." I said as I thought back on his day again. The first day of the rest of his life, really. "I think you're right. I think he's going to be okay now. Because of *you*." I looked up at him again. His face was calm. So were his feelings on the subject. Impassive. No gloating, no pride. It was a little unexpected, I had to admit.

People were people and they were usually pretty predictable. Especially to me, since they rarely managed to hide much from me, or to surprise me. His completely selfless behavior *did* surprise me though. I wondered again where all of that came from.

"It's a good thing, what you do." I said, but in a way that made it sound like I didn't understand how it was possible. Because I didn't. He stepped back another step and looked out at the moon. I couldn't help wondering again, what it was that made him the man he was then. I could also tell quite easily, that right at that moment, he didn't want to share that with me. I could respect that. I would try to understand. Hadn't he respected my boundaries?

"Well, I should get back in case she wakes up." I said. I started to turn to head back up the steps, giving him both his space and the opportunity to bring it up himself some other time.

"Okay." He spoke up. "But hey, I won't be around for a couple days. I figured I would let you know, if you were still up while I was running by. Kill two birds with one stone. Just in case you decided that you *needed* me." He said with a wink. "I wouldn't want you to think that I was ignoring you, but I'll be in the city at Mass General's Eye & Ear building with Jeremy and my cell phone will be off. They're not allowed in there. They interfere with too much of their equipment. This is one of those rare times where we need *their* equipment, so we have to go there rather than have someone come out to us."

"Unfortunately, there can be no *guests* along on this one either. This exam is a lot harder to pull off *'unofficially,'* but the information that we will get out of it is invaluable." He said, explaining why I wasn't being invited along on that leg of his journey. "If you do need to reach me for some reason, text me or leave a message and I'll try to get away and check my phone whenever I can." He was thinking about Jeremy and what they would have to put him through at least one more time to get the results they needed. He felt bad but he knew it was necessary.

"Hopefully we'll know everything we can about his particular physical changes by the end of his stay. We should know everything there is to know, even on a molecular level, by the end of the week." His disposition lightened at that prospect.

"Is that really possible?" I asked. "To pinpoint and identify *actual* physical differences?" I was surprised by the notion that you could actually see what I do under a microscope. Well, sort of anyway.

"Yup. Like I've said, it's a permanent change. That's because it's a *physical* change in the tissues, the muscles, tendons, even the bones that takes place in whatever area is *heightened.* Everything from the blood vessels to the nerve endings can be altered afterwards. It's like puberty in that you can only go through it, you can never go back. The process is a one way door and it *does* leave a visible trace behind when you pass through it." He revealed and I was enthralled.

I glanced curiously down at my hands while he talked. I tried to be nonchalant but I could tell that he noticed it. However brief. He looked at me for a minute then continued his explanation.

"We've seen it affect every major system in the human body. Nothing is immune to its reaction. These changes are not things that are visible to the naked eye." He said with a slight, sideways grin at me. "But if you know what to look for, they are right there in black and white in the test results. Time and time again. Of course like everything else about H*g*T, it always differs somewhat from person to person. So although we can document each case quite clearly, we still never know exactly what to expect from a new case until we've tested them." He admitted.

That got me thinking about myself again momentarily, and what it would be like to have those kinds of answers. Once it was a possibility, it was actually a little scary. I still found it all fascinating though and of course I wanted to learn everything that I could about it. That's just how I am, that constant *need-to-know* that drives me. Not only was this new information fascinating all on its' own but it also provided answers to questions that had been lingering, *unanswered* in my head for years! Unfortunately, I knew it was not the time.

"That is so cool! You are going to have to tell me more about that. A *lot* more. Just another time, okay?" I offered diplomatically.

"Okay." He agreed.

"When will you be back?" I asked.

"Sunday night, if all goes well. It'll be easier to just stay in the city until all the testing is done." He pulled me up against him then and I went willingly, wanting to indulge in that incredible feeling just one more time before I went inside alone. I leaned up on my tiptoes and wrapped my arms around his shoulders and buried my face in the crook of his neck. He was still slightly damp from his run, but somehow he managed to smell fantastic. I was pretty sure that pheromones had to have something to do with that.

"Will you miss me, just a little?" He asked in a gruff voice from behind my ear. The breath from his words tickled the tiny hairs on the back of my neck and a shiver floated slowly down my spine.

"Mmm hmmm." I confirmed. "I'm afraid I just might." My eyes were closed and I was just absorbing as much of it as I could for a minute. I knew I would regret it later when I was alone in my bed, but right then I didn't care. Waves of sensuality were rolling off of him as he kissed my sensitive skin and I was just breathing it all in. I had found that I *really liked* the way he felt about me. *I* liked feeling what he felt!

He reached up and brought my hands back down by my sides. He turned my palms to face him and then slid his palms along mine as he went. He clasped our fingers tightly together, like he could hold on to the things that he saw there. His head came back up and he looked at me with a fire burning in his eyes and I knew that we were walking a fine line.

I tipped my chin up towards his, not ready or willing to turn back just yet. Daring to push it just a little bit further. He reached our intertwined hands around behind my back and leaned in closer to me so that my head tipped back even more as my back arched. Then, when our bodies were pressed tightly together, he dipped his head low enough to brush his lips across mine. I felt him let his passion go, just a little. I knew better then, than to think that's all there was. No he was just giving me what he knew I wanted. Just a little taste.

I closed my eyes again and felt myself get weaker. I was almost at my breaking point. Almost, but not quite. I opened my eyes, but he came right back for more and as much as I loved to watch him, I couldn't keep them open while he kissed me. Before long, I could feel myself rising higher and higher, involuntarily trying to get even closer to him. Okay, that was it. I broke the kiss and pushed him back a little. *"Phew!" Deeeeep* breaths.

He smiled at my obvious state of arousal but he was breathing pretty heavily too so he couldn't gloat too much.

"I'll see you Sunday night." He said deeply, intently and I was not about to argue. *It was going to be a long two days until then!*

"Sunday." I answered just as adamantly, confirming the "date."

I did finally escape up the stairs then and he just chuckled as he took off again at a slow jog. "Guess I'd better get back to my running!" He said, shaking his head.

I laughed too. "Goodnight." I called back as I reached the deck.

"Goodnight, Simone." He said softly, already at a distance but his deep voice carried easily across the quiet night.

I went back inside and locked the doors. I checked on Liliana and found her still sound asleep in the exact same position that she had been in when I went outside. I took a *very* long, hot shower, knowing the white noise wouldn't wake her up. Even though it would seem to be counterproductive, it was extremely relaxing. I was actually able to fall asleep after that.

It didn't stop me from dreaming about him though.

When I woke up in the morning, I missed him before I had a chance to remember that I shouldn't and I was instantly pissed at myself for that. It was always fresh and exciting whenever you started a sexual relationship with someone new. I knew that. I needed to remember not to be blinded by that, which with Ethan would be only too easy.

It's actually also quite easy to understand how the natural progression works, if you pay attention to it at all. And I do.

Great sex will leave you giddy for days. Weeks. Months even if you're lucky. While you're walking around in a fog of endorphin's, unable to trust your own judgment, you end up all caught up in the relationship. You learn to count on the other person being there. And *that* was the trap! That instinct that makes us want to connect on as many levels as possible before that fog wears off. Because no relationship can sustain that kind of heat permanently. If you have what it takes together to balance those times out with something other than just the physical side by the time that fog wears off, then the connection is solidified and nature has done its' job. That's how we pass from casual acquaintances to committed partners.

Problem was, I didn't *want* to get past the casually acquainted *lovers* phase! I was really hoping that if we didn't lose sight of what was important to each of us separately, then we could manage to exist permanently like that, somewhere in the middle. In the easy going, fun phase. I thought it was at least worth a shot. And that wasn't going to work if I kept doing things like missing him the second that he left.

I groaned and got up. I sat on the edge of the mattress and ran my hands through my hair while I looked at the clock. It was still only 6:45. Liliana was already up and was eating a bowl of cereal at the coffee table while watching her new #1 favorite, "*Toy Story.*"

"Good morning sunshine!" I called to her on my way over to the coffee pot. Just seeing her there, right upon waking, instantly made me happier.

"Good morning, mama! You're early! Do you wanna watch a movie with me?" She asked sweetly.

"I'd love to, but first I need some coffee, okay?" I got the pot going and then went to brush my teeth and wash my face while I waited for it to brew.

When I came back she had set up a stack of pillows on the floor next to her so I smiled and sat down with my mug. We sat and watched the rest of "*Toy Story*" and I happily sipped my coffee. It was stress free and as always, it made me happy just to sit and watch her giggle. I should have learned to recognize by then, the calm before the storm.

Chapter 23

Once we finished breakfast and the movie, we got dressed into our customary Saturday uniform of comfortable jeans and t-shirts. Then we headed over to the riding area for Liliana's weekly lessons. Jack greeted us with his usual warm, weathered smile and a wave.

Liliana went straight over and took Cookie's reins from him. They were like old friends already. She pet Cookie's cheek as the horse leaned down and nuzzled her in greeting. Jack helped her to mount and then he let go of Cookie's bridal and let her have her head.

They walked slowly around the paddock unassisted. I was so proud and so scared by how easily she could move on to the next step in life. I also know now, why people constantly tout that *"It goes by so fast!"* bullshit all the time. It's because it's *true!* It's ridiculous really, how fast it all seems to go by. You spend your whole life hearing people say it but it's simply staggering when you suddenly see it for yourself firsthand!

I would never want to hold her back from learning something new, or stop her from growing. I look forward to every milestone she will someday reach. Privately however, I knew I would acknowledge and mourn each stage's passing along the way, at least to myself.

I watched as she rode slowly but confidently around the paddock. I also noticed that Jack didn't feel the need to stay right next to her anymore. He was watching from the far side while he saddled up another horse. I was pretty sure that it was for Jonah, who usually came every other Saturday. On the weeks that they were both here, they liked to ride together.

My suspicions were confirmed only moments later when Jonah and his mom pulled down the long driveway. I had met her once before when she was dropping him off. Her name was Elizabeth. That was about all I knew since she wasn't the friendliest person in the world. She hadn't stayed long enough to say much other than hello.

I didn't pick up any animosity though, just a slight indifference. I was fine with that. It made things easier on me. I waved to her but didn't bother to go over there, knowing that it was preferable to both of us. It was nice not having to go through the motions sometimes. She waved back. A quick flick of the wrist, then she let him out and pulled around without ever getting out of the car herself. A moment later she was gone.

Jonah didn't waste any time getting mounted and heading out to ride with Liliana. I heard her squeal in delight as he galloped over to her and I smiled and closed my eyes as her joy hit me. I looked over at Jack and he was smiling too, at both of us.

He walked up to me then, still smiling. "I don't know which one of you is happier right now." He said with a shake of his head. "I guess it would be you though, since you feel both sides, right?" He winked at me.

"Right." I agreed easily. "I win." I smiled back at Liliana as her and Jonah passed by again. "I always win where she's concerned." I squinted and grinned at him with that admission. "I know, you probably think I'm corny as Hell, but I just can't help it." I said, slightly embarrassed. I didn't need to be though. He quickly disagreed.

"Not one bit. You're not alone on that one, missy. I've got kids too, remember. I know exactly what you mean. They make me so proud sometimes, I think I'm gonna burst. Other days... Well that's why God also made whiskey." He said and we both laughed.

"Speaking of children, are you planning on bringing yours to movie night next week? Supposed to be real nice weather again. We're having one Hell of a spring!" He stated happily. "I figured I'd give you fair warning, since I think Jonah may have already let the cat out of the bag." He said with a nod in their direction. I watched again as they laughed and rode side-by-side. I could feel the excitement coming off her as she looked over to confirm that I got it. I smiled back.

"Sure. She had a lot of fun last time." I said then. Actually, so had I, I remembered. Although some parts I had originally tried to block out. I smiled to myself at the memory. I noticed then, that Jack was smiling at me too.

What was that about? Did he happen to know just who was and wasn't up there that night? *Hmmmm...* Knowing Jack? *Probably.* He really didn't miss much.

I could feel him being humorously smug and I could tell that he was having fun with me, but I couldn't feel whether he *knew* or not. I got the distinct impression that Jack had learned how to keep his feelings close to the vest long ago. The most important ones anyway. How did he learn to do that? I wondered. How would he know to separate them? An old favorite "C+C Music Factory" song played in my head then. *"Things that make you go, hmmmmm!"*

I thought back to when Jack had first brought to my attention that he was aware of my particular talents. He had been showing me around the property at the time, about a week after I had first moved in. We had still only talked a few times by then, but I'd already had a sense that he was *aware* in general. Guarded, even. He was also sharp as a tack and quick to notice little things, so it didn't surprise me too much when he figured me out all on his own. He had just come right out and asked me about it. At least he asked though, unlike Ethan, who had *told* me what I was, I thought in comparison.

I had been following him around the orchard, ducking under tree limbs, when I mentioned what I was picking up to him directly.

"You put a lot of love into this place, don't you?' I had asked honestly, impressed by his devotion to the property. He nodded but then was quiet for a while afterwards. Eventually he spoke up.

"So, you seem to be pretty good at picking up on what people are feeling, huh?" He asked outright. Since I was going to live there and I didn't sense any ill will from him or his wife, I decided to be honest as well, right from the beginning. It was unusual for me but I trusted him completely already so it wasn't really a risk in my eyes. I couldn't pinpoint why exactly, but I was sure of it just the same.

"Yup. Kinda' my thing. I try not to bother anyone because of it though and I only ask the same in return." I looked him in the eye while I said it and I could feel that he understood. He smiled, nodded.

"Works for me." He turned and kept walking.

We discussed it briefly, and only that one time. He had asked honestly. I had answered honestly. He actually thanked me for that. Then he proceeded to tell me that it didn't matter and he wouldn't mention it to anyone else, besides Shirley of course. He told me flat out that he didn't keep secrets from Shirley or the family. I immediately respected that as well.

The truth was, anyone who really wanted to, could figure me out in time. All anyone needed was a reason to pay attention to me long enough. Like I've said, I don't *hide* it necessarily. I just don't offer it up with the first handshake. Though I guess having someone living on your property was a good enough reason to pay that close attention. I had been so grateful that he wasn't bothered by it, that I hadn't even thought about *why* he would have recognized it so *easily*.

I wondered about it then though, as I watched the horses sauntering around the riding area in slow circles.

I was about to start fishing a little, when his attention was diverted by the soft peal of his cell phone. He looked at the screen curiously before holding up a finger to me as he walked away to answer it. I went back to watching the kids while he walked slowly around the outside of the fence, talking to whoever it was. I watched him as he talked and he watched them. He never took his eyes of the kids once as he paced back and forth.

The call only lasted a few minutes but I could tell that his mood had changed. As usual, he was keeping it a dull impression at best, but I got the clear sense that he was not happy about whatever news he had received. Just then, we heard the lunchtime bell ring for Jack up at the house. We all knew that sound meant that their time was up. They were always the last two riders before he stopped for lunch.

Jack went back over to the kids to help them dismount and then they led their horses to the water trough to have a drink. Once they had their fill, they led them into the stables where they brushed them out and finally, left them with a pile of fresh hay.

I eventually gave up on getting answers form Jack for the day, but jotted it down on my mental "To Do" list for another time.

We stood in the driveway in front of the main house and discussed the time for movie night next week. It was starting to stay light out later, so he had pushed it back to nine o'clock. Liliana and Jonah ran around in circles while he waited to be picked up.

It was another beautiful day. It was even warmer than last week and like Jack, I had heard that next week would be warmer still. I shielded my eyes from the sun and when I did I could see Shirley in the front window, so I waved. She waved back on her way by with an armful of folded towels. It was all so Norman Rockwell and peaceful, that I breathed deeply and easily for a while. If I had to have neighbors at all, these were the ones I wanted to have, I thought to myself.

After Jonah left, we said our goodbyes and headed back into the city a little early so we could go by my parents. They could see Liliana any time they wanted really, being closer to her than I was. Plus, they were also two of her four favorite babysitters. But that didn't stop them from loving our impromptu visits as well.

They squealed in delight right along with her when we got there and then immediately took her out back to show her all their spring vegetables that were sprouting. I watched them through the big picture window, having the time of their lives when my phone rang. I was both glad and slightly disappointed when it didn't come up as *"unknown,"* but once I got over that initial annoyance, I was happy to see that it was Mack.

"Hey Mack." I greeted him as I answered the call. "How are things on the home front? You holding down the fort okay?"

"Eh. Holding it down..., watching it float away. It's all the same, right?" He answered cryptically.

"Huh? *Floating?* What are you talking about Mack? Do I even want to know?" I asked skeptically.

"Ahhh, probably, not. And I was perfectly happy to handle the initial discovery and investigation into the matter while you took the day off. But, seeing as how you *are* the boss, I figure you're bound to find out sooner or later." He was joking, but I wasn't hearing a lot of laughter. Dread started to sink heavily into my chest. I didn't want to say the words, but I knew I had to.

"Hit me." I said, gearing up for disaster. I was not disappointed.

"Well, we got a chance to get some of the big machines working yesterday, just finishing up clearing the main path. Things were going really good too, I have to say. Shoulda' been my first clue." Mack said with a chuckle. He and I shared a *"glass half empty ...and probably cracked"* kind of attitude. "Anyway, we got all the way up to the top of the "S" curve before we had to stop. It seems that particular section of woods hadn't been cleared in decades and so no one was even aware of the *brook* that runs right across our main trail."

"*A brook!* What! Are you serious?! How did no one know that? *Shit!* How did *we* not see it?! We've been out there checking over that whole site twenty times over the last six months! Where the hell was the damn thing hiding?" I demanded, mad at myself for missing something so huge.

"Well, they're saying it's actually less 'brook,' more 'underground spring.' And it's not so much 'across' our trail, as 'underneath' it. We knew that it existed in the area, remember? It runs underneath a lot of the surrounding terrain. It's fed way up high somewhere by a natural spring or something. But it was never an issue on our plans, because it was only previously known to surface miles and miles away from there. Nowhere even close to us!" He paused for dramatic effect and I could tell that there was more. The waiting was killing me.

"*Sooooo, congratulations!*" He continued, finally. "You officially get to add and name this newly discovered '*well!*'" He laughed in the end. "Of course, you also have to figure out what the hell to do about it sitting smack dab in the middle of our main trail. Not to mention that the Conservation Committee is now officially involved." He addedd, and I could tell that he was finally done then. *Thank God!* That was going to be more than enough to throw a wrench into my plans.

"*Shit!*" I groaned loudly at the new development. The Conservation Committee was to landscapers what the building inspector was to a general contractor. A giant pain in the ass. Lots of hoops to jump through and tons of red tape to hold things up at every step. *Great!* That's exactly what I needed on the biggest job of my career. Oh well, it may truly mean the end of that particular career. I wondered then, what I could do next in life at that point. Sadly, it wasn't a very encouraging thought.

"They said they'd likely be there all day today, if you want to go by and talk to someone yourself." He offered.

"*Ugggghhhh!!* Alright, I can be there by 5:30. I'll go check it out." I said with a sigh. "And Mack?"

"Yeah?" He answered.

"Thanks. For everything." He knew I meant it. Mostly for being the kind of *second-in-command* who could handle a disaster without immediately calling for help. I was grateful for every extra moment he had given me in the end, whether I could properly express that or not.

"You got it, boss." He said, seeming to understand and he hung up. It was my problem to handle essentially. We all knew that. He had only bought me a temporary reprieve, but I was still grateful.

I put my phone away and sighed again, heavily. It was probably the worst time for something like that to come up out of the blue. I had been more than happy to divide my time between the Gardens and Liliana. Then I wanted to make space for Ethan in that mix somewhere too.

It wasn't even just about time to spend with him. I could manage that in the wee hours with no real problem. I was also really excited to explore his whole *"organization"* once I had decided to embrace it. Along with all the things that he could teach me, *about me!* How would I find time for all of that, if this turned into one of *those* jobs? The kind where everything that should take one day, ended up taking three.

Not to mention, the amount of time that I had left to

complete that project before Mr. Wu Xing's planned "Opening Day" event, would not allow for that type of expansion. As usual, I had left myself only slightly longer than I expected it to take to finish. A *small* buffer, built in for '*unforeseeable's.*' It was not going to be nearly enough for something that big.

If I had known that there would be any type of *Conservation* issues to consider, then I would have planned accordingly from the beginning. Allowed for a *much larger* buffer. But nothing like that had ever come up in our original investigation of the site and no one from the city even mentioned the possibility when Mr. Wu Xing pulled the permits. It should have been clear sailing, from beginning to end.

I guess I really should have known better then to count on that though. And that brings me back around to why I am usually a *glass-half-empty....Blah, blah, blah,* kind of girl.

Dammit!

My parents were having such a nice time playing with Liliana in their small back yard that I decided to leave her with them and let them have their fun. They had no problem dropping her off at Ben's later, which gave me the opportunity to head up to the site early. I was useless *'fun-wise'* at that point anyway. I called Ben to let him know the new plan while I went and got Liliana's stuff from my car. I gave her a big hug and a kiss, thanked my parents and I was off.

All sorts of worst case scenarios were running through my head on the drive up there. So far the biggest obstacle I had thought of besides Conservation, was the fact that I didn't normally do a lot of water features. It wasn't really my thing. That also meant that I didn't have a *"water feature expert"* either. Natural or otherwise. I would have to hire someone new to help me handle that part of the job. I hated that even on a *good* day!

I tried to stay calm until I knew just what the situation really was, but it was still a long, *long* ride. As soon as I pulled up, I could see commotion way down at the end of the trail. I took a deep breath, got out of my car and started up the path.

It was a little different being there in my sneakers, not having intended on going by the site when I left the house. It gave me an excuse to take my time on the uneven terrain. As I got closer

I could see a few handfuls of people, just milling around a roped off area. Some I recognized as workers from the hotel, others must have been guests. There were only two people currently in the center of the *almost* clear, clearing though. As I approached, I could see Mr. Wu Xing talking to another man who was kneeling down by the group of large rocks that my crew had been moving.

I knew that area was the biggest section left that had to be cleared. There were four large boulders in the center that we had to move but the areas on either side of them had important, fully mature trees that I wanted to use, rather than remove. It seemed like the path of least resistance at the time to leave the trees and clear the rocks. I hoped that was still going to be the case since it would be near impossible to change that so late in the game.

"Good afternoon Mr. Wu Xing. I hear we've had some excitement." I said, greeting him with a lightness I didn't really feel.

"Good afternoon, Miss. Harrington. That appears to be the case, yes." He answered as politely as ever. I wasn't sensing any anger or disappointment directed at me or the situation in general. Just curiosity. He was as calm and as confident as ever.

I wished then, that *I* was handling it as well. He was standing on the dirt path in a suit and dress shoes and yet he still managed to appear completely cool and collected, like he belonged there. Entirely comfortable in his own skin. That's what it came down to really, and that was about so much more than just being appropriately dressed.

The kneeler stood and introduced himself. He was a small guy, only my height and as much as I hated to admit it, probably a few pounds lighter. He had brown hair and blue eyes in a soft face. He had to be at least in his early thirties I guessed, but he still looked more like a child than an adult. He spoke then and his voice did little to change that impression.

"You must be the designer," He said while extending his hand to me. I shook it while he introduced himself unnecessarily. "I'm Warren, Warren Wright. I'm with the Conservation Committee." He was wearing pleated khaki's and a white button down shirt with a name badge pinned prominently on his chest. Even aside from all that, he could have been a mute and I could've been an illiterate and I still would have known exactly who he was. It was that fast sometimes that I had a person pegged.

"Simone Harrington." I said back. "It's nice to meet you, Warren." He was a little smug, but I couldn't figure out if he had a reason to be yet, or if he was just that way normally. "So? What exactly are we looking at here, Warren?" I asked kneeling down myself then to peer into the space left by the first boulder that my men had moved. Even if I couldn't see the water moving past slowly through the darkness under the rocks, I still would have been able to hear it. It wasn't loud, but it was a distinctive sound.

"Well what it is, is a small part of a large underground aquifer system. Let me guess. You're from Massachusetts, right?" He asked like it was the obvious reason for some unknown infraction.

"Yes. I am." I said without hesitation or apology, since I wasn't sorry for it.

"You see Simone, in most of the country aquifers are more uniform and usually run much deeper underground. But here in New Hampshire they typically lie only ten to twenty feet below the surface. Most of our fine state is made up of well sorted sediments left by glaciers, and layers of highly fractured bedrock. That makes the groundwater here very shallow and easily accessible. Maybe *too* accessible." He looked at me again like I had broken some unknown rule. Then he continued.

"The land and surface waters are of course all connected, and therefore much more drastically affected here by things like the changing climate or shifting geology of a specific area. *Or,* by a poorly placed or improperly functioning well further up the system." He said, again with obvious disdain for any such offenders. "That is why the regulations governing the accessing of the aquifer need to be so stringent." He was warming up to his subject, so I decided to let him continue and to wait for the question and answer period. I secretly hoped it would be soon.

"Since sixty percent of our public drinking water comes from groundwater which is basically unseen, it's imperative that we are consistent with vigorous testing. Any time a new well or access point is exposed the water quality at the site must be evaluated and documented. Otherwise, it would be impossible to maintain any type of control over the pollution and contaminants in the water that can come from unwanted runoff. It would also be impossible to determine after-the-fact, *where* a pollutant has come from." He was still only focused on the telling of his tale, so I tried to get a question in to see if I could hurry him along.

"How is it that no one knew this particular aquifer ran under here? Shouldn't those things be all mapped out by now? Shouldn't you know where they are and what's over them, so when someone pulls a permit to change the landscape, you would know if that area poses a risk or not?" I could sense his indignation at my inference so I quickly tried to assuage his ego a little, knowing I would get further with honey than vinegar.

"I don't mean to imply that someone's not doing their job, quite the opposite actually. I just think it must be very hard for you to police the system, without the basic tools you need to do your job properly. It must be difficult for you, always playing catch-up, *after the fact*." He was mostly placated by that, enough to keep answering my questions at least.

"Well, it would be nice, but the truth is it wasn't until 2008, when the amount of landscape development happening and the increased reliance on the groundwater system, finally prompted a study on its' use and the hydrogeology of the region. That's when we got our very first updated and seamless map refining all of the '*currently known*' locations of the aquifers. But even *that* is a constant work in progress." I could tell it wasn't his first time giving that speech.

"There are more occurrences like this one than you would think. Every week there are updates being added, and I can tell you now there will be another one this week." He looked at me like it was my fault again, but I understood what he meant then. I guess I couldn't blame anyone for this any more than Mr. Wu Xing could. I *would* have to find a way to deal with it though. And fast!

Mr. Wu Xing had stood listening intently, but made no comment. I could tell that we both thought it was my place to handle it, so I did.

"So Mr. Wright, forgive my ignorance on the subject, since this was unexpected to say the least, but what does all of this mean to us and our plans here specifically?" I asked with as much sweetness and patience as I could muster. He seemed to be enjoying his lecture too much to want to answer questions still. Well that was just tough. My patience had officially run out. There were more important issues there than geology and groundwater regulations. Like my future!

"Well first things first." He answered annoyingly. "The New Hampshire Department of Environmental Services will have to come in and check the water for contaminants for their Groundwater Hazard Inventory. Once that clears, if indeed it does, then you will have an opportunity to submit plans for the construction and flow rate on the new well, just like everybody else." He finished and his smugness was back.

"What if we don't intend to access the well at all? What then?"

"Either way you'll have to contain it at the very least and make sure that it meets safety regulations, now that it's been exposed." He handed me a card when he finished. "This is the number you need to call to set up the appointment for testing."

"How long does this whole process generally take, from start to finish? We will need to adjust our work schedule around this area in the meantime. But what we do, and when, will depend on how quickly we'll be able to get back to work on this spot." I explained, trying to appeal to his logical side. Unfortunately, I was disappointed again.

"Oh I don't think so, Miss. Harrington. All other work permits are hereby suspended until this issue is resolved." He was enjoying that delivery immensely. I was in shock.

"What! Are you serious?" I asked, stunned by the news.

"Oh yes, quite. Any newly constructed site accessing the aquifer must have all its' well and water usage permits submitted, approved and completed before any other construction permits can be obtained. Since you had yours prior to discovery, they are automatically null and void until further notice."

My jaw hung open for a moment while I tried to absorb that.

"How long?" I asked again in an unnaturally calm voice that time.

"If you're lucky, you might get an appointment by the end

of this month. If not, then most likely the beginning of the next. It just depends on how busy they are and how many are before you. This time of year though, there's likely to be a bit of a wait." The asshole actually smiled at me after that before he walked away. I let him go. Partly because I was still in shock and partly because when it wore off I was likely to slug him, and I didn't need that just then on top of everything else.

I turned back to Mr. Wu Xing after Mr. *"Always"* Wright left. He was surprisingly still calm. "Well, this changes things a little." I said understating it purposefully with a weak but honest smile.

"Let me know what you decide." That was all he said. He smiled at me with his ever-present calm fully intact. He bowed slightly towards me and then he turned, bent under the barrier and walked back down the long rocky trail like it was something that he did every day.

I wondered at his unwavering faith in me, and not for the first time. I didn't know why he was so sure that I was the right person for the job, or why he was equally sure that I could handle anything that came with it. But he was and apparently he did, and I really didn't want to let him down.

I vowed to find a solution and not to let it knock me off track completely as I followed the route the others had taken under the ropes and back up the trail to my car.

I just wished I had an idea *how* I was going to do that.

Chapter 24

I drove home in a daze, wondering what I could do about the situation at the gardens. I was temporarily stumped and I knew that I just needed to get it off my mind for a while and the answer would come to me.

I really wished then that Ethan was going to be playing at The Tavern that night. What I needed then was to turn off my conscious brain and succumb to the peace his music created. Too bad that wasn't an option. *Damn* the bad timing!

I thought about going home too though. About how I was no good at running or sitting home alone when my brain was on overload. In the end, I decided to go to The Tavern after all. Have a drink, just be with people for a little while.

I knew it wouldn't be as good without his music to block for me, but it was still preferable to sitting in my apartment pulling my hair out. I knew myself well enough to know that there would be no rest until I had worked the issue out. The scary part was that I could see no immediate solutions. I was at a momentary loss. I knew I would have to start with some research on the aquifer at the very least, but I also knew that I couldn't absorb anything else just yet. After that kind of overload came a temporary shutdown, a mental reboot so-to-speak.

I wasn't in a frame of mind to figure out the answer yet but I knew where to go to avoid it for a while until I was. With or without Ethan.

I walked in and dropped heavily into my usual booth, beyond grateful that I had caught it momentarily empty on a busy

Saturday night. It was a stroke of luck and I needed a little of that at the moment. It really *was* a different atmosphere without Ethan's music, I noticed. Louder certainly but it was more than that. It was more chaotic, too. I liked it though, at the moment anyway. I wanted to disappear into the crowd and let the outside emotional buzz drown out all the noise in my own head. I was really hoping I would be able to think clearer afterwards, kind of like my own version of shock therapy. The original practice was horrific, but the theory is valid to an extent.

Maybe I would come up with the solution. Maybe I would just get a regular buzz. Either one would do, I decided.

The jukebox was playing and the crowds' selection did a mediocre job of keeping some of the noise out but I really didn't care. I was on my second glass of wine and it was keeping me, at the very least, slightly humorous and more forgiving than usual. After a while I was so relaxed that I almost didn't notice the searching element in the room. I probably wouldn't have either, except that a small part of me thought that it was Ethan for a split second, and that of course caught my attention before I had time to think about it.

Dammit! *Arrrggghhh!!*

I knew right away that it wasn't him though. The intensity level wasn't even close. Since I knew then what some people came there looking for, I was instantly curious who was looking. I scanned the room carefully with my eyes, trying to connect the search that I was feeling, with the searcher.

The bar was crowded by local standards. A good thirty to forty people anyway. I recognized the regulars like myself more easily by then though, which was most of the crowd that night thankfully. That made it pretty easy to pick out the strangers. It was not hard to see anymore, why Ethan had pegged me so easily in that crowd. Just like I could easily peg the guy in the corner in the dark grey suit, as the searcher. He was definitely a little overdressed for The Tavern. Stood right out. To anyone who was looking anyway.

He was sitting by himself, scanning the room. Dani tried to pass by him on her way to a table full of rowdy softball players, but he waved her down as she passed. It was too loud to hear what he was asking her but I could feel his disappointment when she shook her head "no" in answer. I could tell that he thanked her. Then he got up, dropped some money from his pocket on the table and walked out.

He definitely wasn't a local. He obviously wasn't a young new *height* looking for guidance either. I was pretty sure then, who he was and why he was there.

Fifteen minutes or so later, Dani came over to check on me. I wanted to just ask her outright if she knew one way or the other, but I was thinking about what Ethan had said about not talking to anyone outside of camp. So while I declined another glass of wine, I tried to think of a way to confirm what I suspected. Quickly, before she could run off again, I decided to ask her as casually as I could manage if she happened to know him.

"He just looked so familiar to me!" I lied "It just drives me crazy when I can't figure out if I know someone or not. Does that ever happen to you?" I asked innocently.

"Oh yeah! All the time." She agreed enthusiastically. "The problem for me is that I never know if I really *know* them or if I've just seen them in *here* before. It makes me insane sometimes trying to distinguish between the two!" She laughed at that and I laughed with her, waiting patiently for the information that I really wanted. I had no choice though. I couldn't tell what I wanted to know from what she felt about him, her feelings always moved so fast. They were just as quick and as unstoppable mentally sometimes, as she was physically, as she ran around the place. Thankfully, I didn't have to wait too long. Unfortunately, it was no help.

"You know, I have seen him in here once or twice recently but I don't think he lives around here. He was looking for Ethan though, so maybe he's a friend of his that came from out of town to hear him play?" She ventured. She was being sincere. "He really only plays here so that happens a lot. He was definitely disappointed that he wasn't working tonight." She shrugged her shoulders and then went to get the order from the next booth. Learning that he didn't play anywhere else was something I could use. Unfortunately the rest was less than helpful. Somehow I was still convinced that I'd just had my first glimpse of our overly persistent government agent.

I didn't know if Dani knew what Ethan really did or not, and I wouldn't be able to tell unless she brought it up which wasn't likely whether she knew or not . Since asking her was out of the question, I was left wondering if she was really as clueless as she proclaimed. There was no way to know without asking Ethan himself and that was impossible as well, so I let it go. It was definitely frustrating though to have gone there thinking I would come up with answers, and as usual all I had found were more questions.

I wondered for just a second if he might be part of Ethan's *"organization,"* but I was almost sure I could rule that out just based on the hostility that I could feel underlying his search. It wasn't a *happy, expectant* kind of anticipation he had been feeling, like you would expect from someone coming to *"see a friend perform."* No, it was much more of an, *"Oh, just wait till I find you, I'm getting closer!"* kind of thing instead.

I paid my tab and said good night to Dani, who was still running around trying to keep up with the crowd, poor thing. She waved to me on her way by.

I drove home in silence for a change. I put the windows down, opened the moon-roof and listened to nothing but the sound of the breeze blowing by. In it, I finally found the peace that I had been looking for. I laid my head back against the headrest and held my arm up high out the window into the wall of wind, diving up and down against the air current like a dolphin. It was pure fun and it made me feel like a kid again.

It didn't help me solve my problems but it did help me to forget them for a little while. Sometimes that was more important and it was all I really needed. If I was going to tackle a problem as big as an unexpected, underground water system, then I needed some serious recharging of my brain first. *Balance.* That's all. *I could do this!* I insisted to myself.

At some point, I knew, I would figure out *how.*

I pulled down my driveway and felt the outside world fall away. Finally having achieved some sense of peace for the moment, I went upstairs and changed into some shorts and a tank top. Feeling refreshed if not necessarily recharged, I went to sit out on the deck for a while.

It was late and the half moon was high in a cloudless sky. I sat there with my knees bent and my feet up on the bench, feeling very small and not fighting it. I felt as if I could practically disappear out there and I loved that. I breathed slowly and evenly for a long while until I was ready to feel connected to myself again. I really didn't like to complain, but it wasn't always easy being me. Living inside my head. Sometimes I needed a little time off.

Occasionally I would wonder what a shrink would have to say about that. Though when I considered all I'd been through and how things could have turned out, *eh,* I didn't really feel too bad about it. Heck, it could have been a lot worse. Just then a small voice inside my head thought about how for Ethan, it obviously had been. Somehow, it had been much, much worse.

I had no idea what his childhood had been like, he still hadn't told me. I could tell how the memories made him feel though and it made me sick to *my* stomach. It certainly gave me a clear indication that things weren't peachy. I wondered then, who had come along and finally helped him?

So many pieces still missing. Did I really need to fulfill the constant urge to put them together? Couldn't I ever just let anything go? I wanted to resist. A part of me was still afraid to know him that well. To get that close.

There were no answers out there for those questions though, so after I decided to send him a text and let him know what I suspected about his new friend at The Tavern, I tried to change my chain of thought to something more constructive. *Like my livelihood.*

As I sat there, plenty of ideas finally started to come to me at last. The only problem was that each one ended with why it was completely impossible. Oh well, at least the brain was working again. I guessed that I could give it a little time. I just hoped that it wouldn't take more time than I had.

Maybe if I slept on it, I thought with my usual hopefulness, since that so often worked for me. At that thought I gave up and I headed inside.

Chapter 25

As it turns out, I slept great. But I still woke early on Sunday no closer to the answers than I had been when I went to sleep. Unfortunately, they had not chosen to come to me in my dreams. Not that time anyway. I decided it was time to get back to basics. Back to square one.

I threw on a pair of jeans and grabbed a t-shirt from the drawer. I skipped breakfast and even my coffee. I slipped on my work boots, to help me get in the right frame of mind. I grabbed my keys and my phone and slipped out the door.

Twenty minutes later, I was walking up the main trail just as the first rays of sunlight started to shine. It was completely deserted at that time of day. No workers taking their break outside to watch the action. No guests milling about curiously behind the ropes. No annoying little man in khaki's, telling me that I was screwed.

Just the birds declaring it dawn by singing to each other high up in the trees. The moisture in the air from yesterday having laid down across the ground overnight, refracted the emerging sunlight making it look like glitter. It was a beautiful illusion and it would exist for such a short time that I walked slower to appreciate it. I didn't mind. It was refueling mentally just to be there. I absorbed my surroundings while listening to the only other sound, which was the noise my boots made in the rocky dirt as I went. As I got closer that noise was joined by the soft echoing sound of gently trickling water.

I stood still and just listened to it for a few minutes, eyes closed. The sound was not unpleasant. In fact it was quite the opposite. It reminded me of wind chimes a little in the distinct variation of tones that rose up through the opening in the boulders. *Hmmmm.*

I opened my eyes again and walked all the way around the center of the clearing, slowly. I took my time. Absorbing it for a while from every angle. It was my way of *connecting* with the area. Letting it speak to me. I waited for *it* to tell *me* the way that it was meant to be.

I know that sounds ridiculous, but it was something that I *always* did whenever I was left in charge of a space. First and foremost, before anything else. The original idea was based on the things that Ben had taught me back in the very beginning. They were lessons that had served me well when working with a living medium.

I needed to comprehend the inherent beauty that existed, regardless of and in spite of me. Then I could use my designs to emphasize that rather than accidentally cover it up, or flat-out betray it. It resulted in a harmony in the space that you couldn't create artificially. It was something that felt very natural to me once I understood the idea behind it.

The point was just to relax and not put anything out. To just perceive what existed there already. I try to keep my major idiosyncrasies to myself for the most part. Those who know me best are quite familiar with this one particular quirk though, and the fact that I trusted it completely. I needed to start again from there, since things had changed so drastically.

What I felt quite clearly, was that the beautiful trickling water was as much a part of the area as the trees were. It was all in harmony. I didn't know how I could have missed it before, even without it being exposed. I also didn't know how I was going to complete my plans for the garden without betraying that. I sighed deeply and climbed up onto the highest boulder to sit.

As the sun rose higher and the air grew warmer, I realized that I knew then at least what I had to do. I just had no idea still how I would pull it off.

With that one decision made I just sat for a while,

enjoying the sun and the relief at having accomplished even that much. Unfortunately, once my mind was free of that worry, the next one popped in right on cue.

My mind wandered easily all on its' own, back to the suit in the bar from the previous night, who had been looking for Ethan. I also thought about how funny it was that I too, was already so protective of him. That was another thing he seemed to inspire in those people who really knew him. I knew our new friend *"Tie-Guy"* could be a real problem but I had no idea what to do about that either.

Of course, thinking about that inevitably reminded me that Ethan would be home that night and at *that* thought my heart started to beat a little faster. I tried to fight it. I even thought about yelling at it again, but I decided there was just no point. Physiological responses, much like rich foreign Princes with diplomatic immunity, just don't give a crap what you or anyone else *thinks*. They're gonna do what they're gonna do, and no one's gonna stop them. They have their own personal independent approval process which takes *nothing else* into consideration.

I took a few deep breaths and worked to calm myself, then jumped down off the rock and headed back to my car. I had killed quite a bit of time there, since the site was completely quiet, but the rest of the world was getting on with their day and it was time to get back to it myself. I needed to figure out a way around my new friend from Conservation. That was first and it was going to require a few phone calls.

I thought about that on the way back to my car. I was still thinking about who to call for help with my water issue, but I knew who to call for help with local politics. That one was easier.

He answered on the third ring. "Hey Honey!" He said happily when he answered.

"Hello Daddy. How are you?" I asked.

"I'm just ducky dear, and you?" He said cheerfully, always a morning person.

"Well, I hate to bother you but I think I might need a little help. Who do you know on the New Hampshire Conservation Committee? Or in the courthouse? Or anybody at all with any connections out here? I've run into an unexpected issue on the job and I may need some assistance getting things resolved in a timely manner." I explained somewhat despondently. "I get the distinct impression that my newest friend there, Mr. Wright, is not inclined to take my current time-line situation into consideration. That being that I can't wait two months for someone from the New Hampshire Department of Environmental Services to come and test the new well we accidentally uncovered." I inhaled deeply trying to catch my breath after that mouthful.

"Well? Are you branching out to include water features now too?" He asked innocently, and I had to laugh.

"I guess so. *Hmpf!* Though truly, not by choice." I insisted as I told him the details. He listened quietly until I finished.

"You know what? Let me give Dom a call. If anyone can help, it'll be him. He owes me one from that last bocce match anyway." He said laughing at the memory.

"I hate having to ask you to call in a personal favor for me, you know that. But right now I really would appreciate any help I can get. I just can't afford these kinds of delays. Especially not just to entertain a smug little man on a distinct power trip." I said, with a bit of an attitude.

I really did feel less than awesome at having to *"ask daddy"* for help. I always tried to avoid things like that whenever possible. I was also a realist, couldn't really be anything else. I know it's not always possible to succeed without asking for help from those who love you, *if* you are even lucky enough to have some of those people in your life in the first place. Thankfully I was and I did.

"I know you hate to ask honey, believe me. I also know that you can do anything you *really* want to do. I've always known that about you." He said as if reading my mind. "Of course I'm proud of you every time you accomplish something amazing all on your own. As far as the whole parenting thing goes though, we really do *like* to be needed once in a while." He laughed again but with me that time. "I'm always happy when you throw me a bone." He was only half joking and I knew then, being a parent myself, exactly what he meant. It was strange to be able to see it from both sides so clearly, but I did.

"I'm sorry, daddy. I promise I'll try to be needier." I joked back. He thanked me for being such a considerate daughter and said he'd get back to me as soon as he could.

I hung up the phone and let out a sigh. I relaxed just a little bit more. I wasn't sure if he would be able to do anything to help me or not but I was sure that he would try. It was only the second step of many yet to come but I felt like at least I was finally going in the right direction. I was sure that it had to be the right direction, since it was so hard.

Next up! To find an aquifer accessing specialist, I thought laughingly to myself. I didn't know where one would find such a person but I had an idea at least of where to start looking.

He picked up on the second ring. "Hey sugar! What can I do for you?"

I relaxed just a little bit more at the rustic, calming sound of Jack's voice. "Save my butt, I hope. I need to find someone trustworthy and local that has experience working with the underground aquifer systems up in New Hampshire. Someone who is available to help me immediately at my work site. And last but surly not least, someone who knows their way around the laws and regulations, 'cause I sure don't and I need a miracle right now! So, any chance you know someone who fits the bill?" I asked with a laugh. I knew it was a long shot, but I figured if anyone would know who to call around there, it would be Jack.

"You decided to tap into the aquifer? Won't that set your job back an awful lot this late in the game?" He asked unknowingly.

I couldn't help but laugh again. "In ways I could never have imagined! But I didn't *choose* to access it, so much as it *decided* to come and play in the middle of my site. Needless to say, I'm scrambling to get the situation under control before time runs out. *Hah!* I'm open to any and all suggestions." I said, surrendering mentally.

"Hmmm. I might have an idea. Give me a few hours. I need to see if it's even possible right now, before I get your hopes up." He said a little mysteriously. I wasn't going to argue.

"Thanks. I really appreciate anything you can offer at this point." I told him

"If there's anything I can do sugar, you know I will. You're just like one of my own already." He assured me.

"Guess that means I'll be driving you to that whiskey soon too, huh?" I joked.

"*Hah!* Probably, sugar. Prob-*a*-bly! S'alright though. It comes with the territory." He agreed with a chuckle before he hung up.

I just shook my head. Issues. Definitely issues, but still pretty damn lucky.

I let out a huge sigh and sank back further into my seat.

A few minutes later, I called Mack back and filled him in on what I knew so far. I asked him to send a group text and let everyone know that until further notice, we were shut down. Hopefully, not for long. I would send a mass email later that day with all the details and another once we were back up and running.

I was still stuck, but at least I didn't feel like I was running in place anymore. At that thought, having wasted another half hour on the phone, I was ready to get moving physically as well.

I started up the car and pulled away.

Chapter 26

I drove home, but I didn't plan to stay there. I was back in motion and it felt good. I left the keys in the car and ran upstairs.

I took a quick shower and threw my wet hair up into a tight pony tail. It would give me a headache later and dry with an ugly bump, but for the moment it was up and out of my way and that was all I cared about. It was starting to get more "hot" than "warm" lately. I decided to go to my "spring/summer clothes" bin in the closet, where it still waited to be switched over to the *"current season"* drawers, to find something to wear. I would get to that task sometime very soon, I reassured myself.

I picked out a pair of red denim capris and a black and red bandana print top. I pulled my little flat black sneakers out again and threw them on. I got my sketchbook and my pencil case and headed out, thinking I might take a ride up to the beach and start drawing up some ideas. Let the nearby sound of the water inspire me.

I decided the first stop would have to be lunch though. Someplace close. It was well before noon but I wasn't going to make it much longer!

I drove the short trip to the diner with thoughts of a chicken kabob salad making me practically salivate. Skipping breakfast was not really a good idea for me. By lunch time, my eyes tended to be much bigger than my stomach. Inevitably, I would get way too much food and then end up throwing half of it away while moaning in pain from the half that I ate way too fast.

I was aware of my patterns at that point in life, but that didn't mean that I could stop myself from following them. They are patterns for a reason, after all.

I went inside and luckily, sat right down. That was nearly impossible to do early on a Sunday morning, but by late morning the breakfast crowd had thinned out to a more manageable size. I got the table farthest from the door and I sat facing the wall for added separation. Even at its' max capacity, it was still smaller and much less crowded with emotional noise than any other place around. That was part of what I loved about it. I was too hungry to pay much attention to it then anyway, so I wasn't worried.

I ordered without looking at the menu. It was the same waitress that I usually saw there, the one from movie night and she didn't bat an eye at my hurried attitude. I drank half of my Sprite while I waited in hopes that it would keep me from inhaling my entire chicken kabob salad in under five minutes when it came.

She was back with it a short time later and I dove in unabashedly anyway, my good intentions completely forgotten right along with everything else, even the noise. Sometimes it paid to be so single-minded about food. I both heard and felt, only vaguely, the noise from the people coming and going behind me while I ate. I was quite happy to ignore it all.

The salad was cold and crisp and the chicken was perfectly grilled so that it was still tender but just warm enough to stick to the feta cheese. The only thing that could distract me from the perfection drizzled in creamy Greek dressing in front of me, was the warm, freshly baked pita bread in my left hand.

It was exactly what I wanted just then and it was all I was focusing on. I was in heaven. I know I probably sighed loudly, more than once while I ate. I'm not kidding around when I say that I am an insatiable foodie at heart.

I was so momentarily engrossed, that I was shocked by the powerful but familiar feeling that finally broke through. It was a deep, vibrating ripple of heat. It hit me *hard, and quick!* I gasped and looked up at the wall in front of me. Swallowed, before I choked. Then I took a deep breath. *Ethan!*

He was there. Of that I was instantly 100% sure. I didn't even have to look, but I did anyway. I knew that feeling too well already. No one else had ever come close enough to feeling the same way, on the same level, for me to possibly mistake it for anyone else. It was pure Ethan and I *had* missed it, damn him!

"You should not be allowed to do that in public!" He said from the table diagonally behind and across from me. He chuckled, but the feelings coming off of him were no joke.

My heart hammered in my chest and I wondered if he could hear it. I took another deep breath and just stared at him over my shoulder. Sitting there in the sun by the window, looking like a summer afternoon daydream from my teen years. His hair was slightly damp, like my own. It looked like he had simply shaken his head and ran out the door, wet black half-curls sticking out in every direction. He had on a well-worn soft grey t-shirt and heavily faded Levis. He grinned at me with a wide smile full of bright white teeth and his mirrored aviators completed the comfy-classic look. I couldn't help but laugh and shake my head.

"That work that you used to do. *Before.* Was that *modeling*, by any chance?" I couldn't resist asking with a broad smile of my own. I couldn't help it. It was impossible to wipe the damn thing off my face! It only grew larger as he stood up and walked over to my table. He pulled out the chair, hooked his sunglasses on his shirt and sat down across from me.

It was weird, because he really hadn't been gone that long, but so much had happened that it seemed like it had been *much* longer. I had to admit that it felt good to have him back, sitting across from me, sending wave after wave of those powerful, wonderful feelings right through me. *Oh boy.* I was starting to get the impression that I might be in *big* trouble. I promised myself that I would worry about it later. Right then all pathways in my brain were occupied.

He didn't answer me. He just kept grinning. He leaned forward with his elbows on his knees and I felt his warm fingers sweep gently over my knee under the table. The contact was so light, so inconsequential. Yet it made my stomach quiver for just a second and a warmth began to spread. *Whoa!* Okay! Still in the diner! I had to remind myself. *Deep breaths.* I stared back at him.

Being around him in public was either going to help me to finally master the art of mediation once and for all, or it would make me hyperventilate and pass out, whichever came first.

"You're back early." I stated matter-of-factly, in an attempt to put the fire out. He slid his hand higher up the inside of my thigh and I stopped breathing altogether for a few seconds.

"I couldn't hold out any longer." He admitted quietly in a deep voice and it was the last thing that I needed to hear right then. I was already getting lost in things I had no business feeling there. Another ripple of desire came across the table and it rode on the back of my own that time, as both waves passed through me simultaneously. Between the two, my hands were throbbing in the end and I was sure, putting on a fantastic one man show right there in the back corner of the town diner. Especially if the look on his face was any indication.

His hand slid even further up my thigh then and sent a shock wave right through me as it continued up and passed right over the very center of me, warm skin over denim. Just once. *It was more than enough.* The throbbing was resonating in other places after that as well. *Damn!* We needed to get out of there! Before we did something to get us *thrown* out and never allowed back. *Check please!* I thought frantically. I looked behind me to see if anyone had noticed the open seduction taking place in the middle of their lunch.

Luckily, it didn't appear that anyone but me had been affected by what he was doing. I looked back at him and he smiled, then he brought his hands up and clasped them together while he rested his forearms on the table.

"That's right. You just keep those where I can see them mister." I said, trying not to sound as breathless as I felt. "So I can't enjoy my food in public, but what you're doing, that's okay?" I laughed and he just went right on grinning.

"Are you finished?" He asked, looking down at my forgotten salad.

"Um, yeah." I said with a laugh, remembering how excited I had been about it only moments before. Eating half had taken the edge off my hunger and seeing Ethan had short circuited my sequence before I could eat the other half and make my stomach hurt. I was actually grateful then for the distraction. *Hah!* What a distraction!

I laughed again and he just looked up questioningly. He didn't expect an answer though. He *was* starting to get me by then, at least on some levels. For some reason, that didn't bother me as much as I thought it should anymore. I didn't want to dwell on that right then either though.

"Where are you headed now?" He asked, and the heat flowing over me simmered just below a boil. I could almost feel it blistering my skin.

"With you." I answered without missing a beat. The rest of my former plans were more flexible and happily forgotten. At least temporarily.

He sat perfectly still and smoldered a minute more at the joy and the surprise that my response gave him before he took a shaky breath himself. He had clearly been thinking we would make a plan to meet later and that he would have to contain the desire building in him so dramatically until then. He had a tight hold on it as he sat there, but after my answer it was questionable for a moment or two. I could feel the intensity swirling like a raging bull behind the gate, frozen in anticipation, hyper focused, waiting for that pin to fall.

He started to reach for my hand and push back his chair, but he looked over my shoulder at the same time and he stopped himself. I could feel his control stretch a little tighter to include another attempt at patience. It didn't feel like it would last very long.

I turned to see what had held him up and saw Gabby walking over to our table. *Jesus!* Could she possibly have worse timing?!

"Simone, I'm so glad I caught you!" She said smiling her normal, *too huge* smile. "Hey Ethan. I didn't realize you two knew each other." She said offhandedly, as she sat down next to him, completely oblivious to the storm raging inside each of us.

"Afternoon Gabby. Yeah, actually Simone has been coming into The Tavern since she first moved here." He answered simply with a smile. He said it so calmly and smoothly, that no one would ever detect the sexual tension reaching a fever pitch behind that facade. *No one but me.* I could feel it *much* too clearly. It was making it hard for me to breathe never mind think straight. Meanwhile he sat there looking as though he didn't have a care in the world. He was *so much* better at hiding it than I was! I was instantly a tad bit jealous.

"Hey Gabby. What's up?" I asked a little shaky, hoping to get right to the point.

"Well, my boss came in the other day with tickets for the new "Cirque Du Soliel" show that she couldn't use. I know Mary wanted them but that, excuse my language, *selfish bitch* got the last two sets. Count 'em, two!" She shouted holding up two fingers angrily. "Now no one is supposed to get them twice in a row but she thinks that doesn't apply to her for some reason." She pushed on with barely a breath in between.

"See my boss is a season ticket holder at the North Shore Music Theatre and whenever she can't go, she gives the tickets to someone at the office." She informed us as an aside. "Well I just couldn't let her get them again. It's just not fair. So I spoke up and I took them, saying I would take my niece. Just love her. She is such a doll! She lives in the city and I don't see her nearly enough. Anyway, long story short." She said and laughed again too loudly, as I was already thinking, *way* too late! She just continued on, unaware of my thoughts or of our general discomfort.

The feelings I was fighting to control had already been put on hold for a few days and they weren't really interested in being put off anymore once the source of said feelings was sitting right in front of me. I tried to keep *my* patience while Ethan held precariously onto his as well. Just... *barely!*

"So, I don't want to give the tickets back now." She said obliviously. "She might get mad that I took them before I checked if she could actually go. Her mother-in-law just happens to be a volunteer usher in her section and, if the seats are empty, she'll notice. Then she'll definitely be mad! I would have to explain then anyway. *So!*" She said, taking a deep breath and finally getting to the point, *I hoped desperately!*

"I thought maybe you might want to use them and take Liliana." She finally said, hopeful that I would get her out of the mess that she was in.

I could let her suffer the consequences for her own actions. I do believe in karma and all of that and leaving things to the higher powers sometimes. But Gabby had never been anything but kind to me and that made me part of the *good* karma that she had out there, so I decided I would help her out if I could. Which would *hopefully* get her out of there faster in the process!

"Sure. Thanks for thinking of us." I said sincerely. "What day is it on?" I asked. As I did, I could feel Ethan's patience slip another notch and I looked at him with wary eyes. He made eyes back at me and then he let loose another short, but powerful wave that washed through me as a warning of what was going to happen if we didn't get out of there. *Soon!*

Holy crap!

"*Don't!* Do! That." I said in a muffled gasp, and then realized too late, what I had done. Gabby just looked at me for a second and smiled awkwardly.

"Sorry." I said quickly. "Not you. I was just thinking about something else. Uh... Sorry." She didn't look convinced, but she let it go. We *really* needed to get out of there! That thought brought me back to what she was saying.

"The show is this Saturday. Oh, do you think you'll be able to swing it?" She asked squinting, as if she were afraid of my answer but still hopeful.

"Well, I will have to check with her father and make sure it's okay to keep her an extra night. As long as he doesn't have plans I know he won't mind, so it should be fine." I assured her. She was beaming.

She wasn't the only one.

"Oh, that's awesome! Thank you so much! I hear it's a great show! You guys are gonna love it" She insisted, hugging me unexpectedly. "Alright, I have to run. Hey, do you want to follow me and grab the tickets?" She asked innocently and I felt actual *pain* come off of Ethan at the mere suggestion. I gasped, as quietly as I could.

"Uh no, sorry, now's not the best time for me. Why don't you just bring them to movie night on Friday?" I offered. "Were you planning to go?"

"Of course! Alright, sure. That works." She said satisfied and got up finally. "I'll see you then and thanks again." She gushed.

"No, no. Thank you." I answered with a laugh.

"Oh right! *Hah,* you're welcome! Okay, I'll see you later Ethan." She said on her way out.

"Bye." We both said at once, and relief instantly swept through us.

He looked at me intently then grabbed my hand and stood up. I stood too. He took out his wallet and left a twenty on each table and led me out the door. It was way too much, but he didn't seem to be in the mood to wait for change and I wasn't going to argue. I figured it was better than running out short.

I tried not to notice who else might be in the diner that would recognize me, or him for that matter as we walked out. I felt like I should try to be more discreet but I couldn't seem to make myself care enough just then. All I could think about was getting somewhere alone with him. *Fast!*

"Should I follow you?" I asked.

"No. We'll take my car. It's faster." He said and again, I couldn't argue with that logic. When we reached the curb he held me back without thinking. With his arm around my waist and my hip held tight to his hip. He stopped and looked for cars. It was so natural for him. So gentle and so protective... It stopped me short for a second. It had been quick, instinctual.

I just shook my head. I wanted to be mad or protest as usual, for his presumptuousness with such an intimate act. I could cross the street by myself just fine. But all I felt was warm at his kindness instead and happy that he was so close to me again. He was making it very hard to keep an emotional distance, the jerk.

The cars passed and so did the moment. He dropped his arm from my waist and reached for my hand again. I looked down as I took his. Just that simple touch and the heat came flaring back. We stared at each other for a beat then quickly jogged across the street hand in hand.

I really wasn't big on overt PDA's, especially with someone who wasn't supposed to *"officially"* be my significant other. It was as though after the recent absence though, the need to touch each other was much greater. I guess that old saying about distance and fondness and all was true too. It felt almost *too* good!

We did have to separate when we reached the car though and it was probably a good thing for the time being. The alarm bleeped as we approached and the doors whooshed open. We climbed inside and in seconds we were moving. The familiar smell of leather and *him*, along with the familiar pulsing heat storm raging inside the small space, had me more anxious to reach our destination than I could remember feeling in a very *long* time!

He was concentrating on driving as fast as he could safely, but his desire simmered *just* below that. Nothing else was coming across. Just those two emotions, neck and neck.

After a few, tense minutes, I gave in to it a little. I reached around the gear shift and slid my hand onto his thigh. *Just to see.* I felt a quick rush of that knee bending heat and I looked up at him, surprised by the intensity of his reaction. Thank God I was already sitting down!

I was even more shocked when he down-shifted and swerved back and forth while slamming on the brakes! My hands went to the "oh shit" bar and the dashboard automatically. He came to a stop and turned to look at me with zero humor.

"Did you want to do this here then? This car's not big enough though, so we're talking you, me and a bed of pine needles." He waited a beat, completely serious, teetering on the very edge. I could feel the strength of his desire nearing levels that I recognized from before, and I knew we were reaching the point of no return.

I looked around at the trees and the thick underbrush. Actually considered it for a few, weak seconds. Luckily, it didn't look too comfortable and I wanted to enjoy it, not have to worry about a rock in my back or someone driving by. I looked back at him and just shook my head no. I put my hands back in my own lap, and he shifted into first again.

After that, his hand stayed on the gear shift and mine stayed in my lap. We were both burning up, even without touching. I was pretty sure the moment our skin made contact again, it would be complete and total combustion! And that really wasn't a good idea in the middle of the road. Or even on the *side* of the road. *Not in a small town like Pinegrove!*

I found myself wishing for the first time ever, that he would drive faster. I gave him a look and he seemed to understand. He sped up. I just grabbed the *"oh shit"* bar again and held on.

Chapter 27

I was glad when we drove up my street, since it wasn't far from the diner, that being part of what had persuaded me to go there in the first place. I was temporarily confused however, when he turned right before we reached my driveway. It was at that point that the cloud cleared just enough for me to remember that he lived right down the street from me. I was glad he chose to go there actually, I thought once the neurons in my brain began to fire again, since there was likely to be people out and about around my place in the middle of a Sunday afternoon. It was a farm after all.

His driveway wasn't as long as mine but it did turn a few bends around two very large boulders, one on the right, then one on the left, that blocked the house from view. Once we came around the last curve though, I was duly impressed with the modern structure of glass and white stucco built into the side of the hill. He pulled all the way up to a garage that opened onto the right side of the bottom floor. He reached up to the visor and pushed a button that was clipped onto it and the glass door slowly rose. He pulled in and I was immediately struck by how clean it was. It was made wide enough to hold four cars but there was also a whole room sized area left over beyond that near the back, for working. The walls were all painted a deep blue color and the expansive floors were an uninterrupted sea of battleship grey.

There were natural stained wooden cabinets and sturdy butcher block counter top surfaces running the span of the room and I guessed that they contained all of the usual garage items since not a single one, not even a can of oil, was visible anywhere. I turned to look at him with a clear look of surprise, *again.* He just smiled that winning smile of his.

"What? So I'm organized." He laughed. Then he grew serious again. "Do you really want to discuss this right now?" That fast the heat was back in the forefront, and the curiosity was forgotten. I just shook my head. Sitting was starting to become uncomfortable by then and that was not exactly conducive to conversation anyway.

He pressed the button on his visor again and the garage door closed. Then he opened the doors to the car and we both climbed out. We ran around and met at the back of the car, running into each other. I would have laughed at the absurdity of it, but the urge was buried too deep under the need. The need had finally been given free reign and all I could do then was surrender to it.

The breath escaped out of me when I hit the hard surface that was his body, but I didn't mind. *At all.* His arms wrapped around me and I couldn't help but let out a huge sigh of relief.

It was *crazy* how amazing it was to have him next to me again! Everything about it was immensely satisfying. The way he felt, pressed so tightly against me. Unyielding, but so warm. The way he smelled. I could breathe it in all day! The way he held me like he would never let go. And last but certainly not least was the way *he* felt while doing it! I should have known something that good would be addictive, dammit!

Right then I didn't care though. I would have risked just about anything at that point, to fulfill the desires coursing freely through me. As well as *from* me!

He was only kissing my neck at first and I was already melting like a complete amateur. I hated it and loved it at the same time. His hands came around meanwhile and quickly undid my jeans. Between what he was doing to me and what *he* was feeling, I couldn't even hope to contain it. I couldn't control it either and I stopped trying. I surrendered completely once and for all. Just let go, and let it take over.

He lifted his head and looked at me, as he pushed my capris down over my hips. I kicked off my sneakers and he lifted me up and he *actually sat me* on the back of the car momentarily, while he slipped them off the rest of the way! Oh boy, he really *was* single-minded I thought, petrified I would leave a dent!

He threw them towards the leather couch that was against the wall behind him and then quickly lifted me back up again. His mouth found mine while I wrapped my legs and my arms around him. He didn't head in the direction of the couch though. Instead, he carried me over towards the long counter while we tried to devour each other. We slammed hard into the cabinets in our haste when we arrived, but neither of us cared in the slightest. His arm behind me took the brunt of the impact. I didn't feel a thing other than his lips sliding over mine and the soft wood surface beneath me, when he set me gently on the edge. He reached in his pocket for a condom then undid his own jeans.

Within seconds he was inside of me and my jaw dropped as my head fell back hard against the cabinets. I heard the air rush from him loudly at the same time. He looked up then and pulled my head back up with a hand under my ponytail. He tilted my face toward his so he could continue to devour my mouth. I wanted to cooperate, I really did, but I was having trouble getting enough air into my own lungs and I needed my mouth for that. My nose just couldn't seem to move enough oxygen by itself to keep up with what he was doing to me.

I pulled back and took as full a breath as I could get into my lungs, then looked back down at him while he moved. His eyelids were low and he was watching our bodies where they met with great interest. Then I was watching too.

His shirt was in the way though and it was suddenly extremely offensive to me. I pulled it up and he helped me to get it over his head and I dropped it on the floor. Better. *Much better.* You really couldn't beat the freakin' view!

My reaction set off a similar one in him and I felt it come back to me all over again. Our momentum was rocking me off my center emotionally, as he rocked me back and forth on the countertop again and again, physically. I wouldn't have stopped him even if I could have. The feelings were crashing over me, one after the other and I couldn't think about anything else. *Didn't care* about anything else just then, for that blissful moment in time.

I didn't let go *completely* very often. It wasn't easy for me to do. Generally when I did though, it was worth it.

I was starting to wonder how much more I could take when he looked up at me to check in. He wanted to see how I was doing.

"You alright?" He asked in a shaky voice. I could tell then, that he was a little worried about his lack of control.

I let out a huge gust of air at that.

"*Huuhhh*! Are you kidding me? I've never been better!" I said emphatically, staring him right in the eye.

He held more tightly onto my hips.

"*Uuuahhhhh!*" He exhaled loudly, as he pulled me closer again, *slowly*. "I'm not going to last much longer." He admitted easily. Then he looked back up at me. "But don't worry. This is only round one." He said intently as he lifted me again and carried me over to the couch.

He laid me down on the baby soft black leather and I got lost in the cushions completely when he came down on top of me. Once there was nothing for either of us to hold up, we relaxed fully into the feelings. It didn't take long for either of us to find fulfillment, and I know for a fact that neither one of us was the least bit sorry.

Afterwards, we stayed on the couch for a bit, recouping. I was lying there considering how very *un*-me it all was. It was *crazy* what he did to me! It wasn't normal! At that thought I looked at him curiously, like the explanation would be written on his face.

I shook my head again. "How do you *do* that?!" I asked him seriously.

He was lying comfortably beside me, breathing slow even breaths, each of us only half clothed but completely comfortable. His energy, entirely changed. He was very relaxed by then. *Serene*, even.

"Do what?" He asked simply in return.

"Make all my bones turn to '*Jello.*'" I said more honestly than I was normally comfortable with. "Make me forget where I am. *Who* I am. *To breathe! Hmpf!*" I just looked at him in wonder.

"I do that to you?" He asked, while he reached over and

took out my pony tail and began to run his hands through my hair. He was quite pleased by the idea.

"Mmmm hmmm." I answered with my eyes closed. Just his fingers gliding slowly through my still damp hair was enough to make me practically purr! It was ridiculous and I said so.

"You make me feel like I'm some out of control teenager again, and I am soooo *not!* At least I'm not *supposed* to be!" We both laughed at that, but I was serious again afterwards.

"The feelings... that I get from you... *Hmpf!* I'm no rookie when it comes to blocking that kind of stuff. Especially when it's unwanted." His mood dipped low for just a second at the thought of that I noticed. I went right past it. "With you, I don't want to block it, but then I forget every intention I ever had and I get completely lost in it instead! Like I'm seventeen all over again." I said in wonder. His joy came back around then.

"Well, I for one sure am glad that you are *not* seventeen! 'Cause I'd be in jail for sure!" He joked and we both laughed again. "But I don't think it's me." He said more seriously. "I think it's *you.* In case you haven't noticed, I've hardly escaped unaffected. I don't know what it is about you that constantly brings out the absolute *animal* in me!" He insisted quietly, the memory clear in his eyes. It hit me a second later. *Ahhhhhh.....*

"I'm not going to lie Simone. I've enjoyed a pretty active sex life in the years since I started working on '*catching up.*'" He informed me with a wiggle of his eyebrows. "But I can't remember *ever* failing to make it out of the damn garage before being entirely overcome!" He admitted with a rough laugh, looking around us in wonder of his own at our situation. "This would be a first for me. We officially just christened it." He proclaimed with a nod and a satisfied smile.

He jumped up then without warning and I was curious what he was up to. Not enough to get up however. I waited patiently for once and was rewarded when he came back a minute later with a glass of water from the sink near the counter that we'd just thoroughly *'christened.'* Once he was standing there offering it, I suddenly realized how *totally* parched I was.

"Oh, you are the *best!*" I exclaimed, as my eyes practically rolled back in my head. He laughed and then held his hand out to take it back after I drank my fill.

"So now that you've had the deluxe tour of the garage..." Another eyebrow wiggle. "Would you like to see the rest of the place? Or are you content enough right here?" He teased.

I grinned in spite of myself. *Like a freakin' teenager! Uggghhh!*

"Care to throw me my pants?" I asked innocently, trying to keep it in check.

"Hmmm. Not really, but I will." He grinned and tossed them over to me. "You may have them back, but only temporarily." He joked and pulled me up after, so I could zip them up and button them.

When I was reasonably presentable again, he took my hand and led me barefoot, through the door at the far end of the room.

The interior was as modern and as immaculate as the garage had been. It was similar to his cabin at Camp, in the high ceilings and an abundance of glass. But that's where the similarities ended. His home was done in soft white tones and it was bathed in sunlight.

It actually reminded me of my own place a little and I said so.

"That's not as much of a coincidence as you would think." He confided with a smug grin. "I actually helped Jack to remodel that place originally." He admitted with a satisfied smile. Once he said that, I could totally see it. The same clean lines. The same sweeping views, only his looked out over the forest.

"It's beautiful." I said. "But I guess you already know how much I like it." We both smiled knowingly at each other and he pointed toward the back of the house with a tilt of his head.

"Come on. I'll show you the rest." He said. He took my hand again, but not because he needed it to get me to follow him. We were still having a hard time not touching each other for any length of time. That was still not quite back to normal yet. I wasn't worried about it anymore though. It was just a physical need and with the physical side of things, I had no complaints. I wasn't holding back on that anymore. I was a living breathing human and that came with urges that needed to be fulfilled. He was equipped for the job and he was up for it. It was as simple as that.

It was funny to me that I could be so *"all-or-nothing"* with that part of my relationship with him, and yet so contradictory when it came to others. I chalked it up to multiple-personality disorder and followed him guilt free, into the kitchen.

Our places differed there in more than just size. Where my kitchen was light and bright, like the place was as a whole, his was an exercise in contrasts. With the rich deep cherry cabinetry and a black, gold, and brown speckled granite surface that went on for miles. That was accented with a thick blue-green glass that looked like the ocean on a sunny day that made up the doors and various shelves around the room. The dark cabinets were lit from underneath and the whole room was bright with sunshine from the huge skylight over the main island. Dark and light coexisted everywhere in perfect harmony.

"So you were a contractor and a decorator, before becoming Camp counselor?" I tried again, always looking to make sense of him.

"No, not a decorator." He joked. "I did go through a period where I had a lot to learn. Jack was a good *"on-the-job"* teacher." He half explained.

Hmmm. Jack again. "Just how close *are* you and Jack?" I asked flat out, even more curious about him then than ever before.

He laughed again. "Jack and I go way back. I told you, I grew up here." He smiled, but it faltered in the end for just the briefest of moments and I felt that sickening sadness sweep through him again. He was quick to push it away. Quick enough for it not to show on his face, but not quick enough to keep me from feeling it.

He knew that of course. He took a deep breath and walked out through the sliders off of his kitchen onto a large deck. I followed him but I kept my distance. He stood at the railing with his back to me, looking out into the treetops. I sat down gently on a wooden deck chair and looked around while I waited. I still didn't want to push him, but even if we were just going to be friends, I felt sure that he would have to tell me about all of that at some point. It was too much a part of who he was not to. That much I could tell already.

There were flower gardens around the houses edge and a few well-worn trails marked out in river stones that led from his property into the woods. Other than that, it was mostly untouched. Just the rocky hills and the beautiful, natural woods and sky to set the scene behind him. He stood still and quiet for a while and I let him. I could feel him battling his indecision and I wouldn't force it. A part of *me* was still afraid to know just what had hurt him so badly. I felt that deep pain come and go a few times as he considered whether he wanted to talk about it or not. Finally he decided, and he spoke.

"Well, I guess if you really want to hear this, then I have to start at the beginning." He stared out into the forest, his back to me still. He took a deep cleansing breath and began his tale.

"My father Joe was a *height* too. Though he never really came to terms with it. My grandmother had died when he was young and my grandfather was trying hard to survive as a single parent in a time when such a thing didn't exist. He had no idea how to deal with my dads' issues and no time to do it in, even if he had.

My father saw a few doctors over the years, physical and psychological, on urging from my grandparents church. But Joe was mostly resistant and he ended up being labeled mildly schizophrenic in the end. Mostly due to the things he said he '*saw.*'" He took a moment and a breath, obviously believing their skills to be very similar at the very least.

"He finally learned to just shut up about it, but he never did *deal* with it." I could feel anger and resentment towards this man, Joe, but there was a sadness, too. I could tell that Ethan would have liked to have been able to help his dad. Unfortunately that had been way before his time.

"Instead, he dropped out of High School and started drinking pretty heavily by age sixteen. He was in and out of jail a few times throughout his early twenties. Mostly for misdemeanors like public drunkenness or domestic assault on one of the many women who were blinded enough by his good looks to try and love him anyway." I could feel his fear at that point. I realized for the first time that he felt somewhat negatively about his looks, considered them to be false advertising. The difference was that his father took advantage of it, whereas he felt guilty for it. Huh. I felt a definite click when that mental piece fell into place. He took another deep breath and kept going.

"According to the stories there were a *few* unwanted pregnancies along the way. Apparently, he didn't care about using any sort of protection. It was still way too *un*-cool back then. My dad had a foolproof way of persuading them to get rid of any "unfortunate accidents" though. He basically told them to take care of it or *he* would. No one had ever doubted him. No one ever dared to defy him either. At least not until my mother came along." The pain was much greater when he spoke of his mother I noticed. *Wow!*

"Jillian was a pretty girl and she could have had any guy she wanted back then, but for reasons unexplainable she only wanted Joe. They were quite the beautiful, manipulative, conniving, untrustworthy pair. She'd had enough of her own anger built up at the world, to hold up the longest in the face of his. They had been together for two whole years when she told him the '*good*' news."

"You can imagine her displeasure when she received the same ultimatum that all the others had. She had known all along that he wasn't good for much, but she had been certain that he would marry her or at least let her move in with him if she got pregnant. She wanted out of her abusive fathers' house and he was supposed to be her ticket." He didn't stop to feel sorry for her I noticed. He kept up his tale instead.

"When that didn't happen she wasn't just disappointed, she was *furious!* She took the abortion money that he threw at her and left town, screaming that she wouldn't want his *"fucking bastard"* anyway. Those were probably the truest words she ever spoke." He finished and my heart broke into tiny pieces as I finally realized without a doubt where that deep chasm of pain originated from. My chest ached at the picture that was taking shape in my mind. He wasn't done yet though. Not even close.

"She went and stayed with a cousin who lived out of town until I was born. Then she immediately came back and filed for child support, thinking she had beaten him at last. He managed to kick her one more time though, when instead of quietly giving in, he contested paternity."

"That was the first battle. In the end the test came back positive that I was indeed his bouncing baby boy and she thought for sure she *finally* had him. Then he surprised her again by filing for full custody rather than agree to pay child support. Claimed her to be an unfit mother." He just shook his head but I could feel the pain again quite clearly.

"Even though it was completely true, she had no intention of giving up her meal ticket. Not after she had done all the work of carrying me. They fought tooth and nail over the baby that nobody *really* wanted. For three years. I bounced back and forth, and occasionally in and out of foster care when they were at their worst."

"In the end the judge was tired of both of their antics and didn't want another ward living entirely off of the state with both parents present and accounted for. So he finally settled it by awarding joint custody with permanent, provisionary support from the state, as long as they stayed out of trouble."

"It kept the situation mostly out of the courtroom from there on out, but it also left me a perpetual pawn in their constant battle for power over the other. When I was really small, it was just about treating me like a possession to be passed back and forth. Once I got older and could talk and *spy*, I was used mercilessly by both sides in their constant quest for revenge and control." I could feel how much he detested their lack of conscious.

"I eventually moved permanently with my mother, back into her father Mike's, house. He was always "Mike." Never *"Grampy"* to me. I wasn't allowed to call him that. I didn't count as a *'real'* grandchild." I felt the pain of the little boy again and I was getting really pissed.

"The only rewards I was ever given were for betraying one to the other. But the joy wore off as soon as the ice cream melted. It didn't take me too long to get tired of it and start to figure them out. I finally realized that it was never really about my earning their love. It had always only been about them hurting each other. By the ripe old age of seven, I'd had enough." He was a little stronger once he got past that part and I was glad. I wanted so badly to go back in time and protect him.

"I told them that I was done and that I wouldn't be a part of their fight anymore. Well, then they had no use for me at all. Fortunately, they left me alone after that. *Unfortunately,* they left me alone after that." I could *feel* that emptiness as he spoke. That surety that, the only reason that they had ever tolerated him, was to use him. That and for the monthly check.

"Other than to smile and look good when the people from the state came by to check on me, they had no use for me at all. I was left completely to my own devices." I wanted him to be kidding, but I knew that he wasn't.

"Basically, I was told that if I wasn't going to help them, that they wouldn't help me either. Never mind the fact that they were the parents and I was seven." He looked down over the edge of the deck and shook his head at the memory. I was tight lipped, trying really hard not to cry *real* tears with the pain that was coursing through me. His *and* my own.

Mostly his. On his own. At *seven! Holy Jesus!*

I remembered then my thoughts that day at the cabin about what an adorable child he must have been, and I was instantly, *incredibly* pissed. Not only had that someone obviously *not* loved him to pieces but they had apparently been downright *cruel* to him on top of it!

That bitch!! That was all I could think for a few minutes. I tried to pay attention, but I really just wanted to hit something! The anger wasn't his though, surprisingly. It was all my own. He was still moving swiftly through his tale, and I could tell that keeping it moving was important to him finishing.

"They couldn't throw me out, not and still get a check. But they could ignore me. So for the next eight years or so, that's exactly what they did. I washed my own clothes. I did my homework alone and if I had a question, then I asked it the next day at school.

I was also responsible for my own meals. My mother refused to share hers with a traitor." He said plainly, like it was common policy. Alright, I knew exactly who I wanted to hit then! What the Hell had been wrong with this lady?!

"I was not allowed to leave the house to play with friends, and the ones from school were too far away to help me, so a lot of my meals came either during school time or out of the neighborhood trash cans for the next couple of years." That part had been particularly hard for him to tell me and a sob caught in my throat. I fought hard to keep it there. He did not want my pity. Of that, I was absolutely sure. I refused to let him down. If he could get through it, so could I. I slowed my breathing a little and he kept going.

"I had some small amount of childish hope that she would give in eventually but to her credit, she never did." He laughed humorlessly at that backhanded compliment. "I was never invited to her table to eat again once I stood up for myself. Declared myself my *own* team." He said and there was still a little bit of that wonder in his voice, even then.

Hmpf. A one man team. Sorry, no. A one *"boy"* team! I had to shake my head to lose that one quick, but I managed to keep it quiet.

"It was lonely, but it was still *better.*" I could not only picture it perfectly from his words, but I could also *feel* the loneliness of which he spoke and I had personally never felt anything like it before. I closed my eyes and tried hard to keep it in. I didn't want him to need to stop himself because of me.

"My father was no help. I went to him a few times over the years, but he wasn't shy about reminding me that he had never wanted me in the first place. Or that, he wasn't going to drive around in a shit box, just so that I could have fancy new clothes. Basically, it wasn't his problem. He did his time on the weekends in order to get his part of the check. But he did it with even less interest than my mother. Mostly, he left me with my grandfather and went out to drink, but that was fine with me. Grandpa Stone was the only person I ever remember being nice to me back then." He lightened a little at the mention of his Grandfather I noticed gratefully.

"He just didn't have the strength or the means to do anything to stop Joe and Jillian from hurting me the rest of the time. He was dependent on Joe at that point for his roof and food, and too afraid of being thrown into a nursing home if he caused trouble. And *not* a nice one either. I didn't blame him then and I still don't." Again, there was no anger coming at me at all. He was being honest as usual, and quite selfless. *As usual.*

"I knew I had no options for at least the next few years, so I tried to make the best of it. I had a few friends in school that didn't care if my clothes were old and stained. We played at school, also before and after in the schoolyard. I never went to their houses though and they never came to mine. It wasn't allowed. Anything that she could do to hurt me that wouldn't leave a mark, she would do with true joy. The game then was how bad she could be, while looking really good on paper." He shook his head and smiled like he understood. In the memory I could mostly feel his deep disappointment in her, even more than his own pain at being that little boy.

"I got a little older and decided to try talking to the school guidance counselor about my situation, but she thought I was greatly exaggerating the severity of it. They refused to believe that she really did the things I told them. Or, if anyone did believe me, she would come in and scare them off with her threatening manner and the whole thing would be dropped. Either way, nothing would ever come of it." I could feel how helpless a time that was for him and that feeling was in the running for the worst of them all so far.

"I know now, that she was a true sociopath and had no regard for the consequences of her actions or anyone's feelings aside from her own. I think on some level, I always knew that she was different that way. The thing is she wasn't just crazy, she was *smart!* I'm talking *Mensa* level smart! Unfortunately all her guile and wisdom was used only to get what she wanted, fool who she needed to, and hurt who she felt like hurting. She had nothing else to do, quite frankly. She never worked a day in her life." Even when he wasn't trying to earn her love anymore, I thought sadly, just to stay out of her path as much as possible. She still went out of her way to hurt him.

"My father's sins were mostly crimes of neglect and indifference. My mother on the other hand, she worked actively over the years at hurting me." I kept quiet but she was hurting me too at the moment.

"I eventually also came to realize that it was her way of hurting *him,* even though that was something that she could never really accomplish. His defense was that she couldn't use me to hurt him, if he didn't care. I think that drove her the craziest. She never gave up trying though. She just kept practicing on me. Just in case. It was almost just as good in her book. Because I was *his.*" He didn't stop to reflect on that too much. He seemed to have had some help working that part out and I could tell that he still wasn't really comfortable with it. He pushed on through his explanation and it was obvious he hadn't spoken most of it out loud very many times. It still felt raw to him even then.

"I was never allowed to play a sport or learn an instrument. Those things required fees and rides back and forth and that was simply out of the question." He was reliving it and I was feeling it all right along with him. He would know that, too. I wondered suddenly if that was part of why he had avoided telling me all of that, because he wanted to spare me what he had experienced. It seemed like something he would think of.

So many things about him made sense then. The joy he found in simple things like his music and running. Not just because no one could keep him from them anymore, but also because he needed those things for their therapeutic benefit as well. *Hmpf.* Kind of like I needed his music for *my* peace of mind. What an interesting circle that was, I thought to myself while he was quiet.

He sighed again and finally turned to lean his back on the railing and face me for the first time since he had started. He was calmer. He didn't feel the need to hide that particular pain from me anymore and he felt better about that. For that at least, I was glad. I had no idea how to ever make up for the rest of it, but I was happy to help him in any way I could. I smiled a small half smile in encouragement and he went on.

"Even with the daily life of her disdain and neglect, I was getting by alright. I don't know why I never believed all the bad things they always said about me and to me. I always just knew somehow not to. That I really was going to be okay, eventually. Once I was old enough to get out. That inner strength was enough to get me through an awful lot over the years. Just holding on for *'eventually.'*" He took a breath. Gearing up.

"Then I got sick." He said that, and the bad feeling in the pit of my stomach was back. It was an ugly, dark place kind of

feeling. He kept going. *Deeper.*

Damn! There was more! Uggggghhh!

"Then I wasn't just an unobtrusive monthly check that stayed out of her way anymore. Suddenly I was a real problem that required possibly expensive medical attention. Or worse, someone who needed to be taken care of long term. That was unacceptable of course, and that was when I was no longer even welcome worth the check anymore. I was no longer welcome in her house at all. She had a new boyfriend by that time and the possibility of greener pastures, so I was just a nusience at that point anyway." He said plainly.

"I was dumped off at my fathers' house. That was right over there, back then." He said, pointing across the lot towards an empty space that the forest had since reclaimed. "Of course, I was subsequently left in my grandfathers' care, with instructions not to bother to return." I was feeling how he felt when he realized for sure once and for all, in the most undeniable and permanent of ways, that he was truly and completely unloved and unwanted by his own mother. That wasn't even the darkest part of his seething wound yet. He was still going deeper. *God help me!* I took in a deep breath and tried to keep it from shooting back out all at once. I must've done a fair enough job of keeping it in, because he continued.

"No one was allowed to know that I was sick. No doctors were ever called. They didn't want it on my record for the court to see. My father surely recognized the illness that had destroyed his own life, or at least had flash backs of it and he took off for the next few months without a word. My grandfather did his best to care for me but he was really no better equipped the second time around." He took a deep breath of his own then, to fortify himself for what was coming next. I couldn't even breathe then, it was so heavy.

"I lied up on a cot in that small attic, sweating profusely and vomiting into an old metal bucket. It was the same bucket that I used for all my bodily functions during that time, since I was too sick to make it up and down the stairs." Again, he was mortified at having to even remember such a thing, never mind admit it out loud and I found his courage truly inspiring. He just kept pushing through the darkness. I held on to it all, and my cool. If he could not only re-tell it, but *live it* in the first place, then I could certainly sit through the telling of it without falling apart, I determined again. *I would be strong!* I vowed silently.

"My ears were ringing in a way I'd never heard before. My head felt like it was going to explode! Like it was already too big for my neck. I could barely lift it. Every new smell was so strong that it would make me sick again. And *any* light at all hurt my eyes in ways I had never felt. My eyes were the worst. They felt like they were swollen shut, even though they were wide open. It was the weirdest thing that I had ever felt and I had no idea what was happening to me, or why." He took a slow breath.

"I stayed there in that attic, alone for the most part, in fear and in total darkness for eight *long* days." He said with less energy in his voice than before. I felt what he remembered as he did, and I compared it to my memories from the virus. They were very similar. I had also lived that particular hell firsthand. I, on the other hand, had gotten the best possible care at the time and still could hardly bear the memories. I found his to be that much more uncomfortable to experience. I had to physically swallow it down in order to keep it in at that point.

"My grandfather brought me soup or ice cream depending on what I needed. He also brought me water and later, when I got a little better, some toast. *And he emptied that damn bucket!*" He proclaimed fiercely. "The most I had ever asked for or received from another human being in my life to that point. I was grateful for that beyond words." I could feel it, so I knew exactly what he meant. It helped me to breathe a little easier again even though I knew he wasn't done.

"He couldn't really do much else. I thought many times during those days that I would die. Sometimes I even thought that might be better. But I just continued to wake back up again. It was hard to be sure half the time, if I was awake or asleep. What was real and what was a hallucination or maybe the afterlife. It was so dark all the time that it was all a guess." I was breathing deeply, silently.

"When the fever broke on the eighth day and he finally opened the blinds, I wasn't the same person anymore. He wasn't either. Not in my eyes, anyway. He looked different to me after that day and it took me a long time to figure out why." He stopped for a minute, took another deep cleansing breath. Obviously it was strong in his family lines.

"Are you sure you still want to hear more of this?" He asked, not oblivious to the fact that I had to go through it with him. I could instantly feel that little boy inside of him coming through. The one who was not afraid to stand alone, or to stay that way. Because it was safer, and it was easier. For everyone. He was trying to make it easier for me. Again.

For the second time, I wished I could go back in time and rescue him but I was not delusional enough to think that it was really possible. It was probably a good thing though because if I could go back there, *I would kill that bitch for sure!* I thought with satisfaction in a rare moment of viciousness.

Well, I could be there for him then. Much too little, much too late but I would savor the opportunity to be someone who does right by him.... That made me start to understand why people always felt the desire to protect him. It was because no one ever had before and the universe owed him that. It was part of his karma. That realization made me feel a lot better. I took another deep breath.

I nodded. "Please." I asked, and he resolved to continue.

He looked down at the deck and I felt him let it all back in. It was like getting hit in the chest, but I held it together.

"I didn't understand the things that I woke up seeing and hearing. I didn't know enough to try to hide it either. I was scared and looking for answers, and *help!* But no one knew what I was talking about. I pushed my grandfather incessantly until he finally set up an appointment for me to see a couple of different doctors that he found through a court appointed psychologist. He really didn't know what else to do. Unfortunately, they looked up my family history first and found my fathers' prior *mis*-diagnosis of schizophrenia." He didn't have to explain. It was easy to see what they would assume.

"Schizophrenia is a condition that almost always develops during adolescence. Most people also become *heightened* sometime during adolescence. *Coincidence?"* He asked provocatively.

"Anyway, when they couldn't find anything physically wrong with me, quite the opposite in fact since my sight and hearing suddenly tested off the charts, they decided that sadly, I was probably just following in his genetic footsteps." Of course they did, I thought. That's much easier than trying to find the truth. Especially when the state was footing the bill.

"I was left to go back to my regular school but I was labeled then. I thought life had been hard before that. I was wrong. Being poor and neglected was *nothing,* compared to being ostracized and bullied all the time." He admitted painfully.

"The bullied part didn't last too long since I had learned to stand up for myself a long time before that. I could handle that part easily enough. The segregation hurt a lot though. I never felt accepted after that, even at school." He sighed. "That was harder." I just choked it back again, stuffed it down *deep,* and waited for him to continue.

"Before that, I'd had that one place that I could go and escape the hell that was my home life. I could pretend to be almost normal there. *Almost.* After I lost that, I had nothing. I had never felt bad for myself and my situation before that. It was bad, I knew, but I always had that hope, that once I was older everything would be okay. It seemed I had lost even that possibility then." I felt the desolation hit me then and it was almost suffocating. How he had kept finding the strength to hang on, I couldn't imagine.

"I tried to talk to my father about it but he flat out refused. He left town for good without a forwarding address a year later, after my mother was killed while driving drunk. Shae had crashed into an SUV full of kids. She took two of that family of six with her on her way out." There was a deep regret that I could feel in him there. Not for her passing though. No, it was clearly for that family that she had hurt, and also because he would never get a chance to confront her himself, as an adult. That she had gotten off so easily. That part bothered him and it was quite understandable.

"If there had been a single soul in town with an ounce of sympathy left for me still, it was gone after that horrible incident. Guilt by association." He said with an accepting shrug of his shoulders. Ah, that good old small town mentality, I thought as I pursed my lips in disappointment.

"The only good thing was that the check still came from the state. For the first time in my life, *I* actually got to benefit from it." I could feel a little of the confident Ethan that I knew currently within that statement.

"I took care of my grandfather and the house with that money and it was the best time of my life to that point. Things were finally looking up a little until he passed away a year later. Then I was *truly* alone." Just like that, the glimpse of *"now-Ethan"* was gone. It was so fast. The deep despair I felt in him at that moment instead, reminded me of Jeremy and how desperate he had been that first day to either feel normal again or to escape completely. One or the other. Thankfully, Ethan had been there to pull him through that.

No one it seemed, had ever been there to pull Ethan out of that dark, scary place. He was back to blocking that old pain again when he finally started to speak of how it all changed and I was grateful for his ability to do that then. I needed the break. I took a quiet, but deep breath.

"He left me the house and the family property though, that it turns out had always been in his name, even though my father had always laid claim to it. I think it was his way of finally helping me in some worthwhile way. It was mine free and clear, to do with as I pleased." He said with a broad smile that was backed by genuine happiness.

"So of course, I promptly set the house on fire. I sat and ate a steak dinner on a nearby rock and watched happily while it burned to the ground." Still the grin. "It wasn't the smartest thing I ever did, but it *was* one of the most satisfying." He admitted continuing to smile at that memory. "The fire department hadn't even bothered to come." He explained matter-of-factly. I took another breath with the change in atmosphere. I was even more amazed then at how he managed to still be such a commendable human being after everything he'd been put through. It was nothing short of a miracle. *Truly!*

It seemed as though someone, somewhere had other plans for him in this world. Like the work he did now. It was obviously pretty important, I thought to myself, for him to have had so many guardian angels watching over him through the years. They weren't able to get him *out* of that situation, but they had made sure that he had gotten *through* it and that he survived it with his heart intact. That was the most impressive part, I thought. I wasn't sure where that impression came from, but it felt right.

"I lived in a tent for the next three months but I didn't care. It had been worth it. I needed that time anyway. To be by myself. To try and get a handle on my new *'abilities.'* Night time in the woods was certainly a lot different than it used to be." I could feel his wonder then as he remembered the discovery phase with his new skills.

"I had to relearn how to interact with people, too. Once I got a handle on myself again." He took a deep breath and I felt him move past that part too.

"I was finally on my own and out from under their thumb, but I found I still couldn't get anywhere. I couldn't get a job. Not even pumping gas. I was still labeled things like *'just another Stone family trouble maker'* and *'not mentally stable.'* They weren't true, but no one seemed to care. *Nobody* wanted to hire me. That was tough for me to take because I was tired of living on the state's dime. I wanted to earn my own keep, once and for all."

"I really thought I was finally beaten for a while. I even tried to take after my old man and be a drunk for a time. Unfortunately I wasn't any good at that either." He laughed humorlessly at himself. "I would go out drinking without having eaten any food, since I couldn't really afford both and I'd end up on the floor after two drinks. *Quite the failure.*" He chuckled at the memory, shaking his head back and forth. His nickname made more sense to me then also, as I realized why eating would have been more appealing and more important to him than drinking, by the time he had met Pete. *Hmpf.*

"I would have kept trying and eventually I'd have gotten it right." He joked confidently. "Instead someone finally came along and kicked me in the ass." He said it with a smile and some pride which seemed contradictory to his statement.

"I had been drinking too much in the bar and trying to hustle some guys at pool for money, when I woke up in the back of Jack's truck." He laughed again and shook his head at his own stupidity.

"Apparently the fine gentleman that I had actually somehow beaten, didn't like to lose. So he and his buddy decided to crack me in the head and leave me in the alley rather than pay up. Jack had driven by to put some paint cans in the dumpster and found me lying there unconscious." He laughed again.

"He dragged my sorry ass into the bed of his pickup and brought me to the farmhouse where he threw me in the shower, clothes and all. Shirley gave me ice for my head and something to eat. Then Jack let me sleep it off in his guest room. When I woke, he read me the riot act." He smiled again at the memory instead of getting angry and that was also very telling. There was definitely affection there.

"He told me that he had known my father and he also knew what a screw up he was. Told me that Joe had needed help but that he never cared enough to try and get it." He was quiet again for a minute thinking about that. Apparently he wasn't the only one who had wanted to help his father.

"He said, it was too late for him, but not for me. He also said he knew that my life had not been easy up till then, but then he pointed out that what happened to it from then on was entirely up to me. That if my life didn't go the way I wanted it to after that, I had no one left to blame but myself." His strength was back again at that statement and I really liked the way it felt.

"It was the most important thing anyone ever said to me. It was all I needed, to find the strength to change things. Just the belief that I could. That it was *finally* really up to me. 'Eventually' had officially arrived." He said with a smile. I could feel the Ethan that I knew in there again and I couldn't help being grateful for his presence.

"He gave me work on the farm. Small jobs, things that I could actually do. I had led an oddly sheltered life and I had an awful *lot* to learn. He was patient with me though. Took the time to show me things when it was painfully obvious that no one else ever had. Simple things like 'righty-tighty-lefty-loosy.' I can't begin to tell you how much I learned from him." I could feel that affection again.

"I was grateful, but mostly I was ambitious then. I finally felt like a real human being, with just that small amount of support and encouragement. I felt I had a lot of lost years to make up for. People's lack of understanding about my *special skills* was the one thing still holding me back. I couldn't get around it or seem to find a way to fix it though."

"That confusion about my *"mental health"* still lingered and I just couldn't make a real place for myself in the community with that hanging over my head. I could leave but where would I go? I had land here. I had nothing out there. I asked Jack to help me fix it and he agreed. He knew that I wasn't crazy and he took me to a psychiatrist out of town that would give me an unbiased diagnosis once and for all to help me prove it." I could feel his strength again then and I took a big drink of it while I could. I was starting to realize that it could change again at any given moment as he tried to squeeze his thirty two years down to thirty minutes. We were only about three quarters of the way there by my estimate.

"That's when I met Dr. J." He said with another genuine smile. *Hmmm.* Another new connection, Jack and Dr. J. Huh. I realized then that his level of involvement in the things going on behind the scenes was a lot greater than I had originally thought. I would add that to the growing list of things to remember to ask him about at some point.

"Of course he knew I wasn't schizophrenic or bi-polar or anything else. He knew immediately that I was a *height* and he spent the next few sessions explaining it all to me. I had never felt so... disconnected, and yet... so completely sure of my place in the word at the same time." He tried to explain, but we knew it wasn't really necessary. We had both felt that way at one point.

"I was pretty scared at first, by the sheer scope of it all. Though I knew the truth by then when I heard it and what he said made more sense than anything else in my life had before." He smiled at me and we both remembered again that scene having just played out for me so recently. I smiled back, a little more understandingly then.

"It took six months of hard work and sheer will to overcome the initial shock and the desire to just deny it all, but eventually I did get over it. You actually came around a hell of a lot quicker than I did. *Thank God!*" He admitted with a chuckle, feeling proud of me again. I remembered him feeling that gratitude along with his surprise that night in the car as we had left Jeremy's house and I understood that better then too. I smiled again but only a half-smile, trying to be modest.

"Well I had more time, don't forget." I interjected. "To adjust to my skills at least, in between. I never had to deal with it all at once." I said being honest. His expression didn't change nor did his feelings on the subject. He was still proud of me. I smiled the whole smile then and he happily went on with his story.

"In the meantime, I managed to graduate high school, in spite of all the people that had encouraged me so strongly over the years to just quit." He said with another roll of his eyes. "Jack and the rest of the family were there in the audience to clap for me when they called my name and handed me that piece of paper." He remembered fondly and I liked Jack even more then.

"I also survived some pretty intense therapy sessions in that first year, during which I finally found out for sure just how messed up I really was." He laughed humorlessly again. "But I also finally got confirmation of just how wrong my mother had been to treat me the way she had. I mean I always knew it, but it's one of those things you actually need to hear someone else say, just once, in order to make it stick. Dr. J explained quite easily that she *had* obviously had serious mental issues and had most likely been abused and or neglected herself, which was easy to believe having lived with Mike. He told me that it's often a cycle that, if not broken, tends to repeat itself and I was very lucky to have escaped it." That helped him to put that pain away a little. It wouldn't heal it, but it helped him to let it go. For the most part.

I still wanted to slap the bitch. I'm sorry, but she really brought out the *not-nice* in me.

"I also found out for the first time, that the state on the other hand, was seriously, *legally* negligent in its supervision of my case. Or more accurately, it's lack thereof. There were no excuses for them. With the help of a group of really good people, who understood me and my situation, I finally got the help I needed and I took my case to court." He was even brighter after that. I was still a little afraid to trust it yet. I imagined then that he must have felt the same way at the time!

"What I wanted was just to have the community at large acknowledge that I was not only perfectly sane, but that I had been a victim of my parents and the broken system all along. I just wanted to remove that stigma that they had forced me to live with. I finally did, but that wasn't the only good thing to come out of it." He brightened a little more then and I liked the way that felt, a lot!

"The state couldn't defend itself against the things that I had lived through. Things like my attempt to involve school officials numerous times with little or no response also bolstered my case. The fact that the state didn't have a record of a regular physical exam on file for me for twelve years prior but had not so much as made a phone call to ask why, didn't hurt either. Not to mention the fact that I had been wrongly diagnosed with schizophrenia on one of the only doctor visits I'd ever had, but then subsequently left with no treatment or follow up care for it after that. There was also the small fact that no one had picked up on my mother's *obvious* mental illness or her complete inability to *'mother'* anyone." He took a breath, but didn't stop. He was much easier to be close to at that point.

"These were all things that the state could not explain never mind defend. So then I went from being practically invisible around town, to being the local poster child for everything wrong with the system." Another eye roll, this one with a little more patience though.

"Anyway, the publicity was fun in the beginning but it became a real pain in the ass before long. The settlement that I received when I won on the other hand, sure went a long way towards my *'getting on with the rest of my life.'*" He was smiling again. That had been the real turning point for him and I could feel it. Not the money, but the official victory over his past. *Ahhhhhh....* much better.

Then I thought about what he had said during his original tale of Camp *Height* and the "settlement money" that he said had helped him start it. "Aha." I said out loud, The pain that went with that memory made sense now too, but it was his past. He didn't live in that place anymore and I was more than a little impressed by that.

"A few more years of various college courses and some self-realization in therapy and I got to a place where I knew I could actually help *others*, too. That was when I knew I had really, finally won. When I found my life's purpose. When I realized that those who were simply ignorant or cruel, not only couldn't hurt me anymore, but that I could *stop* them from hurting others like me as well. Once I knew there *were* others like me. Like my family. Finally being in a position to do that, gave me the greatest satisfaction of all." He finished with conviction.

That was where that selflessness came from, I realized at last. It was so simple to understand then. It was another small part of his victory over his own mistreatment every time he saved another person from that fate.

"Ironically, the day I decided to help others, is the day that my life finally became my own." He said then, nearly voicing my thoughts and I smiled. "That's when I finally felt like I was free to just be me and live my life. *Enjoy* it even. Like I finally had the same right to that everybody else did." His broad smile was back in the end. Thank goodness for the joy he was still somehow able to feel!

I breathed in the good feelings coming off of him again. It was much easier for him to expunge those demons than it was for me and I could finally see why. He'd had a lot longer to perfect it. I shamelessly used his refined ability to help me in my efforts. They were old ghosts for him at that point. It had happened long ago. However it was a fresh new pain in my head and heart. I was happy to let it go for the moment if he could, though. I felt like I understood so much more about him then and I didn't want him to regret telling me.

"Anyway, I lived and worked with Jack through those last couple of tough years. He gave me a real home within his family, the first one I'd ever had, and he taught me what a supportive, kind relationship was like. He and Shirley had four kids of their own already, but they treated me like I was one of their own too. Much better than the ones I had actually belonged to ever had. It meant the world to me." He looked up at me and I could feel the love he had for them. That was much more than I had expected when I asked originally.

"He wouldn't accept money for rent. Only work in trade, so I poured my blood, sweat and tears into fixing up the old garage for him and his kids to use to show my appreciation. They were there for me, to help me learn to socialize. *Hmpf.* They made a cake for me on my seventeenth birthday. Also, the first one I'd ever had." He admitted with a small grin.

"They invited me to go places, to do things with them. They weren't just the only people in the crowd for me at my graduation, they were also there with me in the courtroom the day the verdict was read." He was beaming with pride for his makeshift family then.

"Jack has the farm, the horses, and the orchard and yet he always makes time to spend with his family. He's never held them back either though, so I wasn't surprised when his oldest decided to move out to the city for a few years and go to school instead of moving over the newly finished garage. I *was* surprised however, when he invited me to stay there instead." That was an unexpected revelation and all kinds of thoughts went through my head at that!

"His next oldest was still too young to be on his own, he said. It was mine for the next three years if I wanted it." He grinned at that happy memory and I was so glad that he'd had at least a few.

"I lived in that apartment while I built this house. *Your apartment.*" He said with that usual grin on his face. That made me think about all the new memories we had made in *his old/my new* apartment!

"It only took me two years to finish though, not the three he had so generously given me. I can never really repay him for everything that he did for me. But I will spend the rest of my life trying." As he finished with that, his mood had returned to normal and I was very happy to bask in his current feelings some more.

"Wow. I'm glad I asked." I said seriously as I stood and walked over to him. *"Thank you,* for telling me all of that. I *know* that it wasn't easy." I said feeling that the obvious needed to at least be acknowledged.

"I'm just sorry that you had to live it vicariously through me." He said honestly with a cringe, confirming my earlier suspicions. "I spend a lot of time and energy trying to keep others from feeling what I felt. So for me to do that to *you,* knowingly, is extremely counter-productive to what I'm about." He said sadly. I could feel his remorse.

He reached up and held my cheek in his hand then looked me in the eye intently. "So I guess I've found one thing about your skill that I don't like, because I didn't like doing that to you." He pulled me in and kissed me once. "I'm sorry." He said, meaning it and I didn't want him to feel that either. That was not an improvement in my book.

"I know you would rather suffer the worlds' sins in silence and all alone, but you don't have to anymore, so just stop it okay? My discomfort lasted a mere handful of minutes. and it helped me to know you in ways that I never could otherwise. I am truly grateful that you decided to share the whole story with me. It goes a long way with the *need-to-know* side of my brain that is always trying to make sense out of you and all of this." I admitted.

"But I'm not gonna lie. I am also incredibly glad that I know you *now!*" I said as I wrapped my arms around his shoulders. "And that you're telling me all of this *after the fact,* while you sit here so well adjusted and so strong, fighting so nobly for so many others." I slid my lips over his lightly and I could feel his mood change drastically but I wasn't done yet.

"I am *so proud* of who you became, or more accurately, who you *remained* in spite of what you were up against!" I slid my lips back the same way they had come. "Besides, if it was still back then when you were telling me all of this, then I'm sorry but I would have to *kick* your mothers' *ass!*" I said and he laughed, *hard.* I really liked that sound!

"No *seriously!*" I contradicted myself with a laugh of my own but I meant it. "It would have been the biggest bitch fight you ever saw! *Arrrghhh!!*" I laughed again to release some of the pent up frustration. I felt better and I fell back in his arms. He held me there for a few seconds then he brought me back up to face him again.

"So that's still not enough damage to scare you off, huh?"

He half joked. I just shook my head. "You are certainly tougher than you look." He smiled that heart stopping smile at me again and I held his face with my hands.

"I *hate* what they put you through." I said quietly but emphatically. "It's a tragic story and it never should've happened." I was angry about it and he could tell. I didn't try to hide it at first. Then I sighed and softened consciously. I brought my hand up and ran it through his hair and around the back of his head to pull him closer to me. "In spite of that, I *really am* very fond of the person that you are and nothing that they could ever do to you could change that." I said confidently, although I didn't know why. It just felt true.

"It's funny." I said. "You were so proud of me for turning out okay on my own but look what *you* did! My life, outside of the *height* issues, was pretty ideal. I mean I had everything in my background on my side." I just shook my head. "No, what you did. *Hmpf!* You have an inner strength in you that I will never understand. The best part is that it's governed by such a pure, unselfish heart." I chuckled a little at his expression. "I know it sounds like something out of a movie script. I'm sorry. It's true. I don't know how else to say it. I call 'em like I see 'em and that's how I see you." I grinned and tried to explain.

"It's like you're some sort of warrior, born to fight for the good side. An angel, sent here to help the other good people on Earth." I said with a playful smile. "So the Devil, knowing you would be a formidable force, sent his top minion to try and stop you. *That bitch!*" I allowed myself one last time. He grinned, pleased with my protectiveness and I continued.

"*She failed.*" I said simply, while I stood on my tiptoes and wrapped my arms around his neck again. "She used every evil trick in her book and she still couldn't break your spirit. In the end, she couldn't defeat *'Ethan-The-Good.'*" I finished triumphantly with a giant smile, warming up to my story. He was enjoying it to.

"I like your version much better." He said happily, wrapping his own arms back around me and lifting me tightly up against him while he walked us back inside. "I am being a very bad host. Let me try this again." He said as he set me back down inside the kitchen.

"Are you still hungry?" He asked seriously and I thought about it for a minute.

"Nope. You?" I asked in return.

"Ut uh." He answered. "Alrighty! Then we'll call the kitchen tour complete and move on to the upstairs." He said with that brilliant grin again as he led me through a large archway into a sleek looking den/office area. We went up an open stairway made of chrome metal runners and highly polished, blond wood blocks for treads. It was an absolute piece of art, like so many other features in his house.

'You built all of this?" I asked, taking it all in as we went.

"Well not singlehandedly, but yes. I worked on it from start to finish, inside and out. It was very therapeutic actually." He said with fondness and wonder as he led me around the corner at the top of the stairs.

Just then my phone, that was miraculously still in my back pocket, had the nerve to ring. I took it out and looked at it. "Awe crap, it's the real world calling." I joked disappointedly.

"Do you have to answer it?" He asked hopefully.

"Sorry, I do. It's actually Jack." I said ironically, which just confused him. Of course he had no idea about my new issues yet. I hadn't had a chance to tell him. There had been more important matters to attend to. I just grinned at him mysteriously as I said hello.

"Hey Sugar! I think I may have found someone who can help you out." He said excitedly.

"Oh my God, are you serious? That's fantastic!" I said with great relief.

"I've got 'em coming over to the house in half an hour. They were gonna be passing by anyway. I know its short notice. Think you can make it?"

"Absolutely! I'll see you then. And Jack...? You're the best! I mean that." I said seriously, looking right at Ethan. He waited patiently for me to finish before asking questions.

"What'd I miss?" He asked me after I put my phone back in my pocket.

"Oh no, unfortunately, it's what *I* missed!" I said by way of explanation. He looked at me perplexed, waiting for more. I told him as briefly as possible about the situation with the aquifer at my job-site and the snotty little Mr. Wright who had shut me down. He laughed. I did not.

"I know the guy. He's a tiny little putz with a great big Napoleon complex. I've met him a few times working up there myself." He shook his head at the memory. He didn't elaborate and I decided not to ask. For the moment anyway.

"So I took a shot that Jack would be a good place to start for help in finding someone with this kind of experience and as I'm sure you just heard, it paid off." I looked at him meaningfully as I finished that last part.

"Well, thirty minutes is still not enough time to do this properly." He said looking down at his watch to mark the time. "But I'll take *every second* I can get!" He said as the waves started rolling over me again, one after the other in quick succession. I matched his enthusiasm almost instantly.

"After last time, thirty minutes actually seems dangerously long." I said with a wicked grin, reaching around his shoulders.

"Are you kidding me? If we had a week right now, I could easily fill the time with the things I'd like to do to you and still never do the same thing twice." He said with his eyebrows raised suggestively. He turned us around and started coordinating our tandem walk toward the massive bed. "I'll still completely *wreck* you in ten, if that's all I have!" He said gruffly, his intensity bowling me over once again.

"*Ahhhh...* yes, please." I said enthusiastically, my eyes closing as we fell back together onto the sea of white.

Chapter 28

We reached the farmhouse with two minutes to spare. I had bolted into action after feeling like I had surely left the stratosphere entirely. I had decided *during,* that I didn't care, but when I looked up and saw that a mere twenty minutes had gone by, I was massively relieved. *We could still make it!* He was a man of his word.

We jumped up, and took turns spending twenty seconds in his luxurious shower. I definitely needed to revisit that when I had more time, I thought happily. Then we threw ourselves together like we were late for the school bus. I managed to get my hair back up into the ponytail, although not as tightly or as neat. Ethan finally relinquished my clothes. He threw his own back on too which I must say, did nothing to dampen the desire for me. His teasing antics in funny voices about how "we'd never make it" did help though and we ran out the door in record time still laughing.

We took Ethan's car since mine was still downtown and we hadn't left enough time to retrieve it. I wasn't sure how I felt about showing up together, but since it was obvious to me then that Ethan didn't need an invitation to Jack's house I hoped no one would make a big deal out of it.

We parked Ethan's car over by my place, trying to be at least somewhat discreet and walked the short distance over to Jack's. As we approached we saw a big shiny black and chrome Humvee 3 in the driveway and when I looked at Ethan, he was smiling to himself. It was clear that he knew then, exactly who was inside.

"Am I in trouble?" I asked, worried by his obvious amusement.

"No." He assured me with his eyebrows raised like he was surprised by the truth of his own words. "Not at all." *Still smiling.* He put his arm around my shoulders then, seeing that I was unconvinced. "Come on."

Jack met us at the front door and we followed him into the parlor. There, he introduced me to his recommendation for the job.

"Simone, I'd like you to meet my *eldest* reason for the occasional evening cocktail, Genevieve." He said, gesturing towards a tall woman with straight, blonde hair that fell half way down her back. She had been sitting in the high backed chair in the corner by the window. She stood up and walked over to greet us.

She wore dark blue jeans, running shoes and a Red Sox t-shirt, but still looked every bit the professional. *Polished.* The jeans were designer and the shirt was obviously her own. Cut to fit a women's figure. Not some old college shirt that she had stolen second-hand from a boyfriend.

We shook hands. She had Jack's warm blue eyes and Shirley's easy smile. She was giving off only kindness and mild amusement, very much like her dad. It made me feel comfortable around her very quickly and I knew that she had already passed the most important test.

"It's nice to meet you Simone. I've heard so much about you." She said and smiled a conciliatory smile with an eye roll in the end, like she knew first hand exactly how annoying small towns could be.

"I get that a lot around here." I confirmed with a nod and a laugh.

She laughed with me politely at first, but then caught me completely off guard by hauling off unexpectedly and punching Ethan in the shoulder. I would have judged her too feminine for such a thing but she proved me wrong. That didn't happen too often and I found it very amusing.

"What's up, E?" She said teasingly. "I wasn't expecting to

see *you* here." She accused with a smug smile. "Are you two dating?" She asked straight out. So much for going unnoticed, I thought. I looked to Ethan, wondering what he would say.

"We are, whatever she says we are." He answered with a defiant smile. They all looked at me. *Awe, crap.* Genevieve spoke up again, giving me a little more time.

"Sorry. I hate to put you on the spot like this, but I've waited a longtime to issue a little payback where the bitch is due with this one. You have no idea how much fun Mr. Protective over here had with any boy who dared to attempt to date *me!*" She gave big, angry eyes at Ethan, but he acted completely unaffected, like a big brother should. "Now you unfortunately, are simply collateral damage." She joked mercilessly and I decided that I definitely liked her. "Please, call me Gen." She said, and then finished with, *"So?"*

I looked at Ethan and a million things went through my mind at once. The one image that stuck was the memory of the little boy who so proudly stood on his own when no one would stand beside him. He would do that again with zero argument if I asked him to. At just that thought alone, I already knew right where *I* wanted to stand.

"Yes. We're dating. Moving on?" I said as matter-of-factly as I could. Jack jumped in to help thankfully, bringing the conversation back around to business, but he grinned that *all-knowing* grin again when he spoke.

"Why don't we all go sit at the table and you can tell my Gennie here about your situation in a little more detail." He suggested, making me appreciate him even more, since I was never psyched about my personal life being the center of attention.

Except with Ethan. I enjoyed being the center of *his* undivided personal attention very much, I thought to myself in true ADD fashion. I don't really have it, at least I think I don't, but that doesn't stop me from trying to use it as an excuse from time to time. *Hah!*

"She has a degree in geology and has recently branched out into environmental law. I can't claim complete innocence from nepotism, but it seemed like a perfect match to me." Jack provided.

"From the sounds of it, I would have to agree." I said, trying to focus as we walked over and sat at the dining room table. It was a long, well-worn tabletop of solid walnut that had enough chairs to comfortably seat sixteen or so. You could almost smell and hear the years of family dinners that had taken place there as you approached.

Jack was telling Gen about my work and I was trying to follow along but no matter how hard I tried to pay attention to the conversation, I couldn't block out the overwhelming joy that was coming at me from my left where Ethan had sat down next to me.

I looked up at his face and it was as serene looking as ever. He was in complete control. His expressions would never betray his feelings, unless he allowed them to. But *I* knew better. I would *always* know better. I found I liked that.

He was *very* happy about my proclamation. Yes, he hid his elation beautifully, but it existed just the same. Instead of the fear I expected to feel, I found that I also liked being responsible for any small amount of his happiness.

He smiled at me. One small, knowing smile. Then he turned back toward Jack who was still talking, but he slipped his hand into mine under the table. I couldn't help thinking that the fact that he could still feel such joy at all was an absolute gift, and perhaps something else that I had to thank Jack for.

"So there was no prior documentation of the aquifer's path in that area, right?" Gen asked, bringing my attention back once and for all.

"Not before now, no." I answered finally really listening.

"Good. I know they love to act like you're a villain for coming across it accidentally, but it's more common than you would think and it's better for your case than if you had knowingly ignored the regulations and the proper channels. Which believe me, too many try to do." She explained.

"Whatever you say." I agreed easily. "I will take your word for it because I have no experience with any of this. But I can assure you that I had no idea it was there and absolutely no intention of ever *accessing* it. If it could have been avoided, it would have been." I could feel right away that she knew I was telling the truth. I was glad. That would help speed things along.

"I'm basically just left doing damage control." I said letting my exasperation show a little. "Unfortunately, I only have a little over a month left to complete this entire job. I don't have a few extra weeks to spare, hanging around waiting for new permits to clear. Tell me, is there any *above board* way to hurry this process along?" I asked hopefully.

"No. Not really." She answered much too quickly, dashing my hopes. "But there are any number of *"slightly below-board"* options that I can think of." She answered with a grin. I knew for sure I liked her then. "First things first." She said standing up. "It would be good if we could take a ride up there and I could get a good look at exactly what we're dealing with here, before we commit to a plan of action. Especially if time is of the essence."

"Absolutely. Whenever you want to go." I said, willing to be extremely flexible.

"How 'bout now?" She offered, and I was surprised but immediately onboard.

"Sure! Let's go." I agreed. Then I remembered that I didn't have my car. "Oh, but would you mind driving? I don't have my vehicle at the moment." I explained vaguely. I ignored the waves of heat that rolled over me from Ethan's direction, as he obviously remembered our earlier trip in his car.

"Sure. No problem. We can *all* fit in my car." She said, smiling at Ethan again, but he refused to be baited. He did however, tag along.

I grabbed my original plans and sketches from my apartment and then we all climbed up into what she referred to as her *"car."* Jack climbed in front and Ethan and I got in the back. It was so spacious that we were actually pretty far apart though and that was probably a good thing for the time being. It was surprisingly luxurious and comfortable inside and I was immediately reminded of Ethan's super-sized SUV. They seemed to have not only similar taste in vehicles, but also some sort of rivalry going on between them about each one's superiority over the other.

I enjoyed the dynamic going back and forth between them on the ride there as they sparred verbally, continually delivering cutting comments and one-liners at each other's expense. For the most part Ethan was feeling much more entertained by it than annoyed, so I sat back and enjoyed it all silently.

There were statistics given for the "well known fact" that women were better drivers. There was back-handed disparaging of both vehicles shortcomings and how inferior one's intellect would have to be to want to own one. There were even a few jibes about the size of the vehicle being used to overcompensate for a corresponding lack in anatomy. That one of course was the funniest, since it was the furthest from the truth. I kept that information to myself however. I could also feel Ethan's deep sense of content to leave that information a mystery to his family. He would take the hit. I smiled at him but left it alone.

They never said too much though, or stepped over the line between playful and rude. Jack was enjoying it immensely as well since it was all intended in the most loving way, of course. I had to laugh. It was nice to know that he had gotten some of that good old sibling rivalry in his life after all. Better late than never.

I'd had only cousins myself, but they were the next best thing and when you're close enough, it works the same way. We managed to stir up enough of that loving, competitive environment to develop into adults with proper consideration and appropriate social skills. Well, for the most part anyway.

We reached the site fairly quickly since there was no traffic. On a Sunday, it would all be going the other way, with all of the weekenders heading back down South to the city. I hoped silently that we wouldn't hit too much of it on the way back.

We got out and walked together up to the roped off clearing. There I set my designs down on a nearby rock and started to explain the plans to Gen while I pointed around the site at various features. She just nodded a lot but seemed to have no trouble following along. I noticed both Jack and Ethan were quietly smiling while looking at the plans. I could feel the happiness coming from the child inside each of them and it was apparent that they liked it. I had felt sure that they would, but it still felt pretty good to have my hunch confirmed.

Ethan looked up then and interrupted. "I want to help!

Can I help?"

"Me too!" Jack chimed in quickly. I wasn't really surprised by either of them. Gen was waiting patiently, so apparently she wasn't either.

"Sure." I agreed, realizing that it may not be a bad idea. "If we ever get back to work on it, anyway. By then we may need all the help we can get in order to pull it off in time."

"Mr. Wu Xing has a big opening night planned for the official beginning of the summer season the first week of July. I know that he has family coming in from China and everything has been booked for months. A week's worth of events have already been scheduled around it. There is no renegotiating. If I don't make that deadline, I don't get paid." I explained, knowing how bad it sounded out loud.

"That seems a little drastic. Are you telling me that you don't have any clauses built into the contract to cover yourself in the case of natural disasters and such?" Gen asked with obvious surprise.

"Yup and nope. It was a 'take it or leave it' kind of deal, settled mostly on a handshake. But I agreed to the deadline, no conditions. It was the job of a lifetime. I wasn't going to argue. At the time I had another job that paid the bills anyway. So the money wasn't so much of an issue." I explained in my own defense. "Things have changed since then. A *lot!*" I admitted with a humorless chuckle. I looked over at Ethan, where he talked excitedly with Jack. He grinned back, the child in him absolutely beaming. Just then, a small part of me thought, maybe I *can* go back and save him... *just a little.*

"Well I can't say that I blame you but the lawyer in me sure *wants* to." She said sarcastically. I smiled weakly back and shrugged my shoulders.

"It is what it is." I said plainly. "Now I just have to make it happen. Somehow."

"Well, that's where I come in. Hopefully!" She said, trying to be positive.

Jack and Ethan were doing some pointing of their own by then, matching up my sketches with certain parts of the terrain. Their grins were getting bigger and bigger. I smiled a tiny smile to myself and shook my head.

They kept talking and pointing, even when we took the plans away temporarily. I followed Gen around as she drew a rough, *guesstimated* map of the path of the aquifer beneath the site, onto a tissue overlay of my original plans, before mercifully giving them back to the boys.

We went back to the opening in the rocks after that, and she took some water samples of her own to do independent testing.

She also explained to me the steps that were usually involved in accessing the aquifer and installing a pump and a well. All important information for me.

Unlike Mr. Wright, it was actually beneficial to listen to her talk. She wasn't feeling superior, or annoyed at my ignorance. She was very patient with my questions too. I appreciated that. Smart people weren't always patient or kind. I would often notice them feeling like it was too tedious for them to have to bother with the pretense. Like it just wasn't worth their valuable time. In a small way, I get it, but I also know they are smart enough to know that their attitude is not helpful to others. It's an innate selfishness that they don't see a problem with. Gen was not that kind of person and I was glad then to have her on my side.

"Mostly they are looking for contaminants." She went on. "Not that they expect them to be from you, but if a test is positive, they can test a grid in the surrounding area and eventually track it back to a source. They're still left trying to fix it after the fact but at least they know when a threat or a problem exists and where to test to know when it's cleared. It's the only way for them to ensure the safety of the aquifer's water." I could tell that she was educated on the matter because she actually cared.

"Both its' purity and its' future viability rely on how we treat it today. Frankly, it's more than they've been able to do in the past and I'll be honest with you, Simone. I'm a big advocator of protecting our local resources." She informed me without hesitation.

She also explained as she took her samples, that it was the best way to avoid any potential problems that might arise in the form of discrepancies with the results. Since, she also informed me, there was the occasional question of hidden agendas when it came to the state's results.

"Really! Wow, that's great news." I said with plenty of sarcasm.

"I'm not going on record as making any specific accusations." She said, covering herself in true lawyerly fashion, her hands raised in mock innocence. "But it has been my experience that questionable sites in places where the state wants wells, tend to pass, and no brainer sites in places where they don't want wells, often don't. That's purely an objective observation." She finished with a backwards smile at me. "It is one of the things that prompted me to get into the law side of things in the first place though." She told me, warming up to her subject.

"We find that we can avoid that battle somewhat of trying to prove foul play after the fact, if we inform them right off the bat that we will be doing our own testing simultaneous to theirs. If they have their way a law will be passed preventing "personal" testing being done but until they block us there we have a pretty good way to stop that from happening." She said with some satisfaction.

"I'll set up an appointment for them to come do theirs A.S.A.P. and of course, only under my direct supervision. We will do our second test then simultaneously so it will compare directly with theirs and to back up our original results. Most people installing a well though, the middle-class single family, can't afford that kind of "insurance" necessarily so it doesn't always work across the board." She said, and I could feel her annoyance at that situatation as well. It didn't take her long to voice it.

"So believe me, I know how frustrating it can be, trying to get anything done. Especially since I've sat and watched helplessly in the past as permits for wells that had no right going through have been approved, issued and operational overnight." She added without hiding her anger.

"Somebody had to represent the interest of the actual people who live and work around here. Too long everything has been geared towards serving those large corporations that only want to generate revenue here and then take it home with them somewhere else to spend or hoard it. The main problem with that is that they don't care what they do to the local resources in the process. They'll just leave when it's all used up and polluted, then go begin again somewhere else. It doesn't matter to them. It's not their backyard." She took a breath.

"I know I'm getting up on my high horse here." She said without feeling bad about it. "But it is my intention to live in an area just like this one for the rest of my life. I'd like to raise a family in the beauty of the hills and forests by my home. Then I'd like to see my children still have that same option when they are grown, to raise their families there as well. Do you know how rare that is these days? For an undeveloped area to still be that way, even just one generation later?" She asked seriously.

"I do. Completely. That's a big part of what attracted me to Pinegrove in the first place. *Really!*" I answered trying to express just how much I agreed with her.

"I am lucky enough to know that I will have that option." She continued. "Only because my parents have protected it so vigorously for me. I knew I could go off to school, live in the city for a while, take advantage of the many resources available there, and still be sure that they will never sell out my future while I'm gone. Most families cannot say that. Most families cannot afford to keep up a vast amount of empty land without at least giving in to the temptation to develop some of it themselves. If they can't farm it, or raise cattle on it to sell at market, they can't afford to keep it and not every person is cut out to work the land. It's not an easy life." I could tell she spoke from firsthand knowledge of those particular hardships.

"The demand for space is high and always growing. Economy's fail, jobs go away. Land gets broken up and sold off just so people can survive. It's just the way it is. *If* you don't do anything to stop it." That brought her back around to her original topic.

"The same thing happens to our natural resources if we don't take steps to preserve them for the future. I will work hard to see that there is something left to hand over to my children someday." She was being honest with me and she seemed to be waiting to see if I would change my mind about wanting her help before continuing. She was stating her position. She would fight hard but only for the right side. She had decided that long ago. Very unusual for a lawyer, but it certainly worked for *me.*

"My goal is always to leave nature in the same or better shape than I found it." I answered as honestly as I could. "I'd like to do the same thing here." I said looking her in the eye.

"Good." She said, deciding that she believed me. "Then we're on the same side and we can focus on what needs to be done to make this happen quickly. So what are you thinking?" She asked.

"Well, I have a root of a plan, if you think you can help me make it happen. *If* it turns out to even be possible." I added on, in doubt. "In the end my main goal is to ensure that the aquifer remains safe on both sides. Nothing going in or coming out that shouldn't be." I said as I started to explain what I had decided to do.

"Essentially, I want to keep it the way it is. Exposed but just a beautiful, acoustically pleasing passerby." I said with a half-smile. I made a few rough sketches with a stick in the dirt and I was sure she understood because she smiled too. I recognized that her joy at the prospect resembled my own.

"I think we can do it! I also think it's going to be really cool!" She said excitedly, officially taking the job. "Ethan can easily help you out with getting the guts of it right. I can handle the legalities and make sure all the safety codes are met. As long as your guys can build it fast enough, we could pull it off with enough time for you to finish here." She said with growing excitement.

"We just have to get the plans for this approved through a special permit application to save time. If we can get an emergency hearing to push that through, we may be able to bypass your old permits all-together, rather than waiting for another hearing to reinstate them." She said, thinking out loud.

"*Ooooh,* I like the sound of that." I said and we went over to wrestle the plans back from Jack and Ethan. "Come on." I said over my shoulder as I headed back to Gen's truck. "Gen, you have time for a drink?" I asked. "I need to get to my office." I said by way of cryptic explanation, still the only one walking.

Chapter 29

"I don't get it. Is she joking?" I heard Gen ask Ethan.

"Hmpf. Nope. She's referring to my place of employ, where she gets all her work done while ignoring me most thoroughly." He answered with a smile and a touch of annoyance. Both Gen and I smiled at that I noticed, as I looked back covertly over my shoulder. "Though I wasn't planning on working tonight." He called out louder, to my back.

"Is someone else playing tonight?" I asked, turning back towards him and the group.

"No. Sunday's are usually pretty quiet. Family crowd, mostly kids and they close earlier.

"Will they kick you out?" I asked, not willing to be deterred. He had intercepted me and my brain function during my earlier attempt to get it done, and I wasn't going to let him derail me again. Especially not when I had an actual plan, and willing help! One way or another, I had to get the drawings done; so Gen could get them approved; so we could get to work and get it built; so I could finish my job before I ran out of time! .... *Ahhhhh!!!!*

I wasn't going to say all of that though. The look in my eyes said enough, I was sure.

"They can't kick me out." He answered simply. "I own the place."

"Hah!!" I laughed humorlessly as I turned on my heel and headed towards the truck again. 'Now why doesn't that even surprise me?" I asked rhetorically. At least that explained how they afforded to pay him to play so many nights. *They didn't.* I climbed

up into my seat and waited for the rest of them to follow suit.

"Come on people! Daylight's a wasting!" I yelled from inside. Alright, I didn't say I waited *patiently*. Patience would never be my strong suit. I had learned to be okay with that long ago.

I heard Gen get on board first.

"What the Hell. I'm in. Let me just call Travis and tell him not to wait up." She agreed. I heard Jack next.

"Well I'm too old to need an excuse. I can do what I want and right now, I want to go have a drink." He proclaimed confidently as he came back over and climbed in.

Ethan was just shaking his head back and forth and smiling to himself when he finally joined us.

"To The Tavern, James!" I joked to Gen and we were off.

Thankfully we seemed to have missed a lot of the late afternoon traffic. Either that or everyone got out of her way. I couldn't be sure which, but I wasn't complaining either way as we flew back down the second lane of the highway like it was a Tuesday afternoon. I did get in on the banter a little though. I couldn't help myself.

"So Jack, was the NASCAR driving class part of a bonus package that came with living under your roof, or is it just a personality thing that they share?" I asked. He laughed, but didn't bother to answer. I noticed that neither one was offended either. They were each actually a little bit prouder and I had to shake my head again, while grinning to myself.

When we got there, it was a little more crowded than I would have liked or Ethan had assumed, but we only waited fifteen minutes for my favorite table. Ethan offered to ask the people to move, with their meal on the house of course, but that seemed like overkill to me. I could exercise a little bit of patience for that, I told him. It was good excercies for me.

When we sat I spread the plans out on the table. Once we each had a glass of wine or whiskey in front of us, and all elbows were down, Ethan squeezed my hand and silently walked away. Then we all went to work.

A short time later, he was up on stage playing Paolo Nutini's song, "Million Faces" and it was perfect. Between all the *"decompressing"* we had enjoyed earlier, the walk up to the site, the wine, the music and the perfect company, my mind was in a state of complete Zen. The work was flowing easily and so was the conversation that took place over it. We laughed and made jokes about the impossibility of the biggest problems as we encountered them. We eventually figured out a way around each one and then we laughed some more as we patted each other on the back. Having all our combined experience working on the problems at once made all the issues and therefore the solutions appear a lot faster.

We ate dinner as we worked but kept it to finger foods that we couldn't spill on the plans. I was too stressed out already to set myself up for that potential disaster. Nobody seemed to mind.

Ethan played mostly softer music that worked well as a background for both our working group and the diners. He added a handful of upbeat tunes in as well to keep the energy up and thankfully, no one else came looking for him that night, *height* or otherwise. By the time closing came around, we were already alone in the place other than the few staff members left and our combined work was mostly done. On *that* step anyway. It was a huge relief to at least have taken a step in the right direction though!

We packed it up and sat back comfortably in the booth, finishing our drinks while Ethan finished the night with Jason Mrazs' *"Bella Luna."* It was one of my absolute favorites and it was a great way to end that day. Maybe things really were just better when he was around, I considered then being uncharacteristically fearless. Why was I so sure that had to be a bad thing, anyway?

Damn. It really was scary where my mind would go sometimes while I sat listening to him play.

He finished and we all clapped while he took a dramatic bow in front of his meager audience. He packed up his guitar and brought it backstage then came back out just as we all stood and started stretching.

"Do you guys need a ride?" Gen asked.

I thought the answer was obvious but Ethan surprised me

by answering anyway.

"No. We're good. I'll take Simone to her car." He said. I was confused but decided not to voice it and we all hugged goodbye.

"I'll call you as soon as the testing is done and I can get a date on the docket." She assured me.

"I'll be waiting with fingers crossed." I said

"Hopefully, not long." She added as she hugged Ethan. Come on, Pops. I'm gonna let you put me up at '*Chateau de Jacques*' for the night." She said with a chuckle. I noticed that it made Jack quite happy though.

"Oh yeah? Well lucky you, because we just happen to be running a special tonight. One night only. Stay for free, with blueberry pancakes in the morning included." He added and I watched her face light up.

"Pancakes! Oh yes!" She said with an over exaggerated fist pump. She wrapped her arm around his waist while he rested his across her shoulders. They walked out like that and I yelled to them to drive careful. Gen, who had only had one glass all evening, assured me with a wave that she would.

I looked back at Ethan with a knowing grin. I had an idea then where he had gotten his secret pancake recipe from. I looked at him and he just grinned back at me as usual. Neither confirming nor denying anything. Underneath that perfected exterior though there was affection towards Jack again and I knew I was right.

He let it go and held his hand out to me.

"Now what?" I asked, leery but grinning a little anyway, in spite of myself.

"I'm gonna take you back to your car." He answered simply.

"How? You don't have your car either." I said, stating the obvious.

"Are you afraid again?" He asked teasingly.

"Should I be?" I asked back, placing my hand in his anyway.

"Not with me." He assured me quietly, looking down at me as I reached his side. And I wasn't. I kept thinking that I should be, I just wasn't.

It doesn't take me long to really *know* someone, and I could honestly say already by then that if he ever hurt me purposefully, it would be a huge surprise and surprises for me were rare!

"Let's go." I said looking up at him. Ready for whatever came next.

"You trust me?" He asked completely serious and *very* wary of my response.

I knew that I did, but I still thought about it before I spoke, not willing to take such a thing lightly. "Yes." I finally said. It felt good. To say it. To mean it.

I also felt as if I had leapt off a cliff as the word passed by my lips. Free falling. I finally understood where that saying came from. It was exhilarating but numbing at the same time in its' extreme danger level. Why was I letting it happen? Did I really want that?

I did. That was the long and short of it, dammit. Let it be known, that I went willingly.

He was beaming again. I wanted to enjoy it. His feelings and my own. But I was still holding back. Just by a hair. I guess I *was* afraid again, if truth be told. I gave what I felt was a fair and honest warning.

"Be careful what you do with that." I requested. "I will only give it to you once." It was ominous sounding but I couldn't help that. It was true and he needed to know it.

"Simone, what you're getting out of this is not the normal deal to say the least. We *both* know that now." He said referring to himself as somehow less than perfect, which of course was ridiculous. I looked at him in a way that spoke of disbelief.

He looked back at me with a challenge in his eyes. Then he silently ran through his feelings on the many issues that influence the matter. It was clear he definitely didn't have self-confidence issues, but he did believe that he was less than a perfect prospect, boyfriend-wise, because of the life he lived. Both in the past *and* currently. Those feelings were easy to recognize in him. Unfortunately, it was all actually true to some extent. His situation was not ideal, but somehow it didn't matter. He switched the conversation back to being verbal again.

"I get to be at least *95%* open and honest with you and I know that still sounds like a negative, but it's actually pretty fantastic in my book. It's the most I've ever been able to share with anyone!" He pulled me closer while he talked. "I would never *want* to do anything to ruin that, and as long as I have a choice in the matter, I never will. But with everything else I've already vowed to protect, that's really the only promise I can make, without knowing the future. Or endangering *you*." He waited.

It did sound bad, but I knew what it really was. It was more of a commitment to honesty and sharing than any other man had ever made to me, Ben included. And what's more, he *wanted* it that way. Wanted more, if truth be told. I could feel that he would tell me everything if it wasn't a safety issue for me.

"Well then, I guess until you're somehow left with no choice but to screw it up, we're good." I said, trying to lighten things a little.

He laughed at me. "Isn't that pretty much the standard contract?' He asked. He was joking, but he was right. Who was I kidding, thinking I could put a disclaimer on it anyway? Wouldn't that be nice?

Hmpf!

"Yeah. I guess you're right." I agreed with another laugh. "Oh well. Life's too damn short not to live it." I said as I leaned up and placed my lips carefully on his. He responded with a lot more abandon. It was all I needed on Earth for that one moment.

Once we came up for air, he pulled me through the dark area backstage and out the back door.

Sitting there off to the right, behind the dumpster and a chain link privacy fence, was a beautiful, fast looking motorcycle. I had no idea what it was and I knew my fair share of bikes. Of course, there just happened to be two helmets hanging from pegs under a nicely camouflaged shelter on the back wall.

"What the hell is it?" I asked, never having seen one like it before. It sure was pretty.

"A BMW K 1200 S, *of course.*" He answered with a smirk.

"Oh, of course!" I jokingly agreed. "Because..." and we both said at the same time, *"You/I have an uncle with a BMW*

dealership." We both laughed.

'He's not really your uncle, is he?" I guessed, as I twisted my hair up into a knot and tucked it under the shiny, black helmet that he handed me.

"No. Well, not by blood anyway." He confirmed and smiled at me again as he lifted one leg up and over the sleek looking black and silver bike. "Though he's close enough. I really do think of him *like* an Uncle." He slipped the silver helmet over his head and instantly, he could have been anyone. Well, anyone with a gorgeous physique anyway, I allowed with a secret grin.

I walked up and slid my leg over the back of the bike and settled onto the back of the seat. Instantly my senses were full of his scent and his joy at our closeness. *Deep breaths.*

He started the engine and I felt a jolt of energy from each of us as well. The bike roared with power, but it was not a jarring sound like the big bikes often prided themselves on having. They were going for show, which often just meant a lot of noise. Loud worked in your favor when you wanted to get noticed. Ethan on the other hand was still more interested in stealth than show and he appeared to have chosen well. My ears and I were grateful.

"Hold on tight." He called back over his shoulder, and just as I did he twisted the accelerator and we took off like a rabbit from a hole. I held around his waist and leaned slowly with him into the first turn out of the parking lot.

"Very nice." He offered through his helmet. I was pleased that I still remembered how. I hadn't ridden a bike in years but it all came right back. *Hah!* Another cliché confirmed. I guess there is a reason that these sayings last throughout the years.

He sped up once we hit the main road and the wind was magnificent. It had been a beautiful day but it was getting more and more humid as the days grew longer and the night time breeze was a welcome sensation.

We whizzed smoothly around the bends for a while. Leaning left until our knees almost scraped the pavement. *Almost.* Then to the right and our bodies moved as one in the opposite direction. It was like road ballet in the moonlight with the evening breeze blowing over us and I couldn't help thinking what a good choice it had been. It didn't take long to reach my car though and he slowed down about a half a mile away.

I let go of his waist, sat up straight and held my arms out in the breeze like a plane for a little while on the last straightaway. I lowered them down and sat happily after that for the last few seconds while he pulled up next to my car.

I slid off and pulled the heavy helmet off my head. He took his off too and sat up straight with his feet out, holding up the bike. I stood next to him and shook my hair out dramatically like a shampoo commercial and he laughed. It was such a deep, rich sound. I loved it and hearing it always made me want more. I walked back up to him. I didn't stop until our faces were very close.

"Thanks. *That was fun!*" I said with a genuine smile and a quick raise of my brows. I handed the helmet back to him and he strapped it down on the seat behind him.

"Anytime." He answered like a pro.

I just shook my head and grinned again. I kissed him once, lightly on the lips. I pulled my key out of my front pocket where I had stuck it what felt like days ago. Then I turned to get in my car.

"Tell me, Mr. Insomnia." I called back over my shoulder. "Are you tired yet?"

"Actually, I think I am." He realized with a sigh. He raked a hand through his own hair. "Hell, I might even sleep through the night." He added and I could tell that it was half prediction, half hopeful thinking. I thought about it for all of two seconds and decided that I would risk it.

"If you're interested, and you promise to try and get some *sleep,* you can follow me home and sleep there. Since we *are* 'officially dating' now." I reminded him with a roll of my eyes.

"They probably have the billboards up already. I hope they used a good picture." He joked while I visibly cringed. That just made him laugh even harder. *Ahhhhh, joy!*

"Go ahead." He said, trying to reign it in. "I'll follow you."

I got into my car thinking that, although he was annoying, that had still made me way too damn happy.

Was I even fighting it anymore? I couldn't remember at

the moment. Oh well. I was too tired to worry about it then. I thought I detected a distinct pattern forming there also, but I chose to ignore that too.

Tomorrow. I could worry about all of that tomorrow, I thought as I drove home mentally on auto pilot. What I needed then was a good night's sleep. Company really wouldn't matter that much once my head hit the pillow. Still I knew already that I would sleep better with him there.

Chapter 30

I could feel the breeze again, flowing steadily over my body. It was more concentrated than normal, though. Because we were wet. We caught more of the passing breeze with every water droplet that clung to our skin. It made the warmth of the air tolerable and the friction between our bodies nonexistent.

His thumb slid across my bottom lip, just barely grazing it and it sent a shiver running through me. He leaned in and bit down on it next. *Hard,* but not *too* hard. Just hard enough that it surprised me. Then his thumb was back again, to wipe away the insult. *Gently.* It was confusing and *very* stimulating at the same time!

I opened my eyes to look at him while I took a deep cleansing breath. I wondered if he would ever run out of ways to drive me crazy.

I sure hope not, I thought almost instantly.

He swept his hand up and into my hair. He grabbed a handful of it from underneath and held tight. Not tight enough to make me knee him or anything, but tight enough to make me feel *held.* I liked it. For whatever reason, instead of making me feel dominated, what he was doing actually empowered me.

I kneeled down onto the circular cushion and pulled him down next to me. I pushed his shoulders back until his full length was laid out flat along the oversized, wicker chaise. He was perfectly willing to go where I led him. I was very happy about that. I stretched one leg over him and came to rest gingerly on top of him. I thought with great relish about what I wanted to do next, eagerly anticipating seeing his reaction. And then I ...woke ...*up.*

...sitting over him... *in my room!*

...wh ...*huh?*

He saw the look of shock on my face and immediately shot up, holding onto my shoulders.

"Simone? You alright? What happened?" He asked innocently and I thought that I would *die* right there when I realized the answer. *Oh no, no, no, no, no, no. no, no, no!* I screamed mentally. Verbally, I was completely silent.

I slid off of him slowly, in a state of shock. He didn't stop me but he didn't let go of me either.

"Simone? *Talk to me!* Please?" He asked patiently. I looked down at him. He was naked. I looked further. So was I. Had I been when I fell asleep? I tried hard to remember but I had been so tired that it wouldn't come. I looked back up in a daze. Trying to find words.

"Um ...*sorry.* Sometimes my dreams can get a little ...*animated.*" I said and he seemed to understand. His eyes widened and he looked stricken!

"You were *asleep?!*" He asked, obviously completely unaware.

"Uh, yeah. Sorry." I said sheepishly, with one eye closed in embarrassment. He was still sitting with his mouth hanging open. "But if it helps, *this* is basically what I was dreaming about. I just didn't realize that it had become *more* than a dream." I laughed. "That's never happened to me before.

"Huh! Yeah, I have to say it's a first for me too!" He said in a strained voice but he did finally laugh. "Clearly there is no shortage of firsts when you are around!" He shook his head again.

"Simone, I had no idea! I'm ...*sorry too,* I think?" He offered, scratching his head. "Now that I think of it, I can't say if your eyes were opened or closed when it started. But you *talked* to me! *You said my name!"* He explained desperately.

'Wow. Good thing it was yours, huh?" I joked, hoping to lighten the mood a little. It worked. He couldn't help but grin.

"Well I think that's the first time someone has ever been *present* when I happened to have one of *those* dreams about them." I guess it makes sense that you would misinterpret it." I offered, feeling amused and a little more forgiving by then. Of him and of myself.

"*Jesus!* This is a regular thing? One of *those* dreams? What does that mean?" He asked then.

"Um, yeah. Fairly regular. It's a little side bonus that I enjoy from time to time." I said sarcastically. "I have these extremely vivid dreams that sort of... *happen.* Once in a while." I admitted, scratching my head in nervousness. "Not a lot." I added, trying to sound like slightly less of a freak than I knew I currently did.

"When I do though, I tend to be, um, *vocal.*" One eye closed again. Somehow that made it easier to keep going but don't ask me how. "Usually I'm alone though, so it doesn't matter anymore. But uh ...yeah. *Usually.*" I smiled a conciliatory smile at him in the end. I held it as long as I could, before I burst out laughing.

"So much for sleeping through the night, huh?" I said somewhat apologetically through my giggles.

"Eh, sleeping is overrated." He answered casually while lying back and folding his arms behind his head, though I could tell that it wasn't really true.

"*Hmpf!*" He was thoughtful for a few seconds more then he finally started to laugh too. That made me laugh even harder.

'Is it wrong to tell you that you're a better seductress, even *asleep,* than most women are wide awake?" He asked. He was feeling somewhat more humorous but still just a little bit disappointed too. I just chuckled some more and looked down.

'Um, thanks?" I ventured. I laid back myself and took a deep breath. He looked over at me then reached around to pull me up against his side.

"You're welcome." He smiled harder. "Every time I think I have you figured out, you throw me another damn curve ball woman. Would you like to help me out at all, by maybe just telling me how many more of them you have left in your back pocket?" He asked with a chuckle.

"Uh, I think that might be all of them now. I'll let you know if I remember anything else." I said and laughed again too. "Just trying to keep you on your toes." I offered still grinning.

"It's a kind of a strange perspective for me to consider though." I said more seriously. "Because I constantly feel like you see way too much of me at every turn. Much more than anybody else and way more than I *ever* intend to allow." He could tell that I was serious, even though I tried to make light of it.

"*Hmpf!* I don't know about that, but I can tell you that every new piece of you that I finally get to see just ends up making me more curious!" He said emphatically while pulling me up on top of him. Back where I had started. "It's crazy! Usually the more I learn about a person, the more my curiosity fades. But not with you. You surprise me constantly and I find myself more intrigued instead of less every time." He looked at me thoughtfully in the end and it was funny because I could feel his genuine curiosity at how I did that.

I wished I knew. No one else had ever felt that way about me before him. At least not that I had noticed.

He reached up and kissed me then, softly. "Now that you're awake, how would you like to make your dreams come true?" He asked with a cocky grin.

I chuckled automatically. "Well how could a woman say no to *that?*" I asked sarcastically. "Oh well, since I *am* already awake..." I didn't bother to finish my sentence. Not with words anyway. I let my actions speak for me as I leaned down and kissed him back. On purpose that time.

He stopped me though. "How 'bout we make that an official rule. To start every *middle-of-the-night* encounter with that specific phrase from now on, *'Since I am already awake...'*" He suggested playfully. *"Just to be safe."* He said as he laughed. I hit him in the shoulder for making fun of me as he pulled me back down close to him. Though I could hardly argue with him and I eventually gave in and laughed too.

For about a half a second...

Chapter 31

The next time I woke, the first morning sun was shining in the windows. Apparently I had forgotten to draw the blinds the night before. I was still tangled up with him and I liked it. I remembered exactly how we had gotten that way that time around and I had no regrets.

I was trying to feel if he was awake or not without moving at first. It was too hard to tell. It was too peaceful. I knew that didn't necessarily mean that he was asleep thoguh. I stretched just slightly and carefully turned my head. I was greeted by the sight of him laying still, eyes closed, on the pillow next to mine.

He did appear to be sound asleep and it was the first time I had ever seen him so calm. So *completely* relaxed. Not in motion. He was even more handsome without the lines of stress and worry that usually framed his features. I just laid there with a smile on my face at how very young he looked when he was asleep. Until my nagging bladder finally nudged me back into action.

I tried to separate myself carefully, not wanting to wake him. *Again.*

He surprised me though, by holding on to my hips. Tightly. *Mmmmm.* I sighed and smiled in spite of the fact that I really did have to pee.

"You are such a faker!" I accused. "His only response was to reach his arms tighter around my waist and pull me closer to him. He nuzzled his face into my neck, under my hair and wrapped one leg over both of mine. Then he tucked his right foot between my feet to complete the connection and I was suddenly so comfortable, that I totally forgot about having to pee and we both fell back asleep.

It only lasted about a half an hour, before my bladder reminded me again why it had woken me the first time. I didn't want to give him a chance to waylay me again, so I quickly slipped stealthily out from under his arm and rolled silently off the side of the bed.

He startled me by laughing at me almost instantly. "You're a regular *James Bond.*" He said, still chuckling.

I gave it up and stood up straight beside the bed. I laughed myself then. "I thought you were asleep." I said in defense of my overly-dramatic actions.

"I *was.*" He answered plainly. He laid there, strictly content. He was all spread out, staring openly at my nakedness. Clearly wide awake at that point.

I on the other hand, couldn't help thinking again for just a moment, about the depths of the demons that resided deep within him. Demons that still kept him so *completely* on edge, all the time. *Even* when he was *sound asleep!*

I had gotten the highlight reel of Ethan's nightmare childhood but I was still missing the individual episodes. Somewhere, in one of those smaller sub-stories, was the reason for that particular issue I was sure.

"It's your turn to make breakfast." He said then interrupting my thoughts, as if that had been a pre-established part of some imaginary contract.

"Oh really?" I mused aloud. "Well, I don't remember agreeing to any such thing but I *do* like to eat."

"Mmmmm hmmmm." He agreed whole-heartedly, reminding me of my lunch from the day before. Suddenly it was hard for me to believe that had really been just a day ago.

I grinned and continued egging him on. "Breakfast *is* supposedly the most important meal of the day. And I have to admit, when I skip it, I do tend to embarrass myself a little at lunch." I agreed, making fun of myself that time.

"Alright. I think I have eggs and cheese and some fresh fruit, anyway. *Mmmmm.* That actually sounds pretty good now."

I realized aloud. "Okay, give me ten minutes to shower and I'll get started." I said.

"Deal." He agreed, rolling back over and taking up the whole bed once he had it to himself. He certainly looked as if he belonged there. It was easy to understand then though, why he felt so at home there. Because he literally *had* been *"at home"* there. *Hah!*

Normally that would probably creep me out just a little, but somehow it didn't. Not with him. Not there. That place had nothing but good vibes built into it and that was also apparently mostly because of him. It was so easy to see after I knew the truth. You could take the man out of the house but the house still carried the essence of the man. Clean, bright, no frills, solid and strong but without pretense or apology. He easily fit right back in, anytime he chose to.

I grabbed some shorts and a tank top from the bin that I still hadn't switched out yet. Maybe tomorrow, I thought humorously. Then I got some clean underwear and a bra from my drawers and I headed for the bathroom.

I showered quickly and brushed my teeth. I threw my hair up in the towel for the moment and went to start the coffee.

"Do you mind if I borrow your shower?" He asked so politely from the bed that it was comical and I had to smile.

"Please. Make yourself at home." I played along hospitably. "Let me know if you need help figuring out how anything works or where anything is." I called sarcastically over my shoulder. I heard him laugh as he walked into the bathroom.

"Oh if I call for you from the shower, I promise it won't be because I need a towel." He taunted as he closed the door and turned on the water. I didn't doubt him for a second. I just shook my head while I started to get things out of the fridge.

He was pretty fast, but the coffee was ready when he came out. I was still beating eggs and shredding cheese but I had some cantaloupe already cut and set out on a plate, along with some sliced golden delicious apples. I threw a handful of freshly washed blueberries on top to finish it off and set it down on the island in front of him. He sat down and worked on making them all disappear. I picked out a few pieces here and there as I cooked.

All he had were yesterdays' jeans but they still looked pretty damn good. His hair was wet and he hadn't bothered with a shirt yet and I had to admit to being more affected by that than I should have been. *Really?!*

I shook my head in disappointment at myself. *Jesus, Simone! Come on!* I mean, I'd seen good looking guys before, for *Christ's* sake! *What the hell was wrong with me?!!*

In... Out... Deep breaths. *Dammit!* I tried to ignore him while I went back to scrambling the eggs. He really did make it hard for me to focus on mundane things sometimes!

"So, I haven't had a chance to ask yet, but I've been wondering what you found out about Jeremy?" I said, trying to distract us both from the physical tension as usual. It was like my part time job lately. I was getting a little better at it though, I thought to myself while I waited for him to answer. He was amused by my tactics, I could tell. He did something else that I was getting used to, where he didn't say so out loud. We both knew he didn't have to. He let it go.

"Mostly what we expected, except for the depth to which the effects extended. It was a lot deeper into the layers of the eye then we have seen in the past. We're not really sure what that means yet in its' entirety, but it raises flags." I could feel his worry for Jeremy as he spoke.

"His vision tests were certainly exceptional. He's testing at 20/2! That's the same as a *hawk*, which has the best vision in the entire animal kingdom." He said with obvious wonder.

"Mine is only 20/4, and I had the best that we knew of. Until now." He wasn't upset that he had lost his title. He was sad that someone had surpassed his level of *heightening* though, which in his eyes meant they must have also surpassed his level of suffering during the viruses run. That part bothered him. He was remembering that particular sickness again and I was feeling it too, whether I liked it or not. I knew that part was nothing that he could control though and I found myself wanting to reassure him.

"With all of our medical and technological advances, there is still no way to cure a virus. Simple or complex, natural or manufactured. The body has to fight. And it either wins or it loses. That part is still not a variable that we can hope to control yet.

Jeremy was in an induced coma through the worst of his from what you told me. I can't help thinking that has to be the best case scenario." I offered, and I could tell that he was hopeful that I was right about that.

I sprinkled the cheese on the eggs to melt and in another pan I grilled the one bagel I had left in some butter to share between us.

He took a deep breath and instantly set those old feelings aside. I really would have to make him tell me his secret at some point I thought, getting slightly off track in typical fashion.

I went and brushed my hair out and just left it to air dry. I hung the towel and when I got back, everything was done.

I scooped half of the fluffy, cheesy eggs onto each plate before they could start to brown on the bottom. I spread some cream cheese on each side of the bagel then added one half to each plate as well. I brought the plates over and laid them down on the bar and came around to sit beside him. He smiled at me and we both dug in. Conversation stopped for a time. I stopped worrying about everything but the plate in front of me for a few minutes and he did the same. He finished before me but he sat sipping coffee and sighing quietly, until I caught up.

"Thank you. That was delicious." He said.

I grinned at his obvious satisfaction "You're quite welcome." I said with a smile as I got up and cleaned the plates. I would have been surprised by how great an appreciation he had for such a simple thing, but I knew why by then. I put the rest of the cantaloupe in the fridge and wiped the counter but not before he managed to get down a couple more slices.

"How's he doing?" I asked, getting back to our conversation. I was really concerned with his state of mind most of all.

"He's still going back and forth a lot more than I would like." He admitted reluctantly. "One minute, he's taking it all in, handling it all so well. I start thinking he's acting *so* mature and so wise beyond his years, that I'm actually a bit wary. Then the next minute I realize I'm right unfortunately, because he's off hiding in a dark corner again, ignoring everyone." He said and sighed. "It's the classic 'two steps forward, one step back' scenario."

"He'll get there, but he definitely still needs more time to come to terms with all of this. I'm really hoping he's a lot further along by next week. I would hate for Pete to try to take him back from me now." He said in a warning tone, and I could feel his honest foreboding at that very real possibility. The atmosphere cooled a few degrees.

"Why?" I asked warily, suddenly afraid of his answer. "What happens then?"

He just looked at me. Straight at me. No wavering. No apology.

"I'll do whatever I need to do to help Jeremy. I told him I would and I meant it." He answered without so much as blinking. He could see that I wasn't sure what to do with that, so he tried to explain.

"Look, I know not everyone has parents like mine, but the time kids spend as a responsibility to their parents is relatively short anyway, when you compare it to the length of the rest of their lives." He looked at me meaningfully, knowing I may have a problem with that attitude. "I'm sorry but it's true."

"Childhood is temporary. The change in them is permanent. They have to learn how to live with it before it destroys any chance they have at a decent life. Not just for their sake, either." He insisted.

"It's important that they get help before they inadvertently take down everyone around them, too." I could tell that he really was concerned. "Sometimes, the parents are good people, who just don't know how to deal with it. They need and want our help as much as the kids do. It's a lot easier to do our job then, with everyone on the same team."

"Other times though, that's just not the case. I've seen it too many times already. Unaffected family members don't *have* to do anything. They don't *have* to work to find a solution. They start to remember that their own lives would be perfectly happy and normal, if it weren't for that one family member constantly screwing it all up. No matter how much they love them, they can start to become resentful. Then they eventually start to distance themselves. It's not even their fault really. It's just human nature. In the end though, the result is always the same. The *height* ends up on their own." He sighed.

"Besides his learning to deal calmly and rationally with his *height* abilities, there's another element coming into play here that I have to worry about as well. The well-dressed gentleman looking for me at The Tavern? You were correct in your assumption. That would be *Agent Anderson*. Left me his card." He said by way of explanation. "He's the Federal Agent that's been trying to contact Jeremy. From what Department, we have no *'official'* idea. I can only guess. Supposedly he's CDC, Center for Disease Control. If he really is CDC, than he belongs to an undocumented, unofficial branch of it because his name doesn't come up in any database anywhere that we could find." He informed me with raised eyebrows and I was appropriately scared by that little revelation. He ignored my worried look and kept going.

"He has way too much interest in Jeremy still for my comfort level. As I've said, the positive result would have tipped someone off, somewhere. I guess we've identified the *'someone'* now at least. He's been to the Hoffman's house twice since I took Jeremy with me. Pete keeps putting him off, but he's persistent." He said in annoyance with a shake of his head.

"He's been spending all his free time trying to track down exactly who else has had contact with Jeremy since his DOI. He's also trying desperately to find out where his newest *'specimen'* has gone to so unexpectedly, before he even got a chance to interview him or have him tested. Of course, he's suspicious of the timing." He wiggled his eyebrows again at that.

"He really has no legal right to any information as to Jeremy's whereabouts though, or his medical records. Pete's smart enough to know that too. Though his proclaimed position with the CDC gives him a lot more freedom in those areas than we would like. Obviously that's why they use that particular branch of Government as a cover. As long as he can claim it's for *'public safety reasons,'* they can gain access to pretty much anything they want, eventually. That kind of power to cut through red tape can be extremely dangerous." He was leery again.

"Really? What about you? Didn't you also mention talking to Jeremy's doctors?" I asked with raised brows of my own. He smiled.

"Well, here in my backyard, I do have a little pull of my own." He agreed. "But in this particular case, I am also a close friend of the family who happened to have given the doctors permission to talk to me initially." He laughed sheepishly at that admission. I smirked again but tried to stay on topic.

"So what happens if he talks to Jeremy? What's the real threat here? Help me understand. Is it just a war of information? The first one to figure it all out wins? Or is there real fear for Jeremy's safety?" I asked all at once, trying to catch up.

"Possibly both, it depends on the situation. Sometimes they show up, ask a few question and leave. Never to be heard from again. In those instances I think they're just keeping track. It still feels like *'information to be used at a later time,'* but they go away pretty quickly. Other times the initial questioning leads to *'further testing'* being necessary. Again, it's always to *'ensure public safety.'* That gets them a lot of cooperation, especially these days. I personally believe however, that it's more so they can document and verify the most *'unusual'* claims for their own records." He said with his worry more than clear. "We hear that quite often. A lot of times *those* particular individuals, the ones with the more *'unusual'* abilities, are the ones who later disappear without a trace." I could feel his very real fear again at that, so I didn't need to question his sincerity.

"The fact of the matter is, it's just not safe for him out there right now. He's still too vulnerable." I could feel a real love for Jeremy and his family underlying that statement.

"Quite often, by the time someone goes missing, they have already been labeled a *'high risk'* teen based on their most recent behavior. So of course, it's no big stretch to write them off as a runaway. Everyone accepts it, no questions asked. Case closed. I'll admit maybe some of them are. I'll tell ya though, it's hard not knowing what really happened. Especially when a parent had been counting on you to help them and you can't find a single shred of evidence of the loved one that once existed. It's even harder when they're found dead, supposedly of a suicide. Too many people are ready to believe it, evidence or not." He was remembering specific instances. I could tell that not only had each one hurt him deeply, but each loss had also left its' own separate scar that he still carried.

"There have been times that we couldn't say for sure either, whether they really ran off or not, trying to escape it all. Neither could we say for sure if they were *'drafted'* into some type of *'service for their country,'* whether of their own free will or otherwise." He definitely seemed to have some strong feelings about what their motives for that might be and they weren't comforting.

"The uncertainty is the worst, and it works in their favor. Anything that can't be proven, doesn't *'officially'* exist. You just can't get the masses to accept it. We aren't willing to lose any more people to the unknown. Not if we can stop it. We plan to hold on very tightly to our own from now on, and when I say our own, I mean all the *heights* we help, but I *especially* mean the ones that I personally call *'family!'*" His vehement statement left little room for doubt.

"Any way you look at it, Jeremy needs me still. Pete can't even handle what's going on inside his son right now, never mind the forces hovering around him. If I let him go home now, knowing what I know, it would be equivalent to abandoning him. I could ...but I won't." He insisted quietly.

"Not out on the street abandoned, obviously. As you are well aware, there are many ways to abandon someone." He didn't have to say more for me to understand. He knew that.

I couldn't help thinking about Ben just then and how I had felt alone for so long, even before I left. Yet I definitely still considered *him* one of the *good* guys! I hated it, but I knew he was right. It wasn't Ben's fault, but it happened.

"I will not abandon them, Simone. I will fight for them until they can fight for themselves. I've made it my job to see that through. To the best of my ability, I will always stand by them when everyone else would just write them off or shut them away." More painful memories. I tried not to cringe.

"It's such a crucial time. Helping them during that time has to be my first priority. It has to be *someone's!*" I could feel nothing but the strength of his conviction then. He was unwavering on the subject.

That worried me even more. It was the first time I truly

felt the weight of what could happen, if someone disagreed with what Ethan was trying to do. Or tried to stop him from doing it. I had no doubt that he would fight *hard.* He would do whatever he had to. I was just as sure of that then as he was.

I knew why he did what he did and I applauded him for it. I knew his motives were good and that what he was doing was necessary. In Jeremy's case especially, I would most likely agree with his decisions.

I also knew why he kept it all a secret. It was easy to see that the public at large would not be able to understand. Most would never believe the things that he knew to be fact. Things that I now knew. I had experienced many of the things that he spoke of firsthand and I still didn't want to believe any of it at first. Why would someone else who couldn't see it, hear it, or feel it ever believe him? How can you ever hope to defend yourself without being able to use the truth to do it? While standing up against the ever powerful hand of the United States Government at the same time to boot, the original inventors of *"clandestine operations."* He was very brave and extremely selfless, to do what he did.

Still, I was *very* frightened by the vigilante attitude. I couldn't deny that. I *understood* it, but I couldn't pretend that I didn't fear it just the same. It was not a position that came without consequences. Very real and *frightening* consequences.

I was decidedly willing to throw my fears of intimacy aside and be with him *physically.* I had accepted that. Was I also as willing to risk the legal problems and the public battles that could potentially arise? Especially in a small town like Pinegrove, where everyone knows everyone? Could I throw my fate in with his, socially? Professionally? Personally? Knowing the risks that he is willing to take?

Was I prepared and willing to take on *Federal Agents?!*

That one was a little harder to answer. Again, it wasn't just about me anymore. No matter what *I* believed in, I had to take Liliana into consideration in any major decision that I made from there on out. Whether her future would later present her with those same decisions or not was irrelevant at the moment.

I had been quiet for a long time, but it wasn't awkward. He didn't press me. He just sipped his coffee and waited. Either it was a deal breaker for me, or it wasn't. He had stated his position plainly and honestly and we both knew that it wouldn't change.

He was just giving me time to decide how I felt about it.

Chapter 32

When I finally put my own mug down and spoke, it was still noncommittal. "For right now, can I officially go on record as saying I also hope it doesn't come to that?" I asked, sheepishly but hopefully. I was just putting it off and we both knew it, but he seemed willing to let it go. For the time being. He smiled that beautiful smile of his at me.

"I won't blame you Simone. Either way. I know why you're hesitant to get involved in all of this. I understand that you are concerned about being a good parent to your daughter, first and foremost." He brushed his hand down my cheek and held one finger under my chin. "You know how much I can appreciate that." He said with just the tiniest flash of the old pain. It was replaced very quickly with admiration and understanding. I was grateful. But I was also feeling a little guilty and I didn't like it. I confessed.

"It feels hypocritical though, knowing full well that the very reason that I would keep my distance also has the potential to someday put me fully on the other side of this situation. It's a lot of perspectives to try and consider all at once." I explained.

"You don't have to decide it all right now." He said, letting me off the hook. "If it comes down to that, I'll do what I have to do, and you do what you have to do. We'll just deal with it as it comes. Okay?" He offered.

"That is unusually kind of you." I said, more than a little surprised. We both knew very well that at some point, it would come up again. \7]/I *would* have to choose a side.]]=

"But for now, I'll take it." I agreed thankfully. "Will you see him today?" I asked wondering what came next.

"No." He answered quickly. "I want him to gain a little of his independence back. It will be good for him. He needs some time away from me and Camp for that. Dr. J. will be with him. He has a few more days before he has to get back to his normal schedule, and he's going to spend them taking Jeremy on a sort of field trip. He will help him practice being around people again, but in controlled situations. A little at a time." He explained.

"Right now, he's Jeremy's best tool. He's still got to get him to stop fighting it so much. Doc's very good at what he does though." He said and I could feel him remembering how well he had handled *him*. He was very appreciative. After all this time, he was still just a little in awe of the good doctor.

"I'm good at 'the big picture,' but I'm still learning new things myself every day. I know I'm not always the best person to assist with every step of the journey. That's alright. I know other people that are and I'm good at delegating. If anyone can get him past this part, it's Dr. J." He took a deep breath in and let it out all at once.

"So, for now, I'm all yours." He said with a definite gleam in his eye. "What can we do to work on your problem?" He asked eagerly, switching mental gears.

"Actually, you have the only job left that can still be worked on off-site at this point." I explained. He seemed pretty happy about that. "I've got the basic structure of the well and the surrounding area down, but I need you to help me figure out how to make it all work internally." I said with a grin and a raise of my eyebrows as I thought about the finished product. It was a disaster of a situation that had led me there, but I had to admit that I was excited about where we had ended up.

He grinned back at me. "This is like a dream job, combining lots of my favorite things. Including spending time with you. I like it!" He said and his smile expanded until I could see molars.

I went and grabbed the sketches that I had made with Jack and Gen's help. Meanwhile he put his shirt on, which was also sadly a big help as far as concentrating went. He sat on the sofa and I sat Indian style on the floor. I spread the pages on the coffee table in between us. We dove right in and I started to go over all of it with him. How I had envisioned it. Where I wanted things to go, and what I wanted them to do.

He fought me on a few points, but his suggestions helped lead to surprising improvements on a few others. I was drawing while he talked, feeding off of his ideas and his energy. He took his time, explaining things to me as we went, what would give me the results I wanted and why. I was fascinated by both his vast knowledge and his complete willingness to share it.

I had to acknowledge then, that he wasn't just good looking. He was obviously smart, too. I mean, *really* smart! I had always known that he was intelligent. With all the things that he had managed to accomplish, with all that he was up against, he would have to be. But it took more than just your average mind to pick up the working knowledge of so many completely different sciences, and with a bit of a late start to boot!

I had always done fairly well in school, despite my own issues. Went to college. Got a good education. Yet he was *clearly* smarter than me in so many different areas. I imagined for just a moment how dangerously successful a man he *could* have been, had his intellect and his soul been nurtured properly from the very beginning.

A strange kind of realization came over me at that thought. It was so clear that I could almost see it for a moment. He kept talking, and I kept drawing, but I slowed down a little and the images passed through my mind while we worked. I'm not sure where it all came from, but I got a very distinct impression of *another* him. Another version of him.

One where his self-confidence had never been shaken and tested to its' limits, but instead nurtured and allowed to grow, reinforced. A 'him' where his caring heart had never been shattered at so young an age by utter carelessness and pure evil. Where his intelligence was challenged and encouraged instead of stifled and ignored. It was staggering to think of who he could have become.

He was someone that I admired *greatly* already! He was a fighter. He had a beautiful, selfless heart. He possessed real character and conviction in his principles and a faith that I could never hope to match. But he had fought *hard* for every scrap of that, every step of the way. I imagined for just a brief moment, an Ethan who'd never had to put so much of his energy into fighting. It was almost too much to comprehend, but I could *see* it somehow. The sense of peace in his eyes. The rows of diplomas from multiple disciplines lining his walls. The scores of beautiful women hanging off of him, mesmerized by his every word. *Yikes!* That one snapped me out of it a little bit.

I still longed for that vision to be the truth for him. He deserved it. Though I had to admit that I was a little bit glad that not everyone would be able to really *get* him the way I could. I found the sudden idea of having to compete for his attention, *very* unsettling. Huh.

Besides, Ethan's past *had* made him who he was, and regardless of whether it was right or wrong, the results were spectacular! I thought then, that perhaps that peaceful version of Ethan could still exist. I imagined purposefully that maybe he was a *future* Ethan, rather than a past, missed possibility. That made me feel a little better. I truly hoped it could still be a reality for him. Well, *most of it* anyway.

What? I'm still human. That hasn't changed.

I shook off my selfish tendencies and paid attention to the work at hand again after that. We were actually making pretty good progress. Even with the occasional mental wandering, it felt really good to be doing something constructive and the morning flew by. We'd had a late breakfast, so we didn't care about lunch and we worked right through. Before we knew it, it was late afternoon and we decided we finally needed a break.

"Let's go for a walk." I suggested, gingerly unfolding myself. "I need to stretch my legs." I stood and laughed a little at the pain.

"Sounds like a great idea. We can kill two birds with one stone, because I could use a change of clothes." He added, standing up himself and stretching his arms high over his head. I looked up, watching him and laughed. If he was under a standard height ceiling doing that, his elbows would have been scraping across it.

"I understand now I think, why you built the high ceilings everywhere." I said with a laugh.

"Yeah, my construction lessons kind of came at the same time that I outgrew everything averaged sized. I guess it was a natural progression." He made light of it, as if it were a lucky happenstance. Again there was admiration for Jack in his feelings, for knowing what he needed to learn and teaching it to him. I just smiled to myself and went to use the bathroom and get my shoes.

I grabbed my phone, my keys and two water bottles and I was ready. It was actually really nice not to have to try and reach someone to tell them I was going for once.

We headed down the back steps and up the path towards the orchard. We walked across the right side in the just recently cut green grass. We moved at an easy, but steady stride and waved to Jack on the undone side as he rode by mid-mow. It was nearing dinner time but the sun was shining brightly still and it was actually pretty hot out. With the blinds drawn to block the glaring sun and the windows open to catch the breeze, we hadn't noticed just how warm it had gotten. I was glad then, that I had chosen shorts. I could feel Ethan wishing he had a pair on too. I looked up and saw him starting to sweat. I watched absentmindedly, as he peeled his t-shirt off again and hung it from his back pocket.

I was momentarily mesmerized myself then. I had to remind myself to watch where I was going, when I tripped over a tree root that was sticking up out of the ground.

We both laughed hysterically as I ran to catch up with myself, since it was blatantly obvious what had diverted my attention.

"How I resisted you as long as I did, I have no idea." I said with a shake of my head and a self-deprecating laugh.

"Me either." He joined in from behind, quickly catching back up. "But it nearly killed me." He added, beside me again. "I sure am glad we're not doing *that* anymore!" He grinned enthusiastically.

We followed the trail to the right that time and I enjoyed the terrain immensely. The trails wound up and down hills and around a few more large boulders. The trees were just as tall on that side of the forest and with the sun filtering down through their leaves, the backdrop was as pretty as a picture. I wished for a moment that I had thought to take my camera. Just another example of why I would never be a successful photographer. I enjoyed it anyway.

"I really love this area back here. There aren't enough places left like this, where nature still has such a firm hold. Where man has yet to intrude, abuse and overuse it. I know I sound all preachy." I chuckled. "And I know it's all hip and trendy these days to be 'green.' I promise you I'm not normally a bandwagon jumper. I just can't help it. I still feel that way anyway." I said without apology. He was not really judging me, but I still felt the need to explain myself further as we walked.

"I remember when I was little and my dad would take me out to a beautiful section of woods out on the edge of the city to go walking on the weekends. Fully entrenched in the naivety of my childhood innocence, I just assumed those woods would always be there. We could spend hours hiking around and never travel the same trail or climb the same rock twice." I allowed myself to remember it for a few seconds then I moved on.

"Every square inch of forest in that particular area is gone now. It's all a big industrial park with lots of useful, job giving taxpaying companies. Don't get me wrong. I know that it's great for the cities' economy. I still hate that I will never be able to take Liliana there and walk those trails with her that I once walked with my dad. That makes me sad, dammit. That's all there is to it. No real mystery there." I said, thinking again about what Gen and I had discussed.

I looked at him and I could feel that he understood and that he felt bad for me too. Immediately, *I* felt bad for bringing him down.

"Sorry. I didn't mean to depress us." I explained. I smiled in an attempt to get him to mirror me. It worked.

"Don't worry darlin,' it would take a lot more than that to depress me." He admitted bravely, being brutally honest as usual.

"Anyway, I would have to agree. I spent a lot of time in these woods while I was adjusting to my new senses, my new *world.* It was so much easier here than out there in the big, loud, concrete jungle with all of the *normal* people." I felt how stifling that could be as he felt it and I knew that feeling all too well.

"I needed the room. To run. To learn how to see and hear everything in a whole new way. To explore, slowly. *Just to breathe!* Away from everyone and everything." He explained, and I realized then why Camp *Height* was built where it was. He knew firsthand the peace that the trees and open sky could give you. Another piece of what made Ethan, Ethan.

"It was time well spent and I still come back to it over and over to help me maintain my peace of mind. I don't know what I would do if the forests around here ceased to exist." I could feel his very real panic, just briefly, at the thought. It was quickly replaced by a very strong sense of determination. "I don't intend to find out either." He added seriously.

"Let me guess. You bought them all." I said sarcastically.

"Not all. Not yet" He answered simply. "I'm working on it." He was serious. My jaw hit the ground.

"What! You're talking about over 2000 acres in this area alone! That's insane! No one can *buy* that!" I stopped dead in my tracks for once and stared at him across the trail. "Explain." I demanded calmly.

"Okay, but only if you walk while we talk. I'm sweating my ass off and I'm not inclined to go *au naturale* so far out here and chance an awkward encounter. The forest *is* a public place after all." He said, leading the way and pulling me along.

"If I remember correctly, you were willing to do a lot more than go naked in the woods at one point not too long ago." I reminded him with a huge grin.

"Right. That was an emergency situation and would have been well worth any possible encounter." He said with a wiggle of his brows.

"Speak for yourself." I said with a laugh. "I certainly don't want to have to have that conversation with say, the bag boy from the supermarket." He just laughed harder. "Besides," I realized and said at the same time, "wouldn't you hear or see anyone coming long before they happened upon us?" I asked suspiciously.

"Sure, if I happened to be paying attention to anything *else* going on around me." He admitted with a guilty grin. Right.

That made sense.

"Anyway. The explaining please. You're stalling." I accused.

"Alright. Alright." He gave in. "Like Jack, my family has been here for more than a few generations, and they too had acquired quite a vast amount of land over the years. As people began to sell off plots in the beginning of the development boom, my family was buying them up. Anywhere and everywhere they could. Quite often, any *way* they could." He said with a look that made it clear what he meant.

"Mostly they looked for connecting parcels that they could piece together and sell later for a bigger profit, or break up according to their needs. Especially properties near or including the open forests. To them that meant even more room for future development. They took smaller, separate properties when they could get them as well, in the hopes that they would someday end up being next to something else that they could buy." He stepped over a small stream with one foot and lifted me from one side to the other before bringing his second foot to the opposite bank.

"There were great intentions, but not always great results in their following business endeavors. There were marriages that gained more land. Then there were affairs and divorces that re-divided them in different ways. There were often local politicians and career criminals eating dinner side-by-side. Mistakes were made. Prices were paid. Reputations both good and bad were earned and assigned. The Stone family soap opera. It's quite the saga." He said with a half grin.

"Eventually though, our numbers dwindled. So did the money, which has been long gone for at least the last four generations. By then it was all my grandparents could do to keep up with the taxes on the properties, stubbornly refusing to sell. Most fell into a massive state of disrepair over the years. A lot of the properties were no longer rentable or even habitable by then. Plenty turned out not to be buildable at all. They were tough times and my family weren't the only ones out there trying to make their way any way they could. They were duped into buying unusable properties probably as many times as they swindled someone out of a decent one." He admitted openly.

"Besides that, personal problems have always plagued our family, for one reason or another." He said with a sideways glance. I could think of at least one recurring problem that I would assume might have made things difficult for his ancestors. I voiced what we were both thinking.

"Well, it seems that being a *height* runs strong in your family. I imagine it would have been just as troublesome a situation back then as well, if the virus goes back that far. Do you know whether it does or not?" I asked.

"Not exactly. We don't have access as of yet to any records that old, but it goes back at least seventy five years that we can prove. Before that, it's still a guess right now. It may very well be a big part of the why every generation got a little smaller though. There really *wasn't* a next generation this last time around, so to speak. There was just my dad. And after that, against all odds *and* his own vehement wishes, there's just me." He was still a little bit sad about that and I wondered for the first time about whether he ever wanted to have children of his own or not, knowing what he knew then.

As soon as I considered it, I wondered how on Earth I had never considered it before! Especially since that topic opened a myriad of other questions for *me* that I couldn't even stop to *consider* then. There were just too many. I placed it in the mental HOLD/BUT DAMN IMPORTANT bin and went back to listening to Ethan.

"The land, in one state of development or another, has remained in our family regardless. Which it still is to this day." He raised his eyebrows and his hands and gave a grin at that, as if to say, "*Wa-la!*"

"The forests themselves of course for the most part, are Government and Federal property and are not available for private sale. They're also mostly open to the public anyway, and protected. For now at least."

"I'm fine with that, but I still personally feel a lot safer owning as much of what borders them as humanly possible. I don't trust others not to slowly but continually encroach from every direction, just as my ancestors had originally intended to do, until there's nothing left." I could feel his determination return again then.

"I currently own and maintain about 750 surrounding acres in total, just from the Stone Family Properties alone." He had some pride at that fact. It may have been the first time that I felt him feel anything like that towards his family and it didn't go unnoticed. "Then of course, there's what I have added in the last ten years myself. Just in this area, that adds almost another 200 acres. So technically, I'm about half way there." He said with a wink. I was sufficiently awed.

"That's incredible. I think I'm officially jealous now." I said seriously.

"Well you're welcome on any property that I own, at any time, so don't be." He assured me. He stopped me, turned me by my shoulders to look at him. "Seriously, Simone. Regardless of whatever happens between us personally, you can always bring Liliana walking *here!* And in twenty five years, you can come back with her and bring your grandchildren too." He said. "I promise. Okay?"

"Thanks." I said simply, knowing that he meant it and that he really understood how much it meant to me. He squeezed my hand and we started walking again. He was right, it was too hot to want to stay still for any length of time. He wasn't the only one sweating by then.

A few minutes later, we reached the top of the next rise in the trail and we could see the back of his property. Well his *own,* personal property anyway. It was my first time seeing it from that perspective but I could instantly tell from the way that Ethan was feeling that it was a very familiar view to him, and a welcome one. He was *home.*

He finally had that, even if he'd had to make it himself. Looking at it as we approached, I could see the whole facade for the first time and was surprised to find that the "front" of his house had been designed to face the forest and not the street like one would normally expect. That made me smile for some reason. I just shook my head again and we started, still hand in hand, down the last hill and up the stone lined path towards the entrance.

At the doorway, he reached up underneath the overhang and came back with a key. He unlocked the door, then replaced the key in a place that I could never hope to reach.

We walked inside and we were greeted by a heavenly blast of cool air.

"Oh, it's nice in here!" I said, happily stating the obvious.

"Yeah, it's all automatic here. Programmable thermostat. The heat or the AC will turn on if it drops below or raises above my baseline settings. It comes in handy, not having to come home and check and adjust it all the time.

"*Phew!* I bet! Works for me." I said plopping down on his sofa in a dead straight fall. No programmable thermostat at my place, huh?" I asked jokingly once I stopped bouncing.

"Sorry. It was a later revelation. I learn as I go. If it makes you feel any better, Camp is even more high tech than my place here." It didn't, and my look said so.

He was amused by my lack of amusement, which of course amused me immensely.

He stood there looking indecisive for a few minutes. Then I felt him settle on something and suddenly he was excited. I looked up at him.

"What?" I asked warily.

"I was going to take another shower but I'd just get sweaty again walking back. I have a better idea. Wait here while I get a few things." He ran up the stairs and I laid back on the sofa, enjoying the cool air while he was gone.

He came back a short time later in a pair of brown cargo shorts, a grey tank top, and a pair of flat, ankle height, lightweight hiking sneakers with no socks. He looked a lot more comfortable. He also had a small black backpack in his hands. He threw me a new water bottle and held out his hands to catch the old one. He took the empty bottles back to the kitchen, no doubt putting them straight into the recycling bin. I chuckled a little to myself at his OCD-like tendencies. Then I thought, I guess that's what you get when you make a child act like an adult from the age of seven. I had to admit to myself that it wasn't quite as funny but it did make an awful lot of sense.

He came back with two sandwiches that he rested on the table while he placed a new bottle of cold water for himself in the pack and then put it on.

"Are you sufficiently cooled enough to start back yet?" He asked teasingly.

"Awe, do we really have to go back? Are you sure that we shouldn't just stay here until the sun goes down?" I joked.

He pulled me up. "Come on. I'll make it worth your while." He promised. "We need to get back to your place first though, and a vehicle."

"Are you telling me that you don't have three or four other vehicles tucked away around here too?" I asked disbelievingly.

"No. Not at the moment anyway. I try not to keep too many toys here. I know the townspeople in general don't think too much about my occasional extravagances. A lot of them still see me as, *"That kid who won his case against the state."* so they think they know where it comes from. Still, I try not to overdo it and push my luck. I *am* just a local performer these days after all." He joked with a wicked grin in reference to my initial curiosity about his expensive toys. I chuckled and understood easily enough.

"I do have a pickup truck that's usually here, but it's currently in the shop. And both the bike and the F1 are at your place. So we're walking. Come on. Up!" He commanded while holding his hands out to me.

I groaned like an old person while I took hold of them and used them as leverage to stand. There was no real reason. It was just fun sometimes to be overly dramatic. He just grinned and shook his head, completely undeterred.

"Take this." He said handing me one of the sandwiches. "We'll eat on the way." I hadn't been hungry before, but I was then. I took a bite. There was smoked turkey, avocado, romaine lettuce, cucumbers, and a thin slice of cheddar. All on fresh scaly bread that was wrapped up tight in wax paper so none of it could fall out. Again, I was impressed with his culinary skills. *"Yum!"* I said and finally made for the door voluntarily, sufficiently bribed.

Chapter 33

We made the hike back in half the time, our leisurely attitudes somewhat squashed by the unexpected heat. It didn't take long to finish our sandwiches and we moved with more purpose in our strides after that. I was aware that he was shortening his stride to match mine but we were moving at a good pace none-the-less.

I made the climb up the back steps a little slower than usual, still waiting to hear what had him so excited. I looked at him questioningly at the top of the stairs, but he just smiled and followed me inside. He walked right through, grabbed his keys and headed straight out the front door. On his way down the stairs, he told me to pack a bathing suit and a change of clothes and meet him outside.

Ahhhhh. Swimming! That's right! Apparently Camp *Height* was empty again, at least temporarily. Oh, that sounded *really* good right then! I ran to my closet and quickly dug out a one piece that I remembered hating the least, from the bottom of the bin that was *still* there waiting patiently. I reached in a little deeper and grabbed a soft grey cotton skirt that had multiple thin, but figure forgiving layers. That made it a nice concealing piece to wear over a bathing suit. It was just easier than sucking it in the whole time. I also picked out another pair of shorts, a t-shirt and clean set of undergarments to go with them but I still didn't know for sure why.

I threw it all in an oversized beach bag, along with my keys and my phone and I met him out front. He was waiting in his car with the windows up and the doors closed so I knew he would have the AC cranking. I hopped in and sighed happily in the cool interior. He revved it once then slipped it smoothly into gear and we were off.

He drove straight to Camp and I followed most of it that time around. I was pretty sure that I could get back there on my own at that point if I wanted to. In theory anyway. In reality I never really memorized a route until I had driven it myself at least once. I tried not to be too distracted by the scenery and the setting sun. I watched out the window as the beautiful day began to turn into a beautiful night, but I paid as much attention to the route as I could.

He pulled into the garage and we walked over to his cabin to change. We entered and he headed towards what I still could only assume was his bedroom there. I could feel his anticipation growing. His arousal wafted back over me as he went. That unfortunately, made me think about how sweaty I still was. I decided to keep up with my part time job and try to derail things a bit. At least for the time being.

"Which way to the ladies room?" I asked with false innocence.

He chuckled, only mildly disappointed and nodded toward the second door. I walked past him with a forced smile and into the large, luxurious bathroom alone just to find a second door inside that connected the two rooms. I rolled my eyes as I heard him laugh through that door from the other side.

A moment later he called out. "Meet me out back when you're ready." Then he was gone.

I pulled my bathing suit out of my bag to change. It was a solid black one piece, with wide straps over the shoulders and camouflaging gathers up both sides. It was pretty basic and not terribly sexy, but it covered everything well enough and held things firmly in place for the most part. It hadn't been cheap but that one feature made it worth the money.

I was still somewhat of a work in progress and I knew that. I had no problem with the slow but proper process that we know we're supposed to follow these days, nor did I have the impatience for the perfection that I battled in vain to maintain in my youth. It's just that sometimes, standing next to Ethan in all his physical glory, I did feel just a little bit softer and flabbier than usual. I was really proud of what my body had accomplished already, creating a whole other person and all, and then somehow bouncing back. I would never take that for granted. That didn't mean I didn't understand and appreciate the benefits of keeping it tightly wrapped in spandex whenever possible.

With all of its' technological advances, it was still warm in the cabin since the AC hadn't been running before we headed over. Of course that was because everyone had expected that the Camp would be empty, so it had been purposely turned off. Why waste money? I understood. It had been on for a few minutes by then but it had yet to make a difference and I was still eager to get back outside. I realized then that I had forgotten to grab a pair of flip flops. I was mad at myself for the oversight but there was nothing I could do about it, so I decided in my impatience to just go barefoot.

As I stepped out the door, I was instantly relieved by the soft breeze that hit me. It was constant, but it was very light and still far too warm. It was coming across my body in a steady stream, but it wasn't nearly enough to cool me. I wanted it to be though and I pulled my hair up and twisted it over my head to allow more air to reach my skin. I didn't clip it, I just held it with my hands while I walked. I inhaled deeply as I stared up into the canopy and appreciated the way the last rays of the late day sunlight were beaming down through the leaves and lighting things in an orange and black speckled pattern. It all looked very surreal.

When I stepped off of the deck, I was acutely aware of the way the cool, damp leaves felt under my bare feet. It was slightly shocking but not in a bad way. With the heat of the day still lingering, it felt good to connect with the cool Earth, down where the heat didn't really ever reach. Not completely. By the time it would start to warm, or dry that far down below the canopy, the sun would set and the cooling cycle would resume its' reign again. Just then I was glad for that. I let my hair go and enjoyed the cooling effect under the soles of my feet instead while it lasted.

After the short trip across the path, I stepped up onto the warm concrete slab surrounding the pool, where Ethan was already opening the solar cover. He had left the outside lights off, I assumed so he wouldn't attract bugs, but the lights inside the pool were on and the water was glowing a bright neon shade of purple. He had changed into a pair of white and navy blue swim shorts and as usual, he looked like a damn ad for Abercrombie & Fitch. I just shook my head.

"When do you find time to work out exactly?" I asked, genuinely curious, rather than simply being complimentary. "You're often here during the day, at The Tavern in the evenings and *busy* at night." I said, purposefully exaggerating the situation. "I don't understand how you have enough time left over to look like that!" I said incredulously.

He just laughed. "I've mentioned that I occasionally have trouble sleeping, right?' He laughed again. "Except when I'm with you of course, then I have no problem at all because I am so physically exhausted that I have no choice! It's satisfying on so many levels." He said through half closed eyes and with a smile that illustrated his point just as nicely as the wave of pleasure that hit me.

"The other nights...? *Eh.* I find the repetitious nature of things like crunches or running to be almost as recharging an activity as sleep." He kept working while he talked, like it was no big deal.

I wanted to laugh, but I could tell right away that he wasn't kidding. *Holy shit!* That was his idea of relaxation? I was bound to be a huge disappointment to him in that department if that was really the case! At that thought I pulled my skirt up a little higher over my slightly rounded mid-section. He walked over to the ladder on his side and climbed down into the water. He had seen me naked already and seemingly approved wholeheartedly. That didn't stop me from judging myself a little more harshly than usual.

I did enjoy a nice long hike through the woods or a long walk around town. But when I really wanted to *relax*, I much preferred to watch a movie, or the sunset. Or some other activity that finds my ample ass comfortably seated.

"You just never cease to amaze me." I said while shaking my head back and forth.

"Well, the feeling is mutual and you certainly don't need that damn skirt, so take it off... *please*... and come in here already." He added without pretense as he stared into my eyes.

I had to admit that I was pleased that he would feel that way about me too. Whihch of course I could feel that he truly did. I may be a little self-critical sometimes, but I knew my own worth. Somehow, like him, I had always believed in that. I had never really considered myself to be super-model material though. I was tall, but not ridiculously tall. My legs are strong, but they aren't three miles long. My curves were probably a little better than average, if I was going to judge myself honestly, but I felt like I could pick out bucketful of bad parts as easily as the handful of good ones. Still overall, I had always felt like it probably averaged out as a whole, to about *"average,"* humorously enough. With Ethan though, each and every little thing that I *was*, he seemed to *genuinely* appreciate. *All* of it!

It was like playing cards and having your mediocre hand suddenly become the winning hand. Not because you had changed your cards for better ones. Rather because the rules of the game had suddenly changed to suit the cards you had been dealt.

I thought about that as I watched him walk through the shallow end towards the middle of the pool until he sunk down up to his neck with a dramatic sigh of his own.

"Aaahhhhhh!!!"

"How's the water?" I asked sarcastically, as I finally gave it up and slid the skirt off. I walked over and sat down near the steps that led into the deep end.

He dove under and swam towards me. When he came back up, he shook out his hair and then answered me. "A perfectly balmy 85 degrees, as a matter of fact. Just cool enough to feel like heaven. The heater for this runs continually. Otherwise, it takes too long to warm up since the sun doesn't reach down here. I'm not a big fan of cold water, personally." He said with a grin. "Too much *shrinkage.*" He added in reference to an episode of an old popular sitcom and we both laughed.

I held the hand rails and put my feet in. He was right, it

was perfect. "Well you don't have to worry too much about that." I said with a laugh. "I think you could absorb a little shrinkage and still be better off than most." I added, only half joking.

He was swimming slowly over to me while we talked. He chuckled again before responding. "Well thanks, but it doesn't matter what size you are. No guy likes to look down and feel like something's gone missing." He said casually. A laugh burst out of me at that.

"I guess I can understand that." I agreed. *"Hmpf!* All this and funny too, huh?" I said, sliding into the water in front of him as he reached me. "How did I get so lucky to find such a well-rounded swimming companion?" I asked as I wrapped myself around him.

"I sure as hell don't know." He pulled me close to him in the water. "But you won't catch me complaining." I just smiled happily at him in response.

"Ahhhh." I said myself then, sinking down. I let go of him and sank all the way under. I came back up and sighed again. "Oh, that feels good!"

I pulled away from him and decided to swim a few laps, thinking a little more exercise wouldn't kill me, since I was blissfully cool again. For once he was the lazy one and he just floated around on his back. It was a nice change of pace.

I swam back and forth for a while. Not particularly fast but with long, even strokes. I blocked out everything but the sound of my hands hitting the water with each length of the pool. It was heaven and it brought me back to the lessons I had taken as a kid. It was another activity that I had found loud with emotions, but it was usually things like excitement and joy. I also discovered that the water could drown out the noise to some extent, so I didn't mind it too much.

Eventually, I tired myself out and I decided to join Ethan. I turned over to float on my back. I laid my head back in the water and stared at the moon in the sky above me while my breathing slowed back to normal. The sky wasn't quite black yet. It was currently a deep, dark blue. The crickets were beginning to chirp and the fireflies were popping on and off high above me, where they danced around against the dark silhouette of trees. All in all it was quite beautiful and I found myself wishing I had a camera again. Well, maybe a waterproof one that time.

I stretched my arms slowly over my head until I felt the cooling water reach all the way under my arms. Then I brought them back down to my sides again, moving my legs in unison to make water angels. I was enjoying the way the water rippled over me as I moved. I continued to swish around like that, slowly, aimlessly, lost in the scenery. Until his face suddenly became part of the scenery above me.

I had been so relaxed that I hadn't heard him get out. Hadn't noticed his mental change of location either. His mood had been pleasant and resting happily in the background, mostly unobtrusive. Leaving me free to feel my own for a while. It had been nice. I winced just slightly at the surprise and he smiled. He was definitely amused.

He was sitting on the edge of the diving board with his feet dangling in the air. He smiled down at me as I floated past. "Feeling better?" He asked.

"*Mmmm.* Much! This is *really* nice. I could float around in here forever!" I answered freely. I was so used to always trying to keep everything close to the vest. Not to overwhelm others with the exuberance of every single thing that I felt. Somehow I always seemed to forget about that when I was with him. The truth constantly just flew right out of my mouth without my permission.

I think it may be because part of my subconscious was still waiting for him to freak out and run away. So me being me, I had to push it. No holding back, you know. To see how much he could really take. Let it all hang out, so-to-speak. Not that that side of me was exactly scary or anything. It's just brutally honest and I know firsthand how scary *honest* can be.

But... so far so good. *Hmpf.* That was new.

I could feel his patience. He was happy that I was happy and he was content to leave me be. I could feel his desire too. It was currently revving steadily in neutral. He had it completely under control, but just the knowledge of its presence was enough to kick start my own. I picked my head up out of the water and looked back at him as he sat contentedly, looking at me.

I liked knowing what he was feeling, but I still hated not knowing what he was *thinking.* Just like everybody else. Well alright, not exactly like everybody else, but I still had to guess sometimes, what thoughts had led to certain feelings. It was like a puzzle with only *most* of the pieces. You could get the overall picture, but it was still somewhat unsatisfying not to be able to complete it to confirm it. I swam over towards him and I felt his excitement grow as I got closer. That was pretty clear at least and it made me feel a little better.

When I got so close to him that he thought I would reach up to him, I dove under instead. I grinned under water as I swam away from him and towards the ladder. When I came up, I tilted my head back and let the water sweep my hair back out of my face for me, and then I pulled myself slowly up the ladder. I could feel his appreciation and his anticipation increase with every step. So of course I took my time, my self-consciousness of earlier completely forgotten.

As I was walking around the corner towards him, he stood up and backed his way off of the diving board. He came and met me on the warm concrete with our bare feet, toe to toe.

I could feel the small rivers of water running down my body and dripping off of me everywhere. It was catching more of the gentle evening breeze as it wafted by and it felt so good that I didn't bother to wipe it off. Any of it. Not that I had thought to bring a towel anyway.

He seemed to be enjoying it as well. I stood still for a moment, just taking it in. My own feelings and his. No resistance what-so-ever. A single drop of water finally reached its maximum gravity defying weight and fell from the tip of my nose to land on my top lip. From there it ran straight into the bottom one. He reached up and swiped the pad of his thumb gently across my bottom lip to catch the drop. It was so slight, that I couldn't swear he had even really touched me.

Then he leaned in, and I thought he would kiss me, but he shocked me when he bit down on my bottom lip instead. Quick, but *hard!* I looked up at him, surprised. His thumb was back already, to gently rub away the sting. I thought about whether I wanted to complain about it or not. While I was deciding, he started to lean in again, very slowly. I instantly forgot what my complaint had been and I didn't care anymore.

He did kiss me then, once he had my full attention. Softly. The whole thing was disorienting but very titillating at the same time. And ... *something else*, I thought to myself at that moment. Something *familiar*, somehow...

He reached up the back of my neck with one hand and grabbed hold of a handful of dripping hair from underneath. He held it tight. There are instances where something like that would just piss me off, but that was not one of them. I liked it. He knew how to be forceful, but still not cause any pain. It was a tricky combination and very easy to get *very* wrong. He had it down.

It only took me another moment of searching my memory before I identified the ringing bell. *It was the dream!*

Riiiiiight!!! I remembered then what came next. A shiver ran through me at the memory flash and I suddenly grinned like the Cheshire cat. He noticed my change of expression but was left to quietly wonder what had caused it. He didn't ask though. He just looked at me curiously.

I placed my hands on his chest and backed him up until he bumped into a round wicker chaise lounge that was on the extended concrete patio behind us. I kneeled down on one side and pulled him down next to me. He didn't fight me. I kept pushing until he was lying flat right down the center. I kept right on grinning in anticipation all the while. The mosquitoes didn't seem to realize that we were out there yet and I hoped silently that it would last for a while because I was on a mission.

I slid one leg up and over and settled comfortably on top of his hips before he finally gave in to his own *need-to-know.* *"What?!"* He asked with a chuckle, sensing he was missing a punch line.

My grin expanded, but I found that I had to look away for a minute as I prepared to tell him. "Remember that dream I was having when I um, woke you up last night?" I asked, rather tellingly.

He looked at me wide eyed. *"This? Really?"* He asked in return. I could feel his surprise but also his joy at that.

"Mmm hmm." I confirmed, remembering again while I

looked down at the real thing. I was secretly very glad then, that I wasn't going to wake up in the middle and miss what came next that time.

"Wow, *nice!* No, wait. That's not fair! *I'm* jealous now. That means you get to do this *twice!*" He said with obvious envy at the thought. We both laughed a little at that and I didn't argue. "That was fast though, wasn't it? Is it always that quick?" He asked, momentarily sidetracked by that new bit of technical information.

"It depends. Usually the clearer it is, the closer it is. This one was pretty clear, almost real." I said with wide eyes and a grin. He smiled for a second at the memory then his eyelids relaxed a little and his intensity started to wash over me again. I leaned down and just barely grazed his lips with my own. Just a hint of what was to come. I pulled myself back up to sitting and enjoyed the onslaught of heat for another minute. Then I spread my knees wider and sank down on him more thoroughly. I slid back, then forward a little, fitting myself just right. I could feel his reaction instantly, both emotionally and physically. Then I bent my arms and leaned my top half back down again as well. Not touching, but close enough for my breath to warm his ear.

"Shall I show you how the rest of it was going to go, before I woke up?" I whispered quietly. I almost fell off the chair when his pleasure hit me a second later. My elbows buckled further, but I held on tight to the edges of the chair's giant cushion with my eyes closed while it passed. Damn, but he sure was fun to tease! *Whoo!*

"*Yes, please.*" He answered quietly, recycling another familiar phrase. Hearing such a humble response, spoken in such a deep, strong voice was confusing for my brain. It fired off all sorts of endorphins in response to the new and confusingly pleasant sensation. My arousal shot up to levels rivaling his and suddenly I felt like I was swimming again. Floating happily on the waves of *heightened* desire along with all the plain old hormones rushing through me.

It swept through every part of me, but was strongest when it passed through my palms as usual. I felt that welcome cyclone of sensation build and expand, over and over each time it traveled by. It made my breath come faster and I could feel my heart forcefully pounding the blood through my veins.

Ethan turned his head to one side and smiled brilliantly at the light show taking place that only he could appreciate. His feelings were stronger than mine again then, and as they washed over me the whole process began again.

After that, there was less 'his and mine' and more 'ours' as the feelings mostly blurred together.

I pulled myself back up to sitting and took a few deep breaths as I sat looking down at us. Then I reached down and untied the string on his damp shorts. I lifted myself up. He took the hint and did the same, so I could slide them down and off. I settled down again further back on his thighs, slowly. I looked back up into his eyes.

"Are you holding on tight?" I asked with a sly grin. He grinned right back at me. Utterly fearless.

"Oh you'd better believe it! To everything that I can get my hands on!" He said, illustrating his point nicely by grabbing my knees and pulling me a little closer.

"Good." I squeezed my thighs tight over him and leaned down to kiss his neck. I worked for a minute to send his passion rocketing back up to where I wanted it. Then I sat back up and waited in anticipation for the next amazing waves to hit me.

As the first shiver ran through me, I held my hands up in front of him, so he wouldn't have to twist his neck to see it. I *wanted* him to see it. He smiled a broad, satisfied smile at my generosity. *He had no idea!* His arousal shot up even higher and out of the rabbit hole we flew once more. Only that time, *I was driving.*

I didn't intend to stop there. I waited until I felt the next ripple sliding through me and preparing to reach that all important, visual *'window.'* When it did, I dropped my hands down. As he watched very closely, I placed them lightly on his bare chest.

He breathed a quick unsteady breath when I made *brightly-lit-skin* on skin contact. He followed my hands with his eyes as I slid them slowly down his body. I timed it so that they ended up wrapped around *his* one man show just as the next wave crested. Another sharp intake of breath. That was good. I liked that reaction. *A lot.* My grin was back. It was fun to have a turn in the drivers' seat.

I watched his face as I began to move my hands up and down over him and I was immediately rewarded by the depth of pleasure that was evident in his expression. It was as enjoyable to see as it was to feel physically, pouring off of him.

He watched my hands, and I watched him, and although I couldn't see it myself, I could envision each ripple's presence remarkably well strictly through the joy reflected on his face. It was a strange new experience for me, for my gift to be a whole new part of my sexual side in that way. It was a dynamic that I never could have even thought to consider before meeting Ethan, but I was suddenly extremely grateful for its existence. I felt almost *...lucky* for once. *Huh.*

When the idea had occurred to me in the dream, I had been dying to try it out. Wondering how he would react. I was actually annoyed when I was waylaid the first time, but I had forgotten about it as soon as I woke to my complete and utter humiliation.

As it turns out, I had been dead on about how he would react and I couldn't be happier. Judging from the look on his face and the amazing feelings coming off of him, I was guessing that he couldn't be either.

I played with the pressure levels, but I kept my movements slow while I pushed at the limits of his control. His eyes kept closing, but he tried to keep them open as much as he could. I could tell that what he managed to see was more than enough. He looked near the edge already and he was as hard as I had ever felt him. My grin grew even bigger then.

In between light shows, I leaned down and placed feather light kisses along his chest and stomach, making my way down. I could feel his anticipation building. His feelings were stronger than anyone else's that I had ever felt before and I was just as excited trying to ride them as he was.

I slid back even further down his thighs as I leaned down. He let go of me and reached back over his head, past the cushion, to hold onto the edge of the chair.

As another powerful surge of his desire crashed through

me, I spread my hands wide and looked up to see that I had his undivided attention. Then I wrapped them slowly around him again. I held him steady while I closed my mouth over him as well. Between the two, his hands almost came through the edge of the chair. I heard it crack and groan as I watched his muscles tighten along his entire length, but apparently wicker is *very* resilient.

After a few minutes of that I took my hands away, thinking they had done the job that I had intended quite nicely, but that I had teased him enough. I focused on the part that I had been leading up to, but he actually relaxed a little then and started to catch his breath. That was *not* exactly the reaction I had been expecting.

He looked down at me, suddenly wary of revealing too much again and I stopped momentarily. He decided it was worth it.

"Forget that. Bring 'em back!" He said quietly. *"Please?'*

I lifted my head up and grinned. "Really? Are you sure?" I was surprised that a guy would ever prefer hands to lips and my expression I know, conveyed my disbelief.

"Don't get me wrong." He laughed, but then quickly turned serious again. "Your mouth is amazing." He brought one hand up and ran his fingers over my lips again for emphasis. I sighed deeply. "What you're doing. a*lso* amazing. I really don't ever want you to stop." He smiled brightly.

"But the truth is, and believe me I never imagined that I'd say these words." He laughed again. *"Your hands are hotter!"* He admitted, shaking his head. He was breathless again just thinking about it. He threw his head back again. "God! *So much fucking hotter!* Damn, woman! It's not even fair, what you can do to me!" He said in a way that made it clear he didn't really mind.

It was the first time I'd heard a serious curse word out of him and it was just more reinforcement of what I was getting from him physically. He really wasn't messing around. *Huh.* Of course that information just made me happier and I took the opportunity to go back on the offensive.

I reached up and gave him what he wanted. As I grabbed hold, his breath caught in his throat again and my smile broadened. He waited just the right amount of time before opening his eyes again and looking down at me. He timed it just as the first onslaught hit. I realized then, that he was getting the hang of it too. We both smiled hugely at each other.

I sat back up straighter and thoroughly enjoyed driving him crazy, while he enjoyed every ounce of pleasure that he knew he sent right back to me. It was a viscous circle but it was the kind of endless loop that I didn't mind. It was steadily building and building, like a roller coaster rising slowly but steadily toward the top.

Just as we approached the peak, he grabbed my hands and tried to hold me still. We were both breathing fast by then. He was working hard to maintain his control. I could feel him teetering precariously on the edge and my goal then became to push him over. When he opened his eyes again, I shook my head back and forth, indicating that stopping was not an option. He looked up at me for mercy. He tried again to argue with me.

"*Oh my God!* Simone! *Wait.* I need to... *huf!...* stop!" He tried again. He didn't really need to though. We both knew that.

"*Ut uh.*" I said, allowing no room for negotiation. "*Keep going.*" I ordered. I tried again unsuccessfully, to peel his hands off of mine. I sighed and sat still a moment, waiting. He stared into my eyes for a few more long seconds, unsure. Then, giving in, he finally let go of my hands and reached down over the edge again. He reached further and held onto the legs of the chair that time. He let out a deep groan from between clenched teeth and closed his eyes.

He inhaled and exhaled deeply as I started to move again. His honest and open reactions eventually sent new waves of heat soaring through me and he opened his eyes again, just as they hit home. It was the last push that he needed and he finally stopped fighting it and let himself go. I have to say, I was truly impressed with the tensile strength of the wicker, when the legs miraculously stayed in place throughout.

Afterwards, for just the briefest moment, I was rewarded with the sight of the peaceful, relaxed Ethan again. The same one I had seen sleeping next to me in the bed. It was "*Ethan-with-his-guard-down*" and I got the impression that it was a side of him that didn't see the light of day very often. I liked it and it made me extremely happy as I sat, reveling second-handedly in the pleasure storm still pouring off of him.

After a few moments had passed and he'd had a chance to catch his breath just a little, I leaned in and whispered in his ear again.

"I thought you might like that." I said it with a most devious smile. His eyes popped open for just a moment.

"Holy shit, woman! Definitely another curve ball!" He huffed out between two giant breaths and my grin grew even larger. That was all he had to say for a while. When his breathing had at last returned to normal, he looked up at me again where I still sat over his thighs. He didn't say anything then, either. He just looked into my eyes for a bit. I could feel his happiness. I could feel his deep sense of satisfaction too, but also his very real surprise behind that.

I could feel a separate curiosity there too. About what exactly, I didn't know. It was that *half-a-picture* thing again. He didn't explain and I decided not to ask, content to let the moment be.

He reached up a few quieter breaths later and unceremoniously this time, peeled the straps of my bathing suit down off of my shoulders. He held it for me while I slipped each arm out, then he pulled it the rest of the way off as I lifted myself up and off of him momentarily. Once he passed my knees with it, I rested myself back down and slid it off the last foot, then flung it with my toes off the chair.

Then I waited to see what he had planned, because I could feel there was something coming. He smiled and sat up, wrapping my legs around his hips. Then he stood up and holding underneath me, brought me up with him. He grinned like a man with a plan and ran straight over and jumped back in the pool with me clinging to him in mid-air. We landed with a hugely satisfying splash and came up laughing.

He pulled me up close to him again and the laughter died away. I instinctively wrapped myself around him completely and we floated around treading water together like that while we kissed. I forgot about being a *height* just then. We both forgot all about my hands and the pretty lights. I just lost myself in kissing him and being kissed back. It was more than enough to distract me from everything else.

In fact, it started to keep me from remembering to tread water, I realized in a momentary panic as I felt a wave hit my ear. Suddenly I remembered where I was. I looked at him breathless and wide eyed then, and he understood right away.

"So, would you like to see the bedroom *now?*" He asked, enjoying teasing me as usual.

I didn't care. I nodded. Then I gave him the humble, *"Yes, please."* right back. He grinned and swam for the side, pulling me by one hand as I half-swam along behind him.

We got out and grabbed our bathing suits but made our way back up to the cabin without stopping to put them on. Instead we held them in our arms in front of us in a vain attempt to cover the essentials and made a run for it. It felt strangely liberating to jog up the forest trail with nothing but the light evening breeze and the moonlight on my bare skin. There really weren't very many opportunities for something like that to happen and I took it all in as I went. I knew it was only an option then, because I had the luxury of being absolutely certain that no one but Ethan would see me.

He held my free hand as we ran and his expression bore his open approval. It actually made me blush and suddenly I was a teenager again.

We reached the back door and he pulled it open, letting me go through first. Whether out of chivalry or to take advantage of the view I wasn't sure at first, but I ran in ahead of him anyway. Then I knew. It was the view. I felt him smile without looking back and I just shook my head. A second later the rest of me shook as well. We slowed down once we were inside and I was suddenly wishing we hadn't left the AC cranking. He was right about the high efficiency systems installed there. My place would never have cooled off that fast!

"Brrrrrr! Damn, it's cold in here now!" I said laughing and huddling close to him for warmth. He didn't mind.

"Isn't that a good thing?" He asked with a laugh, slightly confused.

"I don't know anymore." I answered, laughing myself but

with a slight shiver in the end.

He gave up on trying to perfect the overall climate and wrapping his arm around my shoulder, brought us to a smaller and more controllable area instead. His bedroom.

Chapter 34

He turned on the lights as we entered and I could see immediately that it was the polar opposite of his bedroom at his house. He went into the bathroom and came back with an oversized fluffy black towel wrapped around his waist and another in his hands. He walked over and wrapped the second one around me and I gratefully tucked the edge under my arm. Then I wandered around a bit, taking it all in.

Where his room at home was bright with the many tall windows and done in varying shades of soft whites, this one was a lot *darker*. It was also more private, secure.

There were lots of windows, but they were too small for anyone to climb through and they were placed way up high. The walls were painted a deep chocolate brown and the ceiling was done in stained wood and beams just like the main area. His furniture was all a matte black and appeared to be made of a thick, solid wood. The curtains and carpet were a nice coordinating shade of dark gold. The bed however, was covered in blankets so soft, and so dark black that the edges were practically invisible.

It occurred to me that we had seen and learned so much about each other already, yet there always seemed to be something else that was new and unknown left around the next corner. He called them curveballs, but I liked that and I wondered how long it would last.

"Very nice. It's so different from what you did at home and on the farm though. So tell me, did you actually bring a decorator in here?" I asked, genuinely curious at the sleek, masculine room.

"Nah. Roxy helped me out in this cabin, since I finished this one last. Said she was tired of everything being *'strictly utilitarian and boring.'* She convinced me that I needed a little bit of style along with the functionality, at least in here. She also insisted that she could make it nice without making it *girly.*" He smiled at that.

"I'm sure it's not easy being the only woman around here. So I try to be accommodating once in a while to make up for that. Of course I never expected anyone else to see it anyway. So it really was a non-issue. Roxy knows me pretty well though and I think she managed to pull it off. I don't know. I like it." He finished, totally content with the situation.

I understood immediately what he meant about Roxy and I knew firsthand what it was like to work in a place that was basically a boys club. I was glad that he was aware as well, and sympathetic. Still I can't deny that for some reason it bothered me a little that another woman had already put her *stamp* in there so-to-speak. It was ridiculous I knew, but I would have to lie to say it didn't. The room was nicely done though. I honestly wasn't sure if that realization made it better or worse.

I pushed the pettiness aside and continued my wandering. There were no family photos. No vacation souvenirs. Though there were other traces that it was his private space. The universal gym placed prominently on the far side of the room, next to a state of the art treadmill, presumably for the colder months. The guitar sitting in the opposite corner by a lone straight backed, black leather chair.

"I'm going to go get us a drink. Be right back." He said, heading back out towards the kitchen.

I made my way back to the adjourning bathroom door. I decided to take advantage of his absence and kill a few birds at once. I went inside and quickly used the facilities. Then I attempted to drag his brush through my hair. Finally, I dug my phone from my bag so I could call Liliana to say goodnight. With all of that done, I smiled happily and dropped my phone back on top of my bag. I came out just as he came back with two cans of Sprite and handed one to me.

We both took a long drink. It's funny, how incredibly thirsty spending time in or around the water always seemed to make me! I tried to let the CO_2 back out as ladylike as possible. Him, not so much. We laughed, but then a small shiver went through me again.

The AC was still cranking and the soft, fuzzy, black blankets suddenly looked very inviting.

As if reading my mind, he walked over and lifted one side of the covers then looked back at me. I didn't need any more encouragement than that. I dropped my damp towel and climbed in. I nuzzled deeply into them happily, while he dropped his towel on top of mine and climbed in behind me. He wrapped his arms around my waist and pulled me tight up against his slightly chilled body. It warmed up quickly though, where our skin touched. I had every intention of continuing to ravish him further once I was warm. Unfortunately, I was so comfortable then, that I fell fast asleep instead.

I woke a few hours later. I was facing away from his bedside table where the clock was so I had no idea what time it was. I just knew that it was still dark. With the AC on, we remained snuggled tightly under the covers. My hair however, was still wet. I had noticed already in my half-awake state, that he was worried about that. He pulled the damp strands up off of my back and laid them gently across the pillow to dry. That made him feel better, but of course it also led to my bare neck being exposed. That he found, he could not resist.

I was too comfortable to move when he first started placing kisses down my neck. When I felt his desire awaken, I just smiled. As the soft kisses started to expand down my back and across my hip however, parts of me began to move all on their own, whether I wanted them to or not.

I got on board then and turned to face him. I slid up close to him. As close as I could get. Touching, *everywhere.* I wound my legs over and through his and then I kissed him, softly, but thoroughly and for what seemed like a long time. When I started to move again after that, he moved with me.

He separated himself just long enough to jump up and wrestle a condom from the little pocket inside of his swim shorts where they were hanging in the bathroom. He ripped off the package and threw it in the trash. He came back and set it down next to him on the table and jumped back in the bed.

"Really?" I asked, surprised at the disruption level of the maneuver. He was usually so smooth about it. "No condoms in the headboard?"

"Nope. Never needed them here before now." He answered simply. I wasn't sure I understood. I thought about it for a minute then I said as much, looking for clarification.

"I don't understand. Are you really saying that in ten years, you've never brought a woman here? Not even once?" I asked, clearly disbelieving.

"Um, yup and nope, I *think*." He said trying to follow along with my babbling questions.

"*Huh.*" I said, momentarily speechless.

"There have only been a few women over the years that I was close enough with to even consider it. None of them were *heights* though and that always kept me from crossing that line into this part of my life. It's just safer for everyone involved. I couldn't allow myself to break that trust that was put in me, purely for selfish reasons. You know, just to make my love life easier. So the two never crossed before. It was better that way." He explained quietly.

"I never wanted to pick someone who was a *height* either, just for that reason alone and use them like that. That wouldn't have been any better. Not to mention, most of the *heights* I meet are either too young or in no shape to be starting a relationship. Besides, mixing sex and business is never really the best idea either. So it was just easier to keep it separate. Less conflicts." He smiled again then.

"*You* on the other hand, are a different story all together!" He said with a deep sigh while he rolled his eyes and straddled himself up and over me. He lowered himself down and sat lightly over *my* hips that time reversing our roles from earlier, though he rested his weight mostly on his own heels. He smiled and he shook his head.

"The more I noticed you, the more you pulled away. The more I determined to just stop thinking about you, the more you would show up. Every time I managed to put you out of my mind, you would disappear and it would drive me absolutely *insane!*" He admitted shamelessly, shaking his head again.

"You suspected that your using me for blocking was responsible for what Carson saw between us, and I let you." He confessed. "But I have to at least consider that my own overly obsessive interest in you could have just as easily been the cause." I could feel his guilt at that possibility. I was surprised by the admission. I hadn't even considered it. "Now I suspect it was the result of both our unconscious intentions combined. So powerful." He said in an almost whisper.

"And that was before I even got to *know* you!" He finished practically shouting. Another deep sigh. He quieted down and stared at me again. "All of *'wonderful'* you." He said looking down appreciatively and then back up again. He pulled my hands up to his lips and kissed each palm gently, one at a time.

"You Simone, are somehow the exception to my every rule. My *kryptonite.*" He grew very serious then.

"You see now don't you, why I was so suspicious about your motives in the beginning? You know now, just how dangerous you could be for me, right?" He asked quietly and for the first time that I could remember since I had met him, he felt scared. *Truly* scared. It was extremely unsettling. He didn't hide it though, or run from it like I always wanted to. I could feel it and he knew that, but he spoke his most vulnerable feelings out loud anyways.

"I'm not backing away from this though. If it's all been a set-up, designed to do me in? *Hmpf.* Then I can tell you right now. You win. Because you've got me with more than just my *guard* down." He said with a humorless laugh.

"That's a first for me. If it also turns out to be the 'last,' well then I'll go down with a smile on my face and no regrets." They were nice words. By themselves they were just that, but what struck my heart strings was that I knew for a fact that he meant every one of them. "And as another first, *lucky you*, you're not just getting one half of me and my crazy life, either. No my friend, you are the lucky recipient of *all of me!* Like I said before, *as much as you can take.*" He grinned but I could feel how serious he was.

"I don't know how to do all of this right. I'm still trying to figure it out. This is all new for me. I've never *known* anyone like you, Simone. Anyone better suited for *me!* It's crazy, but I never even thought to hope that someone like you existed!" He explained honestly.

"Now that I know you *do* ...!" His eyelids lowered and a searing heat washed over me that had nothing to do with the blankets. "...well, good luck getting rid of me. That's all I can say." He finished with a chuckle. He tried to laugh it off but we both knew that I felt what he was feeling and it was very real.

The intensity was still a little scary for me. I didn't want it to go away either though. Of course, that realization was scary too. I decided that was enough heavy for one night and I worked to try and change it up.

"So a night just full of *'firsts'* then, huh?" I asked suggestively. He caught on quick.

"I guess so." He agreed, waiting for the rest of the reason behind my smile.

"So how should we do this?" I asked playfully. "After ten years, the maiden voyage is under a lot of pressure to be memorable." I said enjoying the look of horror on his face.

"Oh gee thanks! No performance anxiety there!" He joked back and we both laughed harder as he tackled me. He chose that time to remember my weak spot and held me down and started to tickle me for revenge. Of course I screamed in surprise and managed to get away, but not for long.

We laughed and wrestled around in the big bed for a while like we didn't have another care in the world and I was glad then that my simple reverse psychology plan had worked. By the time it got back to being serious again, we had both forgotten all about where we were and what it meant. We were just focused on the heat when it returned.

He picked me up from the edge of the bed where I had managed to end up, and flipped me back around to the top. He dropped me down in the middle with great relish and I giggled one last time as I landed.

Once I came to rest, he leaned over me on his outstretched arms. We certainly weren't cold anymore. He kicked backwards.

Just one time, with just one foot, and sent the entire mountain of blankets sailing to the floor as one solid unit. He came back over me then and grabbed the condom from where he had left it on the bedside table. He straightened up onto his knees while he put it on and I couldn't help thinking that he could sell tickets to something like that.

Then he came back down over me, thankfully oblivious to my mental musings, and started to kiss my neck. He nibbled my ear next and just one tiny but hard bite had me reliving the earlier part of our evening all over again in my head. I was liking very much, the new connections that were forming in my brain because of him.

"Now it's your turn to lie back and let *me!*" He said with a brilliant smile as he lifted himself up and moved slowly backwards down my body with his kisses. "Go ahead and try to argue." He looked up, caught my eyes. *"I dare you."* He taunted.

My body shook a little in anticipation at his words alone. Just one quick shiver, but it was all the motivation that he needed to continue. He groaned low in his throat at my reaction and stared intently into my eyes for a breath, before he bent his head back to his task.

Just the trip down was enough to get me squirming wildly beneath him, but when he actually arrived on point I thought I would fly right off the bed! He held on to me though and it was a damn good thing. He didn't waste time. There was no need. He reached one arm around my right thigh but pushed my left leg up and out of his way. I was only too happy to oblige. I would turn sideways and balance on one elbow if need be. As long as he didn't stop doing what he was doing.

I reached down to grab fistfuls of the sheet on either side of me at one point, and I heard him groan again just as I felt the familiar tightening pass through. I hadn't been paying attention to that at the moment but the impeccable timing made me smile. I noticed it after that. The waves were coming fast and furious, quickly approaching the only thing I had ever known that could surpass them, pleasure-wise. He was holding me tighter, moving faster. He knew where I was, even without the visual cues that the colors gave him but whether he needed them or not he had that too.

He looked up at me again briefly. He waited patiently while I caught my breath. He had figured out already, just where to hit with his tongue, and just how hard and how fast to hit it. He also knew how long to keep pushing it, and when to stop and let me breathe. He smiled with the knowledge of inevitable success and went back to work without mercy. I would have come off of the bed then for sure if he hadn't been holding on to me so tightly! I could think of nothing at that moment that I was more thankful for.

He brought me to the very edge once more, paused, then delivered the last merciless push and I was officially a lost cause. No hope what-so-ever of holding on any longer. I was gone on a sea of my own pleasure that time. A vast, undulating, wide open sea that I could happily float around on forever.

I did eventually start to feel his joy come back into the forefront and join mine again, but it took a while. He came up over me then. He was very happy but also *very* determined by then so it was not a "smiling" happy, *per se.* I was sure I mirrored his expression for once. All humor was gone. All that existed then was the intensity.

When he finally sank down into me at last, it was so amazing that I was *instantly,* already lost! *Again!* That was all it took. Just the entering. It was completely crazy but I wasn't exactly complaining. I just held on.

He held on too. Somehow. By the skin of his, *uh... teeth.* He waited it out. He looked me in the eye. Molars ground together hard, but otherwise calm. Controlled. Watching. Enjoying what he was seeing very much. When he saw that *I* was calm again, slowly, purposefully, he began to move.

Holy Sweet Jesus! How could this really be just the beginning?! I tried hard to hold on, my breath feeling already two inhales behind. He was truly enjoying his payback for earlier, but that was okay. So was I.

He looked down at me and he did manage a smile then. At least half of one before it was swept away by the next sensation. I reached up to find something, *anything* to hold onto. But the headboard was flat aside from the sliding cupboards on each end and it afforded me no purchase.

He noticed my dilemma and mercifully, found a way to help. He reached up to clasp his hands in my searching hands. He pulled my arms up straight over my head. Then he leaned his weight on them so that I was free to use that hold for leverage without fear of flying out from under him.

He smiled down at the vision that created, glowing palms and all, and with his pleasure soaring ever higher, he started to move again. I inhaled as the first blast hit me and I was extremely grateful for the stronghold.

By the end of the night, I was extremely grateful for two more things as well. One was that I had decided that fateful night to answer my phone. And two, that there were no neighbors *anywhere* near there!

Chapter 35

I woke to the sound of my phone ringing from the bathroom early on Tuesday morning. I was snuggled up nicely into the soft mound of black blankets and Ethan's warm body. I cracked one eye and could just see the first rays of dawn glowing through the high windows. I considered ignoring it since I wasn't ready to be awake yet, but then I thought about Gen and the court date and I changed my mind. I slipped out and headed for the bathroom. I dug it out without turning on the light. It wasn't Gen though. It was Ben. *Ben? ...*why would *....Liliana!* I panicked and picked it up as fast as I could.

"Hello? Ben? What's up? Is everything okay?" I asked hurriedly.

"I'm sorry to wake you, but it's Liliana. I'm on my way to the E.R. I just wanted to let you know. She's been sick." He said, sounding tired and worried.

"Do you have any idea what's wrong? Have any of her friends been sick lately?' I asked pulling my change of clothes out of my bag. I didn't bother trying to be quiet anymore. Ethan was already up and moving around his dark bedroom getting dressed. That exceptional hearing and all.

"I don't know. I have my theories, but it's just a guess, really. The fever only lasted a day. That's not what I'm worried about. It's her wrist." He said. "I think it's broken." He admitted, and I was completely lost then. I stopped mid-way through getting dressed.

"Her wrist? I don't get it. What happened?" I asked

wanting desperately for it all to make sense. I was worried about the fever and I was also more worried because Ben didn't even know to *be* worried! We would have to talk and *soon*, I decided. Somehow. I'd have to talk to Ethan first, but not yet. First I needed to figure out what was going on!

"It was just a nasty stomach bug." He said calmly. "She threw up a bunch of times but had already gotten through the worst of it. She was feeling better, but she was still dehydrated and hadn't eaten. So when she tried to jump up out of bed too fast, she fainted on me! Scared the shit out of me, I'm not gonna lie." He admitted and I could hear an appropriate amount of fear in his voice then. *Good!*

"I was walking down the hall to check on her. She saw me coming and tried to run to me. It was like watching it in slow motion because I was still too far away to catch her when she fell. It was the landing that hurt her wrist and I'm just praying that it doesn't need to be reset. I'm sorry Simone. I don't know what I could have done differently, but I feel terrible anyway." He said tiredly.

"You don't have to be sorry. It's not your fault. Don't beat yourself up over something you couldn't possibly hope to control." I told him, really meaning it. "I really appreciate you calling. I'm sure she's going to be fine, but I'll meet you there just the same. Are you going to the Northeastern Medical Center?" I asked using Ethan's brush again, not having the foresight to bring my own. I noticed that was not going to be enough to make it look presentable, so I gave up and just twisted it up into a tight knot. I pulled a clip off of the handle of my bag where I always kept a spare and clipped it up and out of the way.

"Yeah, Northeastern. Alright, I'll just see you there, okay?" He said.

"See you there." I agreed and we both hung up. I pulled the rest of my clothes on. Then I grabbed my bathing suit off of the towel rod where it was hanging and threw it in my bag along with yesterday's clothes. When I walked back into Ethan's room, he was ready and waiting, keys in hand.

Okay, I wouldn't go so far as to say that it was a *good* thing to have a paranoid, insomniac with super hearing for a boyfriend. But occasionally it *was* handy.

"Ready?" he asked. I nodded and followed him out.

When we got in and not needing me to repeat what had been said he asked simply, "Northeastern, or your car?" He didn't have any feelings invested in either answer I was glad to see, because I was thinking *'one thing at a time.'*

"My car please. That's probably best for now." I said, stuffing my bag down by my feet. "I think an introduction when we're all in a better frame of mind will be worth the wait." I answered somewhat weakly.

"It's fine Simone. Don't worry about me right now." He said with the same confident smile that I was used to. I let out a sigh of relief.

"Thanks." I said and flopped back in the seat for the short ride back to my place. That made it a little easier, because we both knew what I was really worried about. We didn't need to say it out loud.

When he pulled up, I leaned over and kissed him once, slowly, not thinking twice about it that time.

"Don't worry. She'll be fine. *Either way.* "He said gently, trying to reassure me. It helped, but only slightly.

"Thanks. I'll call you later and fill you in, okay?" I said. He just nodded. He was keeping it very neutral. Trying to make it easier on me. I smiled a little, then I took a deep breath and jumped out. I ran up the stairs as I heard him pull away. I dropped my bag at the door. Then I went to use the bathroom, which I realized I still hadn't done yet in my haste, and brushed my teeth real quick. I skipped everything else and grabbed my purse on my way out the door.

Of course the Northeastern Medical Center Hospital was in the city and that was exactly why I could only handle being so far away. I was extremely relieved when I made the trip in only twenty two minutes.

I found a spot in the small emergency lot, which was nothing short of a miracle and headed through the big revolving doors to find Ben and Liliana. I had been doing nothing but scaring myself with thoughts of her potential *heightening* all the way there. Twenty two minutes was far too long when you had nothing but worst case scenario's running through your head. I also had plenty of time left over to think about how unprepared we still were to deal with it. I hadn't even tried to explain it to Ben yet. Never mind Liliana! But I knew I should. I was in a position to possibly prepare her for what might happen somewhat. Or at the very least, understand and be there with her, if and when it did. That was a huge advantage that I'd never had and I wouldn't waste it.

I just needed a little more time. She was just a baby still. Barely six years old! *Please!* I begged to whoever wanted to listen to such things. *Please!* Not her. At least not *yet!* I prayed as I made my way inside.

I was starting to hyperventilate and I tried to calm myself down. I was glad for the moment that I was alone in the hallway. I put my hand on the wall for balance and tried to catch my breath before I ended up in there getting x-rays myself. *Slow, deep breaths. In and out.* I felt better after a minute and I pushed off the wall and kept going.

I was trying to remember not to run through the halls like a maniac. Especially since I had no idea which direction to run in. Then I saw Ben and his familiar face was like a lighthouse beacon to my lost ship. He was standing next to the coffee maker in the little kitchen off of the waiting room. I barely remembered walking the rest of the way over there.

When I reached him I resisted the overwhelming urge to fall into his arms. I did stop and rest on the counter for a minute though, while I tried to regain my composure.

"Hey, relax!" He said, laughing just a little at my dramatics. "She's going to be fine. Maybe I should've waited to call you." He considered out loud.

"No!" I protested much too vigorously and his look of uncertainty grew more apparent. "No." I tried again, in a more civil tone. "Ben please don't ever think that I'd be better off *not* knowing! Not ever, okay! I just..." I trailed off, realizing then, that I couldn't really explain. I felt a little taste of what Ethan must go through all the time and my admiration for him grew even more. I wasn't sure how to fix it right then either, but I figured I had better reassure him somehow. Before he had me committed while

he was there.

I sighed deeply again. "I just got a little worked up on the drive down here, that's all. I'm a mother. We worry. That's what we do." I said with calm shrug of my shoulders, back to trying to keep it all under control. That was important around Ben I reminded myself, but I had been away from him for a while and I was out of practice already. "I'm sorry. I'm okay now, I promise." I said, adding a little bit of a smile. He didn't look entirely convinced but thankfully, he let it go.

He handed me a Styrofoam cup of coffee. I noticed then that he had already fixed it how I liked it. He turned back to fix another one for himself. He nodded towards the lime green pleather chairs in the waiting room and we went and sat down.

"What are we doing out here? Where is she?" I asked with as much patience as I could muster, which still wasn't much. It was definitely an adjustment being around Ben again, since I also couldn't feel everything from him for myself instantaneously. I had to wait for him to offer information up to me. Again, not my strong point. That complete lack of patience thing.

"She's with Lisa." He explained and it suddenly made sense. Dr. Lisa Sherry was a local doctor that he knew originally from school. They didn't attend the same college obviously, but they had both been part of their prospective schools Ultimate Frisbee teams. They had met originally while competing against each other. They are both fun loving and easy going, but *extremely* competitive when it comes to sports. So they each ended up becoming the other's favorite opponents. Over the years, it eventually also made them great friends.

I remembered briefly how we used to have game nights with her and her husband Thom at least once a month. I hadn't seen her in quite some time, myself. I didn't know about Ben. I figured that she was his friend first though, so I guessed that one justifiably went to him in the divorce.

"She just took her for an x-ray. Told Liliana they were going on an *'adventure'* together through the hospital, while *'Daddy got himself some coffee.'*" He said rolling his eyes. He laughed. "I must've looked like I needed it." I looked up at him. *Really* looked at him for the first time since settling down a little.

He *did* look worn out. A tad bit older even. It surprised me. I was always used to seeing Ben and his boundless energy as inexhaustible. I never worried about Liliana being well taken care of when she was with him. Ever. He was as fastidious in his parenting, as he was in every other part of his life. Not just because he was *'supposed'* to be either. That was just Ben. I counted on that. Seeing him look as haggard as I often felt was just a little bit unnerving to me, I had to admit. I was willing to cut him some slack though.

"Well, she's not wrong." I said, but I elbowed him gently when he looked offended so he would know that I didn't hold it against him. "It's certainly understandable. With her keeping you up and stressing you out. First being sick, then this! You must be exhausted. Anyone would be. That was nice of her though." I added. He smiled a tired half smile at my efforts.

"Yeah, the last few days have been tough. I had an emergency call for a breech foal in the middle of the night on Friday. Got home about three hours before your parents brought Liliana back on Saturday. I was tired but she was feeling fine then and I had the Vet trade show that night. So mom and *Brad*-Dad came over for a while and talked me into going. What a mistake *that* was! I didn't come back with anything but a hangover and a second night with little to no sleep." I looked at him confused but only until his next sentence. "I ran into Ronnie at the show."

"Ohhhhhh." I said, seeing immediately how that would end up in a hangover. Ronnie was another old friend, this time actually from Vet school. Ronnie was different though. He was the antithesis of Lisa. Where she excelled at sports as well as her academics, Ronnie excelled at things like keg stands and a drinking game called *"Asshole,"* where he always ended up being the *'President.'*

For some reason, whenever Ben got around him, his IQ would drop about twenty points. Ronnie was Mr. Fun and he could be *very* hard to say no to. Even *I* knew that first hand. Somehow, *"Just one more..."* always turned into watching the sun come up somewhere unexpected. Even still, you always ended up thanking him for an amazing time as you crawled home the next morning with your shoes in your hand. I just grinned knowingly.

Everyone had one friend like Ronnie. At least I thought everyone should. We all needed one, really.

"I didn't even get home until 5:30 AM, so that's when my poor parents got woken up to go home to *their* own beds. My head hit the pillow about 6:00, so of course, she woke me up promptly at 7:00." He said with a conspiratorial smile at me about our rule. "Why did we decide on 7:00 again exactly?" He asked jokingly.

"Because we were trying to get her away from 6:00." I reminded him with a chuckle.

"Oh yeah." He remembered with a tired grin.

"So there was the usual Saturday soccer game followed by the end of season party at *Senor' Cheese's* where I suspect she came in contact with 'patient zero.'" He said theatrically. "We got home late and she was really tired. I took one look at her and put her to bed early, thinking we could both use the sleep. *Hah!*" He laughed again and it startled me a little. I also didn't have the same forewarning of an emotional one-eighty with Ben that I had come to expect with other people. He went on with his story regardless.

"About three hours after we were asleep that night, I got called back in. You know, it really is a good thing that both of our parents are right around the corner from us." He said looking back at me. "I know that you would come, but I'm really glad that I don't have to ask you to do stuff like that in the middle of the night and everything. You know *our* emergencies, that's one thing, but not for my job. No, you shouldn't have to live a life on call like that just because *I* do. So I definitely spent some time thinking about how we really are lucky." He confided. I just stuck my bottom lip out and nodded my head, agreeing easily enough without feeling the need to add to that.

He was right. I would come in a heartbeat if I needed to and he knew that. Though I was just as glad that it wasn't necessary on a regular basis. It really was better for everyone involved. As I said before, I really am not at my best when I don't get enough sleep. Another personal failure I suppose. Doesn't function well, *or* play well with others when sleep deprived. *Check!*

"Anyway, one of the dogs from the city's K-9 unit took off after a suspect and ended up in traffic. His name's Urgo. I'd seen him once before to verify his chip and his shots and so forth when he first came over from Europe, where they are often originally trained.

Because of this it's quite common for them to respond only to foreign commands. With Urgo it's Czechoslovakian. They do that purposely, so that only the handler will know how to speak the command words. That way, if a criminal yells at the approaching dog to *'stop'* or *'stay,'* the dog won't listen."

"That makes sense I guess." I said, seeing the logic behind it.

"Right? The only flaw with the design, is when you have the rare situation like they did last Saturday. When the officer who's his handler, was actually shot on the scene and wasn't *conscious* to call the dog off the chase." He shook his head again.

"Urgo was given the command to apprehend the suspect and he did so, single mindedly. Without any fear or hesitation apparently, from what they said when they brought him in. He pursued the guy through four or five alleys and a junkyard, before they reached the traffic. He *did* apprehend the suspect too." He said with a slight smile. "Even after he was struck." He looked me right in the eye. "By *two* different vehicles." Then he went back to shaking his head again. "He just kept going. All the other officers could do was run after him until they caught up, but he was a lot faster." His admiration for the dog was clear in his smile as he stared at the linoleum floor.

"Anyway, it took up all of Saturday night and most of Sunday morning, putting his hind leg back together. Meanwhile the good doctors here were putting his handler back together. Lisa and I were both working that night, so she knew a little bit about what I've been through this weekend." He explained with a knowing smile.

"I'm happy to say that both are doing really well now. So that's good." He added with a real smile and a deep breath. It was so easy to see where he drew his strength from. It was the success stories like Urgo's that gave him extra energy when he needed it.

"By the time I got home, Liliana was helping Grammy make me lunch and then she reminded me that I had promised to take her to see the new Disney movie." My jaw hit the arm of the chair as I realized there was *more.*

"*Please* tell me you are kidding!" I begged. He just shook his head no.

"Luckily, seeing her excitement perked me up somewhat." He continued bravely with a laugh. "Plus Grammy, sensing my exhaustion, decided to come along, *and drive.*" He admitted with a wink. That made me feel better. "I fell asleep as soon as the opening previews rolled but if anyone asks, I saw the whole thing and I loved it." He claimed with resounding confidence. I just laughed. At least he had lightened the mood.

"We even went to McDonald's on the way home, but that was mostly because I was too tired to cook. In hindsight, it was probably not the best idea. She ate all her chicken nuggets and her fries and asked for a cherry pie to top it off." He said and I cringed at what I could imagine all that would look like in reverse.

"It was around bed time that she started to say that her stomach hurt. I thought it was just too many nuggets at first, but it didn't take long for that stomach bug to kick nugget-butt and send them flying right back out. Them and everything else. *Everywhere!*" He looked at me with wide laughing eyes.

"I mean, it was like the *'Exorcist!'*" He exclaimed with an incredulous laugh. "I haven't seen her throw like that since she was a baby!" He laughed again, more earnestly that time as we both remembered those days. I saw a spark of light come back in his eyes and it made me feel a little better.

"She was up and down all day Monday and into the evening. We napped a little in between but it never lasted too long. By midnight though, she was done. It was finally out of her system and she slept. *Thank God!* So did I, but after the previous few days I slept too heavily Then I woke in a panic early this morning, worried that I hadn't woken up at all to check on her!" I couldn't feel the guilt filling him but I could see it written all over his face. I knew he didn't really do anything wrong but I also knew that I couldn't stop him from feeling that way. That didn't stop me from trying.

"You shouldn't do that to yourself. You didn't do anything wrong." I assured him. He smiled a weak smile and went on.

"When I woke up on the couch and realized that six hours had gone by, I jumped up and ran upstairs to check on her. I was so scared then, that something may have happened while I wasn't there to watch over her." He was feeling bad but he was being honest. It wasn't just a pity-party. He needed to confess, so I listened and I waited.

"I was so relieved to see her up and sitting there, happily playing and waiting for 7:00, that I almost passed out myself. She was fine. I was fine. Everything was fine." He sighed as he remembered it.

"Then she saw me and got really excited to show me what she had drawn." He said looking slightly bewildered. "She jumped up so fast to run over to me, that she never had a chance. She was out cold before her feet ever hit the floor. The way she landed on her left hand, I knew right away it wasn't good." He shook his head back and forth like he could erase the memory. Like a slow-mo replay in football on TV that you immediately wished you hadn't seen.

"There I was worried sick about her and meanwhile she was perfectly fine. Until *I* showed up." He said, back to blaming himself again. It was funny when I thought about how much I worried about big things like horseback riding and being buckled in her seat in the car, only to then have her get hurt getting out of bed! I shared that thought with Ben and added, "It just goes to show that you really can't protect them from everything. I hate it too, but it's the truth, dammit!"

He sat back in his chair. "Now she'll have a lovely cast just in time for the hot weather. *Yaaaaay.*" He said tiredly.

"Okay, now *you* need to relax." I said continuing the reversal of asserting myself in the supportive role so he could take some time off to fall apart a little. I was beginning to think that maybe that was *really* why Lisa had wanted to give him a few minutes away from Liliana. She really was a good friend to him.

"She's going to be fine. She'll get to pick a fun color and then decorate it to match her favorite outfits. You know she's going to love that." I said honestly. That brought another weak smile.

"I was also going to ask you if I could keep her until

Sunday this weekend, but I'm not asking anymore. I'm telling. You can take the whole weekend off and get some R&R. Catch up. A friend of mine gave me tickets for Cirque De Soliel on Saturday and we have movie night on Friday. She'll be so busy showing off her newest accessory that she'll forget it ever even hurt." I assured him cheerfully. He just sighed again, but he seemed a little better.

I thought about mentioning Ethan then, and how I wanted to introduce the two. I was a moment too late though. Just as I opened my mouth to suggest it, a smiling Liliana came wheeling around the corner on a stretcher. She was being pushed at what was clearly *not* the normal gurney speed. Lisa was laughing too as they both yelled, *"We won!"* in unison. The losers came around the corner behind them. It was a male doctor pushing another male employee of some sort on a matching gurney. They high-fived her good hand and pretended to be disappointed as they admitted defeat. Then they made a U-turn and headed back where they had come from just as fast and as loud.

We all laughed then, which was good because seeing her tiny form on the great big hospital bed, with her little arm in a sling instantly made tears spring to my eyes. I fought the urge to rush over to her and ball all over her though, and tried to breathe it away. I could tell immediately that she wasn't in any pain. In fact what I noticed her feeling was a little bit loopy so I knew they had given her something for that already. That was a relief at least.

She seemed to be in good spirits and I didn't want to ruin that. The doctors had obviously worked very hard to get her there. I worked up a smile at Lisa then, in appreciation. She smiled back and I could feel her joy at Liliana's hard won mood and her worry over Ben as well. Then there was the slight awkwardness between us but I'd have been able to feel that with or without my special skills.

"Hey Lisa. How are you?" I asked, trying to get past it. I stood and gave her a hug. Ben stood as well but he was quiet, obviously still worried.

"I'm good. How are you?" She answered politely. "I mean aside from all of this, of course.

"Aside from this, things are pretty good." I said, playing along. "Thanks for taking such good care of her." I added more sincerely.

"Oh it was my pleasure, I assure you. She kept me away from all the craziness for the last half hour. I wish all of my patients were as good as her!" She said smiling back at Liliana. "She was perfectly still during the x-ray. Like a statue!" She praised. "She told us all the funniest jokes while we wrapped her cast. Plus I have to say, she even picked my favorite color." She added with a secret look at Liliana. I watched Liliana's smile grow even bigger at that last part, as I spied the bright neon pink cast peeking out of the blue sling.

"Yes, she does have very good taste, doesn't she?" I agreed.

Ben seemed to have gained enough courage then to ask for the details and he finally joined the conversation. "A clean break? You didn't have to re-set it?" He guessed optimistically, since they had come back fairly quickly.

"Yup. Textbook. Best case scenario, really. If that line wasn't on the x-ray, I wouldn't even know it was broken." She said confidently, understanding exactly what he was waiting for. He let out the rest of the air that he'd obviously been holding and sank back down onto the edge of the chair that he had just vacated. I felt Lisa notice as well and worry again. It wasn't necessary though. He would be fine now that he knew she was fine, I was sure. He just needed some rest. I may not have been his wife anymore, but I could still help him with that.

"So what d'ya say kiddo. How about we get you and daddy home? We can make a huge fort in the living room and have a big family camp out in the middle of the day!" I suggested to a surprised, but appreciative crowd. Liliana was sold instantly.

"Oh yes! Can we daddy?" She asked hopefully. Of course even if he *didn't* desperately need the rest, he would never turn her down at the moment.

He looked at me and mouthed, "Are you sure?" When I nodded, he agreed. "Alright. Why not." He told her and she immediately started planning which pillows and stuffed animals she would bring, her bright new accessory momentarily completely forgotten. Ben smiled at me as I picked her up off the gurney. It felt so good to finally hold her. Just to feel the weight and the warmth of her little body against my chest and know that she was really okay. Those were among the handful of things that I never took for granted.

Lisa seemed content that I had things under control then, so she said her goodbyes and reluctantly went back to work. "Just wait for the nurse to bring you your paperwork with your discharge instructions and you guys are all set, okay? You take care of them now, you hear me?" She said jokingly to Liliana. She hugged both Ben and I again and then she was gone.

It only took about fifteen more minutes before the aforementioned nurse showed up and we were out of there. Liliana said she was hungry and I knew that was a good sign. We both had our cars so I took mine and stopped at the market to get some ginger ale, some eggs and English muffins. Then I went to the Pharmacy to get the prescription that Lisa had given us for Liliana filled before I met Ben and Liliana at the house.

Ben questioned me as I entered about whether I needed to be at the job site or not, since he knew all about my current project and I groaned. He raised his eyebrows at that so I gave him the shortest explanation possible.

"Wow, so you've had a couple of shitty days too huh?" He realized, sympathetically as we unloaded bags in the kitchen. "Must be something in the air." He added. I just sighed and nodded. It was the truth but when I ran it all back in my head, I knew.

It hadn't been *all* bad.

#balance.

Chapter 36

Ben got to the business of filling the living room with all the blankets and pillows in the house. Liliana was already sitting in the middle of the room on a giant mound of her own pillows, by the time Ben started moving chairs and attaching blankets with clothespins to make walls. I left him to it and went back in the kitchen to make us all some breakfast.

It was a little strange, cooking breakfast for the three of us in that kitchen again but I tried not to dwell on it. I cracked the eggs into one frying pan and grilled some thinly sliced Virginia ham in another. Meanwhile, I put some English muffins in the toaster. Then I pulled my phone out of my pocket so I could text Ethan and let him know what was going on.

We're back. Wrist is broke but it's a clean break. She's a trooper. Doing great. I'm gonna stay a while & help out. TTYL

He answered me a minute later.

Sorry it's broke, but glad she's ok. R u ok?

I smiled to myself. He really was too good at knowing when I wasn't.

I will be. Thanks.

Hang in there. :}

His silly smiley face actually made me smile as I started flipping things. The first two muffins popped and I buttered them lightly then put a slice of cheese on each. When the eggs were ready I laid them on top. I put some ham on top of that and finished it with a tiny sprinkle of nutmeg that I was surprised to find in the cabinet, not too far from where I had left it. Then I went and poured three glasses of ginger ale while I waited for the last English muffin to cook. When all the sandwiches were done, I put it all on a tray and brought it into the living room for our little picnic.

I barely recognized the usually neat room. It was covered from end to end in various shades of cotton.

"Hello?" I called out. A sheet to my right flew up and Liliana grinned like the cat that ate the canary.

"Here we are!" She said happily. "Come inside mama!"

I could see Ben too, laying across the middle and taking up most of the fort. "Okay, here I come. Make some room, please." I said while playfully kicking the big bare feet that were sticking out off to one side. I heard a deep chuckle and the offending obstacle slid reluctantly to the right.

I ducked in and set the tray down inside the door then I pulled the flap closed again. Liliana handed me a pillow and a flashlight with her good arm. For the most part she just seemed to be ignoring the other one. I could feel a dull ache coming off of her by then, but nothing serious yet. I really was impressed with her demeanor after all she'd been through. I tried not to think about what I had been doing while she was getting sick, the poor thing. I knew it wasn't my fault and that I couldn't have known at the time, so I tried not to torture myself either. It wasn't easy.

I handed out the sandwiches on paper plates, giving the hottest one to Ben. He sat up as much as he could under the low slung cotton ceiling to take that and a glass from me, with his other hand.

"That looks good! I didn't realize until just now how hungry I am!" He said appreciatively and took a big bite. Liliana giggled. I had cut hers in half to make it easier for her to handle with one hand. She picked up one half and took a big bite of her own, mimicking him. Then they looked at me.

"We're bears, mama! This is our cave!" She said. I understood suddenly and played along. I growled a little and attacked my own sandwich playfully. She giggled some more and it effectively drowned out the last of the lingering pain temporarily. We continued to eat heartily with lots of growls, grunts and gusto until the sandwiches were gone. Then we laid back on the pillow-mountains and rubbed our big bear bellies.

"So what do bears do in their caves after their bellies are all full?" I asked Liliana innocently, hoping her imagination would take her in the direction that I was aiming for. Thankfully, it did.

"They hibernate!" She proclaimed excitedly.

"That's right! Oh boy! We get to hibernate now. Woo hoo! Where's my pillow? I asked pretending that I couldn't find it. She giggled again. If I lived to be a hundred, I would never get tired of that sound.

"It's right behind you, mama." She said through her laughs and I was glad to be able to help her burn off the rest of her nervous energy. I knew she would crash soon, and hard!

I looked over to see that Ben was on board with the direction that our game was going. He made sure that Liliana was comfortable when she laid down, fixing the pillows under her head and her arm.

"How's that baby bear?" He asked her affectionately while he tucked her favorite blanket around her.

"Perfect. Thank you, papa bear." She answered much more tiredly. "You have to lie down too." She added worriedly.

"Oh believe me, you don't have to tell this bear when it's time to hibernate!" He said smiling slyly at me. Once he had her all tucked in, he laid back and stretched out his arms and legs dramatically with a roar of a yawn. Then he folded his arms across his chest and closed his eyes. I knew that he was playing along with her to get her to rest. I also knew that he fell sound asleep about five minutes after she did. I listened to the soft snore he was emitting for a minute or two just to be sure, then I smiled at them both and crawled quietly out of the fort.

As I made my way up onto the sofa, I sat and looked back

on my surroundings. At the comfortable, cozy New England Cape that we had picked out, bought and decorated together. The walls were all done in a cheerful, beach-y palette. A pale, sky blue in the main living area, a soft buttery yellow in the kitchen and a light, sand color in the dining room that stretched up the stairs and into the hallway. The furniture was simple but tasteful and functional. Kid friendly. The floors were all hardwood, with the exception of the kitchen which we had done in a terra cotta colored ceramic tile. Overall, it was a bright, sunny, happy place.

I still loved it, but I was surprised to realize that it didn't feel like *home* to me anymore, at all. I felt entirely like a guest sitting there. Like I wouldn't *really* know where things were anymore if someone asked. It was funny how quickly that had happened when it had taken years to build. I didn't know if it was good or bad. It was mostly just… weird.

I thought about my new home then too. *Hmpf.* Ethan's *old* home. It really is all relative. But that *was* home then and I was happy there, even if it didn't really feel the same. It would be so easy for me to spend all my time being lonely and resentful. I knew how lucky I was to have found a place where, even though I was *alone*, I mostly just felt peace and renewal.

I sat quietly looking around while they slept. Just another new adjustment to get used to. I was sad at the loss of that sense of *"daily home life"* that we had shared. The little things, like putting away the groceries together and sharing meals. Or things like hanging out in a fort in the living room.

I was glad though that while we may have lost the *"daily"* part, we hadn't really lost our sense of *"family."* We did succeed at keeping that intact, I reminded myself with pride. Times like those may not happen every day anymore, but at least they could still *happen.* We hadn't lost *everything.*

Breathing was so much easier on the brighter side.

I decided then, that I'd had enough self-torture for one day and I got up and started to clean to distract myself. I walked around picking up things and putting them away. Even if I didn't know where the right place for them was anymore necessarily. At least it looked better. I washed the dishes in the sink and set them to dry in the strainer. I walked into the small laundry room off of the kitchen and put the clothes waiting there in the washer. I didn't need to do those things there anymore, but I still felt better doing them than sitting still with my own thoughts.

I got to the point though, where there was nothing left to clean and nothing left to put away. I wandered for a little while longer, looking out the windows at old familiar views that I had missed of the street and backyard, as well as the city beyond. Eventually, I ended up back at the couch again. I sat down and rested my eyes for a while. I knew I wouldn't sleep but I didn't mind the opportunity to just stop and recharge a bit.

It wasn't long before I heard Ben start to stir inside the fort. I opened my eyes then and waited for him to emerge. He made his way out a minute later, looking sleepy and disheveled.

I knew that as an adult, waking up someplace strange could be very disorienting. I'd had some very recent experience with it coincidentally, so I gave him a moment to acclimate and readjust. He looked at me as he exited, bewildered at first but he quickly seemed to remember. With that, his expression softened from suspicion to a kind of relief that I was still there.

"I would like to go on record as saying, that while I was a big fan as a child, forts make horrible sleeping arrangements for grown men." He said, slowly standing up. He had only slept about two hours, but I knew that was long enough to wreck an adult's back on a hard floor. I wasn't sure if the nap had made his situation better or worse. He groaned as quietly as he could while he stretched.

"Better?" I asked, choosing to go with optimism.

"Actually, yeah." He answered surprisingly. "It ought to get me through the day, anyway." He let out a sigh and plopped down on the couch next to me. "Thanks for sticking around. *And for cleaning!*" He said with surprise of his own as he noticed his surroundings.

"No problem. I'm glad I could help lighten the load a little. You probably won't be able to find anything!" I informed him with a laugh. "But I really did *try* to help."

"That's alright. It's still preferable to the mess. I just haven't had a chance to get caught up with all the 'little things' lately. You know, the '*non-life-or-death*' things." He joked. I nodded because I knew exactly what he meant. My life had felt the same way lately. Like suddenly all the normal day-to-day things had been replaced by one unpredictable situation after another. "There must be something in the air." I reiterated in agreement.

"Don't worry about the little things. As long as you keep doing all of the big one's right, we're good." I assured him. Just then I heard the 'baby bear' waking up. Right away I could feel that she was in pain so I jumped up to get her medicine. I heard a tiny whimper as I walked by and I looked back at Ben meaningfully. Clearly he had heard it too, and he knew then why I had gotten up. He went to get her out of the fort.

He pulled back the flap and put on a happy face for her. "Is it springtime yet?" He asked innocently and she giggled then, unable to resist.

"*Umm hmm.*" She agreed. "Time to get up now." She sat up on her own but I noticed as I walked by, that she had held her arm carefully still while she did it. He crawled in and picked her up carefully. Then he stood straight up with a roar and busted right through the roof of the "cave." She squealed and laughed even harder. It really was the best medicine of all and I could already feel the pain lessen. It was still too much as far as I was concerned though and I quickly returned and handed her the little plastic cup of liquid medicine.

She drank it all at once but made a sour face immediately after. I handed her a plastic cup of orange juice next and she drank it down.

"*Ahhh!*" She said "That's better. That medicine tastes yucky, mama." She was so serious that I couldn't help but smile.

"Oh sweetie, I know it does. But it will help your arm to stop hurting." I could feel that she wanted to deny that it was hurting but she didn't bother. She knew it wasn't something that she could hide from me. "Don't worry, by tomorrow you'll be feeling so much better that you probably won't even need the medicine anymore. For today though, I think you'll have to be a big strong bear and get it down. Okay?" She decided that was a fair deal and agreed.

"Okay, but only for today. No more after that. *Yuck!*" She

said again, shaking her head.

Ben set her down on the couch and took a few of the pillows from the floor to prop up her arm. We had peanut butter and jelly sandwiches and apples for lunch once she was feeling better. Then we spent the next few hours playing board games and charades. Whatever it took to keep her mind off of her arm. By evening, she'd had a good healthy dose of the *'laughter medicine'* and she was feeling almost back to normal.

"Alright. I'm going to go start dinner. Would you like me to put a movie on for you?" He offered and of course her eyes lit up. He put on *'Toy Story'* for her and asked me if I could stay. I thought about Ethan again. I wondered what he might be doing then and if he would see Jeremy at all or not. I had no plans to meet him though, and I wasn't ready to leave Liliana yet, so I agreed. I settled down next to her and texted him again while Ben went to get dinner ready.

Hi. How's your day going?

He answered me almost instantly and I was ashamed to admit even to myself how happy it made me when his words popped up on my screen that fast.

Busy. Never a dull moment. How's L?

Hmmm. I wondered what that was about. Coming from him, it was certainly worrisome.

She's doing a lot better. Still not ready to leave yet tho. Everything okay? U see J today?

I hit send.

Eh, it will be. Don't worry.

Of course. I noticed though, that he hadn't really answered my question. Then another text came through before I could answer.

Rock hard just talking to u. It's really not normal. But I like it. ;)

I was instantly feeling hotter myself, just reading his words. *Damn!* Then another came through.

Too much?

I smiled. I could picture him doing the same.

Absolutely! But I like it... ;)

I sent another right after that.

Can I call u later? It might b late.

Lol. Really?

Right, look who I'm talking 2. :) Call u when I'm home.

Good. Don't hurry. Just call.

K ;)

Soon I could feel her pain creep into my consciousness once more and I was instantly focused on her again. I know every parent wished they could take their child's pain away. Most would gladly take it on themselves instead, if that were an option. I was no different, except that I *did* take it on. Unfortunately though, that didn't take it away from her. The best I could do was to share it.

Even still, it was far easier to sit in pain with her, than it was to sit there feeling fine while she was hurting. It was kind of masochistic, I knew, but as humans we choose the hard way more often than we realize. Personally, I think that's also by design. The easy way so seldom ends up being the *right* way. On some level,

I think we all know that.

I went to get her another dose of her medicine and she took it with her eyes closed that time. I gave her some more juice and she gulped it down quick. She finished with another satisfied "*Ahhhh!*"

She sat back on the pillows after that and watched the movie intently while we waited for it to kick in. Once that happened, it was a little easier for both of us. I think Ben knew she wouldn't last too much longer and he made quick work of dinner. He came out with the same tray that I had used earlier, only this time it was holding bowls of cheese ravioli's. They were another of her favorites and for the third time that day she was happily focused on something besides her arm. I found I loved that she shared that love of food with me. That, I could definitely work with. Joy from food was easy. Keeping it balanced so you don't pay for it by having to buy an extra plane seat was the key.

"They're not nearly as good as the ones you used to make from scratch, but and as far as frozen goes, we think they're the best. Right?" He asked Liliana as he put it down on the end table and passed out bowls.

"Right." She agreed, though not as energetically.

He set up the TV trays in front of us and then offered me some garlic bread. I thought of Ethan and later and I passed on the bread, but the ravioli's I scarfed down right alongside Liliana. I had to admit they were pretty good. Once her stomach bug was gone, her appetite had come back full force. That was good. It helped to make the medicine easier to take, and keep down. We watched the end of the movie while we ate and she slowly cleaned her plate. She was still a little hungry but she was too tired to bother to ask for more. I reached over and gave her my last ravioli and she smiled as she ate it.

"Thank you, mama." She said in a tiny voice.

When she finished, I picked her up and took her upstairs to show her how to put the plastic mitt they had given us at the hospital over her cast. Then I helped her take a quick bath. She didn't complain about my helping her that time. Ben took advantage of the help and stayed downstairs to clean up.

We finished her bath and I helped her into her jammie's

then I brushed out her hair while she brushed her teeth. Once I had her all tucked in bed and propped up on a few extra pillows, I read her a story. It was a short one. She was fading fast.

Once Ben was done disassembling and relocating the rest of the fort, he came up to say goodnight. Between the medicine, the bath and the super long day, she was out before we tiptoed quietly through the doorway. I turned off the overhead light and her room was instantly bathed in swirling stars as they cascaded around the walls from her nightlight. I closed the door most of the way and followed Ben back downstairs.

As we made our way back into the living room, thoughts of Ethan popped into my head again. They were quite the stark contrast to my current reality. I thought then about trying to blend the two worlds and it seemed nearly impossible. I knew though that at some point it would have to happen, and I didn't want it to be a horrific disaster if there was any way I could prevent it. I decided then, that it was as good a time as any to mention Ethan to Ben.

We got back to the couch and sat down heavily.

"I can't thank you enough for all your help today. Obviously not for what you did for her. I mean the extra stuff that you did to help me. I really appreciate it." He said seriously.

"It's nothing. Just pitching in." I answered simply.

"Well I'm glad that we can still work together so well. That there's no animosity between us. It certainly makes times like these a lot easier to handle, you know?" He said with a deep sigh. I did. I was grateful as well.

"I was thinking the same thing actually, while you were sleeping. We don't have to be married to help take care of each other. We're still family Ben, and in one respect, we always will be." I said and I was glad that it was true. That there was no hate between us. "We are lucky. I know we're all still adjusting, but I think things have finally settled to a point where we can start to be happy again. It's a lot better, for all of us." I ended with a resigned smile. He nodded. I breathed a little easier again too. We really we're going to be okay, I thought with some relief.

I was hoping those good natured feelings would last through what I wanted to talk about next.

"Things are definitely getting better. Not just easier, but actually better." I said with a genuine smile.

"Yeah, absolutely. She's really been enjoying her time with you lately. Things really seem to have improved in that respect remarkably. I think that's great, Simone." He said, still with the warm smile. "She comes home now so excited to tell me everything that you guys did. It's awesome that you're starting to get out so much and enjoy life a little again. It sounds like Pinegrove has really been a positive move for you." *Hah!* If he only knew, I thought to myself. I couldn't keep the smile away completely though.

"Yes, I've definitely been handling things better lately. It is easier to step back and recharge there, so to speak. That helps a lot. But I'm not gonna lie. It's not just because of me. A big part of it also has to do with Ethan." I waited for the question, knowing it would come.

"Ethan? Who's Ethan? Do I even want to know?" He asked, only half joking. He didn't appear to harbor any jealousy though. He was just curious. I thought about how I used to like that I couldn't feel all of his feelings all of the time, but I had come to the conclusion over the years that sometimes it was just easier to know where you stood. Just then I really thought it would be nice, but anyway.

"Just a friend. A *good* friend." I said meaningfully, with my eyebrows raised. I could see from his grin that he understood. "But still, just a friend. For now. I don't know what's right for anyone else, but I know that I'm not ready for anything more than a good friend just yet." He nodded in agreement. "I wanted to mention to you though that I *would* like for him to meet Liliana." His eyebrows furrowed and he looked confused.

"What? Why? I thought you said it wasn't serious? Who is this guy anyway?" I remembered Ethan's comments then about hiding out in the open.

"His name is Ethan Stone. He lives in Pinegrove, right up the road from me actually. He performs regularly at a place in town called The Tavern. He's become a pretty good friend, but I've also found out that he's pretty knowledgeable when it comes to my particular type of *abilities*." Ben looked very surprised by that.

"You told him about that? *Already?* Wow, that's not like you Simone. Are you sure you can trust this guy?" He asked sounding genuinely concerned.

"Yeah, pretty sure." I said with a patient smile. It was a typical response for Ben. I didn't let it shake me. "And I didn't tell him. He kind of has a knack for noticing that sort of thing all on his own. Believe me, it surprised me too. All he wants to do is help and not just me. He's helped a lot of people in similar situations. He has a very good understanding of how difficult it can be to live with these types of abilities." I explained.

"Anyway, the details aren't important right now, I just thought it would be good for her to *know* him. Just in case, God forbid, she ever needs help in that area." He looked at me warily. We both knew what I was talking about, although he didn't even understand the full extent of what that may mean yet. Still, neither of us ever wanted to say it out loud. Like that would give it more power to become real, just by voicing it. I continued anyway, bravely for once. "If she turns out to be more like me than we had hoped. It will be easier for him to help her if he's not a stranger. Do you know what I mean?" I asked hopefully.

He looked away again and shook his head as if that could make it go away. "I don't know Simone. It sounds a little hokey to me. You move up there to the boonies and then you start talking about crazy stuff like this? I thought you were there for the peace and quiet. That it was actually doing you some good! I didn't expect you to run off and join some *empath cult.*" He said vehemently. I sighed and felt some of the ground that we had made slip away.

It all sounded so ridiculous when he put it that way. I knew that firsthand. If I hadn't already gone through that same thought process myself I would probably be angry at him for his predictable shortsightedness. As it was I understood his reaction perfectly.

I just wasn't sure how to change it.

"Look, I know it all sounds a little *'out there.'* I'll give you that." I said with my hands up, laughing and trying to lighten the mood. "But you *know* me Ben. You *know* how easy it is for me to see if someone is lying to me or just trying to use me. Right?" He was thoughtful for a minute then he softened some at that reminder. He nodded.

"I know that he does what he does because he went through similar things when he was younger. I also know that he wants to use that experience to help others in the same boat. He does that because *he* knows that there aren't a lot of people out there who *can* help. Most importantly, I know that his intentions are pure and selfless. That's enough for me." I took a deep breath and started again.

"Anyway, like I said, I'd just like for her to meet and get to know him a little. For right now, that's all but I still wanted to let you know. It seemed like something that I should talk to you about first." I said, trying to get back to that good place that we had been in earlier.

"I think it's important for us to keep an open and honest communication, Ben. I meant it when I said that I am grateful for the way our relationship is now. I don't want anything to build resentment between us and poison that. We've worked too hard already trying to keep that from happening, dammit!" I insisted.

He seemed to be reconsidering it, which was good because I was running out of arguments that I could use without breaking any specific confidences with Ethan. "I respect your right to make decisions for Liliana, Ben. I need you to do the same for me, okay? You have to know that I would never do anything that would put her in danger." He was thoughtful for a minute more.

"Fine. If you want to introduce them, I won't argue with you. But if he becomes anything more than a casual acquaintance, for *any* reason, hers or yours, you have to promise me that I won't be the last to know. Alright?" He still looked wary, but he was agreeing to trust me. That was definitely a step in the right direction!

"I promise." I said softly. I was grateful for his compliance, but I also knew what his fears were and I shared them for the most part. "Especially if it's '*hers.*'" I assured him. He let out another huge sigh and sank back into the couch even more. I was sorry then, about adding to what he had on his plate already. At some point though, he would have to know. I had to start somewhere, while I still had time. Who knew how much?

Still, I hoped to do a little damage control before I left him on that note. I looked him in the eye and smiled. He smiled back. Tiredly, but honestly. I would take that.

"Thank you Ben. I've always thought since day one, that Liliana was lucky to have you for a father. That hasn't changed." I hugged him and he hugged me back for a long minute. "Call me if you need me." I added, realizing only briefly that I had heard that exact phrase just recently myself. That made me smile.

I got up, grabbed my purse off of the table, and I headed *home.*

Chapter 37

The trip home was slower and therefore longer, but 95 was at least peaceful with four wide open lanes of empty highway. I called my parents' house on the way to let them know what had happened. My mother answered.

"Hi mom. I didn't wake you, did I?" I asked even though it was still only a little after 9:00 PM. You never knew.

"No. I was actually just watching a movie. It's a total chick flick and I'm taking advantage of the fact that your father went to the Red Sox game tonight. I finally have the TV all to myself. How are things?" She asked casually.

I jumped right in and told her the whole story while I drove the rest of the way home. She was appropriately aghast at the thought of Liliana getting hurt, and she promised to go and check on her in the morning. And again in the evening. *"Just to help Ben out, of course."* She added with mock innocence. Right. No doubt bearing balloons, toys and candy in obscene amounts with each visit.

It really is funny what happens to people, even formerly super strict parents, when a grandchild comes along. Suddenly they find they're free to love that child as much as a parent does, but without the restriction of also being responsible for their discipline. They just lose all control. It was pretty funny to watch though I thought, smiling to myself while she continued to gush about all the things that *"the poor baby"* would surely need.

I grinned quietly and shook my head while she talked. I felt a little better, knowing I wouldn't be there myself every day.

I would stop by tomorrow at the very least but I figured that there would be a minimum of four unexpected family members dropping in on a regular basis, once Ben's parents also found out. I didn't want to overwhelm Ben by adding myself to that number for the entire time. The good thing was at least I knew I could relax when I wasn't there with her myself. Or at least I could try.

"Thanks mom. I knew I could count on you." I said with humor.

"Oh don't you worry, we'll take good care of her. You just focus on getting back to work. Dad was telling me about what happened. Any word yet?" She asked.

"Not yet. But I have the best people I know working on it for me. There's not much else that I can do right now but wait. Of course I'm handling that about as well as you would imagine." I added with a chuckle. She laughed too. She knew firsthand what a joke that was.

"Well, you hang in there, kiddo." She said, reminding me of how I sounded talking to Liliana and I felt that generation gap close a little more.

"Thanks mom. I will. Kiss Daddy for me when he gets home." I requested. She agreed, and we hung up.

I thought about calling Ethan next as I pulled down my driveway but I decided at the last second to wait until I got inside and got a chance to shower and change. It had been such a long day! I really felt the need to go peel and rinse, as much of it off of me as I could.

I parked my car and put my phone back in my pocket. I was walking absentmindedly across the gravel to my door, when it rang. I sighed deeply, afraid to look.

I wanted to hope that it was Ethan being too impatient to wait for me to call, but even subconsciously I knew that was ridiculous. If he said he would wait, he would wait. Period. I looked down at the screen as I pulled it out.

"Hey Jack." I answered, not hiding my surprise.

'Hey sugar! Sorry to pounce, but I saw you pull in and I didn't want to give you a chance to get into bed." He said apologetically.

"Don't worry about it." I told him. "What's up?"

"Gen and Travis were up here for dinner earlier tonight, and she happened to get a message just as they were about to head home. Something about a possible court date. Said she won't know any more about it until morning, so she wasn't going to call you herself tonight. But she said if I saw you, to give you a heads up." He explained as I unlocked my door.

"Oh, Jack! That's fantastic! Thank you!" I said as I let out another huge gust of air in relief. "I really needed some good news today. Even just a little." I said as I reached the top of the stairs and dropped my keys into the bowl. I kicked off my shoes and dropped down onto the sofa.

"Not more problems at the site, I hope?" He questioned with obvious concern.

"No, no. Not that. Actually Liliana fell and broke her wrist this morning. I guess you're going to be short one rider for a few weeks I'm sorry to say."

"Oh no! Awe, that's terrible. How's my little star pupil holding up?" He asked, sounding genuinely worried.

"She's actually doing really well. Thanks. Don't worry. She's handling it far better than Ben and I are." I laughed.

"Oh, I don't doubt that for one minute." He agreed with his familiar raspy, chuckle. "Well I'll let you go now, so you can get some rest. You must be exhausted. You keep me posted. Alright?" He added. I agreed that I would and told him that we'd most likely still see him Friday at movie night anyway and we hung up.

I sighed and realized that getting together with Ethan then may not be the smartest idea anymore. Not with the very real possibility that I may have to go before a judge first thing in the morning and beg for the future of my livelihood. I sighed again. It was disappointing, I had to acknowledge. I had really been looking forward to his company.

Oh well. There's always tomorrow, right? I decided to call and break the good/bad news. He picked up on the second ring.

"Hi! How is she? Are you home?" He spit out all at once.

"Yeah. She's okay. She was sleeping soundly when I left. Unfortunately, I think that I am going to try to do the same now. Sorry for the change of plans, but Jack just told me that I may have a court date in the morning. After the day I just had, I think I could use all the sleep I can get." I admitted with a self-deprecating laugh.

"No problem. I understand. I'll just go for a run. I could use one anyway. I need to get out of my own head for a while. One way or another." He said with his usual, wicked chuckle. "I'm sure you can relate."

"Mmmm hmmm." I agreed easily. "Everything okay?" I asked.

"I'm not going to drag you into it. It's nothing for you to worry about." He paused for a brief moment after he answered. "You know I wouldn't keep anything from you, if I didn't have to, or if it had anything to *do* with you, right?" He asked gently.

"I know. I answered with a smile that he couldn't see. I was glad that it was true, because I knew what it was like when you had no way to be sure. Every promise, assurance or excuse Ben had ever given me, I'd had to take on faith, just like everyone else. I still don't know how many times I was schmoozed or duped over the years in that relationship, any more than the next trusting girl ever does. It was not my favorite thing in the world and I admitted to myself that I probably didn't have it in me to go back to that again. As I pondered all of that, he continued with his *sort of* explanation.

"The times that it doesn't have to do with you though, it really needs to stay that way. It's smarter and safer for everyone involved but *mostly* for you! Do you understand what I'm saying?" He asked gently. As usual, I could feel his complete openness and I knew that he meant what he said. It was that protectiveness in him again. For all parties involved. That huge responsibility that he had agreed to take on.

I felt for just a moment what it must be like to have the weight of both sides always resting on that one brave person, strong enough and willing to stand in the middle. That thought created another new image of Ethan in my head. One of him standing tall with his arms outstretched on either side. In one hand he carried the weight and the responsibility of the Camp, and everything that it entailed. In the other, he held all the things in his own personal life and his *public* life. He stood ever strong, but had to carry each weight separately. Eternally. Without ever letting them come together in the middle, where he would be able to support it all so much more easily by using both hands together. I shook my head a little and the image faded away.

And still he never complained.

"It's fine. I get it. Can I call you tomorrow?" I asked.

"Darlin,' you can call me anytime you want to! Absolutely *any* time." He said and I could hear the wicked smile in his voice. "Should I be unavailable when you call, *believe me* I *will* call you back as soon as possible!" He said quoting the popular voicemail phrase. "I'll talk to you tomorrow. Sweet dreams." He said and I said goodnight too, but I found that I couldn't stop smiling, even after I hung up. I shook my head again and got up to take a quick shower so I could get to bed before it *was* tomorrow.

I started the water running in the shower while I grabbed a new set of shorts and stuff to sleep in. By the time I got back into the bathroom, the water was perfect. I stripped out of the clothes that I had been in since very early that morning and stepped under the tepid stream of water with a sigh. As much as I wanted to just stand there for a few hours, I knew it wasn't a good idea. I made quick work of my normal routine and got out.

I grabbed the oversized, fluffy beige towel off of the rack and wrapped myself in it. I stepped out and grabbed another one for my hair. I quickly brushed my teeth and then impatiently, pulled the towel back out of my still drenched hair to brush it out. It was anyone's guess what it would look like the next day anytime I went to bed with it wet. I was willing to risk it though for the extra half hour of sleep.

I threw my clothes on and hung both towels to dry. By the time I was in my bed, legs sliding smoothly, back and forth against the cool cotton sheets, only fifteen minutes had gone by. I was just about to drift quietly over the edge into dreamland when I heard a short, sing-song-y whistle echo up from the edge of the woods. Someone else may easily mistake the sound for the call of a nocturnal animal, or some kind of bird. But I knew for sure exactly which nocturnal, *human* animal was responsible for that call. I smiled happily to myself at the shout out, feeling closer to him for just that brief satisfying beat. After that, I slipped happily into a deep sleep.

I woke what felt like minutes later, to the sound of my ringing phone. I had decided to leave it on my bedside table the night before, just in case. I was glad that I had. I picked it up to see that it was 6:30 AM. Hours later, not minutes after all. It was Gen.

"Hello?" I said, trying not to sound like she had woken me up, although I had no idea why. It *was* 6:30 in the morning after all. It was an automatic guilt reflex.

"We're in!" She said excitedly. "We're on the docket for the next open slot! Of course only problem with that is, there's no way of knowing when that will be, so I'll have to hang around the courthouse a lot in the meantime just in case. It's sort of like being on standby for a spot on a plane. Whenever that next open slot comes up, it's ours!" She said excitedly. "We just have to be ready."

"Oh Gen, that's fantastic! You are the best!" I proclaimed happily, completely wide awake then.

"Well I'd like to take all the credit but the truth is, I really have no idea how we got moved to the top of the list. All of my bright ideas were coming up dry and all of my contacts kept telling me their hands were tied. I was banging my head against the wall and really starting worry that I had gotten your hopes up for nothing. As it turns out, *someone* pushed it through! I just have no idea who! Do *you?*" She asked.

I immediately thought of the one other person that could have had a hand in it. *"Hmpf!* Yeah, I think so. I might need to take a moment to thank daddy for that one." I smiled to myself at how lucky I was to be his daughter.

"Sorry, I forgot to mention that to you. I guess it's because I was pretty sure there wasn't much he could do. Apparently I underestimated him." I admitted affectionately. "I hope you don't think less of me for asking for his help, but I was admittedly desperate and it was also before you came along." I confessed.

"Are you kidding me? Without my family, I'd be nowhere! Nobody gets through life without a little help from somewhere, Simone. You're very lucky to have a close, supportive family that you can even *ask."* She said, and I knew she was right. "So am I and believe me I know it too! I would never want to do anything to ruin that for myself, so I would never hold it against you." She said easily. "Anyway, they didn't do anything for you to feel ashamed of. They've only just gotten our foot in the door, that's all. I'll definitely take it though!" She said and I felt better.

"So now what?" I asked.

"Are the plans for the well all done?" She asked in return.

"Yup, about 98% anyway, thanks to the group effort. Just have to 'dot a few *i's'* and 'cross a few *t's.'*" I answered, feeling really good about that and what we all had accomplished together. Yes I had spent a night making love and a day playing "The Three Bears" in that time as well, but I still had no regrets. We had completed a lot of work in a short amount of time, because thankfully, I'd had the right kind of help. Sometimes it was better to be lucky than good. Like Gen had said, I wouldn't look a gift horse in the mouth.

"Alright, get me a copy as soon as you can, and I'll call you as soon as I hear anything. At that point, you'll have about a half hour to get down here. So even though it may or may not be today, you'll have to be ready to go on a moments' notice. Okay?"

"Got it. You should have the plans by 8:00 AM." I said. "That work?"

"Perfect! Talk to you soon." She said and hung up.

I let out a huge sigh and sat back down on the bed that I had been pacing around while talking to catch my breath. A minute later I stood back up and went to make some coffee, even though I barely needed it. My heart was still racing. In the *third* best possible way!

I brushed my teeth and hair while I waited for the coffee to brew and was pleasantly surprised that my hair had dried in a somewhat tolerable wave. I decided to leave it down since it was cooperating after all, and I went to get dressed.

I was a little confused about what to put on. I could tell already that it was going to be a hot one. But I was also supposed to be ready to appear in court on a moments' notice. That meant no shorts or tank tops. *Hmmm.*

I finally decided on a lightweight, swingy, sky blue cotton skirt that looked decent enough for court, but would also mercifully, expose most of my legs to the breeze. Next I found a sleeveless, white button down top that worked as well and threw them both on. I slipped my feet into a pair of tan flats and went back for the coffee I could hear beeping.

Once I'd had my coffee, I put on a little mascara and some earrings. Then I rolled out the plans on the table again and added the last finishing touches. I was in my car with the finished plans, heading for the copy shop by 7:30. Thankfully there wasn't a line of people already waiting when I showed up. I had two copies made, just to be safe, and arranged to have a courier run one set over to Gen's office. I was finished and back home waiting by 8:30 AM.

"*Hmpf.*" Back to waiting again, dammit. Boo. There had to be something else I could do, I thought frustratingly. A few things definitely popped into my head, but the most appealing options all had to do with Ethan and I was afraid to let myself get sidetracked. Being with him tended to make me lose track of time. *Quite willingly.* No, I needed to do something I wouldn't mind stopping when the call came.

I thought about going for a hike but I didn't feel like changing again, never mind having to shower all over again. If Gen called, that would take too long. I turned on the TV, but all I did was flip through the channels for an hour until I realized I was on my third rotation. I gave up and shut the TV off and sighed dramatically. Just then, my phone rang.

I picked it up off the table in front of me excitedly, but my hopes plummeted just as fast when I saw that it wasn't Gen. It was Viv though, and that made me feel a little better.

"Hello!" I said answering it.

"Hi. I'm bored to tears and I hate *everyone* around here! Come have brunch with me!" She demanded.

"Oh thank God!" I exclaimed. "I'm going insane too. I'll be right there! Are you at the shop?"

"Yup." She confirmed. *Perfect!* I would be in town and that much closer to the courthouse when Gen finally did call, *and* I'd have something to do in the meantime. Thank God for small miracles!

"See you in thirty minutes." I said and I grabbed my purse and keys on the way out.

There was a little more traffic than usual for some

unknown reason, but I still made it there in under forty five minutes.

"You're late." Was my greeting as I walked in the door to her shop.

"Traffic sucked." I explained, glad that I had not waited for Gen's call to head down after all. I could feel the annoyance in the air but it didn't seem like it was all about me. I also noticed then, that the place was completely empty.

"Where is everyone?" I asked, surprised that it wasn't hopping as usual. The shop seemed twice the size and almost desolate in contrast.

"Beats me. Not like I have 'em Lo-jacked or anything." She bit back, being purposefully evasive at first.

I barked out a laugh but just stared at her until she spoke again. "I sent everyone home for the day. I had no one to cover Andrea's chair and too many appointments of my own to do it myself. I decided on the "all or nothing" approach of management for today. I couldn't do it all, so I'm doing nothing. I cancelled everything and took the day off so I can figure out what to do next. It's hard to find good hard help these days." She finished sarcastically.

"So you lasted halfway through your 'day off' before you couldn't take the inactivity and solitude anymore and called me?" I teased.

"Are you kidding me? I'm surprised I lasted that long!" She admitted and we both laughed. She locked the door and we headed off on foot to find someplace to eat. You could do that in the city, just head out aimlessly and decide your destination based on the many options that you happened to pass, or on your most recent cravings. Some aspects of city life I did occasionally miss. Having endless food choices at your back door was definitely one of them.

We settled on a little Chinese place three blocks from her shop since it was getting closer to lunch by then. It was a welcome break and it was nice to just vent a little and know that the information would go no further than your breath. We took turns gushing and listening. It was a very effective and beneficial give and take. When I left there, I felt ten pounds lighter. I could tell that she did too and that made it even better. We hugged on the street and I ran excitedly back to my car. I had just finally received word as the waiter brought our check, that it was time to head down to the courthouse. One way or the other, it would be the end of the current situation.

My heart was racing again as I got in my car and I sat for a minute to let it slow a little. I sent the same text to two different people. Separately. One to Mack and one to Ethan. Then off I went to hear my fate.

Just heard from Gen. On my way over now. This is it. Fingers crossed.

Chapter 38

I stood in the doorway and held my breath. I didn't mean to. I tried to stop myself. It was no use. It was too important. I stood there effectively separating one part of my life from another. I remembered the last time I had thought about someone else doing that voluntarily, and how hard I had thought it must be to maintain.

I decided maybe I could lead by example. It was time.

I took a deep breath and stepped back, allowing Ethan to walk inside and follow me up the stairs.

Liliana was sitting on my sofa. She had a pillow in her lap with the book resting on top that she was coloring in. I had told her that a friend of mine would be coming with us to Movie Night. She was only mildly curious about who that friend might be, originally. It was obvious as we reached the top however, that she had been expecting a *'girl'* type friend. Somebody more like Viv.

Ethan however, was nothing *at all* like Viv. Probably her polar opposite, in fact. Most notably, where Viv was decidedly tiny, he was *quite* large!

She looked up, but didn't say anything as he walked in. I could feel her initial desire to back up a little, even though on the sofa, there was nowhere for her to go. I could tell that, just like my reaction to him early on, it wasn't fear that made her act that way. It was more a sense of how much energy had just entered the room. For what was probably the millionth time, I wondered if it was normal for her to feel that too. Did *everyone* feel that around him, I wondered?

He was being very careful not to move in any way that would be intimidating and I could tell that so far, he was getting the desired result. She was wary, but still not afraid.

"Hi!" He said to me first. I could tell that he was *very* excited to see me but of course he had it firmly under control. There was a definite *"for now"* implied in there though. I smiled slyly at that comforting knowledge.

"Hi." I said back, pretty excited myself. *Deep breaths.* I still wasn't as good at dealing with it in front of other people as he was, but I was getting better. *Phew!*

"Liliana, this is my friend Ethan." I said turning back towards her. Focusing on her made it easier. He walked over with his hand held out. I was filled right away with his joy at her sweet adorable looking innocence as he finally met her face-to-face. I wasn't surprised. Most people felt the same way when they first met her. Just as Ben and I had long ago. She wasn't quite *that* sweet and innocent necessarily, but unlike other kids who looked one way but acted another, she actually came pretty close. Meanwhile she was withholding her judgment. Right then she still had reservations regarding his size.

"Hello Liliana. It's nice to meet you." He said politely. He pointed to her cast then. "Ouch! Bet that hurt!" He said with a grimace.

She recovered quickly and shook his hand. Not just to be polite, which she always made a conscious effort to do, but because she was curious too. Plus she was quite happy to talk about her newest accessory.

"Not really. Only a little, in the beginning. Now it mostly just gets in the way. I like to decorate it though." She replied, still not totally sure about him.

"Wow! You're one tough cookie, aren't you?" He asked. I felt her self-confidence and her mood lift a hair. She wasn't sure about him yet, but she didn't mind talking to him, she decided then. I smiled to myself.

"When I was your age, I broke my arm and I cried for days!" He said emphatically and I was surprised to see that as usual, he was being honest. I had to wonder then just exactly how *his* arm had happened to end up broken, and why the pain had gone on for *days.* For a minute, I was furious all over again.

He wasn't though. He was just trying to even things out between them a little, at least mentally, and he was willing to lose face to do it. I could tell that was working also. She would never admit it that easily, but she was starting to think it might be okay to like him.

He had started out looking big and overwhelming. But by showing her a mental picture of himself as small and vulnerable, he allowed her to actually see him as someone more her size. Suddenly he was much easier for *tiny-little-her,* to relate to.

It wasn't long after that, that I even noticed her starting to feel just a little bit protective of him for a brief moment. I almost laughed out loud at that all too familiar response. I knew he didn't set out to evoke that particular reaction in people. It was a natural reaction. I wondered then, to what extent he was even aware of having that effect on everyone around him. I noticed that so far, he hadn't focused on it at all.

"Do you want to sign it?" She offered, still somewhat reluctantly. He smiled at her but she just waited, playing it totally cool. That's my girl, I thought with a mental laugh.

"Sure. What color should I use?" He asked as if he already knew it was the perfect question. I don't know how he knew, but I could feel her warming up to the subject and preparing to explain the right choice at great length.

They weren't necessarily friends yet, but that was okay. They were sitting together, discussing color combinations and the pictures that already covered eighty percent of the space. I would take it.

I turned and left them to it for a few minutes while I went to make the popcorn. I finally let out the breath that, in spite of my best efforts I had still been holding.

Breathing in general had started to get a bit easier over the past few days. Court had been terrifying. I was completely out of my element there and I knew it. It was hard enough to keep my own emotions reigned in, never mind properly separating and handling all the other volatile emotions floating around a place like that. Thank God I'd had Gen on my side and that she turned out to be so good at what she does. I didn't understand a lot of the legal jargon, but I managed to follow the bullet points.

We didn't have a permit prior to accessing the aquifer. That was bad. Though we were able to establish that it was previously unknown in that location. That was good. We were able to provide finished plans for a fully functional well in record time. Also good.

My dear friend Mr. Wright was there, along with a representative from The New Hampshire Department of Environmental Services. Warren's official job was to witness their findings with the water testing for the Groundwater Hazard Inventory report. Which, whether diabolically or just thankfully, did match our own when all was said and done, and were completely clean. However he also had a vote in the approval, or the rejection of our well design. I could tell that the Environmental guy had no interest in our particular case either way as long as the regulations were met. I could handle that. But Mr. "*Always*" Wright was a different story. He seemed to enjoy the negative energy that these types of problems could create. He was definitely the most worrisome of all for me and my deadline.

In the end though, neither the judge nor the committee could find any problems with our paperwork or our plans. And believe me, they dissected every aspect of every part *trying.* Eventually they did reluctantly sign off on them. With that done, the judge had no reason not to approve our newly submitted work permits as well. Just like that, we were back in business. *Thank God!!* I had felt thirty pounds lighter after that.

Gen was a miracle worker after all and I told her that as I thanked her repeatedly on our way out.

There was someone else to thank too though and once I was alone in my car, I called my father to do exactly that.

"I never could have pulled this one off without you! I can't thank you enough!" I had gushed appropriately.

"Your very welcome honey. I'm really glad I could help. Now you get back in there and create something amazing that will blow them all away, just like you always do!" He had said, being his ever supportive self.

"Will do, Daddy. Trust me, I can't wait!" I replied easily.

Next I had made the call to Mack to start the *re*-round up

of the troops. In the meantime, I still needed to get all of the materials for the new well ordered, and shipped to the site. I also had to pull together the specialized manpower required to install it. Gen was still helping me with that thankfully, being the only one with connections in the field and in the area. She was a Godsend and I continued to let her know that daily.

She'd had all the necessary paperwork filed by the end of the day on Thursday and said she'd call me as soon as she had some potential help lined up for me to interview. That would hopefully be by Monday or Tuesday at the latest. I could still pull it off, I was pretty sure. Even with the added workload, since I had a few extra sets of hands. It was possible, *if* things went smoothly from there on out.

I knew better than to count on that though, so I wasn't home free yet. I could get back to actively working at it though and that was so much better than sitting around and waiting! At least there would be something to *do* while I waited to see if my career would go down in flames. Something to keep the hands busy, if not the brain. We were due to be back on site first thing Monday morning and for me it really couldn't come fast enough.

Until I learned how to speed up time whenever it suited me, I still had to wait, at least a few more days. Thankfully in the meantime, we had movie night. Then we had the show at the Music Theatre tomorrow. Of course there had also been the one small issue of Ethan meeting Liliana for the first time to get through.

With that particular situation, came the potential for things to go so very wrong, and I hadn't been sure what I would do if that happened. So I was extremely relieved to have at least the initial meeting successfully behind us. *Phew, did not even begin to cover it!*

The microwave beeped and I pretended that I had been paying attention. I reached up like I had been waiting for it and took one bag out, then put the second one in. I hit the "popcorn" button again.

I stood and pretended to wait, but I was really listening to their conversation. Absorbing and overanalyzing all the different emotions passing back and forth. There was patience.

Wariness. Curiosity. The distinct feeling of being slightly and pleasantly surprised. From both sides. There was plenty of amusement mixed rather heavily with reservation.

Liliana had all but forgotten about me for the moment and was completely focused on Ethan. Ethan was totally focused on her as well, but *he* had not forgotten my presence at all. I let out a smile at that where no one could see me.

They were still talking. Then she was giggling. A moment later I heard his soft, deep chuckle join in. The sounds alone were enough to make me melt. I dared myself to turn around while I waited, and not be touched by what I saw. I knew better than to fall for that kind of pressure tactic though. I held my ground and kept my gaze straight forward until I heard the microwave beep again.

"Alright!" I said grabbing both bags and setting them in the basket by the flashlights. "Who's ready for Movie Night?"

"I am!" They both answered at once and then laughed a little at each other. I smiled. It was definitely a good start.

"Time for the spray-down." I announced, heading towards the back deck to conduct the all-important deet application. Liliana hopped down off the couch and followed me out. Ethan came too and lined up behind her.

I made sure she was downwind. Then she closed her eyes, held her breath and held out her arms, both the bare one and the one in the cast. I sprayed one whole side. Gave her a moment to take a deep breath, then she held it again and turned so I could do the other. She knew the routine pretty well at that point.

I looked up at Ethan when he stepped into the firing zone next. I smiled and he held his arms out and closed his eyes. I only managed to spray most of him, as he stood there feeling silly, before he burst out laughing and sucked in a mouthful of bug spray. Then we were all laughing.

"You're supposed to hold your breath when she sprays." Liliana told him in all seriousness and he and I laughed even harder.

Then he held his hand out to me for the can. Ut oh. "Be nice." I said jokingly, as I slowly handed it over. He just grinned. I raised my arms and closed first one eye. He raised the can menacingly, and I reluctantly closed the other.

He covered me carefully, but entirely. He spun around me and did both sides without my having to open my eyes or move. He was quick and I was relieved. Then I was something *else* too. His super gentle touch always seemed to have that effect on me. He was not unaware, but as usual, no one but me would be able to tell that it had affected him as well. I took a few big steps away from the spray cloud and him and took a deep breath. Needing clean air was a good cover for my current weakness.

We went back in to get the basket I'd put together with drinks for all of us and our popcorn. I folded the blanket and laid it across the basket under the handle, making it all easy to carry. We each grabbed one of the flashlights that I had bought brand new earlier that day. I wasn't taking any chances on a repeat of last time. Ethan watched me double-check each one anyway, and he grinned again at our shared memory. I made a face that clearly said, *'Don't go there.'* He grinned harder but he kept it in check while he grabbed the basket and we headed back outside.

"Come on Mama!" Liliana called back to me as she bounded down the steps. "It's dark already! They're gonna start without us!" She said worriedly.

"Oh, I doubt that sweetie. I know Jack and Shirley are waiting to see you. They wanted to sign your cast too." I said to her as I made eyes at Ethan, who had done so well using that topic for an icebreaker.

"Good thing I brought my markers with me." She said happily, patting the small, lightweight backpack she wore where they were currently tucked away. I had to smile. Ben and I had already joked about how she hadn't gone anywhere without them since my mother had given them to her on Wednesday.

We reached the path and she skipped happily ahead of us, her flashlight beam bouncing left and right as she went. We walked side by side behind her in the warm night air. I felt the change as he allowed his excitement to take center stage a little more. His flashlight switched off. A second later, he took my flashlight from me, freeing up my right hand. He switched it to his right hand then took my free hand with his left. Once all his ministrations were complete, he spoke up.

"I've missed you." He said quietly. That familiar radiating wave washed over me and my eyes closed for a second or two. I knew that I had missed him too. I could try to deny it, but to who? I was a little nervous when it came to holding his hand around Liliana, but I realized that it was silly. She was far enough in front of us and it was dark. His hand was warm and it squeezed mine a little tighter. That warmth began to spread. I gave in and squeezed his back.

"I've missed you too." I admitted, looking up at him out of the corner of my eye as we walked. When I had canceled our plans to meet Tuesday night, I never imagined it would be Friday night before we would get a chance to see each other again. Sadly, Friday night was not a night that I could consider sharing with him. Not to *that* extent anyway. Saturday wouldn't be either that particular week, but I didn't want to think about that just then.

I'd had my issues to deal with earlier in the week, and he'd had his toward the middle. He didn't tell me much about what was going on but I could tell whenever we had gotten the chance to talk over the past two days that he had been busy, *and worried.* It felt good to at least have him with me in the flesh again, rather than just a voice over the line that I wished I could better comfort. For the moment I would take his presence, real and warm next to me and be happy.

"How are things going with Jeremy?' I asked him without worry of being overheard, since we finally had a moment at least *quasi* alone.

He sighed again before he answered. That wasn't a good sign. I could feel him deciding how much to tell me.

"He's supposed to go home sometime this weekend. Pete's been pressuring me to stick to what we agreed on. He misses his kid. I don't blame him. But he still doesn't quite grasp the seriousness of the danger he's in from Anderson. Not to mention, I'm still not even sure he's ready yet. Neither is Dr. J. It could do more harm than good if we make a mistake right now." He sighed again, considering his options. "I'm not sure yet though. I'm thinking maybe I should just let him go, and I could just try to stay close by. I don't want to make him feel *trapped* either." I could tell he had been over it a lot in his head already.

"Mmmm. I'm sure you'll figure it out. When it comes time to decide, you'll know what's right. Don't ask me why I'm so sure." I insisted. "I just am." I squeezed his hand again before I let it go. I bumped him with my hip before separating from him completely as we approached the crowd.

I heard Liliana squeal then, which obviously meant she had found Jonah. I heard his voice next, raised in an excited greeting, echoing through the darkness and confirming my suspicions. Their combined happiness hit me a moment after that. I could hear her telling him about her cast as I got closer. I noticed that her tale of recent tragedy, illustrated nicely for all to see in bright pink neon, was starting to draw a bit of a crowd. I stopped and hung back a few yards and allowed her to get her socializing in.

A lot of emotions began to crowd into the space, but it was mostly the innocent excitement of happy children and I could take that all day long. It was like candy covered emotions. They were sweet and they made you feel happy. Ethan and I exchanged a look and a smile while we stood together waiting patiently.

"She certainly can hold her own, can't she?" He said quietly to me, with clear admiration at her ability to not be overwhelmed by the crowd of mostly older kids. Or by him. "She's a lot like her mother." He added, looking back at me with a sly, sideways glance. I just shook my head in denial.

"I wish." I said longingly.

"Nah." He disagreed. "You're a lot more impressive than you give yourself credit for." He insisted. I wasn't sure how to respond, and thankfully I didn't have to.

Jack and Shirley made their way around the crowd then and came over to us. I had known that Ethan knew Shirley for some time by then, but it was the first time I'd had a chance to observe them *together* since he had explained his background to me. It was easy after that to pick out the familial affection between them as they hugged each other. I wondered how long it would have taken me to notice otherwise. Oh well. No way to know now I thought, letting something go for once.

Jack slapped Ethan on the back in an outwardly jovial manner on his way by. Beneath that though, I could feel a secondary wariness pass between them that I didn't know the reason for. I got the distinct impression that my ignorance was intentional so again, I let it go.

"Is this where we purchase a ticket to talk to the famous Miss. Liliana?" He joked while he hugged me. He looked back at the circle of children huddling around her, jockeying for position to get the last few spots on her cast. I laughed. She did look like a movie star. Between the beautiful night and the crowd of happy faces wanting to be close to her, I could tell that she felt like one too. It made me feel good to see.

"I'm afraid it wouldn't do you any good." I joked back. "Not even I can get you in now." I said coolly. I turned back just in time to see the crowd carrying her off toward the hay bale trailer that was set up in the same place as last time. My chin still hung in surprise that my joke had already turned out to be true.

"S'alright. Don't you worry, darling.' She's in good hands." Jack said, nodding towards the group of kids that she was with. "I'm glad to see she's the same old cheerful, fearless girl as always. I knew a little thing like a broken bone wouldn't keep her down." He said with a chuckle as he hit me in the arm playfully. I could feel the pride in him when he said it. Like she really was his family too. It was amazing how easily he could make you feel that way. Like *real* family. I looked at Ethan again, remembering that I wasn't the only one who could attest to that.

"Now you two go and enjoy the movie." Jack insisted. "We've got things under control here." He put his arm around Shirley's waist and she waved and smiled over her shoulder at us as he swept her away towards the front of the crowd that was waiting to greet them.

"We should probably do what he says." Ethan said then, only half joking. I looked at him with amusement. He was undeterred. "Big or small, I've learned to do what Jack tells me. One thing I know for sure at this point in life. Anytime he speaks, there's a reason." He told me with a shake of his head and great meaning in his eyes." I could feel the purpose in his attitude as well, so I decided to believe him.

I sighed then. "Where?" I asked warily.

"Oh, you know where we're going." He answered with a grin that reached all the way to his eyes.

A shiver ran through me with the memory. "We won't be alone this time." I said, challenging his arrogance.

He took my hand and started walking without hesitation anyway. "I wish that mattered. You know as well as I do that it doesn't." He said with a cocky smile. I shook my head, wishing he wasn't right and I let him pull me along behind him towards the hay loft. I tried to smile politely at all the staring people that we passed along the way.

A lot of the faces were familiar to me by then but there were still plenty of others that weren't. Most smiled back. A few were just being polite and friendly, I could tell. The majority of them appeared to be more than a little surprised and amused to see Ethan holding hands with a new woman. *Geeze, not again!*

I could tell that they were all used to seeing him with women. That wasn't that surprising. It was that I was *there* with him. This was his *"home base"* so-to-speak. I was getting that while this was not quite as rare as my being at Camp, neither was it as common as him being with a woman at The Tavern. I suppose that made sense.

I tried not to look at them with my eyes too wide, while I picked up what they all thought they were doing such a fine job of hiding. I tried not to put too much weight on what they were feeling either. Thoughts about things like that could make me happy and warm deep down inside, if I let them. They also had the ability to send me sprinting madly in the opposite direction, if I thought too hard about it all. My heart started to beat faster and I felt my palms get a little clammy.

I didn't really want to deal with either extreme just then. I just wanted to get through Movie Night with the three of us in one piece. That *should* be doable, I thought to myself defiantly. I took a deep breath and let it out.

He squeezed my hand again. I could feel his amusement at what he could easily guess I was picking up. It wasn't even remotely enough to stop him though. He kept his pace steady and even and plowed forward single-mindedly. Meanwhile, I worked on pretending to be calm and holding onto my wooden smile as we made our way through the crowd.

Eventually we reached the doorway that was our goal and we slipped inside. *Phew!* I hoped that would at least be the last of the awkward confrontations that I would have to navigate. I'd already had more than enough of the shocked looks at our declaration of sorts. It was not my idea of a good time and it didn't make adjusting any easier.

I took another welcome, deep breath and let it out in a huge sigh. The darkness became complete within the first ten feet and I switched on my flashlight. He had his in his hand too, but he didn't bother to turn it on. Anyone passing by would certainly assume we were sharing mine. I found it terribly obvious though, that he just didn't need it. That left me free to aim it solely at the steps in front of me without guilt. Good thing most people didn't notice half of what they saw when they weren't really looking, I thought as we climbed.

When we reached the top of the stairs and rounded the railing, I had a *physical* flashback of the last time we had stood in that same spot together. I couldn't stop the shiver that ran through me then. It should have been too dark for him to see it, or to see me smiling. I knew without a doubt that he saw both. I could also tell that he was remembering it as well. I felt a small ripple of those feelings come over me for real then, as he relived the memory himself.

It was quickly turning into exactly what I had been trying to avoid and I was relieved that we continued right on past that spot. We reached the front area and the other people. I knew that what he said was true, and that it wouldn't stop the feelings from coming. It *would* however keep him from acting on them. His self-control was absolute. That, I knew I could count on. Well, provided he chose to utilize it of course. One never knew which way his determination would go.

Thankfully though, at that moment he chose to keep it under control. I instantly felt the desire ease up to a more manageable level. I took another deep breath and let it back out as we came out into the open area and greeted the other people who were sitting there. There were fewer that night than there had been the last time. Just two other couples. I didn't recognize either but Ethan obviously did and he introduced us.

"Simone, these are the Foster's, Artie and Joan." He said referring to the mid-fifties looking couple sitting on the farthest hay bale. From what I could see, he appeared to be an extremely average looking guy. Probably average height. He had light brown hair, light brown eyes, and a fair complexion. What a detective would call *'nondescript.'* He was emanating a quiet peacefulness that matched his look entirely.

"Joan is Shirley's baby sister." He explained and I could see the resemblance then. Both in her kind brown eyes and her own sweet disposition. Her hair however, was still a pretty dirty blonde. Though whether that was due to her being that much younger than her sister, or just a good stylist, I had no idea.

They seemed to be well suited for each other. I shook hands with both, but they stayed nestled in their cocoon of lightweight blanket shawls, holding their wine glasses. It was a fairly warm night but they looked quite cozy and content.

"These are our neighbors from over on Seven Star Road, Henry and Judy." He added referring to the other couple on the hay nest closest to ours. He was a forty-something, barrel shaped guy with a scruffy salt and pepper beard and mustache. On top of that he had a mop of thick black hair. She was a tall slender woman with a short black, shiny bob and big blue eyes. She looked to be a little younger than him, early thirties maybe.

They seemed a little mismatched as a couple, instantly reminding me of "Bluto" and "Olive Oil," minus the 'Popeye,' but I would never say such a thing out loud. They were also very happy to be snuggled up together. So I smiled at them, and they at me and I left it at *"to-each-his-own."* I shook hands with them too and then we made our way back to the loveseat shaped pile of hay closest to the entrance to make ourselves comfortable.

Ethan laid out the blanket and sat and I collapsed down next to him with a dramatic huff. Then I laughed at myself. He joined me in that of course. I put my feet up on a smaller stack and leaning in on his shoulder, tried to get comfortable.

"Well that could've gone a lot worse!" I said optimistically, thinking out loud then about him meeting my Liliana. He was opening our wine and was thoughtful for a minute before he answered.

He understood my cryptic rambling perfectly. "She doesn't trust me yet. She *likes* me though." He added with a smirk. "Am I right?" He asked, knowing I would know and that *in this instance at least,* I would tell him. That whole *keeping-part-of-our-abilities-to-our-selves* thing would work both ways for us from time to time. It was not always my place to speak other's thoughts and feelings out loud. That was another reason I didn't fight it when he asked me to deal with his limitations. I knew firsthand that it made sense. Sometimes. That was not one of those times however, so I was happy to confirm his suspicions.

"Pretty much. She usually takes a little while to warm up to new people in general. Never mind extremely *large* people!" I said with a sideways grin. "I mean think of the size differential from her perspective." I said in her defense. "She's not afraid of you though, which is good. She's just not ready to let go of *'cautious'* yet." I laughed. "I'll take that though." I said, and I would. He handed me one of the plastic cups filled with the Sauvignon Blanc that I had chosen for us and I took a good sized swallow.

We both sat back then and looked out at the crowd while we waited for the movie to start. We sipped and gazed, but neither of us bothered with the popcorn. It was a good vantage point to people watch from and that was always more interesting. I easily spotted Liliana first, still holding court on the hay wagon. They seemed to have moved on from discussing her cast, just talking and laughing randomly again, the way children should. I noticed that Jonah stayed close to her anyway, feeling a little more protective than usual. It wasn't really necessary but it was sweet. I liked him just a little bit more then. He was a good friend to her.

Seeing her content helped me to relax even more. Ethan noticed. Unfortunately for me, he was in a mood to take advantage of it then. Or *fortunately,* depending on how one looked at it.

He slid his hand down over my shoulder and continued slowly, down my arm. When he reached my bent elbow, he slipped stealthily underneath so that he could slide back up my side. The heat of his palm on my ribs went right through the thin cotton of my top and felt like a branding iron on my skin. Surely that wasn't normal. I found myself squirming up closer to him almost instantly.

I cast a glance out at our perch mates, both visually and mentally. They were each absorbed in their own private conversations. I was picking up only vague notions of what they were discussing, which was good because I wasn't interested. I was more interested in the fact that they didn't appear to be interested in us.

I looked back down and saw the colors start to flicker on the giant makeshift screen. The movie was starting. Once the big lights outside went out, it was night time dark in our loft again. Not ink-black, like the interior, but dark enough for Ethan to feel comfortable sliding his hand a little higher. My eyes closed automatically.

I took a deep breath in through my nose as his desire began to flow out and wash over me again. It had been a few days since I had felt that familiar and welcome sensation. I breathed it in like it was the very oxygen that I needed to survive. I know, *very* dramatic! God help me.

I knew in my head, that I didn't really *need* it. I also knew that given a choice, I'd rather have it than not. I wondered if I was crazy for letting that happen but his next comment made me realize that if I was, at least I wasn't alone.

"I don't like being away from you for that long anymore." He whispered in a low voice behind my ear. "I know I shouldn't admit that. Don't get mad at me." He let out a small humorless chuckle into my hair. "Somehow hiding it doesn't seem as important as being next to you again." He added while he pulled me closer. I wished that I didn't know exactly what he meant, but I did. I still tried to make light of it.

"I imagine it will get easier. You know, once that new car smell starts to wear off a little. Right?" I offered, trying to pretend that I believed it.

"*Hmpf.* Sure. That might happen." He looked down at me and I could feel one half of the very heat that we were referring to wash over me. Even by itself, it was pretty intense. *"Anything is possible."* He added just as unconvincingly.

I groaned softly and leaned my head down on his shoulder. "Okay stop now, because I've missed you too and I don't want to have to get up and walk away from you. But if you keep this up, I'll have no choice." I explained.

I looked back up at him. I was serious but all he did was smile. He leaned in and kissed me then and every nerve ending from my head to my toes came alive. "Dammit! That's it! I'm outta' here!" I said quietly, without moving so much as a muscle. He grinned wider and kissed me again and I forgot where we were. I let out a sound that I hadn't intended to voice and remembered half way though. They couldn't really see us, but if they wanted to pay attention they could certainly hear us! I had quickly turned it into a cough as a half-ass cover.

I looked up again. Not kidding around anymore. "I have to live here you know!" I said insistently, my eyes wide. I ignored him for a second while I felt out our loft-mates current frame of mind. They still didn't seem to be paying attention to us as far as I could tell. I looked back at him and I laughed then started to breathe again. "We are *not* doing this here!" I stated unequivocally.

He stared back with just as much conviction. "We can't be together later. Or tomorrow. And we can*not* wait another two days! It would truly be cruel and unusual punishment Simone. My poor staff will all have quit by then, at The Tavern and at Camp!" He added with another chuckle.

Again, I wanted to be blissfully ignorant of what he meant, but my disposition the last few days hadn't been that much better so I couldn't really argue. I didn't know the answer though.

Then his eyes darkened with delight and I could tell that he thought he did. He was instantly a lot happier! He took my hand in his and said softly. "Come with me."

We slipped out of the loft with a whispered excuse about him escorting me to the little girls room. I rolled my eyes at him but he just smiled harder. He led me easily through the deepest of the dark part of the loft without ever turning on either flashlight. I hoped that no one would come along and accidentally swipe their flashlight beam through the complete blackness and unwittingly land on us. We'd give them a heart attack for sure! For my part, I just held his hand and went completely blindly where he led me.

I thought back to when Ethan had all but surrendered to my theoretic *female-spy* alter ego, admitting that he had no defenses left against me. Like him, I personally couldn't think of a more vulnerable position to put myself in, than I was right then. Yet I had not one ounce of fear left where he was concerned. He was right. Good or bad, it was too late. The trust was there and that was the hardest part.

I could tell that he wasn't leading me out the way we had come, but we did eventually reach another set of stairs. He turned on my flashlight then and handed it to me. I took it gratefully and aimed it down at the treads in front of us. They were as roughhewn as the first set, but these were stained an earthy brown to match the walls in that particular hallway. We went down together and he turned the latch on the deadbolt to open the heavy door at the bottom. We came out on the other side of the hay loft, facing Jack and Shirley's back porch. He let the door go and it closed heavily. I heard it re-latch behind us.

"Ethan, I can't leave Liliana. I mean, I know she's fine, but it's just not right. I'm sorry. I have to stay where I can see her." I insisted, feeling disappointed for him and for myself.

He looked down at me, his confidence undiminished. "I know." He leaned in and kissed me again. Lightly. "It's one of my favorite things about you. So please, don't *ever* apologize for it." He said emphatically, before he continued leading me across the lawn. We headed towards the stables that were to our right from there. I didn't understand yet but again, I trusted him. So I followed.

We walked quickly and quietly in the dark, past the open area in between the buildings where we were semi-visible to the crowd. There were only a few people still up and about, milling around. I assumed that we were shadow blobs at best from that distance and hopefully no one would notice us. Once we passed that open space, we made our way up another path and around the corner of the stables to a back door.

Ethan preformed a familiar task and retrieved a small key hidden under a cedar plank of siding that turned on one nail. He unlocked the small door and replaced the key. He held it open for me and I heard a horse snicker at the unexpected intrusion.

"Shhhhh." He cooed to the guilty party, and it was instantly quiet again inside the stables.

"Does everyone and every *thing* always do what you want them to?" I asked in an accusing whisper.

"Damn, I wish!" He joked. "It would make things so much easier!" He answered a little louder than I ever would've dared. I turned my flashlight back on, careful not to shine it in the direction of the horse stalls. He led the way up another set of stairs directly to our left, there in the back of the stables. They were the skinniest and most rustic treads of them all but I could tell by the darkened, aged appearance in the center of each step, that they had already withstood the test of time and then some.

The stairs led us to another loft. It was long and spacious, but almost entirely full on both sides with dusty antiques, acting as an open storage area. I looked at him waiting for the punch line. Why were we up there?

My only answer was his usual grin as we followed the open path down the center of the room towards the far end. I could see then, as my flashlight reached the other side, that there was a set of doors there. He walked up to the door on the right and did his trick with the key again, this time under a floorboard, and let us inside.

The outside was deceiving, as the inside was beautifully finished. And *clean.* Nothing completely foreign to its surroundings, but still much nicer than I'd been expecting.

The walls were the color of raw butternut squash on the top half and were covered with a golden stained wainscoting on the bottom half. The floor was made up of similarly stained, wide wooden planks. I could only see a little bit of it with my flashlight at a time. I could tell that there was a table and chairs on the left side near some cabinets and what appeared to be a little makeshift kitchen. To the right nearest to us, there was a sofa and an old, large backed TV. Further down the wall near the window, there was a bed. He was hesitant to turn on a light. Since I could see the outline of the entire crowd outside that window that we were facing, I understood why.

L. Pelletier

We were more to their left at that point than behind them, but I still hoped that a flashlight would not be enough to catch their eye. I figured as long as I kept it pointed tat the floor and didn't shine it right at the window, we'd be alright. We could see them clearly from there, but with most of the light on the outside of the window, I didn't think the same was true in the reverse. I imagined all they would see was a reflection. Liliana was practically beneath us. Thankfully though, the trailer was not right under the window, but closer to the back of the stables. The distance would ensure that sound would not travel *too* easily between the two places. Only loud, *something's-wrong* noises would make it across that gap. I could *see* her easily though, anytime I wanted to. And we were completely alone.

I looked back at him as his grin grew to mammoth proportions with each one of my realizations.

"*Damn*, you're good." I said with the increasingly familiar shake of my head.

Chapter 39

"This was the first room here that was all my own. Jack and I finished both sides up here together. It was our very first project. The other room is his office, so he was almost never up here at night. It made sense at the time for an eighteen year old trying to find a little bit of independence." He was walking around, slightly nostalgic as he talked.

"It looks pretty clean, though I'm assuming it's been some time since you've lived here." I said a little confused.

"Yes." He answered with a smile. "Though it hasn't been that long since I've *slept* here." He admitted. "Shirley keeps it up for me. They also sometimes let friends or relatives from out of town use it. Whenever she comes up to clean and dust Jack's office, she does in here too. She knows that I still come here to think occasionally. Or to sleep. The familiar smells and sounds. Sometimes they help." He said and then he was quiet again. I could feel a taste of that old ugliness, some specific horror that still lingered, but also his resistance to go there which was much stronger at the moment. Even mentally he was reluctant, which was mostly for my benefit, I knew.

He turned back towards me after a few seconds and I could feel his whole air change. Effortlessly it seemed! His compartmentalizing skills were definitely enviable! I had no problem letting go of my jealousy over that though. The feelings coming at me from him were so much more enjoyable to hold on to.

He walked back over to me then and took both of my

hands in his. He kissed each palm softly and appreciatively. Then he placed them under his shirt, on his lower back. His own hands slid up my arms as he moved closer to me.

I didn't have the excuse of not having been with a man in a while to blame for the intensity between us anymore. Yet somehow he still made me feel as crazy as he did in the very beginning, just by being near me. So maybe that was never really the reason at all, I considered. Maybe that's just the way it was between him and I. *Hmmm.* Interesting concept, I allowed. *Dangerous* concept, I added more honestly.

I breathed slowly as both the internal and the external desire coursed through me. Then, wanting to be closer, I slid my hands all the way up his warm smooth, back and pulled his shirt up over his head. He didn't try to stop me. He looked at me and I felt the challenge in his stare. It said, *'You can have mine, if I can have yours."* Deal! I thought happily.

I smiled back at him and he didn't hesitate. His hands slid underneath the bottom edge of my fitted t-shirt that was gathered around my hips and ran up steadily 'til he reached my extended fingertips. He tossed both my shirt and my flashlight somewhere behind him, then turned back to face me. He reached down around my waist with both arms and lifted me up to his height, our chests crushed tightly together. It felt like heaven and I wrapped my arms around his shoulders and squeezed him back. For a moment, that sensation of being so close again finally, skin-on-skin was more than enough. I could tell that we were both reveling in it after our *"prolonged"* absence. It was *soooo* ridiculous to have missed it that much! We both knew it too, but neither one of us cared just then. Especially since there was no one else there to call us on it. We just took it in.

His arms loosened a little and I slid down a few inches. Just enough for our lips to line up. Then he kissed me again. I kissed him back that time, whole-heartedly. I completely lost track of everything else for a while after that. The next time I opened my eyes, we were lying together on the bed, though I had no specific memory of getting there. I had to laugh out loud that he could scramble my brain so entirely, but in the best possible way!

I felt like a mischievous teen again, laying there making

out covertly in the little storage loft bedroom, with just the dim moonlight that reflected off of our skin from the window for light, and the faint aroma of bug spray for cologne. As amusing and ridiculous as I found the circumstances, I knew it wouldn't stop me. Those feelings were just too amazing. They were well worth just about all the possible embarrassment that I could imagine at being discovered there. *Almost.*

He reached down and undid the button on my shorts while he stared into my eyes, looking for either permission or protest. I didn't try to stop him and he had his answer. He was pleased. He slid them off and I was momentarily aware of the movie again as the sound track temporarily got louder. We smiled at each other for a second at the sound of Buzz Lightyears' infamous quote, *"To infinity, and beyond!"* which was followed by the laughter of the crowd.

"Mmmmm. My sentiments exactly!" He seconded humorously.

"I can't believe we're doing this." I said with another laugh of my own and an added eye roll.

He stopped short on his return trip and looked up at me. I felt his control take center focus again and the heat eased up.

"Do you want to stop?" He asked, looking up at me.

Oh God! *He was serious!*

"Absolutely not!" I answered very quickly. *"Hmpf!* But thanks for asking." I added in at the end, attempting to re-lighten the mood some. He was very accommodating. The control eased up and the heat rushed back in again.

Ahhhh!!! Suddenly there wasn't enough room in my body for my breath to exist there with it and by default, it all came rushing out. He reacted to that as well and another breath later I was floating away on it all again.

When he finally came back down with me on the bed, the sensation was instant relief. Our lips met and I felt like I had been starving and he was all of my favorite foods! I could not get enough, and I could not get it fast enough! He was doing a fine job of trying, but every sweep of his lips just made me even greedier for the next. It was a really enjoyable way to spend time and I had no regrets for any of the minutes that passed there. After a while I wasn't even aware of them passing anymore.

Next thing I was aware of, *specifically,* was when we *finally* weren't separate anymore. My breath came back to me then. Everything was *perfect* then. I could ask for nothing else at that moment. I just exalted in it as it continued to build and carry me further and further away.

To that wonderful place, where for just that moment, nothing else mattered. It was the happiest place on Earth regardless of what else you've heard and he was my ticket in. I stared up into his eyes so unbelievably grateful for his existence, that again all I could think was, *'Absolutely freakin' ridiculous...'* He stared back with a feeling that was unnervingly similar but neither of us looked away. We watched as it took us up and over the top. Until it was impossible to keep our eyes open anymore.

When calm and sanity returned, he got up and went into a small room off of the kitchen area that I could tell then was a tiny bathroom. Of course. He would've needed one of those to live there, wouldn't he? I took that opportunity to catch my breath.

As reality came flooding back in, so did the need to check on Liliana. I leaned up, wanting to peek out the window at her. I raised myself up slowly beside the wooden pane, trying to get the best view without being seen myself in the process. I balanced precariously on my knees and hugged the wall closely.

I must have presented an enticing picture to Ethan from across the room because the desire that hit me when he came out of the bathroom almost knocked me right back down again. I gasped, and shivered as it passed through me, but I grabbed the window frame and held my ground.

"Seriously?!" I asked incredulously. He just grinned at me with pure joy. "I mean we just finished!" I said, both surprised and duly flattered. I shook my head at him. "Come on! A second, *please?"* I requested, still slightly breathless, myself.

He cooperated then as he walked back over to me. When I felt the intensity ease up, I quickly straightened to my knees again and found her. She was quietly watching the screen with a smile on her face. I looked up at the screen and smiled myself at the scene playing out. It was one where "Buzz" and "Woody" meet the plastic aliens in the claw machine at *Pizza Planet* and I knew roughly how much more time we had based on that. I looked back at him standing next to the bed.

"Thank you." I smiled. Once he knew that I had accomplished my task, his reprieve was immediately rescinded.

A new wave hit me and it reverberated all the way to my newly aching palms, which were apparently, nicely displayed in the shadow beside the window. All I needed to see to know that was his face. He let out a big gust of air and came up behind me. He was also being very careful not to be seen, staying just inside the shadow beyond the window. He reached for my wrists. He held them gently and used that hold to lift my arms higher, until they were fully extended, straight up on the wall in front of me.

"We're just gonna put these away for a minute." He said huskily as he let go. He slid his hands carefully, all the way down the sensitive undersides of my arms. I tried my best to stay still and upright while he traveled. When he reached my ribs, his hands slipped around in front of me and his fingertips grazed lightly over my bare chest before they continued slowly down my stomach. His lips found the back of my neck at the same time his hands found a warm place of their own to explore. I held tighter to the window frame with my right hand, as my body got weaker. I held on with what strength I had left and stayed in the surrender position as long as I could.

He really was going to get me in better shape just from my trying to keep up with him sexually I thought, tired but willing.

I looked out through the window trying hard to hold onto reality while he tried to take it away. I could only see the dark outlines of the people below, where they sat away from the spotlight that lit the little ones. I could see them well enough to tell that they were lounging comfortably and generally enjoying the movie.

It was a very strange sensation. Having a live, first person view, even a dim one, of the other people just casually hanging outside on a summer night, while he did what he was doing to my body. It was *amazing* and incredibly *hot*, but still definitely strange! So I turned and looked up at the stars in the night sky instead. Until I couldn't take it anymore.

When his kisses had almost reached the sensitive spot on the small of my back, I gave up and turned around to face him again. He straightened back up to his own knees with a satisfied smile. He pushed my shoulders back gently against the wall that my hands had just vacated. Then he placed one of his hands on either side of my head and slowly leaned in to kiss me. I closed my eyes and lost my breath for a second in anticipation.

"*Shit!*" He spit out, clearly disappointed and suddenly *very* angry. My eyes popped open instantly. His mood had changed so drastically and so lightning fast, that I was still breathless. A second later I could add wide eyed to that too. As I recovered I realized that he was looking not *at* me, but past me. Out into the darkness, over my shoulder. I wondered then, what he could see, that I had not been able to.

"What's wrong?" I asked with dread weighing heavily on my previously dreamlike buzz. "What do you see?" He answered me in one word.

"*Jeremy.*" It was not a happy statement. He stayed there watching for a few seconds more, before he looked at me again. "I'm sorry. This was not quite the encore that I had in mind." He looked down at me where I was still leaning against the wall in front of him. He took a second to appreciate the view one more time, then he shook his head and reached out to take my hand and pull me back upright. He groaned and dragged his gaze away reluctantly, to stare down at the empty bed instead. I could feel him struggling to push those feelings aside. I was glad to see that it wasn't as easy for him as usual. Of course he was still successful in the end.

He shook his head back and forth again as he turned around and started getting dressed. He stood and handed me my clothes, since he was the only one who had any hope of finding them in the dark.

I was disappointed. I'm not going to lie. Though I was sure that if it was in any way negotiable he wouldn't be handing me my clothes. I took them from him quietly and put them back on while I assessed the emotions coursing through him. There were a lot of them.

Anger. Fear. Disappointment. Uncertainty. *Desire.* Not

gone after all, just moved to the background. Anger again. Helplessness. Confusion. *Determination!* Worry. Hope. They all just kept switching in and out. A minute later, he was texting furiously back and forth with someone on his phone.

I wondered what his next move would be. I would have asked him, but I could tell that he himself didn't know yet. It was still up to fate presently how things would unfold next. It was temporarily out of his control and I could feel him struggling to figure out how to deal with that. If at all.

I saw him quickly make the bed and straighten the few paintings on the walls, before he followed me out the open door.

I turned my flashlight back on and pointed it towards the furniture graveyard and our exit, while he re-locked the knob. We made our way back down the rickety stairway and back outside in silence. Not even a whinny as we passed that time. Obviously, I wasn't the only one who could sense his current mood.

Back outside, he tried to decide on a course of action. We made our way back and stood in the darkness beside the hayloft. He paced back and forth, his mind racing a mile a minute. I sighed and stopped trying to keep up.

He quit pacing and looked around the corner again into the crowd. He stayed there for about thirty seconds, looking around the perimeter before he went back to pacing. I was feeling how worried he was that if he didn't step in, something bad would happen. He was also worried that if he did, he could just as easily end up *being* the *"bad thing"* that happens in a situation that would otherwise have turned out fine. He didn't want that.

I was worried too. With Liliana there the last thing that I needed was a scene that I would have to later explain to Ben. Or worse, to the police! That would just confirm all of Ben's fears for him once and for all. No, that would not help matters settle down one bit.

I was going to go crazy, waiting to see what would happen though! I finally couldn't wait silently anymore, so I tried to get a better idea of what was going on. "Who is he with?" I asked, feeling like that answer would give me the most information about the situation.

"Tina." He answered softly, unfortunately proving me

wrong. I was more confused than ever then. I had been expecting Dr. J, or maybe even Pete.

"Tina?" I echoed.

"You remember, the blonde from the last movie night?" He asked, trying to make me understand.

"Oh. *Ohhhhh!*" I said dramatically once it started to make a little more sense. I smiled at him then. A lot more sense actually. Look what *we* had just gone through for the chance to be together! A persons' libido could move mountains when necessary. He read my expression quite easily and responded.

"It's not the same." He insisted sternly. "He has more important things to focus on. He's not ready for that yet. He can't handle it on top of everything else right now. He's still not thinking straight." He was frustrated again.

"He's setting himself up to fail. What he needs is to get a few successes under his belt, not another failure." I could see his logic, but I also knew that Jeremy would not be thinking about it that way.

"Yeah, he's *how* old?" I asked with a smirk. "You know what his *priorities* are right now." He just glared at me in between laps back and forth. I was not intimidated. "Not everyone has your focus and your super-human level of control." I said through my teeth thinking of certain aches that were proof enough of that. "You are going to have to give him a little bit of slack here. If you don't give it to him, he's just going to take it. Case in point." I said pointing out towards where I knew he currently sat with my upturned hands.

He sighed and stopped pacing again. He turned and looked back at me. "You're right, obviously." He agreed. He was calmer. "The best I can hope for now is that I can handle 'damage control.' Last thing we need is for him to freak out in front of a crowd this size." He looked around again, assessing the disaster potential.

"But I can't just go stand over there and wait to save him from himself. He'll think I have no confidence in him at all. I'll just end up making him look and feel weak and I can't afford to do that to him at this stage either. Especially, not in front of *her!* That won't help his confidence at all!" He turned back around to face me.

"Which is why, *I* wouldn't have brought him here tonight!" He said, clearly still frustrated that someone had taken it upon themselves to make that decision without him. "I can't do anything from here though, either!! *Ugghhhh!*" He groaned in frustration then resumed pacing.

"Listen." I said, trying to be a voice of reason. "For now, why don't we just go back up to the hayloft?" I suggested. "We can keep an eye on things from there without them seeing us, at least until the end of the movie. If anything happens before then, I trust you can get down there pretty quickly. If you do have to rush off and save the day over there though, just do me a favor and make sure you leave me with a damn flashlight, will ya?" I asked with a hushed chuckle. He smiled again and I was pleased with my efforts. His intensity lifted, just a smidge.

"Don't worry about us. Liliana and I can get home on our own if we need to." I added sarcastically. "Besides, at some point I still have to find Gabby and get those tickets from her before I can leave." I added, remembering what we had agreed on. "I haven't even seen her yet." It hadn't exactly been top on my mental list so far that evening but still…

He looked around the corner one more time and feeling content that things were stable, at least for the moment, he came back and placed his hand lightly on my lower back. "Alright, come on. We'll do it your way. For now, anyway." He added. I was slightly relieved. I turned my flashlight back on as we headed one more time up what I thought of as the *"public"* stairs. I really needed to go over there and check the whole place out in the daylight sometime, I thought as an aside while we made our way back up.

I remembered as we came back out to our original spot in the open loft area, what the others up there had thought I left to do. Given how long we had been gone and the looks I got as we returned, I could just imagine the humiliating scenarios they must have been considering. I tried not to hit Ethan as his amusement reached epic proportions. He chose not to offer them any explanation, thinking they were best left to their imaginations.

We sat back down on our "nest" and I could see Jeremy

too then, in the light reflecting off the screen. He had definitely not been there before. They must have snuck in quietly after the movie started, I realized. Ironically enough, while we had been busy sneaking out. He was sitting in the center of the ocean of blankets that covered the grass. Well it was really more like *lying*, with the blonde girl I had first seen him with. *"Tina,"* apparently.

They looked very cozy and *very* content. That was the atmosphere in general down where he was. Nothing was standing out as negative to ruin that. I gave a visual check on Liliana again, although she hadn't moved and I hadn't really expected her to. Again, as a parent, it's just what you do.

Like checking to make sure they are still breathing before you can go to sleep at night. Even when they're almost six years old. It wasn't really necessary, *per se*. You just know you'll rest easier if you do it. It was because of this habitual double-checking, that I happened to notice Gabby, walking into the clearing and sitting down on a bench near the kids.

"Oh! There's Gabby!" I told him excitedly. He was watching Jeremy and he didn't look right away, deeming it somewhat less important. I noticed then, who she was with, who her new *"boyfriend"* was. It just happened to be Ethan's stalker from the Tavern, *Tie Guy!*

"Oh shit!" It was my turn then. *"...and Anderson!"*

"What?!" He asked in a hushed whisper. I had his attention at that point boy!

"To the left of the hay wagon, way in the back on the bench." His gaze switched position like a laser pointer and I knew immediately when he saw them. The fear and anger coming off of him at that development was palpable. His stare grew more intense for a second then eased up. The next minute he was texting again. Breathing. Deciding.

I got the distinct impression that he was only mildly surprised that our friendly neighborhood Agent had shown up there. He looked up with an empty stare, still deep in thought but very agitated to say the least.

"What now?" I finally asked, not able to stand it anymore.

He just stared at me, the intensity that I could feel pouring off of him, my only answer.

Chapter 40

I sat as patiently as was humanly possible, waiting for Ethan to give me some idea of what we would do next and concentrated on not freaking out in the meantime. Ethan sat quietly looking back and forth between the main players. His breathing was even and calm, but his feelings were anything but. They were like a storm, with emotions firing off like lightening in every direction one after the other. He was watching carefully and texting in between. He was much faster than I was, even with hands nearly twice the size of mine and I couldn't help but be impressed by that.

This changed things, *a lot!* That much I knew.

When he did finally speak, he was brutally honest. "I'm not sure yet. I'm still working that out."

Damn! That was hardly reassuring. "So what's the *'best-case-scenario'* here?" I asked desperately wanting to hold on to some kind of hope for a peaceful outcome. Something that wouldn't end with all of us looking like lunatics in front of the whole town, and my daughter, whose father had trusted me when I said that she would be safe around Ethan.

He looked back at me then. He could easily see the turmoil on my face. *"Relax."* He said calmly, as he slowly ran his knuckles down the side of my face.

"Oh sure. No problem!" I choked out sarcastically. He actually laughed. "How are we supposed to get the tickets now? Or even get out of here without them? I can just imagine her chasing me down through the crowd yelling, as we try to quietly sneak off." I said sarcastically.

"Listen, Jack's going to bring Liliana up here in a minute." He said perfectly calm. I wasn't sure if I loved it or hated that he could be so cool while I watched my precariously balanced existence teetering so closely to the edge. I wasn't sure exactly how to define the life that I had been building there, but whether I understood it all yet or not, I *liked* it. I hated the thought of losing it before I could even be sure of exactly what it was I was losing.

I looked back at Ethan again where he sat next to me surrounded by a cloud of calm and patience. I tried to breathe in as much of it as I could so I could calm down too and pay attention. He waited another minute before continuing. I took a slow deep breath and he smiled at me.

"You can take her, and go ahead and get the tickets from Gabby. You're right. She'll never let you walk out of here without 'em. There's nothing for you to worry about. Anderson shouldn't know who you are. Even if he does, you've done absolutely nothing wrong. Just remember that and act natural." He smiled a little at that while my eyes grew larger.

"I admit, it will be the perfect distraction for me coincidentally, to get Jeremy out of here before he draws too much attention to himself. I've worked too hard and too long already at protecting him, to go and lose him now over something as stupid as someone bringing him to *'Movie Night.'*" He said, determinedly.

"If you happen to feel Anderson out somewhat while you're at it, I won't deny that it would be very helpful as well. So we can get an idea of just how much he knows." He added as a request. He wasn't sure if I would be on board with that part or not, but he figured he would throw it out there and see. I wasn't sure how I felt about it yet either. He moved on.

"If all goes well, I'm outta' here. Take Liliana and go home. Put her to bed. At the very least, I will call or text you later once everything's worked out. Okay?"

"Alright." I agreed. It seemed the most reasonable solution. I tried to breathe in a little more of the steadfastness coming off of him. He was calmly and generously offering up his strength and I was not too proud to take it. He smiled at me again, once I started to come down off my panic peak a little. Then he pulled me tightly back up next to him. I sighed and sank in happily. Just for a minute. I could feel that he was glad for the moment as well, however brief it proved to be.

"I'm sorry that our time together was cut short. I *will* make it up to you." He said with a wicked grin and a determination that I had no trouble believing.

"I'll look forward to that." I replied just as honestly. I tilted my head back to look him in the eye and he leaned down to land his lips on mine. It was not nearly long enough, but it was soft and it was slow and it would have to hold us over. I could tell that he was putting it purposely out of his mind after that. Liliana would be coming. He pulled back and leaned away from me, with his elbows on his knees. He went back to scanning the crowd again. Back into, '*Ethan-The-Fierce*' mode. I watched his gaze as it skipped from one area to the next.

A minute later I saw a light bouncing in the darkness behind me and I could hear Jack chuckling softly at something Liliana had said. I looked back at Ethan. He was not surprised. Obviously he had already heard them coming, most likely when they had first entered the stairway and he had kissed me, I suspected.

"I tend to forget about the *hearing* part of your abilities sometimes." I admitted. He just smiled without turning to look at me and continued scanning. *And listening,* I added mentally. Liliana came up behind us and around the corner.

"Hi Mama! She half-yelled, half-whispered. She ran up and jumped up on my left side, away from Ethan. Still a little leery, but ever polite she leaned over me and looked at him. "Hi."

"Hey there Liliana. How are you enjoying the movie so far?" He asked, making small talk back. It seemed silly to take the time, but I knew it made her feel more comfortable. So did he.

"Good! I've seen it before but I love it! It's one of my favorites." She explained.

"*Hmpf.* Mine too." He answered. "I'm sorry that we might have to miss the end. Your mom told me that she had a little bit of a tummy ache and *I told her*, that I thought maybe she should go home. Get some medicine to make her feel better, or maybe just a cup of tea. I don't mind cutting out early, but I wanted to make sure it was okay with you." He lied brilliantly. It was the first time I had personally seen him do that. I was very glad then, that I had a secret weapon that would always let me know when he was lying, because he was *dangerously* good at it. Smooth as silk. Apparently he'd honed his *"acting"* skills as well as I had. They were as sharp as his emotional control.

"That's why I asked Jack to bring you up here. What do you think? Should we go? It's totally up to you." He said innocently holding up his hands, pretending to actually consider it. Of course she would never ask to stay after that and each one of us knew it. She was too good a kid, and he was sure enough of that to be counting on it already.

She played it cool, but not for too long. "Nah. We can go, mama. Like I said, I've already seen it so I don't really mind." She said with a shrug of her tiny shoulders and a smile at me.

I was even more grateful then as I slowly realized that he had purposely stepped in with the explanation to save me from having to lie to my daughter. He nodded to Jack. I also mouthed a quiet 'Thank you.' to him, over Ethan's shoulder. He nodded back, and with a tip of his hat he rolled silently back out of the loft.

"Thank you sweetie. You can put the DVD on at home and watch the rest in your pj's, okay?" I offered.

"Yes!" She said in a whispered, mock-yell with her arms up in the air like she had won something.

"I'm just going to sit still here for a few more minutes. As soon as I feel a bit better, we're going to slip out nice and quietly. Okay?" She nodded and went to play on the farthest pile of hay to our left while she waited.

We sat quietly for a few more minutes before I noticed Ethan's mood take a sharp left turn into defensive mode and I looked up in time to see his gaze shoot back to where Jeremy was.

"*Errgghh!* I knew it! " He let out the emotion, but not the swear words that I could feel behind it. "Remember that distraction we discussed?" He spoke quietly. *"Now,* would be a good time for that." He told me.

"What's wrong?" I asked him quietly, as he stared down

at the young couple on the blanket. I followed his gaze, trying to pick up some hint of what was going on. I could see that they didn't look as casual and comfortable anymore. They were sitting up. Their backs were just a tad too strait, their posture was more rigid and wary and much less lovey-dovey than it had been before. I was a little too far away to get much else. Especially with so many other people crowding around, so I had to rely on him to fill me in. I looked back at him, impatient as always.

He was shaking his head back and forth, like he wished he could mentally stop whatever was happening. "He's seen something wrong with Tina. I'm not sure what. Something about her lungs." He grunted again in frustration. I could feel that he had predicted something like this and was mad that it would come to pass anyway because someone didn't want to listen. I did wonder then, why someone had gone against his wishes that one particular time, and who? I got the impression that it was highly unusual.

"See, here's the major problem that I'm still trying to get him to understand. He has to learn not to fly off the handle every time he sees something. He still doesn't know how to tell the difference between lung cancer and a chest cold! That part's going to take some time for him to learn." He sighed heavily again. "I've got to get down there!" He still held my hand tightly as he stood to leave.

"You take good care of your mom now, okay?" He called over to Liliana, just loud enough for her to hear. "It was very nice meeting you." He said quickly, but without *appearing* to be in a hurry. She waved back and then made another diving roll into the hay. He squeezed my hand once more while he let a flood of different emotions cascade over me for a second or two. I gasped at first at the initial intensity as usual. A second later, he let go and disappeared into the darkness.

I took a deep breath and turned back to Liliana. It was time to make our exit, too. Thank goodness!

"Okay, kiddo. What'dya say? You ready?" I asked with a shaky smile, trying to appear calm.

"Ready!" She answered as happily as always. I grabbed our basket and stood up while I replaced its' contents. She came bouncing back over and aimed her flashlight towards the way out, fearlessly leading the way.

Once we were downstairs and back outside, I gave a quick glance over towards Jeremy and Tina. They were still in the same defensive positions and things appeared to be getting worse. I could feel a ripple of tension strong enough to emanating out from the area by then.

I looked around for Ethan. I couldn't see him at first, but I found him eventually. He was quietly skirting the very edge of the crowd in the dark. It would take him longer to get there, but he would draw a lot less attention that way than if he would if he went stomping through the crowded sea of blankets. I understood immediately why he did it, but I looked back at the escalating tension on the blanket and I prayed that he would make it there in time.

I took another breath and got on with my own task. I was nervous, but I didn't know why since my part was very simple and required that I break no laws. I just didn't want to be the one reason that things went awry.

I knew Gabby and her date were sitting to the left, and I was glad to be heading in that direction, *away* from the potential public disaster about to take place in front of me. I also felt guilty for that instinct but with Liliana there, I couldn't fight it. The maternal instinct that told me to protect her was the strongest of all the feelings I have ever felt. Mine or otherwise. Nothing could compete with that.

I *would* protect her. No matter what. But I could do that and talk to Gabby too, I reminded myself. Liliana was skipping happily at my side and I was glad for that vibe to hold on to. I kept walking and looked back up at Gabby then, sitting with her *"boyfriend."* I watched them as I made my way over.

She had dressed a little too nice, as was her usual M.O. Even from a distance I could see that her makeup was a little too dark and she had on a few too many pieces of jewelry. She did look pretty, it was just a little *too* pretty for a backyard Movie Night.

She was sitting next to Anderson on the bench but she had one leg draped across his lap. She looked beyond thrilled to be sitting there with him. She had no idea who he really was, or that she was being used, I could tell. I felt bad for her then. She really was a sweet woman with a great big heart, who just wanted to be loved. I had sensed long ago, that it probably stemmed from a childhood where she didn't ever get enough of that. Unfortunately, she was still trying desperately to make up for that deficit to this day.

Then of course, I wondered how Ethan had escaped that particular dysfunctional quality himself. The last thing I would ever consider him to be was *"desperate to be loved."*

I knew I didn't have time to figure that one out at the moment, so I put it out of my mind and waved to Gabby as we approached the bench. With the low level of light and her attention being so fully diverted, she was just starting to notice us. Anderson immediately looked up then too, curious who I was. I could feel his intense scrutiny, even from twenty feet away. *Whoa!* Talk about an inquisitive mind! His aggressiveness instantly made me more nervous and it took all of *my* acting skills not to let it show.

"Simone! Hi!" Gabby said, a little too enthusiastically as usual. "Hey there, Liliana!" She added.

"Hi." I said back, keeping it as simple as possible while Liliana simply waved. "I'm sorry to interrupt your movie, but I wanted to get those tickets from you now if I can, since I'm going to head out a little early. I'm feeling a tad bit under the weather." I started to explain.

"Oh no! Will you still be able to make the show tomorrow?" She asked, clearly worried about her original issue.

"Oh sure! Don't worry. I think it's just a little 24 hour stomach bug." I said with a wave of dismissal and a hand on my belly. I was a little embarrassed to say that, even as an adult. Especially to strangers, but I had to admit that it was a good cover. Nobody really wanted to ask for more details about your stomach bug.

"Oh you poor thing! Well I hope you feel better real fast. You should make yourself some ginger tea. That always helps me." She insisted while she got up to retrieve the tickets from the back pocket of her bright white jeans. As she handed them to me, she introduced me to her *"friend."*

"Simone, this is my friend John." She said while she rubbed his neck. "John, this is my friend Simone that I was telling you about." She said and I was instantly worried about the familiarity in that. *Shit!*

"Nice to meet you." I said with another small wave. I kept my distance but I could feel the wheels turning in him. I wondered then if Gabby had told him that her *"friend, Simone"* was dating *"that Ethan guy,"* and if maybe that was why he had come with her tonight. Always assume the worst...

I could feel his inquisitiveness working overtime and I tried hard to keep my panic in check. I decided that it was probably time to go. It would be hard to distract them from Ethan and Jeremy, if he saw me as a direct connection to them. I still couldn't get a handle on how much he knew about me, but I could tell that he was in stealth mode himself. With as much energy as he was putting into trying to keep an eye on everything, it had to mean that he at least knew Jeremy was there.

I wondered then quite stressfully, how much time exactly Ethan would need to get him *out* of there! I wanted to turn around and see how things were going, but I didn't dare give his position away with my pointed attention. Just in case. That was evasiveness 101.

I tried frantically then to think of a neutral topic that wouldn't make him think about Ethan or Jeremy. What I came up with under pressure was, "Nice night, huh?" It was beyond disappointing, but he responded anyway.

"Yeah. It's been downright tropical for this time of year." He said casually. I still couldn't tell if he was playing with me or not. He was good at switching his thoughts in and out very quickly. I didn't know if it was possible for it to be intentional, but it sure felt like it. It reminded me of the first time I had met Ethan. Too smart. Too aware.

"Yeah. Probably means we're in for a bad winter. That usually ends up being the case. We have to suffer at some point, to balance it all out right? It *is* New England after all." I joked with the typical amount of sarcasm. I realized in the end though, that he had enjoyed that statement just a little too much. He was feeling a little smug then.

"Yup. That's justice I suppose. You can put it off, but you can't ever escape it entirely. Eventually it catches up with you." He stared into my eyes when he said it and the certainty that he knew exactly who I was, flowed through me and left me frozen inside. Gabby was still as obliviously ignorant of what was going on as she had been all along. Sitting and snuggling into him again without even noticing his *ready-to-pounce* posture. Liliana was still standing quietly, holding my hand while the adults made small talk. Outwardly, everything appeared to be perfectly normal. But in reality I knew, *everything* had just changed!

He was officially calling me out and declaring himself the enemy. A federal agent was now my enemy.

!!!!...

Again I digested, but I tried not to let it show. I couldn't exactly pick up Liliana and take off at a dead run without some sort of an explanation to Gabby. No, that wouldn't end well either. He grinned and his smug attitude gained strength. He knew I didn't want a scene. Especially not with my daughter by my side. He was prepared to take full advantage of that fact. He was much more familiar with me than he should be, I realized then for sure. He was obviously more well-informed in general than we had originally thought. That made me the most nervous. Know your enemy and all. *He sure knew his...*

One thing was super clear right away about *him* though. From the satisfaction he was getting being momentarily in control, I knew for sure that he had no problem using whatever means were necessary to accomplish his goals. Someone like that was definitely dangerous.

He was still grinning and my mind was racing along with my heart! What to do? More importantly, what *not* to do?! I needed to be very careful around him. Any information was a weapon in his hands.

I wanted to text Ethan, but I couldn't at the moment and by the time I could, it would probably be too late. I needed to get Liliana out of there first and foremost, before he could use that particular weakness against me. I also needed to make sure Jeremy would be safe, although I had no idea how to help with that one at all.

I tried hard not to look and see if he was still there, or if it was safe to offer an excuse and make a bee line home yet. Unfortunately it wasn't long before I knew that all my efforts to divert attention were in vain, as Jeremy's shouted obscenity crossed the distance.

I froze. Anderson and I locked eyes and I tried desperately to pretend that I hadn't heard anything. His happiness knew no bounds then, as he pulled a small walkie-talkie out of his pocket. He slid Gabby's leg off of his lap without paying her any attention and stood, looking out into the crowd for the source.

"Excuse me dear. I think I'll stand for a while." He threw over his shoulder at her wounded complaint. "Stretch these old legs." He said it softly and apologetically and she ate it up. She noticed his walkie-talkie and made excuses for him pointing out that he had a *"very important job"* and was usually "on call" as he walked a few feet away.

Meanwhile, I tried to pretend that the sound had been insignificant. Just some kids talking too loudly at movie night. He was a kind of far away from us for Anderson to know who it was for sure in the dark, but he was still pretty confident that the "scene maker" was most likely to be our guy. I made a slightly confused, funny face anyway and smiled, hoping to dissuade him. Gabby laughed, but I could tell that he didn't buy it. He went back to searching the crowd behind me again. I turned just enough to see Jeremy and Tina standing up on their blanket.

That was it. I was done, because he wasn't going to be *"distracted"* anymore. I decided that my best move then was to get away from him and find some other way to help. I quickly said my goodbyes to both of them and Liliana waved silently as I tried to make a hasty exit. He kept his eyes on me, but he didn't try to stop me from walking away. How could he?

I headed towards the main house and the road, away from Jeremy and the building commotion. Like I had no interest in that situation what-so ever but my heart was pounding. I was glad when I could feel him watching me and following my exit in that direction. As long as I could hold his attention, I could still do my job to some extent and help Ethan. I picked up Liliana and held her in front of me as a precaution, then I continued to walk slowly towards the farmhouse, staying in the lighted areas longer than I would have otherwise. It was working nicely for a minute or two. Until Jeremy's next, even louder comment reverberated across the distance again.

"Fine. Go! I don't care anymore!" He shouted despondently.

We all stopped and turned to look then. It was pointless not to after that. I saw Tina as everyone else did, running away from their cozy spot towards the long driveway and her car, blonde hair flying high behind her in her haste. She'd had one hand over her mouth as she went, in a vain attempt to hold her sobs inside.

While everyone watched her speedy departure, I turned back to find Jeremy. There was no hope of hiding him in the crowd after that. Especially since he was standing tall right in the center of it, also watching her with disbelief on his face and not a single care left for his own safety.

Crap!

Chapter 41

The indecision was paralyzing at first. Part of me wanted to pick up Liliana and run towards the house and safety. Another part of me wanted to run over and help keep Jeremy safe. From himself, from the heartbreak that I could feel from across the property, and from the threat that he was currently underestimating so foolishly.

Then there was a whole other part of me that wanted very much just to be able to help Ethan. He had reached Jeremy's side pretty quickly after Tina had left it. As it turned out, he was just in time to hold onto him and keep him from running recklessly after her, even though he had said he didn't care. It was obvious that it wasn't true in the slightest.

I also hated that Ethan not only had an emotional Jeremy to deal with, but he also had Anderson to somehow evade as well. That was not going to be easy I knew, with only one road in and out of there. I just wished that I also knew what in the world to do about that!

Liliana and I were standing far enough away by then, to have a better view of Anderson than he had of us at least.

I looked back over at him and I could see him staring right at Ethan and Jeremy while talking on his walkie-talkie again. *Shit!* Backup? Sure felt like it. He was definitely taking advantage of the time they were spending arguing. Seeing that finally urged me back into action myself. I let go of Liliana's hand to text Ethan.

"Stay *right* here! Okay?" I instructed her calmly, but seriously when I let go. She listened without question. Empath or not, she was at the very least, extremely intuitive. She nodded and stayed glued to my thigh. Unlike the rest of the crowd, she wasn't really interested in what the commotion was all about. She had noticed, but she had deemed it unimportant and was mostly just bored. That was okay with me too. It was much better than many of the alternatives.

U gotta go. Calls going out 4 b-up!

I typed as fast as the tiny little letters on the screen would allow me and hit send. I looked back up at him where they stood with their arms locked on each other's' shoulders, arguing heatedly. The volume was a little lower then, but it was definitely still drawing attention. Not enough for anyone else to want to get involved yet though. The spectators were content, at least for the time being, to remain spectators.

It was clear to everyone then, *heightened* empath or not, that Jeremy was hurting. *Badly.* Ethan was currently taking the brunt of it. Of course, he didn't care. He just kept trying to reign him in, so he could get him *out.*

How can I help?! I thought over and over frantically. I wanted to go over there, but I knew that Ethan had as good a chance as any at calming him down. I also didn't want to make the spectacle any worse than it already was by adding more bodies to it. Most especially not the tiny, precious body that still clung to my leg. I wasn't sure what to do, but I really felt like I needed to do *something!* I moved over into the shadows to think.

As I stood frozen in limbo, one of the answers I sought so desperately came up and presented itself to me. It was a Godsend in the form of Shirley.

She had two other little ones hanging on her skirt and one in her arms already. Jonah stood quietly behind her, waiting. "I was wondering if Liliana would like to come watch a movie with us, up at the main house where it's quieter? Maybe even have a little slumber party?" She asked sweetly, with a wink at me. *Phew!*

"Oh, that would be great! Wouldn't it honey?" I asked excitedly.

She smiled broadly and agreed wholeheartedly. "Oh yes!

Yay!" She replied, happy to have something fun to do again. It was disappointing to feel like I was going backwards a little where she was concerned, but at the moment her safety was more important. "Are you coming mama?" She asked automatically. Of course that made me feel both better and worse at once.

"Not just yet. I may have that tea first." I offered, fibbing just a little. "See if I can settle my tummy. You go on ahead with Shirley though and I'll join you guys a little later, okay?" I offered.

"Okay, mama." She answered dutifully, already moving on mentally. Shirley smiled at me and offered to take my basket off my hands as well. I was momentarily surprised as I had almost forgotten that I was still carrying it. I handed it over gratefully. Liliana took Shirley's hand then and gave me a kiss before skipping happily, and thankfully quickly with the small group up to the house. When I saw the big heavy wooden door close, I let out a huge sigh of relief. That's number one, I thought. After that I could at least attempt to be ready to help tackle whatever would come next.

I turned back toward my friendly Federal agent, to see if he had noticed the retreat of our "older women and children," worried he would move even faster. Thankfully he was still focused on the spectacle in front of him like everyone else. If he had noticed, it didn't seem to matter to him because it didn't register in his feelings about the situation. Not enough to divert his attention anyway. *Good!*

I looked over to see what was going on with Ethan and Jeremy after that and things appeared to have calmed some. People around them were sitting up and talking amongst themselves in spite of the movie that played on regardless. Some were commenting on the unfolding situation. I could tell who they were by the pointing as well as the wariness of their attitudes.

Many were just taking advantage of the disruption to address their own agendas. Those were the ones not really paying attention at all. There were still more of those so far and that was slightly encouraging somehow. They were just feeling like *"you eventually see everything in a small town."*

I was getting the distinct impression that it wasn't all that unusual for someone's personal problems to be played out on such a public stage around there. I, on the other hand, was *terribly* uncomfortable with the situation taking place. They didn't realize that there was more to it than met the eye. Knowledge could be a double edged sword sometimes for sure!

I scanned the crowd some more, looking for signs of *other* trouble. Quite literally, since I didn't know where Anderson had gone. I just knew that he suddenly wasn't standing over by Gabby anymore.

I spotted a suit skirting the edge of the area and I thought that I had found him. I realized as the suit moved from one tree to the next though, that it was a different color than he had been wearing and therefore didn't belong to Anderson at all. I looked to my right and immediately spotted another, making his way quietly behind the hayloft. *Dammit!* It would appear that the Calvary had arrived. *Geeze! That was fast!*

I could see even more suits then, lining the edge of the crowd. Three or four minimum. It was hard to count since they didn't stay still. Surly that meant that Ethan saw them too though, right? What was it that he had said before? *"If he happened to be paying attention to anything else at the time."* Right! Was he then?

I looked back over at them and I saw him putting his arm around Jeremy's shoulder and starting to head out of the safety of the crowd while they were still talking, quieter than before. He was looking down at his phone while he walked and I saw his posture change. He held Jeremy's shoulder then to stop him tentatively. *Phew!*

I texted him again.

At least 4 surrounding you now!

I hit send and a second later, I saw him look up and gaze around the area slowly. So did Anderson. They locked eyes momentarily. Then Ethan looked back towards me and I felt a small echo of his concern radiating out in my direction as well. My phone chimed. I looked down at the screen.

Got it. Thanks. U should go.

Was his ever considerate response. Of course. That was what we had agreed upon, wasn't it? Always willing to stand and fight alone. To protect everyone else. Who was there to protect him, I wondered?

I looked around at the crowd of people on the lawn and on the fences. Families with groups of teenagers. Grandparents with little kids. Not only were they not able to protect him but if all hell broke loose, he'd most likely be worried about all of them too!

Then there was Jack of course, although I had no idea where he had gone to either. Still, I was sure he would do what he could, like sending Shirley over to help me out. How much more he was capable of, I had no idea. Any scenario I could think of seemed like an awful lot to expect from a lone, middle aged farmer.

I gazed back over where Ethan stood again and I realized that I had already made my decision. I was still petrified of the consequences that may come with it, but I knew that I would stand by him regardless. As long as it was within my power to do so. I couldn't walk away from him. I didn't want to.

Liliana was safe, and it was obvious that Anderson somehow already knew I was involved. So there was really no reason left for me to run and hide. No, what I wanted most then, was to help somehow. *But how?!*

Lil left w-Shirley. I'm good. Tell me how 2 help!

I hit send and waited nervously in the shadows for what felt like an eternity. I switched from foot to foot. I watched them talking, still heatedly, but too softly for anyone else to hear. *Planning something,* I hoped!

I also watched the slow progression of at least two more federal agents, making their way around the stables. I looked worriedly at the spectators, but with Ethan and Jeremy keeping their interest, they were still oblivious to the real action taking place around them. *So far.*

It was easy to be grateful for the things that people could miss. I couldn't help saying a quiet *"Thank goodness!"* to myself for that just then. I knew Ethan had recognized that fact long ago and was good at using it to his advantage.

Unfortunately, so was Anderson. As they continued to enthrall the crowd with their fevered whispering, he was still hiding somewhere, using the time to continue building his advantage against them.

I saw Ethan's head snap up and towards the street then. I followed his line of sight and landed on the headlights of a large black truck pulling an even larger black trailer as it turned slowly down the driveway. There was another coming from the other direction that was slowing as well.

It was bad and getting progressively worse. I had lost count of just exactly how bad.

Jeremy got louder again momentarily. *"It doesn't matter!"* He shouted and tried to pull away again. Ethan held tight. He was keeping his calm as usual. I was starting to think it might be misplaced though. I couldn't see a way out of there for them and I was really starting to get scared.

I wondered how he could still be so calm then. Was it just for Jeremy's sake? I knew he was capable of doing that just for someone else. He was already in the habit of doing it for me, although for much different reasons.

I *really* wanted to know then, where the Hell Anderson had gone to, that sneaky bastard! I scanned the area some more until I finally found him. He was there, lurking in the shadows over by the far edge of the blanket dwellers.

If Ethan tried to head towards the woods instead of the road, he would have to go through Anderson to get there. I was sure that wasn't an accident.

He was still communicating on his walkie-talkie, pacing slowly back and forth. I could feel his confidence from there, once I had honed in on him. That didn't help mine one bit. I wanted to think he was wrong to feel that way, but the facts were not on our side. Two men, one older, one teenager and one woman did not make a very impressive defense. Not against innumerable Federal agents. In fact it was almost comical in its inequality. A minute later, it was somehow even worse. I didn't know how yet, but I was sure that it was based solely on the attitude change I felt from Anderson's direction.

He put down the walkie-talkie and smiled. It was a slow, self-satisfied kind of smile. A short moment after that, an icy cold wave of his ruthless intentions blew right through me and it left me with a very uncomfortable chill up my spine.

I looked back at my "team" and tried to decide quickly, on the most useful form of self-sacrifice. Sadly I could think of no other way to help. Maybe I could at best, distract one or two of them for him with my own arrest. For what, I wasn't sure yet but I would think of something. I just hoped that it would be enough of a hole for him to slip through and that it wouldn't be a totally wasted effort. Because after that one, unoriginal distraction, I wouldn't be any good to anyone. It wasn't a good plan but it was the only one I had the moment.

That was the last conscious decision I remembered giving any thought to. After that thought, everything else happened so fast that all decisions were either made for me, or with lightning speed.

Chapter 42

Anderson called out to Ethan then. Quite loudly and with obvious disregard for the attention he garnered. He wasn't concerned with stealth anymore. His men were in place. He was ready.

Game on.

"Hand him over Mr. Stone. This has gone on long enough! You have no rights over the boy and you know it." He insisted. The crowd was definitely interested then. They all turned to look first at Anderson, wondering who he was. Then they looked back at Ethan to see what he would do. Anderson went on, making his case.

"The boy is not only a public safety hazard, being a carrier of a very rare and dangerous virus, but he's also a danger to *himself.* Look at him! He a mess! This current psychosis is a direct result of his recent illness. He needs proper treatment if he ever hopes to overcome it. Treatment that *we* can give him at our *federally* funded facilities, where every available new technology is at our fingertips. You're only hurting him by keeping him from us." He declared boldly.

That had certainly gotten the crowds' attention. A lot of them were even more wary of Jeremy and his *"mysterious virus"* then. Some even went so far as to unconsciously back away a little. *Great.* That's just what Jeremy needed. Excuse the prepubescent reaction but all that came to mind was, *"Not!!"*

Anderson had counted on it though, that bastard. He continued using every tool available to him to try and control the situation. He was also putting an awful lot of his cards out on the table for the public to see. His confidence was even more obvious in his willingness to do that. It worried me immensely.

Ethan responded in his usual calm demeanor. It was maddening how unaffected he was by it all.

"You'll forgive me if I disagree. On all counts." He replied clearly over the crowd. They were glued to their seats, watching the unfolding situation like it was the nights intended entertainment. "Jeremy is perfectly fine, aside from some normal, teenage relationship drama." He said loudly with a sideways grin, stretching the truth just a little for the communities' sake. He gave Jeremy's shoulders a shake and laughed. He wanted them to know they didn't have to worry. He knew too well how bad it would be for Jeremy to be ostracized so carelessly.

"If you really knew anything about our boy at all, you would know that. Obviously you don't. So as much as we appreciate your concern, we take care of our own around here just fine." The crowd grumbled and nodded in support of that statement. "Thanks anyway *Mr.* Anderson." He answered back, purposely getting the title wrong. He was hoping that *Agent* Anderson would correct him in front of everyone. Anderson caught the slight, but unfortunately he didn't take the bait.

"You're outnumbered Stone, and well beyond your element here. Do yourself a favor and stay out of things you don't understand." When Ethan didn't scare off easily, he moved on.

"There's no way for you to *slip out* on us this time around. Why continue to fight this and endanger more innocent people? Anyone here who is foolish enough to try an assist you in this madness, can and will be arrested for obstructing justice and/or harboring a dangerous person, which you are currently guilty of." He declared loudly for the crowd. "This isn't even about you, Stone. If you were as smart as you seem, you would keep it that way!" He yelled back, signaling the end of his patience.

Jeremy spoke up for himself then, thinking maybe that was all it would take.

"I don't have to go anywhere with you and I don't *want* to! So just go away! Leave us alone!" His voice was shaky but unapologetic. The crowd cheered a little again and looked back at

Anderson expectantly.

"I know you're having a rough time right now, son." He fired back with undue familiarity. "I know you're scared and confused." He slowly moved closer as he talked. "Unlike your friends here, I can actually help you get *better.*" He smiled at the surprise evident on Jeremy's face. Lots of people had talked to him about "helping" him but no one had said anything about him getting *"better!"* That definitely got his attention. Ethan's too. Hell, truth be told *mine too*!

What?!

"That's right. We've dealt with cases just like yours all across the country and *we do* have the ability to *cure* you." I could see Jeremy's shock as well as feel it then. Anderson paused happily to let his proclamation sink in a little deeper. Then he went on, even more confident than before.

"There *is* a cure you know. I bet he didn't tell you that, did he?" He challenged. Trying to confuse and lure Jeremy. Divide his loyalties. "You just have to trust me. I know and want what's best for *you!* Not what's best for my own personal agenda, like *some* who would pretend to be helping you." He was lying through his teeth, but he did it very well. Too well. He kept walking and both Ethan and Jeremy had begun to back up away from the few people left near them, one step at a time.

"We're not here to try and *'acquire'* you into our organization and take advantage of your unfortunate illness, like small, selfish minds would do." He accused. He was working hard at separating Jeremy from his only remaining comfort zone. If he could do that, he knew he would have him. I also knew that Ethan wouldn't let that happen. Not if he could help it, anyway. The odds were stacking higher and higher against him though.

"We just want to help you get well again. Not keep you trapped in your sickness forever, just to serve our own selfish purposes." The comment was nothing short of an outright accusation of abuse and I could feel the burning anger building in Ethan at that. He was reaching dangerous territory traveling up that avenue, and I didn't know whether to hope he stopped or that he'd keep it up until he paid for it. He wouldn't be alone though. If that happened it would cost everyone, so I didn't hope for it anymore.

I could tell that Jeremy was at the very least, suddenly confused by the mind blowing things that Anderson was claiming. He pressed on, smart enough to push his momentary advantage.

"That's all you really want right now, Jeremy. Isn't it?" He asked with a false innocence, knowing very well that he was playing on his absolute biggest weakness. Offering him an easy way out of the whole situation. *"To get better?"* He taunted.

The worst part was, it didn't *all* feel like an outright lie and I couldn't figure out why. I knew for sure that the things he said about Ethan's intentions were untrue. No one could ever convince me otherwise on that even if I *didn't* have my empath skills to rely on. But what was with the talk about a cure? I couldn't help but wonder for just a heart fluttering moment, if it could possibly be true. He knew *something* about it, of that I was sure. There was no way to know what exactly. Still too many missing pieces.

Jeremy was actually wavering momentarily too and that was the scariest part of all. *I* knew that Anderson was lying about the most important thing. The wanting to *"help"* him part. Only Jeremy couldn't know that. Not like I could. Then I thought about it and I realized that he probably didn't even *know* that I could.

He would *want* to hope. He would *want* to believe what Anderson was feeding him, I knew. Anderson knew that too, and just how badly. Of course, he would use it to his advantage. That was quickly developing as his most prominent trait in my eyes. Jeremy was reluctantly becoming just a little bit hopeful in spite of his better judgment. I could feel it. It *was* pulling on him.

I could feel Ethan's worry at that too. He knew very well that it was the ultimate bait. He remembered how much he would have given to make it all just go away when he was Jeremy's age. He was talking softly to Jeremy, working hard and fast to try and undo the damage. With everything in his life currently falling apart on him, and Anderson dangling hope in front of him that he could make it all go away, it was hard and getting harder to convince him. Ethan's task then was equivalent to treading deep waters, while swimming backwards, and trying to get upstream that way.

I was still frozen in my spot. Barely a minute had gone by,

but I had done nothing so far besides observe and analyze all of it in my head. From there, that helped no one. I texted Ethan, even though it was probably pointless. It was something.

He's lying about wanting to help Jeremy. Tell him that! About me too & that I'm sure!

I sent the text and continued watching like everyone else. I didn't mention anything about the *"cure"* part of Anderson's statement, but I would definitely bring that up later. If I ever got the chance, I thought rather dismally.

Anderson had stopped advancing but only because he had them neatly trapped and he knew it. There were men behind them in every direction and he was blocking their front. He was just waiting for Jeremy to either run straight to him and into his arms, or away from him and therefore still into his clutches. One way or the other, he was sure he had him. He could almost taste it.

Jeremy seemed to actually be considering it, God help him. The rapt audience waited with bated breath. Time felt like it stopped.

Until my phone chimed. I looked down. I was surprised to see that it was Jack and not Ethan.

Get ready! Gonna pick u up! We're outta here!

What? Pick me up? I was instantly confused. I tried to think about being *"ready"* but it was hard when you had no idea what to be ready *for.*

I looked up and saw Jeremy pull away from Ethan and start to walk slowly and unsurely over to Anderson. Ethan looked upset, but he gave up trying to stop him. I didn't want to believe my eyes and what I was feeling didn't agree with what I was seeing, so I chose not to. It wasn't easy but I held on tightly to my faith in them both. It had to be part of the plan somehow.

I had to!

But what the Hell was the damn plan?! I wondered frantically. I wished that I could pick that up as easily and as clearly as Jeremy's growing fear upon his approach. Every step made him more fearful and more leery than the last. Surely he wasn't just going to surrender himself after everything he'd been through, was he? Why would Ethan let him? Why would Anderson really believe that he would? None of it was making sense to me and that was driving me crazy very quickly.

I focused hard on Ethan to see what I could figure out and he stared right into my wide eyes. He was pushing off calm but I could feel a very tense readiness also, reminding me of what Jack had said. I took a deep breath and tried hard not to panic but the confusion was killing me!

I couldn't be sure with my average vision, but I thought that he actually grinned at me then! *Ugghhhh!* If we got out of this, I was going to make him pay for that one, I thought to myself. Oddly enough though, as usual the anger gave me strength. Helped me to hone in my energy and focus better. Then I shook my head as the realization hit me.

Dammit, he'd done it again. I smiled back, although weakly, knowing it was more than enough for him to see it. I felt his amusement for real that time. Just for a second, but I could instantly tell the difference. Then we both looked back at Jeremy.

He had almost reached Anderson, who was waving his men in closer to tighten the net. I could feel finally that, that was what Ethan wanted. I still had to wait to find out why though, since aside from being able to fly, I didn't imagine a single plausible exit strategy.

A second and a half later however, it all became very clear. I heard the roar of an engine and turned to look just in time to see Pete on a 4-wheeler racing in from behind the barn and Anderson's line of henchmen! He came barreling towards us at top speed! Anderson looked up as surprised as everyone else as Pete launched off of a strategically placed trailer and through the air right over the line of agents. He landed with a heavy bounce, righted the quad, then and swerved to a stop beside the crowd, right in between Anderson and Jeremy. Literally within *feet* of both! Everyone was temporarily stunned into silence, myself included.

"I believe *my* 'son' said he had no interest in going with you." He said matter-of-factly to Anderson, correcting his earlier familiarity. "Like my friend here said, thank you anyway but don't call us, we'll call you, K?" He said sarcastically. Then he twitched his head at Jeremy who didn't need any more encouragement than that. He swung up and over, onto the back of the seat behind his dad and held on tight.

"See ya!" Was all he had to say as Pete gunned it again and they pulled away directly through the human line that time, sending henchmen diving in all directions! Once he got past them, he headed across the field towards the orchards and the forest beyond. Anderson yelled at Pete to stop but before he could finish his tirade, a second 4-wheeler came gunning around the riding paddock and skidded to a stop right next to Ethan so he could jump on. Unlike Jeremy, he jumped in front of the rider that I was shocked to see was *not-so-wimpy-after-all* Artie. I was definitely a little surprised by *that* surprise!

Before I had a chance to pick my chin up off the ground, Jack burst out from behind the stables on a third 4-wheeler and drove up behind me.

"Hop on Sugar!" He yelled over the engine with a huge grin. Somehow my eyes got even wider.

I looked over at Anderson. He was waving his arms frantically at his men, trying to keep the exits covered. It was all happening almost simultaneously and they were scrambling since they had nearly reached the center of the area by then. They were surrounded themselves at that point, *and* they were on foot. Not to mention that no one was headed for the blocked off road, like Anderson had obviously anticipated.

The crowd was on its' feet and began to clear a path for us, but oddly enough, they didn't just run in all directions in a panic like one would expect. They weren't helping the agents either, who were struggling to get through the mass of people. They got out of our way, but moved purposely into theirs! I couldn't believe it. Was there no one in town that wasn't leading a double life?! *Hah!*

I looked over at Ethan across the chaos. He cocked his head to me in a gesture similar to Pete's that said I should follow. Then he made a quick U-turn and headed back out the way Artie had come rushing in, towards the path in the forest to the left.

"Alrighty then! What the Hell!" I said, officially throwing caution to the wind and hopping on behind Jack. I didn't know where we were headed or what we were in for, but I knew I didn't want to be the only one left standing around after everyone else got away. There were too many questions that I wasn't prepared to have to answer.

I held tight to his waist as we accelerated and in mere seconds we rolled right past a shocked and outright pissed off Anderson. As we flew by on our way into the forest, a wave of pure hatred hit me that almost knocked me off the seat. *Damn!* I was really glad then, that I hadn't hung around to bear the brunt of *that!*

He and his men were pulling it together quickly though. Before we even reached the path I saw the door crop down on the back of one trailer and the motorcycles pulling out. The second door was opening and another black trailer had just come down the driveway when I turned back. Apparently they weren't totally unprepared for that possibility. They had underestimated Ethan just enough to give us a head start, but that was all. I told Jack what I saw, while he drove as fast as he could without knocking us both off.

"They may be faster, but they don't know our backyard. I hope they have a few stunt drivers on their team or it won't even be a contest!" He proclaimed happily. I could feel how much he was looking forward to the chase and I had to rethink my earlier character assessment of him as *"a mere middle aged farmer."* Clearly he still had tons of gumption and vitality left in him yet!

We continued to skid and dip and splash through small streams for another mile or so until, to my great surprise, he pulled around behind a giant rock on the side of the trail and stopped. I was about to ask why he would do such a thing, when I saw Ethan's quad with Artie on back hiding there in the dark underbrush. He smiled, hopped off and started jogging over to us.

"No offense sugar, you're fanny is lovely and all." Jack called back over his shoulder. "But it ain't *my* bitch-seat that it belongs on. I'm just a delivery service." He finished with a devious chuckle. I looked at Ethan and he looked down in disbelief and shook his head back and forth with a laugh of his own. Then he looked back up at me and I instantly felt his deep concern for me mixed in with a stronger than usual desire. The concern was new and even though I instantly felt bad for adding that to his already long list, I couldn't help being warmed by it. The desire, on the other hand, I was getting very familiar with and I found that I had missed it already! I wasn't about to admit to that though.

"Come on darlin.' You're with me. You just purposely pissed off a Fed on my behalf. The least I can do is escort you *personally* out of harm's way." He said, trying to play it off as just a 'tit for tat.' We both knew better though. Based on what I got off of Jack and Artie, they did too.

"Hurry!" He urged then. "We still have to lose 'em!'" He said to me and I was immediately spurred into motion.

I thanked Jack for the lift and slid off of his seat. I ran over to Ethan while Artie hopped on back with Jack. Jack turned his lights back on and headed out in the opposite direction, *"woo-hooing"* the whole way. It appeared that he would act as a decoy at best, but a distraction at the very least.

I slid my leg over the back of Ethan's seat and held tightly to his mid-section. Partly because I needed to and partly because I *really* wanted to. I could tell that he too felt immeasurably more secure once I did. I was right where he wanted me and despite all the commotion around us, I couldn't be happier about that. It was right where I wanted to be, too. Even if I could, I realized I wouldn't change a thing. I had never felt surer about where I belonged before. It was a deeply settling feeling, completely separate from the external turmoil.

I thought briefly about the widely varying possibilities for the outcome by the end of the night. I also thought about the guilt and the responsibility that he would feel if something went wrong. Especially with me. It was a possibility and I knew I had to be okay with that in order to be with him. To *really* be with him. Not just half way. I had to admit that he deserved more than that. I spoke my feelings out loud for once. A big deviance from the norm for me. I leaned up right under his ear.

"As long as I know Liliana's safe, whatever happens from here on out, I have no regrets Ethan. I want you to know that!" I tightened my grip around his waist and finished by lifting up to reach his neck and placing a quick, hot kiss there as he pulled back out onto the trail. He didn't have to respond verbally. I could feel how he felt about my proclamation. His appreciation washed right over me. I would have loved to kiss his neck again but to try that twice was to endanger teeth and arteries both on that terrain.

Ethan made a hard right and we took off in yet another direction. There were three of us out there then, revving loudly and bouncing all over, our headlights flickering madly like lasers through the thick wall of trees. Then I saw two more vehicles coming down the trail towards us and at first, I thought we were already caught. As they came closer I noticed their double headlights and realized that they were additional quads and not the motorcycles that I had seen back at Jack's. They flashed their lights at us as they approached and Ethan flashed back. He veered over to the edge of the trail to let them pass by on our left. As he did, I could see that it was our friends "Bluto" and "Olive Oil" from the hayloft on their own 4-wheeler. Right behind them we saw another one and I could see that it was Hank and Cook on that one. I started to breathe again. Our "back-up" had arrived.

They also drove by on our left side and Hank and Ethan high-fived each other as they passed. I looked back over my shoulder and saw them split up behind us and go in opposite directions from each other. The more the merrier. I was sure then that was the point. Just to keep them constantly guessing which zig-zagging, 4-wheeling duo, was the one they wanted. At least long enough for that *particular* one to get away.

As I looked in front of us again I could see two more sets of lights coming down a trail to our left. I noticed that there were 4-wheelers lights flashing and tires bouncing all over the forest then. They would be hard pressed to find the needle in the haystack out here now, I thought with some relief. Though that would also mean the forest soon would be crawling with agents who would be searching in every direction. No one way would be *"safe."* With that thought, the small amount of relief I had felt went away again.

As I worried about that, I saw the first *single* beam headlights starting to flash through the trees from the opposite direction. There were a lot more than I had expected and they weren't nearly as far behind as I wanted them to be.

Ethan cranked his right hand back on the accelerator again and we flew up and over the nearest hill. Our lights flashed across the trees as we climbed. When we reached the top they leveled out and my heart slammed in my chest as they landed on another motorcycle! *Really* close to us that time! No lights flashing at us then. It was definitely not another '*ally.*'

"Hang on!" Ethan yelled and made a hard left back down the hill. We splashed straight into the stream and I held on for dear life. The motorcycle couldn't maneuver a 180° turn that fast and it sailed on past us. *Phew!* I took the opportunity to take a deep breath as we headed back around a group of rocks to climb the next hill back up to the path.

At the top once again we could see the lights flickering all around us. It was a brilliant light show in the middle of the pitch dark forest. If I wasn't so busy being terrified, I would have thought it beautiful. *Strange,* but beautiful.

Every 4-wheeler I saw had two riders. I knew that wasn't an accident either, as it would keep Pete and Jeremy from standing out. Even to me. So much so, that I still hadn't been able to pick them out.

"Where's Pete?" I finally asked over the noise.

"They're the farthest ahead. If we can slow these guys down for just five or ten minutes, they'll be long gone." He called back over his shoulder.

Just then another motorcycle pulled up next to us on our left side. He was close enough to reach out and grab us if he wanted to, and my heart hammered painfully in my chest again. He turned and looked straight at us then, through his mirrored face shield. Obviously satisfied that we were not the ones he wanted, he sped easily right past us. Then it got even worse. Ethan was instantly worried that he would catch up with Pete and so was I. Ethan cranked the accelerator as far as it would go. We gave chase and watched, horrified as he continued to increase the distance between us regardless. As long as the trail was straight and even, he had us beat.

Then suddenly another 4-wheeling duo came flying up from our right and soared across his path in mid-air. I was surprised to see as they passed overhead, that it was Jack and Artie again. The motorcycle rider threw his arms up defensively against the daredevil stunt and the disruption in balance knocked him off his bike. *Phew!*

Ethan shook his head as he took a deep breath himself. He was very happy to see his friends, to say the least. We watched as they landed safely on the other side of the trail and sped off. I was practically giddy myself after that, as his relief radiated outward.

Generic motorcycle guy #2 tumbled roughly down a small hill. He immediately got back up again though and started to run back towards where his bike had fallen. We passed him as he ran but it was hard to be content with such a small, short lived victory.

The motorcyclists all had matching black helmets with the mirrored shields and black riding gear that was full of built in body armor and padding. It not only made them all appear interchangeable, but it also made them fairly indestructible. Left and right their path was blocked, or their tires bumped out from under them as we all motored recklessly through the area trying to slow them down. Still they continually popped back up and rejoined the chase.

The best we could hope for really *was* just to slow them down some and we were barely pulling that off. I knew we weren't that far from Camp, but also knew without asking that he wouldn't want to lead them there. All I knew for sure was that we were headed deeper and deeper into the forest, swarms of phantom bikers nipping constantly at our tail.

I slid my arms tighter around his waist and squeezed my thighs tighter against the warmth of his as we crossed in front of another biker and then sped off down the incline and into the darkness beyond. It was necessary just to stay on, but it also helped to keep me calm. His body was strong and unyielding, and felt very sturdy and reliable to cling to. It was a warm safe place to me, in the midst of the unexpected storm. I closed my eyes and used the random moment to take comfort in his closeness. As long as I was touching him, the rest of it failed to matter as much.

The roaring engines did have a way of bringing me back though. They were fading off into the background momentarily, but I knew it wouldn't last. Once we found ourselves alone on the trail, he continually doubled back again to keep up with the distraction efforts. It felt like self-sabotage, knowing we also needed to get away, but we had a more important job to do first and I knew Ethan would never abandon it.

We encountered another motorcycle pretty quickly, headed right for us on the trail! We played chicken until I had to close my eyes again, then I held on as Ethan took a hard right and headed back down into the stream. The bike skidded to a stop. I saw the rider raise his right arm to his helmet and look in our direction. Satisfied we were not the main target, he kept going the way he had been headed.

"Crap! How'd he know we weren't Pete and Jeremy from that far away?" I asked.

"Binoculars. Built into the helmet. Night vision too, I would expect." He explained matter-of-factly. That evened things up a bit unfortunately.

"Damn!" I said, both upset and duly impressed.

I could sense Ethan taking mental notes for the future. He took the momentary reprieve to pull out his phone and check on Pete and Jeremy's progress. His worry quickly turned to relief and I knew then, that they had made it out! He knew he didn't have to say it out loud. I could feel his joy. I sighed a humongous sigh and he took a moment to send out the *"all clear/save yourself"* message. Then we accelerated and changed direction again. He turned his headlights off and we finally raced away happily into the darkness.

The next few miles were nerve racking, while we could still see the faint flicker of lights here and there, but after that it finally started to calm down and so did I. I realized after a few more minutes, that no single headlights were visible at all anymore.

We were finally, blissfully, completely alone.

Chapter 43

Once we escaped the cacophony of so many revving engines, our lone steadily running engine in the stillness of the darkened forest around us was a drastic adjustment. It was suddenly incredibly peaceful.

I laid my head down gently against his shoulder for a brief moment, as we enjoyed the much smoother trail. I didn't leave it there long. I knew it probably wouldn't last, but the momentary reprieve was welcome and I appreciated it while I could.

When I lifted my head I tried to pay more attention as he made his way through the forest. I couldn't make out all the details as they flew by so quickly in the dark. Even with just the moonlight coming through the trees, again I couldn't help but appreciate the beauty of it all as a whole.

It was a great relief to be at least temporarily away from the trouble and the threat. That relief gave way to the freedom to contemplate the things that had happened. From our overly dramatic *sex*-capades in the beginning of the evening, to the whole spectacularly cinematic escape from Movie Night. It was all so surreal and so intensely *super-real* at the same time that I had to take several deep breaths in a row to mentally digest everything. He sensed my difficulty from my quickened breathing and he reached down with one arm to hold my arms tighter to his waist.

It was a small gesture but it conveyed so much strength and security that I instantly felt better. We rode like that in silence for another few miles until we began to see the road through the cover of the trees.

Once we were close enough, he came to a stop. He turned off the engine and we slid off quietly, even though it felt less than necessary at that point. He left the keys in the ignition and covered the quad with enough big branches, that it wouldn't be easily visible to any passersby. Then he walked back over to me where I waited, kicking gently through the thick underbrush along the way. He took my hand and I followed him the last twenty five feet or so through the thin hopeful saplings along the edge of the forest. When we reached the road we followed it just around the bend and found a small silver car parked on the shoulder.

He motioned for me to take the drivers' side as we approached from the rear. It was unlocked. We opened the doors and got in, closing them again quickly but quietly. I was worried about the interior light at first but I noticed that it never came on. The keys were in the ignition there as well and I started it up.

"Go." He said, looking out at the road behind us.

I pulled out and automatically went to turn the headlights on but he stopped me by reaching over and holding my hand still on the knob.

"Not yet." He said. He let go of my hand but turned around with one arm still behind me, and moved the other from the knob to the steering wheel. I knew he could see well enough for both of us and I understood that we didn't want to be seen showing up out of nowhere alongside the trails. Not with the number of suits that had to be trolling around town by then covering the edges of the forest. I let go of the wheel completely and kept the gas at a steady speed.

I pulled my cell phone from my pocket and quickly dialed Shirley with my temporarily free hands to check on Liliana. I was relieved to hear that the children had all fallen asleep watching movies. I told her I would come get her as soon as I could but she told me not to worry or to hurry, that they would be just fine. I thanked her again and hung up. We drove like that for another half a mile during which he took a moment to show *his* appreciation.

"Thank you." He said softly, very close to my ear. He wasn't specific, but I knew exactly what he meant. He was still digesting the fact that I had to chosen stay with him and get involved, rather than staying safely on the sidelines. "You didn't have to do that. But I'm really *glad* that you did!" He added honestly. There was more to it than that, but I wasn't sure what it was. It was mostly appreciation, but there was sadness and apprehension as well.

Besides that unknown element, I could also feel that he was greatly but pleasantly surprised by my decision. He didn't bother to voice it though. He knew I knew. We were both beginning to rely on that more and more. I wondered then, if I was ruining his ability to properly date again in the future, since then he would have to remember to voice his thoughts and feelings again. Of course my next thought was, *"I hope so."* Hah! Selfish, I know. Human, remember?

He leaned closer and gently kissed my temple, bringing me back to our present reality. One I was growing very fond of despite its' lack of practicality. Then he sat back and motioned for me to take the wheel.

"Alright. Turn 'em on." He said. I took the wheel with my right hand and switched the lights on with my left. He watched the rearview mirror for a few minutes more, then finally satisfied that we were alone, turned to watch the road in front of us again. I sighed so deeply, I thought I was going to pass out for a second. I tried again to calm down and reorganize my thoughts.

"So where's Jeremy?" I asked worriedly.

"Safe. For now." He answered while texting again. When he finished, he looked up at me and explained further. "They took him to a safe-house across town. It's too dangerous to go back to Camp right now." He said, confirming my earlier assumption. There was still more, but he was hesitant. I was wondering why, but not for long.

"He's apparently a lot more important to them than we had originally realized. Or a much bigger threat. Whatever the reason, they're not giving up and going away as usual like we had hoped." He was feeling very anxious and that seemed understandable.

"We've been putting this off, hoping it wouldn't be necessary, but they're forcing my hand now. We don't really have a choice anymore. I'm gonna have to get him out of here for a while." He said guiltily, looking down at his hand in his lap like it was a confession. I still didn't understand why he felt the way he did about it. It seemed to make sense.

"His parents agree, but neither of them can go. They have too many other dependents, children and animals alike to care for here." He looked back down again.

He was also feeling a great sense of loss that I still didn't quite get. It was pushed way down under everything else but it was too sharp a pain for him to hide completely. I was not only feeling its sting, I was also feeling very confused by it. Was he really that upset about Jeremy having to leave for a while? I wondered. I turned to look at him, the wariness evident in my eyes.

"What is it, Ethan? Just tell me." I demanded as bravely as I could. He looked back at me and held my eyes for a second before he spoke.

"I have to go with him." He said simply. *Ouch!*

He answered without wavering but I could feel the pain again as he spoke the words out loud, cutting fast and deep. I felt it again a second later, when it registered in my *own* heart. I finally got it.

The pain doubled then. It was exactly what I had been most afraid of. I had allowed myself to come to need him and he wasn't going to be there. I completely understood the pain that he was feeling then but I immediately wished that I didn't. *Dammit!*

I had no one to blame but myself. I didn't say anything for a while. I didn't trust my voice. When I did, I finally got up the nerve to ask him the next couple of obvious questions.

"How long? Do you really have to leave? What about Camp?" I asked, my voice cracking only slightly at the very end. He went back to watching the road as he answered.

"It's best just to get him *'out of Dodge'* for now." He looked back at me again and I turned to watch his face in between glances at the road.

"See, when someone comes here from across the country looking for help, hiding them at Camp is our best bet. No one from Philly is going to come looking for their fugitive in *Pinegrove, Massachusetts*. In this case though, they already know that

Jeremy's *from* here, that this is where his family lives. Now that they know I'm the one helping him, you can be sure they aren't going to go away as long as I'm still hanging around town. It's the only way to take the heat away from Jeremy *and* the Camp." He was contemplative again for a minute.

"*Hmpf.* Originally, I had considered it a stroke of luck, that I wouldn't have to completely relocate him on top of everything else he was facing. His road was already going to be hard enough without separating him from his family. In his case, that really is a *bad* thing. His family structure is strong. He needs that right now and I had been glad that I was able to let him keep it. Now it's turned out to be a penalty to be used against him, because it means he definitely *can't* stay." He sighed.

"As for how long, I honestly don't know. It's impossible to say right now. Until they stop looking, I guess." He said solemnly and my stomach fell even further. That was definitely not the *"couple of days"* that I had secretly been hoping to hear.

Shit! Crap! Dammit! I screamed mentally. It didn't help, but I did it anyway.

"I won't tell you *'where'* either, so don't ask. It would just put you in danger." Of course. That was pure Ethan. His energy softened for a minute. He looked back up at me. "I would take you with me in a heartbeat..." He said resignedly. "You *know* that! But *I* know why you would never go, and *you* know that I would never ask you to betray that." He went back to watching the road again. He was right. It was all true, but it didn't make me feel any better!

"Turn here." He said quietly pointing to the street coming up on my right. I slowed and made the turn, not really knowing where I was anymore. Not really caring either.

A few more miles and then we made a left. Half a mile, another right. Before I knew it, he had me driving down an unpaved road. He motioned for me to pull over and park by a large maple tree. I turned off the headlights and the darkness enveloped us completely again. There were no streetlights there.

After a minute my eyes adjusted and he came around to open my door. Who says chivalry is dead? I thought to myself with a humorless laugh. He took my hand and I followed him back into the dark woods on foot. The trust, once again complete. The sadness however, was creeping in. Slowly.

I knew from experience how damaging that could be and I took a few deep breaths. I tried to fight it. I really did, but I also knew that the best I could hope for was to hold it off. Until I was alone... again. Yup, might as well get used to the sound of that. No sense in kidding myself, or putting it off any longer than necessary. I would ignore it then and there though. Just for the moment. I began to rebuild the mental wall that I had gotten so used to counting on for protection. It was going back up, brick by painful brick. Allowing nothing else to reach me. Not yet. *Lock down.*

Deep breaths. *In... Out...* Move one foot. Then the other.

We walked through the trees and the underbrush for about ten minutes. I was glad for the dark, even though I knew it didn't really hide my expression from him. It made me *feel* like it did. That was enough to help me keep it together. His feelings didn't change during the walk from what he had been feeling in the car. He wasn't hopeful. He wasn't mad. He was simply resigned. He knew what he had to do and he knew he would do it.

I was surprised at first, when I began to see the lights glowing out from the windows of the little house. I didn't know where we were going when he had said "safe-*house.*" I still hadn't expected that. It was literally a tiny little house in the middle of nowhere!

He sent a text message as we approached. A minute later, Dr. J. came out onto the little porch and greeted us with a slightly remorseful smile and a handshake for Ethan. Apparently it seemed, he was the one who had thought Movie Night was a good idea for Jeremy, or at least *necessary* in some way. I didn't get the whole picture on why that was, but I was so preoccupied that I easily let it go for the moment. They talked briefly while I stood quietly and tried again to get a handle on my own plummeting emotions.

Ethan had done a fantastic job of shutting his feelings out, as usual. For the second time that night, I wasn't psyched about it. Oh well, it made it easier for me at least I thought, trying to look for a bright side as usual.

Then I smiled and rolled my eyes. *Of course. Hmpf!* He'd done it again. *Damn him!*

I took the first really deep breath since being in the car then and decided that I wasn't going to give in that easy. If he could willingly take on pain and hardship in the name of helping others, then I should be willing to risk at least as much for him. Shouldn't I? I knew *someone* should! Since the thought of someone else doing it made me want to break things, I figured it was time to step up to the plate. I sighed and mentally pushed the damn wall back down. Then I kicked it for good measure. Screw it!! It wasn't going to be easy to love him, but dammit, I was going to do it anyway!

I had spent so much of my life afraid to ever be in too public of a position. I always tried to avoid things that I knew would draw too much attention to myself or to my unusual situation. I basically avoided being *visible* for the most part! That's what I was used to.

It was just easier.

That would be impossible with Ethan though. I couldn't be in his life *and* remain invisible. I couldn't let him believe that he didn't deserve better than that anymore either. He deserved someone who was willing to be at least as committed to him, as he was to those he cared for. I wasn't sure if I was capable of that level of selflessness or not, but it was pointless to deny that I *wanted* to be. *God help me,* I wanted to be!

He sensed my inner turmoil as usual and he reached out for my hand. I wanted him to know that I wasn't backing away anymore either, so I gave it up willingly. It was a small gesture but it spoke volumes and we both knew it. As usual, we were not alone. Dr. J grinned knowingly at us and our small, but open show of affection. He seemed quite pleased. I didn't care anymore. I smiled at him as well.

"That took a lot longer than I thought it would." He proclaimed matter-of-factly. "Too damn bull-headed, the both of you." He admitted, clearly surprised. "Congratulations, though. You *are* very lucky to have found each other at all! Very lucky, indeed." He added shaking his head in apparent disbelief. He added a warm, genuine smile after that but he offered no further explanation. Then he turned and walked in through the little cottage door.

Before I even looked at Ethan I could tell that he was as shocked as I was for once. *"Huh.* He's not generally surprised by much. Nor does he *cop* to it very often." He said with raised eyebrows. "I guess this one even threw *him* for a loop. That makes me feel a little better, I have to admit. *Hmpf."* He said with a laugh.

"I wonder what else he's figured out but isn't telling though." He mused aloud with his eyes squinted in strenuous thought. That of course, scared the hell out of me!

Here we go again, I thought as I led the way through the little white door.

Chapter 44

I worked methodically and steadily, moving from one spot to the next in a hypnotic rhythm. My knees and feet sinking slowly into the soft surface beneath me while I worked. I gave each spot my undivided attention until I was completely satisfied with the results. Then I moved on to give the next area the same individual consideration, treating each spot like it was the most important of them all.

I was deep into my physical task. Focused on that alone. It wasn't accidental. It was what I needed and I could not be more grateful to be able to lose myself in it. So in honor of that gratitude, I gave everything over to it. It was easy though, really. Since it was about all I *had* at the moment to put my energy into anyway.

"You've got mad skills, woman!" A deep voice complimented, shaking me out of my blissfully, numb state. When that happened, the deep longing and emptiness came rushing back and invaded my consciousness.

"Hey Mack. Thanks." I answered, making sure my voice didn't betray my true feelings. It wasn't hard. I was an old pro, well-practiced at the art. I still considered it more *"required acting"* than *"lying."* There was a definite difference in there and that was important to me. It was necessary in order to spare those around me my true feelings. They had always been too much for most people to handle. I had learned that a long, long time ago. Too much honesty was definitely not an option at the moment, since it would be extremely bad for company morale to spend my days complaining and walking around moping all the time. No that wouldn't help anyone.

"It feels good to be back to work." I said instead, and that much at least was true.

"Amen to that, boss!" He readily agreed. "The trucks are here with the materials for the well and the surrounding structure. I sent them up to unload. You ready? He asked. He knew that I wanted to be present to supervise that part. I had made that *very* clear.

Without Ethan there to oversee the project himself, I had promised him that I would give it my personal attention throughout. It had been the biggest stumbling block of the entire job. In the process of that struggle, it had become the crowning jewel of my design. It needed to be perfect. I wanted it to do justice to the person who had brought it to life. Even if he was too busy saving others' lives at the moment to put his own two hands on it. His *touch* was all over it and I vowed to make sure that it stayed that way.

"I'll be up there in twenty and we'll get started Mack. Thanks." I said standing up and pulling off my gloves. There was a bead of sweat rolling down my forehead that I hadn't noticed in my Zen-like state. I lifted my arm and used the cleanest part I could find to wipe it off before it could drip down into my eye. The small innocent gesture instantly reminded me of my swim with Ethan at camp.

I stood and let out a huge gust of air and started down the path towards the trailer. I had always appreciated the bathroom aspect of having it there but there were admittedly other benefits. It didn't hurt to have a place to keep your lunch when the client wasn't feeding you like he was currently. It was also a handy place to keep a change of clothes, for the times when you were practically living on the job. Those days even the microscopic shower seemed like a small miracle! More important than all of that though I had realized as of late, was how important it was to have a place to go when you just needed a moment alone. Like I did then.

I had been dealing fairly well since they left. I thanked God every day that we were able to get back to work right away, without any interference or retribution from Anderson and his associates. In spite of all his threats to arrest any and all co-conspirators, he had in fact completely lost interest in everyone in town once he knew for sure that Jeremy was gone, myself included. Very soon after that, they had all gone too. Ethan had been right about that as well but I wasn't terribly surprised.

The work had been my real savior. Still, there had been other moments along the way that were particularly tough.

I walked up the two metal stairs and pulled the little white door to the trailer open. Every time I passed through it, it reminded me of the little white door on the safe house and the last time that I had seen Ethan. I still couldn't decide if that was a good thing or a bad thing. I was too busy experiencing it.

It had been almost two weeks and I thought the sharpness of it should be starting to fade a little, but it still felt as though he had just held me the night before. It was painful every time I remembered, but it was even more painful trying not to think about him at all. The memories were *very* fresh in my head for sure, but it wasn't even just there. *They were just as vibrant in my dreams.* It was heavenly relief while I slept, but torturous when I would wake up alone. I didn't want to think about that either though, so I purposely recalled that last time that I had seen him again instead.

Pete had greeted us in the small living room of the safe-house and held his hand out to Ethan. He had taken it, but rather than shake, they both used the hold to pull the other closer and they hugged each other tightly. I was overwhelmed by the level of gratitude coming off of him. It was heartwarming to see him finally come full circle. They broke the contact and then he also hugged me briefly with the same generosity of feelings. "Thank you. Both of you!" He had gushed.

I wasn't sure what I had really done, but I didn't bother to bring it up just then. He stepped back and Jeremy came into the small room next. He was really happy to see a few more friendly faces and he hugged us as well. It felt good to get that kind of positive energy from him. He was a little shaken up at the sudden and intense interest in him but otherwise he was no worse for wear. At least not physically. He was still hurting over his argument with Tina but he was trying hard to ignore it, so I did too.

The best part of it all was that his anger and confusion at adjusting to his new reality seemed to have taken a bit of a back seat to the more immediate drama. It was only a temporary reprieve, but it was another step in the right direction. It had given him small moments where he could think about something else. That was an important part of getting on with life. Learning to focus on other things in spite of the difficulty. *Just like I was doing.* It was a learned technique. One step at a time. He would get there, I felt sure.

We went and sat in the little kitchen and he told us about his side of the adventure. Their wild ride through the trails, dodging single headlight beams and forging brand new trails through the thickest foliage where there hadn't been any before. When he was calmer he finally told us a little more about his argument with Tina, who he clearly had very real feelings for.

Apparently he had seen something wrong in her chest and had tried to get her to agree to go and be checked, but without telling her why. She kept insisting however, that she was fine and that she didn't need to go anywhere. He was so worried then, that he couldn't keep it to himself anymore. He'd tried to explain it all to her, to make her take him more seriously.

Yeah, that had not gone very well. We didn't need him to explain that part. Unfortunately, it was far too easy for all of us in that room to understand. After that, he and I ate some frozen pizza that I had found and threw in the oven and played some cards, while the rest of them finalized the arrangements. Jeremy was trying not to think about leaving. Even though he had known that it might have to happen, it wasn't something he wanted to do either, that much was abundantly clear. Though he was handling it extremely well, considering.

Ethan was pretty busy most of the time, but he would come by to check on us every quarter hour or so. I tried to pretend I couldn't tell that he just wanted to be close to me for a minute. It's the same impulse that people have before they quit smoking, where once they know the deadline is approaching, they end up smoking as many cigarettes as they can in the meantime. I desperately wanted 'just one more' as well but it was too late for that.

I could feel it coming and I didn't know what to do with that other than keep pushing it back, especially since I had just so recently come to the conclusion that I actually wanted to try to be *with* him. I hadn't even figured that part out yet and I was already going to be forced to learn how to be *without* him. *Dammit!* That *sucked!* Then I reminded myself that it didn't just suck for me.

I sighed at my present reality as I snapped out of my reminiscing again. I walked down the tiny hallway and into the trailer's little bathroom. I turned on the miniature faucet and let it run while I splashed some water on my dirty face. It felt good to get back to ground zero and actually see my bare skin, *myself*, in the mirror again. Whenever I closed my eyes however, I always saw that last moment with him.

We hadn't stayed in the shed-sized home for very long, and we never got a moment to actually be *really* alone in such a small space. I was okay just being there though. I sat there thinking how glad I was that I had decided to get on the back of Jack's quad. Otherwise, I would have missed even those last small moments. I didn't care if it was selfish and irrational to want to be there with him. I still did. When I saw Hank walk in with Jeremy's mother however, my heart suddenly felt like lead. I knew then that our time was up. I could feel her pain as soon as she walked through the door. It was overwhelmingly clear to me then. She was there to say goodbye. That was the only thing left that they had been waiting for.

Jeremy let go of his control a little then and ran over to hug her. Then Pete came up and hugged them both at once. It wasn't just for show. They really were a very close knit family. I could feel how deeply they all loved each other.

They remained huddled there in the small room, talking softly to each other. Ethan waved Hank and Dr. J into the kitchen for some last minute checks and I slipped quietly out the front door to give them a few moments alone.

I walked out across the front deck again, thankful that it was too late for the mosquitoes to be out, my bug spray having given up the ghost hours ago.

I leaned on the far railing and stared off into the trees, trying to give them whatever privacy the six feet between us would allow. A moment later, I heard the little door squeak and I felt Ethan come up behind me. He slid his arms around my waist and I felt his rough cheek slide carefully along mine. His intensity almost knocked me over as usual, but it wasn't just the good feelings that time around. I could also feel the dread and the fact that he was *really* sorry for that too. He couldn't stop it from coming anymore. I sighed and turned around.

"Well, this is going to make it tough for you to tease me constantly. Whatever will you do with all that free time?" I joked, trying in vain to lighten the mood. The heaviness didn't budge. "I don't know what the rules are here. Will you keep in touch?" I asked, even though it showed more vulnerability than I was usually comfortable with. I didn't care. I knew I didn't have time to hem and haw.

"Yes. *As much as I can.*" He answered quietly and I didn't miss the definite disclaimer in there.

"What about Jeremy? Is he going to be okay? Will he ever get to come back? What about his family, and *Tina?* I have so many questions and I know you don't have the time or the ability to answer them all. It's frustrating." I said, letting my weakness show willingly for once. He reached up to run his index finger slowly, softly, down my cheek and under my chin. He held it there for a beat, before he let it fall. He didn't actually say *"Shhhh."* He didn't have to. I stopped talking and sighed again.

He leaned in closer then and kissed me softly. I could tell that he wanted to answer my questions, but there wasn't time. Fine. I stretched up on my tip-toes and reached behind his neck to hold on while I kissed him back. Time stopped then for a few blissful minutes, thankfully. It wasn't nearly long enough.

He reached behind his head and took my hands in his. He brought them back down and kissed each one slowly. The strength of my desire to hold on to him was so great, that the longing radiated all the way out to my aching palms. It was definitely not the same wonderful sensation that a *good* feeling gave me. I knew he saw it when the pain showed on his face like I had elbowed him in the gut. I wanted to hide it, or to apologize for it, but I knew there was no point. It was what it was. He was not someone I could hope to hide it from. He took a deep fortifying breath and looked back up at me.

"Simone, you don't owe me anything and I can't say how long I'll be gone. I don't expect you to put your life on hold for this." He said, thinking he needed to do the right thing and let me off the hook. It made his pain much worse but he was trying *really* hard to contain it. It was my turn to reassure, I realized.

"Ethan." I said holding his face in my hands. "I'm not going anywhere. You went and made me feel things that I *never* wanted to feel, damn you! It's too late now to try and take them back. I'm sorry, but I'm already addicted and it's your own fault. You've created a monster and you are going to have to deal with that. Sooner or later." I half-joked, while I pulled his face closer to mine and slid my hands down onto his chest. "You go. And you do what you need to do. Then you get your *ass* back here to me! Do you understand?" I asked, with my hands balled up in his shirt, pulling him even closer. He smiled a little at that, pleasantly surprised again.

"Got it." He confirmed softly, before my mouth finally made contact with his again. A few minutes later, we came up for air. "I can assure you that I will do my very best to get back *as soon* as humanly possible." He was feeling an awful lot brighter after that. He reached for my hands and brought them up to his lips once more. "Don't let anything happen to these while I'm gone, okay?" He joked. "Or to any *other* part of you." He added more seriously.

"You either!" I begged quietly, as I leaned up and hid my face in his neck. I could hear them coming out then. The fear and loss that I felt in that flash was too much to hide on my face, so I just continued to hide my face in his neck instead a moment longer. *"Please!"* I added with more feeling, as I hugged him tightly one last time. Then I pulled back and I made myself let him go.

He stared for a few seconds more, then he looked away and turned to say his goodbyes to Pete and Helena as they walked up behind us.

"I can't thank you enough, Eat." Pete said with a frog in his throat as they shook hands. Helena hugged him just as tight as

I had, and then stepped back again. Pete continued. "You keep him safe for us, alright? He has chores to do when he gets home. His brothers and sisters have been saving them up for him." He joked, but the smile didn't come close to reaching his eyes. He was sad too. And he was afraid for his son. Though he trusted Ethan completely by then at least. That helped.

Dr. J was leaving with them. He would take them to their next vehicle outside of town. Then he was heading back to his own life for a while. That was all I knew.

Jeremy hugged his parents once more and then me. Then he pulled his army style duffel bag higher on his shoulder and followed Ethan down the steps and into the darkness. They hiked off in the opposite direction from the way we had come in.

I picked my head up and shut off the water. I inhaled deeply and pulled the towel off the child-sized rack to dry my face. Another deep breath. Almost two weeks and no matter how many times I remembered it, it always ended the same way. With him gone.

Hank had walked us out and I had taken Jeremy's parents' home in the car that I'd arrived in, but with written directions that time. Then I doubled back around the long way to get home. The unmarked, and yet so easily recognizable cars were still milling all around town, not yet having found what they were looking for. I had spotted two of them along the way at a distance. They had no reason to notice my anonymous car though, and I never got close enough for any of them to notice me, so thankfully I made it back before dawn without further issue. The farm was deathly quiet by then and entirely empty again. I parked the car over at Jack's like I was told to do and I went inside to get Liliana.

Shirley had hugged me twice as long as usual when I left. I could only assume that Ethan had already talked to Jack about what was happening, and I knew he kept no secrets from her. I still diddn't bring it up, just to be safe. I just thanked her sincerely, picked up a soundly sleeping Liliana and walked back to my place. I locked up, then I put her down and tucked her in. I took a quick hot shower to wash off the mud and bug spray residue and then fell heavily into bed.

I noticed that the car was already gone when I woke up

and looked out of my bedroom window and up towards the main house a few hours later. Jeremy would be long since gone too. And Ethan was gone. I could feel the void as strongly and as surely as I had once felt his presence.

I hadn't heard from him at all for the next two days. Those had been the hardest of all. I spent half of Saturday's show at the Music Theatre running back and forth up the aisle, looking for a signal to check my phone. Liliana seemed to be having the time of her life. I was glad that she was too distracted by the glitz and glamour of the show to notice my lack of enthusiasm. Of course I felt guilty for that too, but I didn't want to have to try and explain why I was so worried and on edge. I was actually grateful that I'd had no choice but to go through with our original plans to go out. I knew if I had sat home doing nothing, the waiting would have been even worse.

She had noticed at some point though, and smarty pants that she was, she had figured out the reason for it all on her own. We were driving home from the show and it was late. It had been quiet for some time and I had assumed that she was asleep. She surprised me when she spoke up unexpectedly from the backseat of the darkened car.

"Don't be sad, Mama. You just have to think about him doing what he's supposed to be doing. Then you will feel better until you get to see him again." She said very matter-of-factly.

I was blown away that she had pegged my mood so perfectly!

Not only was she mature enough at five to turn my own advice back around on me, but somehow she also knew exactly *what* was bothering me. I had shifted gears mentally from the first worry to considering that unexpected development instead. I was becoming increasingly certain every day that I wasn't just being paranoid anymore. It might be time to admit that there really was more going on there than there should be.

I knew it wouldn't be the worst thing on Earth if she turned out to be like me, but it certainly would make life more complicated and challenging for her. That's the part that really bothered me the most, other than the horror at the thought of her ever getting that sick!

I had decided to put it out of my mind again for the time being though. If it was her fate to be like me, I knew my constant worrying wouldn't stop it from happening. I *would* keep an even closer eye on her than ever though, I had thought to myself at the time. I would also find the time to talk to Ben. *Soon!*

I thought again about Anderson's proclamation about being able to *'cure'* us. I couldn't help it. I thought about it every time I worried about Liliana after that night. Ethan was right about something else that he had said once I thought solemnly, as I headed back out into the burning sunshine, as a parent you'll do whatever you have to do, to help your child...

It was way too bright at first, after the welcome shelter of the air conditioned, closed up trailer. I gave my eyes a moment to readjust so I wouldn't fall down the small metal stairs. As I waited, I lifted my face up to the sun. It felt so good that I was reminded again of how relieved I had been when that first call had finally come, last Monday. It was like winning the lottery, but of course it had been far too short for my liking.

I had been happily burying my anxiousness in my work when my pocket rang. I'd kept my phone next to or on me at all times. I pulled off my gloves and reached for it, afraid to hope that it would be him but relieved beyond belief to see that it finally was! *Thank God!!* I took one huge breath before I picked up! Whooooohhh!

"Hi!" I said, trying to hold back my million questions until I could hear the sound of his voice.

"Hi." He answered simply, sounding just as relieved to hear mine. I melted at the familiar timbre of it and closed my eyes for a while.

"Everything okay?" I asked, trying to keep it general since I knew how easy it was to listen in on a cell phone conversation these days if someone wanted to. I guess it's a good thing that I have always been such a suspicious a person by nature anyway. That frame of mind suddenly came in very handy.

"Yeah. Just got settled." He answered just as cryptically. All I could think was, *"Just got settled?!"* *That meant two days travel time between us!* Ugh! That made the ache a little sharper but I pushed it back and tried not to waste whatever time we had dwelling on the negative. I assumed that he wouldn't chance talking long enough to be traced. Just in case.

"Been pretty quiet here." I said referring to our friends in suits, who hadn't been back since Ethan and Jeremy had left. I was sure that he probably already knew that somehow but I tried to be helpful anyway.

"Yeah, here too." He confirmed. I knew that meant they were safe. That, wherever they were, the Feds were not currently there with them. At least not at the moment.

"Good!" I said, not hiding my relief.

"How are things going at the site?" He asked in an attempt to distract us both from all the things that we weren't saying.

"Things are good here actually. It's moving pretty fast, which is about all I can ask for at this point. We'll be starting on the well next week." I added hopefully, thinking he would tell me to save that part for him. I was sorely disappointed. Again.

"You'll make sure they don't screw up my masterpiece, right?" He chuckled when he said it, but all I heard was, *"I won't be back by next week."* I was instantly a little sadder but I would be damned if I would show it and make it even harder on him. He would never do that to me.

"I will, don't worry. It will be just the way we planned it." I assured him as cheerfully as I could. "Have you slept at all?" I asked, changing the subject to something *else* very concerning to me.

"Not yet. I'll get a couple hours now though." He had said, like it was no big deal to go straight through two nights without sleeping.

"I'll call again soon." He added, letting me know that we were almost done. My heart twisted in my chest.

"K." I said. It was all I could get out at the moment.

"Miss you!" He admitted then and I could hear a wealth of feeling in those two little words. I added two heartfelt words of my own.

"Me too!" I had to swallow hard after that. *So freakin' ridiculous!* I took a deep breath then and pulled myself together.

"Call me when you can." I said calmly.

"Talk to Jack if you need anything or can't reach me in

the meantime, okay?" He said.

"K." I agreed. "Bye."

"Bye" And just like that, even though I was surrounded by workers on all sides, I had felt *completely* alone again. *Deep breaths.* Come on. Grow up! *In... Out...*

I was fine by myself. I knew that. I could handle being alone. I really did have no problem with that concept. It was the missing *him* that I was having a hard time with and that was something all-together different!

I dove into my work completely after that. I was single minded for the most part until the next time my heart lifted, on Thursday, when a CD arrived in the mail. It was postmarked out of our own post office there in town somehow, and was completely unmarked otherwise but I knew right away what it was. The CD that I had dared to hope existed, some time ago. It was really, *really* sweet. He was clearly worried about my peace of mind, since he wasn't there to play and block for me in person. It was such a selfless thing for him to think of with everything else currently on his plate that it gave me strength just in principal alone. It was classic Ethan. It made me smile every time I played any of the songs that I had uploaded onto my MP3 player, to listen to at work. Other than that, and the Friday nights and Saturdays that I spent with my Liliana, I didn't do much else.

I spent very little time at The Tavern. It was both louder and too quiet at the same time without him there. I think the majority of the people came for one of two things. The music or the *height* help. Without Ethan there to do either, it was a very different place. It was nice to go in and sit once and a while, after a long day on site. They had a rotating cycle of local musicians that filled in whenever he was away and they were all pretty decent. Again though, without Ethan there it was mostly just someplace good for me to eat.

I did feel just the tiniest bit closer to him there, especially since I could look at the craftsmanship all over the place by then and easily recognize his handiwork. Sometimes though, that just made it harder instead of easier. It felt familiar but it wasn't nearly enough if that made sense, so I didn't torture myself too often.

Liliana was back to her old rambunctious self, waiting impatiently for her annoying cast to come off. It was of little use to her once it was completely full, with no room left for decorating. She was over it. She asked about Ethan only once, that first Friday with me the next week after he had left. She wanted to know when he would come and hang out with us again. Not *if*, but *when*, I had noticed. I turned away before she could see any discomfort on my face.

All I could tell her without lying to her, which I hated to do and would avoid except for extreme situations, was that he would come back over as soon as he could. I covered for him afterwards though, wanting to protect his reputation by adding that he *would* be very busy for a while. He would come back around though I promised, whenever it was within his power to do so.

At least my breathing techniques were improving with all the practice I was getting, I thought looking for the bright side to pull me through.

Other than that, and the advice in the car, she hadn't mentioned him. Well, not to me anyways. I had half expected her to be more curious about him, or ask me all kinds of questions that would be painful to answer. Even over the phone, during goodnights, as usual she was a dream child and for some reason, chose not to bring it up. She seemed perfectly content that he would be back around at some point. As a child it was easy to always assume that.

I however, was beginning to feel what it would be like if he *wasn't*.

I was no longer a fan.

Life *"before"* him had been fine. Then life *"with"* him had come along and kicked *"fine's"* ass. That unfortunately, had completely changed my outlook. There was still life without him, of course. There was just no real joy in it anymore. I'd never really had that before. I wanted that joy back, and I wanted it *bad!*

Jack was being his usual, supportive self. We didn't talk about the details, but we kept in close touch most days, just in case. He would come by for coffee on Sunday morning and save me from spending my only empty day torturing myself. Or he would send Shirley up with baked goods and fruit that she would leave on the deck for me while I was at work.

I was probably the most grateful for that, since I would often work until I was too exhausted to drag myself to the dreaded market. If not for the food waiting on the little black wrought iron table from time to time, I know many a night I would have simply chosen to fall into bed hungry. It wouldn't have bothered me one bit.

I quickly realized though, after losing a few pounds that neglecting myself wasn't going to help anyone. Not Ethan, my family or my career. So after the first four or five days of struggling to adjust, I'd had enough of the pity party. I got it together just enough to encompass and embrace the new emptiness inside me, and I got back to the task of living. There was nothing I hated to be more than a self-wallow-*er*, so I decided not to be one anymore. He was doing what he had to do. I had to be strong enough to do the same. *For my own good.*

I knew that, but it wasn't easy. I was a big girl however and I *would* find a way to deal with it, I finally determined. One way or another, I vowed to myself to remain strong. For as long as I needed to be.

Until he came back to me.

In... Out...

I squinted in the bright sun and put the ear piece to my MP3 player back in place. With his deep, distinctive voice crooning softly in my ear, I took one more deep breath and let it back out slowly. Then I headed up the rocky trail toward the center clearing, where Mack waited with the rest of the excited crew.

In the meantime, I had work to do.

To be continued in...

EVOLUTION'S CLIMB

BOOK II

Fear of Heights

www.ingramcontent.com/pod-product-compliance
Lightning Source LLC
Chambersburg PA
CBHW061030030726
47504CB00002B/320